GIRLS ONLY LIVE TWICE

Also by Doug Solter

Man With The Golden Falcons

Dr. Yes

Thunderdog

Tomorrow Always Lies

Spies Like Me

Skid Racing Series

GIRLS ONLY LIVE TWICE

BOOK 5 OF THE GEMS SPY SERIES

Doug Solter

To Anna, thank you for all you've done.

GIRLS ONLY LIVE TWICE

Trigger Warning:
This novel contains story elements involving teen suicide.
If you encounter strong feelings towards self-harm,
depression, or suicide, please call 1-800-273-8255
Or go to www.suicidepreventionlifeline.org

CHAPTER 1

Emma groaned as she circled the Mercedes around the city block and discovered there were no more open parking spaces. She was the one who talked herself into a slight detour into downtown San Francisco to check out a sale on Sergei Sackmonov bags at Tousant's right after school choir practice. So when the Gems asked her to pick them up some coffee while she was out, Emma headed to the nearest Kaffee Kadre cafe according to her car's GPS. However, this location didn't have a drive-thru or its own parking, so Emma had to find a place on the street.

The sun moved across the glass windshield as she made another circle and found no spaces had opened up. Emma surrendered to the situation and drove over to the next block, where she found a parking space across from a private Catholic school. It would be a long walk to the Kaffee Kadre, but the weather was mild, and Emma wore flats today.

Emma slipped out of her Mercedes and locked it. Across the street, she caught a glimpse of two little girls walking and talking to each other without a care in the world. Emma guessed they were about nine or ten years old, with both wearing private school uniforms. The girls were loud enough that she could hear them from across the street. The brunette girl reminded Emma of Hailey, her best friend from New York. And the blond girl—well, of course she saw herself under those locks of golden hair. The two girls would constantly touch each other, making new points or wanting the other girl's reaction to a question or a thought she had. Emma could tell they were close, like she and Hailey had been at that age. Then Emma realized she hadn't spoken to Hailey since she moved out to California.

Emma shook off her guilt and headed down the concrete

sidewalk. But then a little girl's scream made her stop.

The blond girl kicked her feet in the air as one man had her trapped under his arms as he ran down the sidewalk. A second man pushed the brunette girl away, causing her to stumble and fall. He ran in the same direction as the first man.

Emma couldn't stop watching. What was going on?

The man with the girl hauled her over to a Pinnacle rental van with the back doors open.

Emma's flats were already crossing the street. This didn't look right at all. The girl screamed like the man was a stranger, not someone she knew.

The first man climbed into the back of the van with the little girl. The second one shut the back door as he ran to the passenger-side door.

Her heart pulsated. Emma couldn't believe this was happening. She took a quick look around, and there was no one else seeing this. She hustled over to the brunette girl, who was still on the ground. "Are you okay?"

The brunette girl nodded.

The van's front rubber tires squealed as it took off down the street.

"Who are those men? Do you recognize them at all?"

The girl shook her head as tears formed in her eyes.

Emma took another look. Still no one else to help. It was up to her. She knelt in front of the girl. "Go back to your school, find an adult, and tell them what happened. Can you do that?"

The girl nodded again. She turned around and ran down the sidewalk towards the school.

Emma jumped into her car. The engine roared as she spun the Mercedes around and gunned it down the street. She drove down one block and didn't see the van. The next block fed into a major intersection. Emma's gut told her they most likely turned there. The big question was...left or right?

Generally, Emma hated left turns. She liked right ones because they were easier. Since the men in the van were in a hurry, maybe they took the easy way too. Emma turned right. She guided her Mercedes on to a six-lane road, which was one of the main arteries heading south to San Jose. The late-afternoon traffic was heavy, but Emma pushed herself to drive more aggressively as she weaved her car through.

Finally, the Pinnacle company logo popped into view...then disappeared in traffic.

Emma changed lanes for a better look.

The Pinnacle van was headed south, moving along with traffic as if everything inside it was normal.

Emma hated driving fast. While training to be a spy, her last evasive-driving instructor had quit in exasperation. Thank goodness Lioness stepped up and did her best to teach Emma basic car control, which did give her some much-needed confidence. Emma knew that if she stayed focused and didn't go too fast, she could drive safely enough for most situations. Trouble is, when you're a spy and bad guys are chasing you...or in this case you have to save a young girl's life...average driving won't cut it.

Emma wedged her car into the next lane. Sped up. Then forced her way over to the next lane and was greeted with an angry horn. She was now behind the rental van. She checked the rear windows and couldn't see anything, but she did recognize the plate. It was the same van.

Emma snapped a picture of the van with the plate, then her thumb danced on her phone as she tried to send an email with the pic to the police. But doing this while driving was more than Emma could—

The seat-belt gripped her chest as the car came to a sudden stop. The Mercedes's auto-braking system had activated to prevent Emma from plowing into the back of the van. Emma then caught a man's face watching her from the van's large side mirror.

The van then scampered off like a scared cat as it crossed over the center line and raced down the wrong side of the street.

Emma didn't want to do this, but she followed the van over to the wrong side of the street and pressed the pedal down as far as it could go. The Mercedes surged forward, cutting down the distance between them.

The van swerved out of its lane to reveal a large garbage truck heading right at her.

Emma almost hit the brake...but used her steering wheel instead, maneuvering her car around the garbage truck, and followed the van back onto the correct side of traffic.

The van swerved in front of her as it cut into a hard right turn.

Now Emma used her brakes as Lioness's patient teaching voice lingered in her head...

Always brake before the turn, then you accelerate through it. That way you keep control of the car.

Emma cranked the wheel and pumped the accelerator, giving the Mercedes enough juice to push through the right turn as she followed the van down a narrow two-lane street. Emma was on him. Close enough to let him know she was there, but far enough away to match whatever turn he was about to make. She glanced at her phone. Emma wanted to send a message to the police, but if she pulled over to do that, then the van and the little girl would be gone.

Then tell your car to call them, you stupid girl!

Her brain was right. Emma totally forgot about that. "Mercedes, call 9—"

The van made a hard left, back onto another major street. She matched the turn and accelerated.

The van was flying now. Swerving in and out of traffic. Driving recklessly.

A pleasant female voice came over the car's speakers. *Who would you like me to call?*

The van sailed through a yellow light.

Emma hated yellow lights. She stopped at most of them. But this time she kept off the brake and bit her lip for luck.

The light turned red as another car moved across the intersection on green.

Emma braked lightly, just enough to coast right behind that car and out of the intersection. Her foot then slammed down on the accelerator.

"Mercedes, call 911," Emma repeated.

I can't find a signal. Would you like me to keep trying?

She wanted to scream. "Yes."

Emma kept up her pursuit as the van raced its way out of downtown and did a sharp turn into a local air-strip. It was a private airport. Or that was what the sign on the gate said before the van obliterated it.

Emma braked hard as she slid her Mercedes through the broken gate. This private airstrip had a series of long "driveways" that connected up to the small concrete taxiway that ran parallel to the single runway. The van raced up a narrow access road that ran along the edge of the taxiway itself, passing by several large houses owned by people who enjoyed the luxury of flying straight home.

4

I can't find a signal. Would you like me to keep trying?

"Yes!" Emma yelled as her car skidded across the access road before she could point the Mercedes in the right direction. After the correction, Emma scrambled down the access road. But then she brought the car to a stop.

At the other end of the runway was a small private plane with two spinning propellers. Its bright take-off lights shined down the runway. The plane was all ready to go. The Pinnacle van skidded to a stop, and the three men carried the little girl towards the plane.

This caught Emma by surprise. Once they flew the girl out of the city...she'd be gone forever.

The men boarded the aircraft with their prisoner. The side door was latched shut. The two engines revved to a high pitch as the plane rolled forward for take-off.

Emma began to panic.

I have a signal. Calling 911, the pleasant lady announced.

It was too late. What could the police do now? There was no van to stop. They'd need a police jet or something.

Oh my God, that poor little girl is about to suffer through some horrible crap because you suck at this.

As panic clouded Emma's mind, a different voice cut through all the emotions...

Focus on your actions. What can you do in this situation? Take those actions. Change the situation. Put it under your control.

Lioness's words filled Emma with new confidence.

Remember, Black Opal, a Gem doesn't call for help. She is the help.

The plane was moving faster. Soon it would pass right by her.

"I am the help," Emma told herself. She gripped the leather steering wheel. She had her car. She had her purse, which had some spy equipment she could use. She could act. And she knew she had to act.

Emma stomped on the accelerator. The Mercedes burned rubber as it drove off the small access road and fishtailed across the grass and mud, finally pulling itself up on to the runway. Emma put the Mercedes on a collision course with the small plane. Its take-off lights blinded her as they pierced through the windshield.

But Emma didn't stop.

The distance between the two objects closed. So much so that Emma didn't want to chance it...

She cranked the wheel and spun the Mercedes to a stop...right across the runway.

The lights grew brighter. The plane was still roaring towards her. Emma realized it might not be able to stop in time.

Instead of saving that little girl...Emma might have just killed her.

She shut her eyes and braced for impact.

Then the plane's noisy engines suddenly veered away from her.

Emma opened her eyes. The aircraft had taken a runway exit back to the taxiway. It was now rolling quickly up that taxiway. Were they going back for another try? Surely they knew Emma wouldn't move her car off the runway.

When the plane got to the end of the taxiway, it did a one-eighty, and the pilot increased power again.

He's taking off from the taxiway.

Emma burned more rubber as she drove up the runway. This time she slid the Mercedes right across the front of the aircraft, causing the pilot to bring his plane to an abrupt halt. Even as their landing lights blew up the inside of her car, Emma did her best to glare at the men inside the plane. To let them know she wouldn't let them take off.

The plane's engines lowered in pitch, as if they were being powered down.

Emma grabbed her bag and dug through the contents. She had her *Forest Fire* mascara smoke grenade. The *Sunburst* hair conditioner and chemical-based flame-thrower. *Raise the Roof* rouge, which was actually a plastic explosive. And she had one *Blitzed* mascara pin dart.

She grabbed the hair conditioner and the mascara pin before carefully moving out of the car.

The side door of the aircraft popped open, and three men jumped down to the taxiway.

Emma stood behind her car with her mascara in one hand; and the hair conditioner in the other.

"Come over here," one of the men yelled over the engines as he came around Emma's car. He was young and muscular with tattoo art running down both arms.

Another man with bushy eyebrows followed. "You deal with her, and I'll get the car out of the way."

The third man stayed near the plane. He was big and tall, but Emma couldn't quite make out his face.

The young man with the tattoo art reached out to grab Emma, but she retreated and pointed the hair conditioner at him.

"Back off or you'll get hurt," she yelled.

The man ignored her.

Emma pointed at the ground and gave a little squirt, unleashing a small fireball that lit up the taxiway.

The young man jumped back.

Emma pointed it at him. "Move away."

Tattoo man held up his arms as he backed away. Behind him, the man with the bushy eyebrows was digging something out of his pocket.

She gave another squirt above the second man's head. The fireball lit up his eyes in terror as his hand froze on the grip of a gun still in its holster.

"Both hands up. Now!" Emma yelled, the actor inside her slipping into the new role of a bad-ass female cop.

The two men backed away. Now Emma would back them up to the plane, force them to take the girl off. Then the little girl would run to Emma's car, and she'd drive her to safety. But Emma realized a flaw in that plan.

Where was that third man who got off the plane?

The answer came from behind as the man's thick arms clamped down on Emma like a vise. His arms were too strong to break out of. Emma did try to roll forward and toss the big man off her, but he quickly lifted her feet off the ground, making it impossible.

She took her mascara pen and rammed it in the side of her attacker, who shook her until Emma dropped both the pen and the hair conditioner. The man's arms continued to squeeze her mid-section, convincing Emma she was about to be literally crushed to death.

Emma kicked the man's shins as hard as she could, making it painful for him to hold on to her.

It worked.

The man's grip loosened enough that Emma brought her foot up and used it to push him off her. Now free, Emma spun around and jumped into a fighting stance. She cocked her arm back for a palm strike when Emma saw the face of her attacker.

It was Aardvark.

Emma rubbed her eyes as if they were malfunctioning.

The man was bald, with a chest the size of a refrigerator. He also had a long scar running down the length of his throat.

Aardvark smiled as he held up his hands in surrender.

"What are you doing here?" Emma yelled, still trying to be heard over the engines. "What's going on?"

Suddenly the plane's noisy engines were both shut off. The two other "kidnappers" put down their hands and simply walked away as if someone on a film set had yelled cut.

A middle-aged woman emerged from one of the small private hangars near the taxiway. Her short blond hair whipped around in the breeze. Emma recognized her too. It was Lioness. Her Authority training instructor. Which meant…this all had been a test.

CHAPTER 2

It hit Emma like a cold wind. Her final. The last test Lioness told her she would need to take in the coming weeks before Emma would be certified as an official Authority operative. A test that would be unannounced.

Aardvark dropped to one knee. The tranquilizer dart that Emma had stuck into the side of his rib cage began to take effect.

Emma knelt beside him. "Oh my God, I'm so sorry. I didn't know it was you."

Aardvark kept his warm smile as he collapsed onto the concrete runway, unconscious.

"Aardvark? Oh my God."

"He'll be taking a nap for a while," Lioness said. "I should've anticipated that you might use your equipment. Thank you for not roasting any of my volunteers."

A fourth man asked Lioness a question in Russian. He must have been the pilot.

"*Nyet*," Lioness replied, then answered him back in Russian.

The pilot gave her a thumbs-up and left. Lioness then yelled something else in Russian, and the side door of the plane popped open. The little kidnapped blond girl jumped out of the plane and skipped up to Lioness without a care in the world.

"Say hello to my niece from St. Petersburg," Lioness said. "Katya, this is my student Black Opal."

"Hello," Katya said. "Thank you for—how you say?" She finished her question to Lioness in Russian.

"Rescue," Lioness corrected.

"*Da.*" Katya then addressed Emma. "Thank you for rescuing me."

"Pleased to meet you, Katya." Emma turned to Lioness. "You

9

brought your niece over from Russia just to test me?"

"Don't think so highly of yourself. Katya was here visiting with her father, so why not give her something fun to do. Besides, she wants to become an actress too. Poor thing."

Emma shot her a look.

"If it hasn't occurred to you by now, this was your final test, Black Opal. I'm pleased to say that you've—"

Katya asked something in Russian.

Lioness shook her head. "Use your English words."

"Where is my donut?" Katya asked in a thick accent. "You promised."

Lioness sighed and removed a small Dunkin' Donuts box out of her bag. She handed it to Katya, who opened it to reveal a maple-iced donut. She bit into it and rolled her eyes like a drug addict. It reminded Emma of her own addiction to mini chocolate donuts.

"Where was I?" Lioness asked.

"My final test?"

"*Da, da*...congratulations, you passed. Black Opal, you're now officially a trained intelligence officer. Now, help me drag Aardvark into your car so he can sleep off your present."

Through the windshield, Emma watched as Lioness directed her men to clean up the "kidnapping" scene. They stowed the aircraft in a hangar and got rid of the rental van. Lioness then made Katya clean her maple-icing-stained fingers with a soft wipe before climbing into the back of Emma's Mercedes, where Aardvark was still out of it. Lioness slipped into the passenger seat.

"Seriously, it's official. I'm now a fully trained secret agent?" Emma asked.

Lioness didn't smile. "You never did pass evasive driving, but you drove well enough on your final, so what the hell."

"Thank you."

"Your advanced skills in other areas far outweigh your driving. Anyway, the Gems are designed to act as a team, and you four ladies have more than enough skills to complement the team as a whole."

"However long that'll last."

Lioness squinted at her.

Emma hesitated. She wasn't sure if she wanted to bring it up now.

"Is there a problem with you and the girls?" Lioness asked. "Fighting over a boy or some other such nonsense?"

"It's not like that. It's more like—do you ever—I don't know how to say this…"

"Don't filter yourself. Not in front of me," Lioness said. "Say the words you mean to say."

Emma sat back in her seat and touched the stitched seam of the leather steering wheel. "Do you, like, ever question what we're doing?"

Lioness paused. "Can you be more specific?"

"You know, the Authority. Our mission. Do you ever think about…why we exist?"

"Didn't Mrs. B give you the official handbook on the first day? It explains our mission in great detail."

"The handbook doesn't explain the motivations of the people who founded us. You know, the Century Group."

"Yes it does," Lioness said. "It details the first twelve families who met after World War I and created a secret organization that only advocated for the good of mankind, not for a particular government."

"That was, like…hundreds of years ago," Emma said. "What about now? Who pulls the strings? Like, are we just pawns who make those families of the Century Group rich and powerful? Are we still the good guys?"

Lioness chuckled to herself. "Isn't that always a matter of perspective? A Russian sees anyone who tries to push him around as the bad guy. An American sees anyone who questions capitalism as the bad guy. A Sunni Muslim sees a Shia Muslim as the bad guy. And vice versa. Yet both of them can agree that the Jews are the real bad guys. Who's the ultimate judge of goodness?" Lioness paused. "It's not God. Too many versions of him or her on this planet. Each version has its followers willing to do horrible things to people to prove how worthy they are to their god."

"Are you saying there's no answer?" Emma asked.

"There's always an answer. Because it depends on the perspective of the person asking the question."

Emma watched the sun disappear over the horizon. Sometimes the world was more complicated than she'd like it to be.

"Having second thoughts, Black Opal?"

Before Emma could answer, an emulated voice interrupted...

Your father's disillusionment had more to do with your mother's death. I don't think it was about the organization itself.

The voice was from Aardvark's phone. Emma twisted around and saw Aardvark was awake. His thumbs were typing on the keypad.

We were sad to lose both of them.

Katya asked a question in Russian.

Lioness answered in Russian. Emma assumed she was asking about Aardvark and why he was using a phone to talk to people. Emma knew that his larynx was damaged, but she still didn't know how. It was a story Aardvark didn't share with anyone.

Your last mission was difficult. You were put in a difficult position. Asset One planted questions in your mind...

"Those questions weren't planted. Like, they've always been there," Emma said. "And I still need those questions answered."

Mrs. B will answer them.

Emma could tell that Lioness was curious. "I'm meeting Mrs. B tomorrow after school. She's going to tell me how my mother died."

Lioness nodded. "I read the report about the *Falcon's Claw* and Asset One trying to recruit you. Those types of missions can be difficult. Too easy for an operative to lose their perspective."

"Or gain new ones," Emma said.

"You're young. I can understand the conflict that such perspectives can create at your age. Just remember that it's human nature to trust what people say because you want to believe they have your best interests at heart," Lioness said. "However, until you can prove the truth with facts, you must assume they could all be lies."

"I want to prove the truth. I can't assume what people tell me is true because it's written in some handbook, you know? I need to hear it from the people who wrote the handbook."

I do not think you persuaded her, Lioness.

"That's not my job, Aardvark. My job is training. I train operatives not to trust what people tell them. Black Opal is a skeptic. There's nothing wrong with that. It only takes one brave woman to refuse the Kool-Aid to prevent mankind from committing suicide." Lioness addressed Emma. "I'll give you my opinion. I believe the Century Group's intentions are honest. I've been around long enough to see the things they've done. The actions they've taken. The people they've saved. A socialist might be angry about their wealth and power. However, I've seen other powerful people squander such wealth, buying meaningless things. At least the Century Group believes in reinvesting that wealth back into the planet, for the benefit of all mankind." Lioness tilted her head. "That's good enough for me."

CHAPTER 3

All the next day at school, Emma's brain could only focus on one thing, her meeting with Mrs. B. Every class, every hour, every minute of the day seemed like it took forever. Finally, the last bell rang, and Emma walked out to the student parking lot, where three girls were waiting near her Mercedes.

"Would you like us to come with you?" Miyuki asked. She wore shoulder-length black hair, and her skin was light with cool, pink undertones. There was love in her green eyes, like a sister who could always tell when you needed a hug.

"You all don't have to go," Emma said. "Seriously, it's not like it's a mission briefing."

"We don't have to be there, but we want to be there. For you."

"Yes, we'd like to be there if you'll find it helpful." Nadia flashed a supportive smile on her warm, orange-brown face. Her blue headscarf matched her fashion-torn jeans as she cradled her lower-leg cast on a leg scooter. Her broken shin was a "gift" from their last adventure.

Nadia shot a look over at her best friend. "Olivia?"

Olivia combed back her curly ribbons of golden-brown hair that covered her eyes. Her beautiful brown skin was accented by cool, bronze undertones. "Emma, you're a member of this team. And we Gems—well, we stick together, right? No matter what. So if you need us there, we're there, love."

It was the worst acting job Olivia had ever done.

Emma turned to Nadia. "Did it take you all day to convince her to say that?"

"Why do I even flipping bother?" Olivia stormed off.

Nadia rolled her scooter in pursuit. "Where are you going?"

"I'm taking the bus. Don't worry about me." Olivia upgraded her walk to a jog as she headed off towards the school bus loading zone.

Nadia stopped. She looked back at Miyuki and Emma, then back at Olivia, who wasn't stopping. Emma could tell she was torn. Nadia had known Olivia way before Miyuki and Emma joined the Gems. But since her injury prevented Nadia from catching up, she retreated to the car.

"She does care," Nadia said. "It's just…after what happened on the *Falcon's Claw*—"

"I get it," Emma interrupted her. "Let's just go, okay?"

It was almost an hour-long drive from Berkeley to Napa Valley. When Emma turned off California State Highway 29, the clock on the dashboard read a few minutes after four. The Burlington Winery sign at the entrance was new. It had warmer colors than the old one, and the design was much more modern. More 2020 than 1920. Emma drove past the winery's public parking lot and took the access road that led to the hidden entrance.

Skip, the long-haired hippie guy with round glasses cleaned his grape-stained smock with his hands before easing up to the familiar vehicle. "Hello there. Identification, please." He checked the Gems' IDs and looked around the entire car before handing them back.

"Can you put a case in the trunk?" Emma asked. "We come here all the time and have yet to taste the wine, you know?"

Skip laughed. "How 'bout I put our fantastic apple cider in your trunk instead."

"C'mon, it's not like we haven't had wine before. We're not kids."

"If I gave you kids wine, do you know what Mrs. B would do to me? I'll get transferred to our Siberian station. All that snow and mud. No, thanks. Now, move along."

Emma put the car in gear and moved on. She parked inside a small garage. The door closed automatically as a hidden elevator in the floor lowered her Mercedes to the underground parking lot.

After clearing the numerous security checkpoints, the three Gems emerged into a huge underground atrium. Aardvark was there, waiting near a golf cart. He offered Nadia the keys.

"Bless you," Nadia said. She took the keys as Miyuki helped her into the cart and stowed her leg scooter in the back. "May I take you to Mrs. B's office?"

"Yeah, but I need a restroom stop first." Emma climbed up and sat down on the back bench of the cart. She gave Aardvark a tiny wave as the cart rolled across the polished floor tiles of the atrium.

Nadia went around the large circular staircase that went up to the second floor, which was an office area cut up into glass-walled cubicles and meeting rooms. There was also a slide that snaked its way around the circular staircase for those who wanted a quick thrill during their workday. The underground atrium connected all the areas of the Napa Valley headquarters. The relaxation room. The jungle. The cafeteria. And the most sensitive area...the Labyrinth.

Nadia parked outside the women's restroom.

Emma jumped off the back. "It'll only take a second."

She ran inside. There were a few women already there, so Emma stepped into an open stall and shut the door. She pulled down her jeans and sat on the toilet, but she wasn't there to relieve herself. She opened her legs and removed a small thumb drive held against her inner thigh by two of Miyuki's Spider-Man Band-Aids that Emma had "borrowed" this morning. It was the thumb drive the leader of Venomous had given her a few days ago. The thumb drive that held the truth about her mother's death.

Emma tore off a piece of toilet paper and dropped it into the toilet along with her used Band-Aids before flushing it all. She pulled her jeans back up and palmed the thumb drive before leaving the stall. Emma turned on the faucet; but only washed the outside of her fist, protecting the thumb drive from the water as she dried her hands with a paper towel and left the bathroom.

Emma climbed back on to the cart, and Nadia drove them over to the entrance to the Labyrinth.

"We'll be in the cafeteria," she said.

"And we'll be thinking about you," Miyuki added.

"Thanks for being here," Emma said. "Seriously."

Emma entered the Labyrinth, a maze of dark blue floors, ceilings, and walls with thin white light strips outlining each wall. This area of the complex always gave her the chills. The weird lighting. The cave-like vibe this place gave out. It made people feel unwelcome. As if they didn't want you to come inside here unless you had to.

The door to the EQ division was open, so Emma went right

inside. She went straight to her equipment locker and placed her thumb over a sensor that read every detail of her unique thumbprint. The light went green, releasing the lock. Inside her locker were two new *Blitzed* mascara darts. Two more *Forest Fire* mascara smoke grenades. And a *Wham Bam* mascara flash-bang grenade. If she were assigned a mission, usually the appropriate equipment would be placed inside her locker. However, for protection, a few items were always available to the Gems because they never knew where or when the enemy would strike.

Emma examined the thumb drive in her palm and wondered what was on it. Would it give her the truth? Was Asset One being genuine or trying to take advantage of her?

She put the thumb drive in her locker, hiding it inside a paper box of tampons. Emma wanted to hear what Mrs. B had to say about her mother's death. Emma wanted someone to be honest with her and tell the truth. If Mrs. B's story matched what was on the thumb drive, then Emma could trust her again. If it didn't— Emma would climb that mountain if she came to it.

Emma navigated through the dark hallways to arrive at the CAC Division or Command and Control area of the Labyrinth. She stopped next to an office door labeled number 99 and pressed a button. A low chime rang while a video side screen came to life with Mrs. B's face.

"Are you alone?" Mrs. B asked.

"Yes, ma'am."

The seals around the door frame deflated with a whoosh as the air escaped from the office and the lock was released. Emma opened the door and stepped inside. Mrs. B's vintage pink steel desk was unoccupied, but her office still had those old concert posters from the 1960s along with some modern artwork. Emma shut the door, causing a sucking sound as the door frame sealed back up again and the lock engaged.

Emma noticed a new concert poster. "Peter, Paul, and Mary... who are they?"

"Have you ever heard the song '*Puff the Magic Dragon*'?" Mrs. B asked.

Emma followed her voice over to the vintage couch. Mrs. B had a small circular coffee table in front of her with a teapot, a plate of cookies, and small sandwiches.

"I don't think so." Emma sat next to her on the couch. "Is it a

'60s song?'"

"A folk song. Quite popular in its day. I played it for your mother once as a child, and she fell in love with it. It's quite a lovely tune. A wonderful diversion from reality. A song full of fantasy." Mrs. B poured Emma a cup of tea, then serviced her cup. "You prefer stevia over sugar, yes?"

Emma nodded. "One please."

Mrs. B tore open a packet and sprinkled it on top. "Cream or milk?"

"Just the stevia is fine. Thanks."

Mrs. B offered her the cup, then finished her tea with a splash of milk before sipping it.

"Was it her favorite song?" Emma asked.

"As a child it was. However, when Angela turned twelve, she discovered MTV, Duran Duran, and finally U2. Her life was forever changed. She no longer wanted to listen to my music…she had her own. She had a good ear for it too. Growing up, I should've exposed her more to music. She could have been a musician or a singer." Mrs. B took a sip and glanced at Emma. "You have your mother's genes. The voice. The acting chops. I'm pleased you're taking the arts so seriously. Your mother would have liked that."

"What was she like?"

Mrs. B smiled to herself. "Angela was strong. Very strong. She was a risk taker. As a kid, she got easily bored. She always wanted to be doing something. Anything to relieve the boredom. She would climb a tree. Jump into a pond. Chase a dog. Angela was always moving. Always exploring. One time she accidentally got trapped inside an old mine."

"A mine?" Emma asked.

"We were living out in Colorado, and somehow her friends discovered an old silver mine. Well, they dared her to go inside it, and of course Angela did, and she fell into a shaft and broke both her legs. Since the rescuers had to tunnel through meters of dirt, they couldn't get to her for days." Mrs. B hesitated. "At that time, we feared the worst. Everyone told us there was no way she could survive for that long."

"And they were wrong."

Mrs. B grinned slightly. "They were wrong. Angela didn't give in to her circumstances. She tunneled herself into another chamber, using only her fingers. She was able to get oxygen through an old vent that still ran up to the surface. Once the rescuers broke into that chamber, they found her alive with her fingernails worn down to the tips and bleeding. Angela never gave up hope. That young girl was tough. She fought hard to survive."

"Wow. I mean, seriously…that's amazing."

"Your mother was amazing. She was one of those women who could tilt a room towards her. And it had nothing to do with looks. Angela's personality and zest for life drew people to her like moths to a light. When she joined the Authority, we had to work on toning down that side of her. We taught her how to control it. How to focus it on targets. Angela became the best operative at flipping assets. She could make any man spill out his life story, and she never once used her body to do it. She was that good."

"Did she want to follow in your footsteps?" Emma asked.

"When Angela turned eighteen, I told her what I did. What I really did. She wanted to learn more, but I insisted that she go to college first before making such a big decision. You see, it's rather common for the Authority to recruit members inside families of existing members. We can more easily evaluate people that way. And if they're loyal to their family, they're usually loyal to us."

"Did you give her a choice?" Emma asked.

"Of course. It was the same choice I gave you."

"Why didn't you wait until I was in college?"

Mrs. B took a moment to glance into her tea, then gave it another sip, enjoying the flavor of the brew. "When you moved out here to live with your grandmother Bernadette, I saw it as an opportunity to approach you."

"Especially since my father was dead," Emma added, without thinking.

Mrs. B straightened at that comment.

Emma was then glad she said it. "My dad didn't want you to approach me."

Mrs. B hesitated. "Your mother would've wanted you to know."

Emma left it alone. "How did she meet my dad?"

Mrs. B sipped her tea. A grin returned to her lips. "When I was transferred to the New York station, Angela came with me. She had completed a few missions as an intelligence op, and people were pleased with her work. I was given a new job as controller for a group of intelligence operatives in North America. We were both settling in to our new surroundings when one day Angela dragged me over to a window that overlooked a large meeting room. This room was filled with people way above our security level…but Angela didn't care about any of that. She wanted me to see this tall, handsome man with blond hair who was addressing everyone in the room. I asked her what was so special about him. Angela replied, 'That wonderful hunk is going to fall in love with me, and I'm going to marry him.' Well, I laughed at her."

"Oh my God. Really?"

"I told Angela that she didn't even know this man. How did she know he would fall in love with her? Yet my daughter had that look in her eye. She stared right at me and said, 'Mom, I want him, and I will convince him that I am the only woman on this planet for him."

"Wow," Emma said. "She was obsessed with him."

"Your mother wasn't crazy," Mrs. B said. "She just knew exactly what she wanted. At first it was Ken's looks; then once she collected more intelligence on him from the people around the office, Angela liked him even more. However, no one mentioned to her that Ken was the New York station head as well as a sitting member of the Century Group. That became relevant when Angela asked him out, because Ken thought she was trying to manipulate him in order to gain favor within the organization. So Ken said no and put her on probation. Soon, Angela was the butt of every joke in that office. Even I took some heat because people thought I encouraged her to do this."

"Then…how did they get together?" Emma asked.

"Angela asked for a transfer to the London station, which was granted. And then she asked Ken out again in an email, saying it had nothing to do with her career. But this time, Angela told him the same thing she told me. That he would fall in love with her, and they would be together. She basically dared him to take a chance on her. That if he didn't, Ken would regret it for the rest of his life."

"Holy shit." Emma covered her mouth. "I'm sorry, Grandma— Mrs. B. That's amazing. I could never do something like that."

"That's my Angela. She was fearless." Mrs. B thought about it. "Perhaps Ken wanted to get rid of her once and for all…or maybe she intrigued him enough that he took a chance. Either way, he flew out to London, and they went out to dinner." Mrs. B stopped and poured herself some more tea.

Emma waited.

Mrs. B put in some sugar and another splash of milk.

The woman was taking forever.

"And?" Emma asked.

"Ken immediately put in a vacation request and stayed in London for about two weeks."

Emma laughed.

"Even though she worked out of the London station, Angela stayed with me in New York and flew out to England when she had a mission," Mrs. B said. "I must give your parents credit, they were committed to each other. They made that relationship work. And it did. After two years of dating, Ken proposed to your mom. They got married, and Angela was transferred back to the New York station, but only after Ken stepped down as station chief."

Mrs. B stopped again. "Would you like more tea?"

Emma shook her head. She was so interested that she had barely even touched her cup.

Mrs. B bit into one of the small cookies. "These biscuits are quite tasty. Would you like one?"

Emma wasn't interested in cookies now. She wanted Mrs. B to keep talking.

Mrs. B glanced at her watch. "I've kept you here much too late. With all the traffic, it will take you at least two hours to get home. But if you start now, you could get home before seven. I hope your grandmother Bernadette won't be too cross with me for making you so late for dinner."

Emma realized Mrs. B was avoiding the one subject that was the entire reason she was here.

"We always come home late after these meetings. Seriously, Grandma's used to it." Emma downed her luke-warm tea in one gulp. "You know what? I will have more tea. Thanks."

Mrs. B nodded and poured her a fresh cup and sprinkled the stevia on top before stirring it.

Emma waited.

Mrs. B didn't smile as she finished off her cookie. "Are you peckish? The sandwiches are tuna-fish salad, I do believe."

"I'm not hungry."

Mrs. B patted her lips with the napkin, causing her lipstick to stain the paper.

She was stalling.

Emma was now about to lose it. She'd better start talking.

"You promised me," Emma warned.

"Promised you what?" Mrs. B asked.

"You know what."

Mrs. B paused.

Emma waited.

"I remember this one time, when your mother was six years old —"

"Shut up." The words flew out of Emma's mouth, the anger pushing her on, nagging her not to back down.

Mrs. B scowled. "Excuse me?"

"Seriously, I won't even give you a week. When I walk out that door, I'm done. Do you hear me? I'm through with all this shit."

"Calm down and watch your language."

"That's your answer? Watch my fucking language?" Emma jumped off the couch. "Why did I even listen to you? I'm an idiot. Of course you wouldn't tell me how my mother died. What do they call this—? Bait and switch? You trick me into coming down here and tell me everything about my mom except the one thing I asked you for. And you did that because...what, you thought I would forget about it? Forget about everything that's happened to me the last few weeks?"

"You must learn to control your emotions," Mrs. B said with an edge.

"You can control this." Emma flipped her off, then marched towards the door.

Mrs. B gripped her cane and stood up. The woman's entire body quivered with anger. "Damn you, Angela, you come right back here and sit down."

Emma stopped in her tracks.

The older woman's mouth hung open. Her eyes in total shock. She sank back onto the couch and closed her mouth. Mrs. B gained back her composure. "Emma. I meant to say Emma. Please forgive me."

Emma glanced at the door, then back at her grandmother. She sat back down and waited.

Mrs. B sighed and flattened the hem of her dress. "What I'm about to tell you...can not be repeated to anyone. I mean... anyone. Do I make myself clear on that point?"

CHAPTER 4

After her anger subsided, Emma discovered she had developed quite an appetite after yelling inside Mrs. B's private office. She reasoned that fury must burn lots of calories. She took a bite of one of the tuna-fish sandwiches, and it hit the spot.

Mrs. B relaxed and sampled her own tuna-fish sandwich. She wiped her mouth with a cloth napkin, laid it out on her lap, and began.

"In the early 2000s, I was a station chief for the Authority in CapeTown, South Africa. It was a smaller station, but it was my first official posting since being promoted from field operations, so I wanted to do the best job I could. After my first year in CapeTown, the United States attacked Iraq, citing that their intelligence services had evidence of their leader Saddam Hussein developing nuclear weapons. Our fear was these nuclear weapons could be smuggled out of Iraq and used elsewhere. Since I was the ranking station chief in Africa, it was my job to coordinate with other stations and search for these weapons or their materials if they made their way into Africa."

"Grandma Bernadette told me that it was a lie. That the White House used those weapons as an excuse to start another war."

Mrs. B scoffed. "Your grandmother has the luxury of history to reflect back on. Those of us who had to make decisions at the time didn't have that luxury. We were dealing with nuclear weapons. Allowing them to fall into the wrong hands was not an option."

"How does any of this relate to my mom?"

"Patience, Emma," Mrs. B said. "One day, some of my operatives working in the illegal weapons trade got wind of an Iraq army colonel who had fled the war but managed to smuggle out a sizeable amount of weapons. Since this colonel was setting up shop in Africa to turn his weapons into cash, we had to check him out.

We tried our best to get someone close to him, but every attempt failed. Then, glancing at the man's intelligence report, there was a note about his collection of VHS movies that he smuggled out of Iraq, most of which were Judy Garland movies. "

"Did he have a wife?" Emma asked.

"No wife or girlfriend that we could find."

Emma smiled. "He was gay."

"It was missed by everyone. We could have conducted a honey pot operation with the appropriate man, but I came up with a more creative approach. This colonel was on the run and desperate. He didn't have time to fall in love. However, he did need someone to support him. A best friend who could help him find a new place to live. That's when I thought about using Angela. She was just coming off her maternity leave after having you."

"Why did you pick her?"

"I needed a rich socialite. A woman who traveled the world and knew all the right people. A rich best friend who could help a gay Iraqi man find a new place to make a life for himself. Your mother was fluent in both French and Arabic. And thanks to your father, she knew all about the lives of the ultra-rich. Plus, your mother was one of the best solo operatives we ever had. I knew if Angela could get close to him, she would be the best friend that he never had before. So I submitted a transfer request for Angela."

"What was her cover?" Emma asked.

"Angela posed as a rich divorcee from the French Rivera on a guided tour of Africa. The colonel and Angela ran into each other, and she took him under her wing. They flew to the UAE on her 'private jet' to go shopping; and so that Angela could show him off to all her 'friends' in Dubai. It was perfect. That colonel opened up to her like a flower. Soon we were getting details on everyone he was selling arms to. That's when Angela found out about crate AOR four-thirty-one."

"What's that?"

"We traced the number back to a chemical weapons facility outside Basra, Iraq. This facility was also suspected of conducting nuclear weapons research. As far as we knew, there was a possibility that a nuclear weapon could be inside that crate. So Angela used a Geiger counter to confirm the presence of radioactive material inside that crate. At that point, we were convinced it was a nuclear weapon of some type, so we coordinated with the South African national police to conduct a raid." Mrs. B paused and cleared her throat. "The crate and all its contents were safely neutralized, but the police took some casualties in the raid. Also…the Iraqi colonel had to be killed."

"And my mom?"

"Unfortunately, Angela became a casualty during the raid. However, her brave actions prevented those weapons from being sold on the black market. Your mother died a hero."

"How did it happen?" Emma asked. "What are the details? Seriously, there must be a report about it."

"The actual details of that raid are classified. I can't give you specifics. But I can assure you that your mother believed in what she was doing, and I couldn't be prouder of her."

Emma finished her tuna-fish sandwich as she prodded Mrs. B for more details, but the woman stayed firm. The details of the raid were classified.

"You should be on your way home," Mrs. B added. "I've kept you here long enough and spoiled your dinner. Please send your grandmother Bernadette my apologies."

It was ten minutes past eight o'clock in the evening by the time Emma pulled into her Grandma Bernadette's driveway in Berkeley. Miyuki helped Nadia out of the back of the Mercedes until she could use her leg scooter. Emma then opened the front door, and the three Gems went inside the house. No one was in the living room.

"Grandma? Olivia?" Emma called out.

"In the kitchen, young one," her grandma's voice answered.

The three Gems followed her voice.

Grandma Bernadette had her long white hair twisted into a single braid that ran down the back of her University of California sweater. She was using her cotton mitts to take out soup bowls from the oven. Each bowl had a thick layer of baked swiss cheese on top. Emma noticed Olivia was already enjoying her soup at the wooden table in the breakfast nook.

"You couldn't wait for us?" Nadia asked with a playful tone.

"I was peckish," Olivia said. "Waited almost two hours for you."

"We both did," Grandma Bernadette said. "I had to snack on an apple." She took out the last of four soup bowls from the oven.

"French onion soup with only natural ingredients. I kept them warm in the oven for you."

"*Hei*, they look delicious," Miyuki said.

"You didn't use vegan cheese again, did you?" Emma asked.

Her grandma sighed. "No, young one, I used real swiss this time. But I still thought that vegan swiss was fine."

Emma could still remember that fake cheese with the nasty aftertaste that made Grandma's last version of French onion soup taste like a sweaty armpit.

"It's actually brilliant," Olivia said. "Tastes like a proper French soup."

Grandma Bernadette placed her soup and a piece of French bread on a small tray. "I'm making a fire in the pit, if anyone wants to join me."

Usually that was everyone's cue to join her regardless if they wanted to or not. But tonight, Emma wanted to. So she followed her grandma outside to the backyard. Everyone bypassed the birch table on the deck in favor of the pebble-stoned ring that surrounded the fire-pit. The four Gems found their favorite spots among the lawn chairs as Grandma lit up the pit. The fire popped and flickered as the smoke rose into the night sky.

"How did your meeting go?" Olivia asked.

Everyone stopped eating and glanced over at Emma.

"It was good," Emma answered.

"What did Laura have to say?" Grandma Bernadette asked.

To Emma, it was still strange to hear Mrs. B being referred to as Laura, even though the two older women had known each other way before Emma was even born.

"Mrs. B told me how my mom died. But she made me swear not to say anything. So I can't."

Olivia nodded. "It was good of her to tell you what she could. She didn't have to do that."

"On the contrary…Laura has a moral obligation to tell her granddaughter the truth," Grandma Bernadette said. "She should've been honest with you the moment she first approached you to join."

The slight tension around the fire-pit eased as they ate their dinner. Miyuki volunteered to clean up, and Nadia went inside to help. Snoopy followed Nadia inside, no doubt feeling empathy with the wounded girl since his own weak back was still supported by a brace.

Olivia felt a slight chill in the air and decided to head back inside. But she hesitated.

"What is it?" Emma asked.

Olivia glanced at the fire, then back at Emma. "Sorry I didn't come."

"You didn't have to."

"Everyone else did so I feel like—look, Mrs. B expects me to look after everyone. Well, today was an important day for you, and I should've been there like everyone else because a team should support each other." Olivia glanced back at the fire again. "But I let my personal feelings get in the way of that." She breathed in the cool air and looked back at Emma. "Like I said, I'm sorry I didn't come."

Olivia then went inside.

"Crap," Emma said. "I didn't say thank you."

"No need," Grandma Bernadette said. "Olivia had to get that off her chest. She was talking about nothing else for the entire afternoon."

"Seriously?"

Her grandma nodded.

The fire burned lower in the pit but still offered a nice overall glow to those around it.

Emma and her grandma Bernadette exchanged glances.

This made her grandma raise an eyebrow. "What is it, young one?"

"Do you want to know what Grandma Laura said?"

"I thought you said you couldn't tell us."

Emma moved her chair over next to her grandma. "I couldn't say anything with Olivia and Nadia around. Seriously, they'd rat me out in a second." Emma paused and gave her grandma a smile. "My mom died a hero. She prevented nuclear weapons from getting into the hands of terrorists. Isn't that awesome?"

Grandma Bernadette thought about it.

"Thousands—no, millions of people were saved by her sacrifice." When Emma said it out loud, the words took on a new meaning. A new reality that Emma was embracing. She was the daughter of a mother who was a hero and a father who created a billion-dollar corporation. Emma was the product of two great people. Meaning she had the potential of becoming great as well, right? What could stop her? No wonder Asset One wanted to recruit her for Venomous.

"Your father never wanted to talk about it."

"About what? My mom?"

Grandma Bernadette nodded. "If I ever brought the subject up, Ken would shut down. He'd stare through the window or at a wall. Sometimes it would last a couple days. Finally I stopped talking about your mom."

"Well, it was because he loved her, you know?" Emma asked. "The same way I loved him."

"Ken loved your mom with every fiber of his being." Grandma Bernadette hesitated. "To be honest, I wasn't one of her fans."

Emma shifted her body to look at her grandma. "What do you mean?"

"When I first met your mom, I thought she was banana-cream-pie crazy. Ken told me about this young woman obsessing over him, and I advised him to seek out a professional to evaluate her mental state before agreeing to date her." Grandma Bernadette relaxed. "However, as I got to know her, I found Angela more high-strung and adventurous than actually crazy. I began to understand what Ken saw in her. She made his life exciting. Shook up his complacency. Gave him a new perspective on life. And there were a lot of things that Ken did that rubbed off on Angela. As a couple, they smoothed each other out. Overall, it was a healthy relationship."

"Does that mean my mom won you over?"

Grandma Bernadette thought about it. "She treated my son well. And he did love her. But I'd be lying if I said Angela didn't take some getting used to. However, I accepted her."

"My mom sounded like an interesting woman." Emma felt the disappointment dragging down her happiness. She would give anything to have both of them back. "I wish I knew more about her."

"What did Laura say about her?"

"She told me the story about when my mom first saw my dad." Emma went on to tell her about Ken having to transfer Angela to London because he thought she was faking her love for him to get a promotion. And about Angela still asking him out despite this. And about her father staying for two weeks to get to know her."

"That's all?"

"Yeah, what else is there?" Emma asked.

Grandma Bernadette sighed as she peered into the flames of the fire. "After Angela was killed...something happened between Ken and Laura. I don't know if it was the anguish over Angela's death or what...but Ken refused to speak to Laura after your mom's funeral. He blamed Laura for something, and he wouldn't tell me what it was. Laura would then call me and ask if I would help her communicate with Ken. But since no one was telling me what the hell was going on, I refused to get into the middle of their fight. Basically, whatever it was soured Ken's views about the Authority. He questioned his own involvement with it and later quit. He also told Laura to stay away from you. That he never wanted you to be recruited into the cause."

"But you let me do it anyway," Emma said.

"I gave you a choice because you were sixteen. And the price of that cooperation was that you would have options moving forward. You weren't aware of this, but I made Laura promise me that you could change your mind. If you don't passionately believe in what they're doing, then you have the choice to walk away. Just like your father did."

Emma sat back. She wasn't aware of such a deal.

"I was hoping Laura would be honest with you. If she wouldn't tell me about the disagreement she had with Ken, she could at least tell her own granddaughter," Grandma Bernadette scoffed. "I suppose protecting secrets is much more important to her than family."

Emma's enthusiasm was gone. Mrs B hadn't told her about the bargain she had made with her grandma Bernadette. And she didn't even touch on the subject of why her father left the Authority in the first place. Was it only about her mom's death? Or was there something else?

She had no choice.

Since the files could only be unlocked using security protocols from an Authority computer, Emma had to go back to headquarters tomorrow and see what was on that thumb drive.

CHAPTER 5

The next day, Emma told the Gems that Kayla wanted her to come over and hang out after school.

It was a lie.

Instead of visiting Kayla, Emma drove back out to Napa Valley. She parked her Mercedes underground, went through all the security, then walked inside the Labyrinth. Once again, Emma stopped at her equipment locker inside the EQ division and changed into a bathing suit she'd brought along in her school backpack.

It was all part of the plan.

Emma grabbed a cotton towel before leaving the locker room and easing her way through the EQ division. A lot of people gave her second looks. Emma didn't shy away from them. She knew she looked good in this bathing suit, and that was the entire point. Emma wanted to be seen because she needed a good reason to be here.

Once out of the EQ division, Emma took the next passageway over and entered the TR or training division, a massive area carved out like a giant cave. Emma passed the indoor gun range. The combat squares with mats on the ground. The various multi-million-dollar simulators that taught flying, evasive driving, and other skills. She passed by the massive rock-climbing wall, where a class was already rappelling down the face of it. Finally, Emma reached the gym portion of the training division.

"What are you doing here?" Lioness asked, standing in place, doing arm curls with twenty-pound weights, her blond hair wet with sweat.

"I'm heading for the pool," Emma said.

"Pool is for training. Not for floating on cushions and eating chocolate truffles."

Emma was way ahead of her. "I know. After that stressful experience aboard the *Falcon's Claw*, I realize that I need to spend more time in the water, improving my swimming skills, which I can't do in my bathtub at home."

Lioness thought about it. "I approve of your initiative, Black Opal. Push yourself hard."

Emma gave her a thumbs-up and headed off to the Olympic-sized swimming pool. She dropped the cotton towel, then plunged into the cool water. The chill invigorated her skin and woke up her entire body. As she did her first lap, Emma's mind relaxed and drifted back to her locker and the thumb drive inside it. The questions it might answer. The truth it might reveal. Despite the alibi, Emma needed to go for a swim anyway. She needed some activity that would clear her mind before she tackled the information that Asset One had given her.

After many laps of swimming as fast as she could, Emma felt like she received an excellent workout. She dried herself with the cotton towel and went back to her locker. Once there, Emma changed back into her street clothes and put her hair up in a pony-tail before she was ready to go. She opened the box of tampons and took out the USB thumb drive. She palmed it before shutting her looker and leaving the EQ division.

Once she emerged from the Labyrinth, Emma had to find a computer to use. She went upstairs to the threat assessment office with all its individual computers, but every station was being used, so Emma went back downstairs. She walked over to the relaxation area, with its tiny one-man pods that allowed a person to rest and re-charge in complete privacy. However, Emma found the computers that ran the pods did not have USB ports.

Then Emma remembered the green pods.

She went over to the area known as "the jungle," which was surrounded by fake trees that made the green private meeting pods look like part of the scenery. Emma climbed inside an empty green pod and sat on the cushy leather couch. Emma found the tablet that controlled the pod and activated it. The green pod hummed as it sealed itself with Emma inside. She scanned the tablet's display. From what Emma could tell, most of the information the pod's computer had access to was through the headquarters' own interior network. It might not need or accept input from an outside source.

Emma scanned through the menus on the tablet and got nowhere. She pressed the help button.

How may I be of service? The man's smooth voice echoed inside the pod. It was kind of like her car's communication system, but Emma liked this voice much more because the dude sounded hot.

"Yes, I have a thumb drive that I want to use. Can I use it inside this pod?"

Are you referring to a USB drive?

"Yes."

Next to Emma, a small door slid down, exposing a USB input.

Of course. Please insert the drive into the flashing input.

Emma plugged the drive in. The light on the drive itself flashed as the system accessed it.

I'm now authenticating this device. Please stand by.

Emma waited.

And waited.

Was there something wrong with the drive? Did Asset One lie to her? Did the drive have nothing on it?

Authentication is confirmed.

Your Priority A access is confirmed.

The 3D imaging system inside the pod came alive, projecting a large report hovering over Emma. The words were crystal clear.

Authority CAC Investigation of FO division's Operation High Society.
Cape Town, South Africa Station
Station Officer: Bluebird
Field Operative: Palomino
October 2004

As Emma began reading, she realized how detailed the report was. This was an investigation conducted by the command and control division, which oversaw every branch of the Authority, in this case the Field Operatives division.

Emma read on. The document went over the operation's goals. Most of which Mrs. B had already told Emma about in their meeting.

Emma skipped some paragraphs. The report went over the Iraq colonel with pain-staking accuracy. It set up the reasoning behind the operation. Why Emma's mom was chosen for the operation—

again, things Mrs. B had already told her.

Emma scanned through the long document, trying to find any tidbits that Mrs. B hadn't told her about. So far, Emma couldn't find anything. But when she found the part about the investigation's conclusions…Emma couldn't stop reading.

Crate AOR431 did not contain a nuclear device. It did contain chemical weapons in the form of field artillery shells. However, the ordnance was old, produced before the Iran-Iraq war in the late 1970s. In Basra, the Iraq Army had stored the crate among discarded medical equipment that used radioactive material, thus giving off higher than normal levels of radioactivity. Even with a higher than normal Geiger counter reading, the amount of evidence to support the claim of a nuclear device was poor at best. No expert on nuclear weapons was present to identify the objects inside the crate. And no images of the device or devices were sent by the field operative to help verify if in fact the device or devices were a nuclear-grade weapon.

Since the level of danger assigned to these smuggled weapons was questionable, the actions of the station officer must be examined since it was her final decision to conduct a raid that resulted in the death of the field operative, the target of the operation, and six South African police officers.

The station officer was given information by the field operative on July 7 of this year that the target planned to move his stolen arms from CapeTown to Yemen by ship, mentioning a possible buyer there. The station officer's decision was to seize the shipment before it left CapeTown. The station officer ordered her field operative using phrases such as—"do whatever was necessary" and "even if you must risk your personal safety in order to prevent that shipment from leaving South Africa."

Due to the haste of putting the raid together, the station officer failed to realize that the captain of the freighter was not only related to the Iraq colonel, but his all Iraqi crew were loyal and would fight any such raid to the last man.

The result was predictable. The raid against the freighter

the *Tigris Sun* was a disaster. As the fifty South African police officers stormed the freighter, the crew counterattacked. The captain made an attempt to put the freighter out to sea, which forced the field operative to blow her cover and neutralize the captain. However, in the fight between the field operative and the target, the field operative was shot as well as the target. Both were found dead on the bridge.

Emma had to stop reading for a moment. The mental image of her mom lying dead on the bridge of a ship was too vivid. Too real. Emma had almost died herself on *the Falcon Claw's* bridge when a missile struck the ship.

Emma lay back for a moment and absorbed the report. There wasn't a nuclear weapon. Only some ancient chemical weapons that maybe didn't work. That was what her mom died for? There must be something else because this report didn't match what Mrs. B told her.

Emma leaned forward and kept reading...

The South African police finally secured the freighter but at a heavy cost.

Under the circumstances, the station officer had other options. She could have kept her field operative in place and under cover. This would have allowed a safe method of tracking the shipment to its new destination, not only allowing our Nairobi station to resume the intelligence operation, but would also have given the mission the necessary time in order to ascertain the exact contents inside crate AOR431.

The station officer could have tipped off the South African Navy to the illegal shipment of weapons. Having the freighter stopped for "routine inspection" within territorial waters would have been a far safer choice, both for the field operative and the target. And this option would have allowed the navy to confiscate the weapons and the crate in question to correctly identify its contents.

The station officer decided to pursue the most dangerous and aggressive course of action when safer, more prudent

choices were available.

This CAC report concludes that the station officer in question acted in a reckless and impulsive manner that resulted in the unnecessary death of a veteran field officer, a valuable target, and five policemen. We recommend that the station officer be removed from duty and placed on probation pending a psychological evaluation.

Emma took it all in. It was all for nothing. Her mom's death was a mistake. She didn't have to die.

But she was ordered to die if necessary. No wonder her mom blew her cover. She was convinced the ship was carrying a nuclear weapon. So convinced that she knew she had to act.

And she did.

And she died.

Basically, Mrs. B had given her mom a suicide order.

CHAPTER 6

The burning started in the pit of her stomach. It lifted into her chest and spread into her lungs. The anger set fire to every cell within Emma's body. Mrs. B had lied to her. Emma's mom wasn't a hero. She was a victim. A victim of someone she trusted. Someone who should've had her best interests in mind.

Acted in a reckless and impulsive manner...

The words of the report echoed in Emma's mind. How could Mrs. B be so reckless? Especially with her own daughter?

...that resulted in the unnecessary death...

Unnecessary death. Her mom didn't have to die.

A sharp pain went up her hand as Emma realized her fist was so tight that her fingernails were digging into her own flesh.

Emma released her fist and pushed the anger down a notch. It all made sense. That was why her dad had stopped talking to Mrs. B at her mom's funeral. She had killed his wife. Emma remembered the sadness in her dad's eyes when she would bring up her mom. It was the only time she saw her dad wilt, as if all the hope in his life had disappeared. When she was younger, Emma thought it was about her. That her dad was disappointed because she wasn't as good as her mom. This only fueled Emma to do more to please her dad.

But as Emma grew older, she reasoned things out and tried to take care of her dad the best she could. Emma knew she wasn't the perfect daughter, but she was sure that her love helped ease the pain and the loss he carried with him. When she was twelve, her father told Emma that she was the most precious gift her mom could have ever given him, and he would always be there for her.

So much for that.

Emma shoved her pity to the side. She refused to be a victim. She would not be used like her mom was. She refused to be manipulated by a grandma who acted like she cared. Or a secret organization who pretended they were doing highly moral acts in the name of mankind.

She had to get out of this place.

She had to go clear her mind.

Emma used the tablet to open the green pod. She wanted to run to her car, but she kept it together enough to walk out of the jungle and into the nearest bathroom. She freshened herself up in the mirror, then forced out a pleasant smile that looked convincing through the glass. Emma wore this disguise until she walked out to her car, pulled out of the garage, and saw the winery in her rear-view mirror.

As she drove out of Napa Valley, Emma's mind picked at the big question like it was a huge meal. What should she do? Confront Mrs. B with the truth? No, the woman would deny it or come up with a clever excuse as to why she didn't tell Emma in the first place. Or worse, Mrs. B could manipulate Emma into believing all the lies. The woman was highly skilled in finding people's vulnerabilities and exploiting them. She could tell Emma the sky was green and also make her believe it.

The Mercedes merged on to the highway that would take her back into the city. Emma picked up speed but flicked the cruise control on so she could think. The report about her mom's death. Mrs. B's lying. Her father leaving the group and not wanting Emma to join—it all confirmed every bad feeling Emma ever had about joining the Authority. Something in her gut had told her to stay away. A feeling that she ignored…until now.

But what could she do?

She could quit the Gems. Really quit, not fake it like she had when she was trying to turn Ryan away from Venomous. Would Mrs. B even allow her to quit? In the past, she had said how difficult such a choice would be. She and her grandma Bernadette would have to assume new identities and live in a new country. And of course her stubborn hippie grandma would probably refuse to go along with any of it. However, her grandma had mentioned the bargain she'd made with Mrs. B. That Emma could walk away from the Gems if she wanted to.

But seriously, how could Emma trust the word of a woman who lied to her and ordered the death of her own daughter? Mrs. B only told Grandma Bernadette what she wanted to hear so Emma would feel better about joining the Gems.

She was trapped. Trapped into working for a group she didn't believe in and for a woman she couldn't trust anymore.

Emma took in the highway. The white dashes zipping by. The humming noise the tires made moving over the pavement. The slight vibration of the leather wheel against her fingers. The Mercedes wasn't moving too fast or too slow. It was cruising in this perfect balance with its environment. It was calming. Something Emma wasn't used to feeling behind the wheel.

Emma's mind wandered as the Mercedes passed under a sign with an arrow pointing to the interstate highway that would take her to Sacramento or Reno. Emma wished she could take that exit. Drive away from the bay area and disappear into the Nevada desert. Never to be heard from again.

Would Mrs. B feel guilty? Would she realize that all the stress she put on poor Emma was too much? Would the Gems finally understand? Olivia and Nadia never understood Emma's concerns about the Authority. They never questioned Mrs. B or the cause. Even if Emma told them about her mom, those girls would tell her to forget about it. That Mrs. B and the Authority knew what they were doing.

Her mind continued to wander. This time to dark places.

What if she killed herself?

Emma imagined her rose-colored casket. Her young body resting inside on a bed of white silk. Her blond hair perfectly laid out upon a pillow with her eyes shut. She imagined everyone from school being there, all dressed in black. She imagined Kayla and Lewis. Mrs. Bracket, the school counselor. Her grandma Bernadette. Ben Gooden and his wife, Rosa. Maybe Aardvark. Would Mrs. B even dare show her face? Would she even shed a tear for her? Would the guilt finally melt through those layers of emotional armor that woman wore every day of her life.

Would Ryan be there?

Of course he would. He would come up to her and he'd kiss her on the forehead. Dead or not. He would do that with tears in his eyes.

Emma allowed the dark thoughts to pass on by, just like the miles.

Killing herself wouldn't change her life. It would just end it. Emma didn't want to give up. What she needed was another chance. A clean restart. Like on one of those video games Miyuki loved playing. Emma wanted to give her life a new beginning.

How could she do that? How could she restart her life and pretend that the Authority never existed? That Emma had never joined.

Before Emma moved to California, her life was far less complicated. She was happy in New York City. She had her friends at Van Dorn Hall. She had her dad. His best friends, Ben and Rosa, were there when her dad was off on business trips. She went to parties. She traveled all over the world with her dad. It was wonderful.

Now she was miserable. It wasn't Grandma Bernadette's fault; she did her best and Emma loved her for that. But joining the Gems had turned her life upside down and not in a good way.

What if she could go back to New York and start fresh? Go back to the life she had before California.

Yes, that was what Emma wanted. To leave it all behind. To begin a new life full of possibilities. She could make that happen in New York.

But how?

Emma would have to disappear.

And the best way to do that—the only way that would cut all the strings and allow her to be free—would be to fake her own death.

CHAPTER 7

As she pulled her Mercedes into Grandma Bernadette's driveway, Emma pieced together the final elements of her escape plan. She shut off the engine and took a moment to think. Emma would have to go late tonight after everyone went to bed. That would give her enough time to set things up and be on her way.

Emma concentrated. The actress inside gripped her purse, using the soft material as a reminder of the old Emma. The version who didn't know what happened to her mom. The innocent pawn who believed what people told her. That version of Emma needed to perform until she reached her room so no one suspected that anything weird was going on. Emma took in a deep breath and opened her car door.

Inside the house, Grandma Bernadette was curled up in her normal reading spot with a thick book, her long white hair free from all its braids and pony-tails. A small clay pot of sage burned on the end table nearby to cleanse the house and provide everyone with wisdom. Or that was what her grandma told her it did.

Nadia was on the floor, her leg cast under the coffee table as she worked on her laptop. Her head scarf was gone and she wore her *Girl Scientists Rock* T-shirt.

Emma's first impulse was to run up the stairs to her room, but the actress inside her played it cool.

"Hi, I'm back."

No one answered.

A collar jingled as Snoopy burst through the rows of blue beads that separated the dining room from the living room. His small leg muscles pumped away as the small Russell terrier made a direct course towards Emma. She bent down and gave him some love. The dog licked her chin as his tail swept back and forth over the polished wood floor.

Emma inched towards the stairs.

"Did you have dinner?" Grandma asked.

"I grabbed something while I was out," Emma lied.

"Please tell me it wasn't a package of chocolate donuts."

Her grandma was obsessed about keeping junk food away from Emma.

"I had a salad at Panera," Emma lied again.

Her grandma seemed satisfied with that answer.

"What damage did you do?" Olivia asked as she came down the stairs.

"Damage?" Emma asked, a bit confused.

"At the mall. Thought that's where you and Kayla were off to."

"Oh yeah, well, we both did a lot of window-shopping."

"You didn't buy anything?" Nadia asked, her eyes free from her laptop.

"No." Once Emma said that, her mind realized how weird it sounded.

"Emma Rothchild went to a mall and didn't buy anything?" Olivia felt her forehead. "Are you coming down with something, love?"

The actress laughed it off, but the real Emma tried her best not to panic. Her weakness for shopping was well known to everyone.

"You should all be proud of me," Emma countered. "I resisted temptation. I think I'm maturing as a woman."

Olivia winked at her. "Sure you are."

Nadia grinned. "You do treat shopping like a sport, Emma."

"Whatever." Emma gathered Snoopy up in her arms. "I'm going to bed."

"It's not even nine o'clock yet," Olivia said.

"I have a headache."

"Do you want some aspirin, young one?" Grandma asked.

"I'll take some upstairs." Emma put a foot on the stairs, then hesitated. She watched Olivia crash on the couch next to Nadia while Emma's grandma resumed her thick book.

Emma took the scene in for a moment. It would be the last time she would ever see them again. Well, someday in the near future—when she was settled in—Emma would contact her grandma. But only when Emma was sure that Mrs. B couldn't find her again.

She went upstairs and noticed Miyuki's door was open. Emma

put Snoopy down and poked her head in the doorway.

Miyuki had her headset on as she played online with some of her gamer friends. Her thumbs danced across the controller as her eyes bounced around the screen. "Oh. I'll take out the green thingy," Miyuki said to her friends. "Look out. The buffalo wizard has a fire wand!"

Miyuki was so focused on the game that she didn't notice Emma standing right behind her.

Snoopy tilted his head up at Emma, his cute little eyes wondering what she was doing.

Emma wasn't sure either. She wanted to say goodbye. Not a real goodbye. Maybe just…one more smile from her friend. One more funny thing she would say. One more laugh that made Emma feel good about the world. That nice people like Miyuki existed. People who could brighten up such a dark world.

Miyuki's game character did a somersault on the screen and landed on a hairy creature that she soon pounded into submission. The girl laughed and giggled as she made her character dance in place like an NFL running back after a touchdown. Miyuki was always so silly. That was what Emma loved about her.

Emma began to have second thoughts. Leaving her grandma was hard enough. But leaving a great friend…

She'd have other friends. Hailey and all the girls she knew in New York would still be there. And when she got a new identity, Emma could get a job and make even more friends. Everything would work out fine.

Emma reached out to tap Miyuki's shoulder but stopped. Maybe it was better this way. If she talked to Miyuki, then Emma might crack and reveal her plans. Then Miyuki would talk her out of doing them.

Emma pulled herself away and silently closed Miyuki's door.

Inside her room, Emma packed her bags. She tried her best to pack only an essential wardrobe because she'd have to buy new clothes once she got to New York City anyway. Emma took out her secret stash of money hidden inside the attic of her old dollhouse, the one her great-grandma Rothchild gave her when she was a little girl. The single rubber band held together at least a thousand dollars in cash. She learned this from her dad, who used to hide large rolls of cash in certain places around the house in case of an emergency.

Once all that was done, Emma paused. Next came the suicide note.

Emma fixated on the blank piece of paper. What was she going to write?

I've had it with my life, so I'm killing myself...

Too generic.

Someone bullied me at school, and I can't take it anymore...

That would be a lie. Besides, there were a lot of kids who were being bullied and using that as an excuse felt...wrong to her.

I feel trapped.

That was more like it.

Mrs. B lied to me about my mother's death.

That's right.

Manipulated me into joining the Gems.

Yes.

I want to leave.

Yes, I do.

But I'm scared Mrs. B will kidnap my grandma and use her as a hostage if I try to leave.

Yes.

I don't believe in what we're doing anymore.

Yes.

I can't leave. I can't stay.

The truth.

That leaves me only one choice.

I love you all.

Good-bye,

Emma

The words flowed out and made it onto the paper. It was all there in black ink. Her real goodbye...disguised as a suicide note.

Emma found more tears to wipe away. The sentences felt honest. Brutally so. It reflected a girl in pain. A girl upset with the situation she had been dealt. A situation that demanded only one outcome. Reading it made Emma believe that she was actually going to kill herself.

Well, in a way she was. She was about to kill their version of Emma so the new version could live in peace.

Emma placed the note on her pillow, where it would be

discovered easily.

That was that.

Another jingle sound announced that Snoopy had managed to jump on to her bed. He nuzzled her hand for attention.

Poor Snoopy. She would have to leave him behind too.

Emma fought back another wave of sadness. "Don't worry. Grandma will take such good care of you."

Snoop cocked his head to the side, as if he didn't believe what she was saying. Or doubted she would leave without him.

Emma stroked his neck. And that was a mistake. His fur was soft and warm. His eyes closed as his tongue came out to lick her hand.

Her heart tightened. Did she have to give up everything? Could she have at least one friend to keep her company?

She could always get another dog. The New York City shelters were full of cute little dogs to adopt.

But Snoopy was her cute little dog. She'd hit him with a car and almost killed him. She still owed him more love. More kisses. More of a life than he started with as a stray dog who was abused.

Emma dug out Snoopy's soft-leather doggie carrier and put him inside it. She then corrected her suicide note…

Snoopy wants to come too. So I guess we'll be doing this together. I'm so sorry.

I love you all.

Good-bye,

Emma.

***

It was after midnight by the time Emma was able to sneak out of her grandma's house with her suitcase, purse, and Snoopy's pet carrier in tow. She drove the Mercedes out of Berkeley and across the Oakland bay bridge into San Francisco. She kept to the highways as her route took her to the Pacific Coast Highway. Once she was on the PCH, Emma headed south.

Snoopy was excited. He barked and pressed his furry head against the cage door, wanting to come out of his carrier. But Emma kept him in for now and talked to him about New York.

She looked forward to taking him on long walks through Central Park and bringing him bones from the local butcher shops to gnaw on.

Fifty miles later, Emma reached a scenic turnout on the PCH. She guided her Mercedes into a parking space and shut off the engine. Her headlights went dark. The glowing clock on the dash reported it was one in the morning.

Emma got out of the car. The breeze coming off the ocean was cold and froze Emma's bare arms. She rubbed her arms and retrieved a coat with a hood from the car. That helped keep out the breeze as she moved over to the railing.

Down below was a small cove that was fed by the Pacific Ocean. In the faint moonlight, Emma could make out the white caps as they rolled in with the waves. The sound of water crashing against the rocks. This particular scenic outlook allowed people to observe the cove from way high above it.

When Emma first came to California, she had driven past this spot many times with her grandma, who loved taking the PCH in order to get out of the city. The cove would be a perfect place to fake a suicide.

She opened the door of the Mercedes and tossed in a pair of cheap sneakers. Next came a pair of pants she wasn't too crazy about. Then a sweater that was difficult to match with any outfit. Emma then placed an old purse on the passenger seat. It had all her credit cards and a few other personal items she could do without. She placed her phone into the drink holder. They wouldn't find her body, but they would find her sneakers, keys, phone, and a purse scattered all over the cove.

Emma took out Snoopy's pet carrier, her new purse, and her suitcase from the Mercedes. She then climbed back behind the wheel.

Everything was ready.

Emma drove the car to the edge of the parking area, then turned it around to aim the front of the Mercedes so it would hit the metal railing head-on. She looked around; no one was in the parking lot at this late of an hour. However, there were still semi-trucks driving along the PCH, so Emma would have to be mindful of that before making her only attempt.

Emma climbed out of the car and left the motor running. She found a good-sized rock for the accelerator and laid it on the floorboard. Emma checked around the area again.

There was a semi-trailer truck approaching from the south.

Emma got into her car and shut off the lights.

The semi rushed past her and finally disappeared around the next bend.

Emma turned her lights back on and checked to see if she had everything ready. Satisfied, she breathed in and placed the rock down on the accelerator. The engine roared to a high pitch, but the car was still in park.

Emma prepared herself. Once she turned the switch to Drive... the car would take off, and she would have to jump before it smashed into the railing and fell into the cove.

She was ready.

Emma rotated the transmission switch into Drive. Her head banged against the leather headrest as the car took off. She used the open door to help pull herself out of the car before jumping clear. Emma rolled along the dirt to dissipate her body's inertia before she turned around to watch.

The Mercedes charged towards the railing and...screeched to a complete stop.

Huh?

Emma ran up to the car. The engine was racing, but the brakes were still being applied automatically. She peeked at the dashboard and realized the anti-collision system was still on.

Emma took the rock off the accelerator and drove the Mercedes back to its starting position again. This time she deactivated all the anti-collision safety systems and tried it again.

The engine roared, and the tires dug into the pavement as the Mercedes headed right for the railing at full speed.

This time, Emma did a much better job leaping out of the car and rolling before the Mercedes slammed into the railing at full speed. The vehicle sailed into the air as the front end dived towards the cove. The car hit the water with a loud splash.

Emma ran over to the broken railing and looked down. The rear of the Mercedes bobbed up and down on the surface of the water before finally sinking underwater.

Her car was gone.

***

Emma and Snoopy arrived at the Oakland AmRail station at fifteen past five in the early morning. Emma had had no sleep. It had taken much longer than she thought to flag down a semi-trailer truck in the middle of the night and hitchhike north on the PCH back to San Francisco. Then she'd had to walk several blocks before flagging down an available taxi that would take her into Oakland.

Emma dragged her rolling suitcase across the tiled floor of the railroad station. Snoopy was quiet inside his soft-leather pet carrier, which Emma had strapped to the top of her suitcase. She was tired and tempted to collapse onto one of the benches, but she pushed herself towards the ticket office instead.

"How can I help you?" a black woman asked, her dark braids all pulled back and tied together. Her gold AmRail badge said her name was Jada and she was a supervisor.

"When's the next train to New York?" Emma asked.

"We don't have any trains going direct, but I have trains going to Chicago, and from there you can transfer to a New York-bound train. Sound good?"

"Perfect."

"The Western Limited leaves in two hours," Jada said. "I can get you a coach seat for one hundred and fifty dollars. That includes the transfer in Chicago."

That name sounded familiar to Emma. Wasn't that the train they used to smuggle out Robert when he was running from the United States Army? Despite having to throw a few Chinese intelligence agents off the train, the trip itself wasn't bad. Emma hoped this journey would be much more chill.

"That train has private cabins, right? I'd like one of those, please."

"Don't have any mainliner privacy cabins available on this train." Jada scanned her computer monitor. "I do have one roomette. Would you like that?"

"What's a roomette?" Emma asked.

"They're semi-private compartments. They have two chairs that convert into upper and lower beds. They're small and cozy, but if it's just you, I think you'll like it."

"Okay, I'll take one of those." Emma brought out her wad of cash. She took off the rubber band and began counting out hundred-dollar bills. Emma hesitated. "Is this enough?" She slid three hundred dollars towards Jada and quickly packed up the rest of her cash back into the wad.

The woman nodded. "Can I see your ID?"

Emma gave Jada her driver's license.

She checked it, then gave Emma a paper ticket. "The one on top is for this train. The ticket on the bottom is for your train to New York."

Emma thanked Jada and dragged her things over to an empty bench. She stood her suitcase up so Snoopy could see her through his mesh window. His little eyes were nervous. They were not sure about where his doggie mom was taking him.

Emma checked the room for police or any sign of security before pulling Snoopy out of his pet carrier. The dog looked around, still a little nervous. But when he craned his little neck to look at her, his tail wagged again. As if to say, *I'm nervous about where we are, but I'm so happy you're here with me.*

Emma rubbed Snoopy's head as she cradled him in her arms. She was nervous about the future too.

CHAPTER 8

The morning sunlight greeted Miyuki with a warm promise that today would be a great day as it reached through her window and kissed her eyes. She took in a deep breath and stretched her arms before slipping out of bed. After taking a shower and drying her hair, Miyuki picked out her clothes for the day. She was in a good mood, so Miyuki chose her pink cotton Kawasaki Motorcycle T-shirt to go with her always-distressed jeans and pink high-tops. Miyuki yawned as she slipped her backpack over her shoulder and headed downstairs.

In the kitchen, Olivia waited by the toaster while Nadia was peeling an orange at the small breakfast table, where Emma's grandma enjoyed some of her breakfast tea. Miyuki gave everyone a hello wave as she went to the pantry and grabbed the Apple Jacks cereal box. Next was the carton of soy milk from the fridge along with a clean bowl and a spoon. She poured in her cereal, then topped off the bowl with soy milk.

Olivia's toast popped up from the toaster. She lathered it with orange marmalade before joining everyone at the table.

Miyuki dug into her bowl of Apple Jacks. Even with the soy milk, the delicious sugary apple taste rose above the soy and made for a yummy breakfast fit for a girl who'd ditched her healthier Japanese breakfast of rice and miso soup a long time ago. Her mother and father would say that America had given their daughter some bad habits. Miyuki would agree, and maybe at this point in her life she enjoyed being bad. American spaghetti. Pancakes with maple syrup. As long as she exercised once in a while, what damage could that food really do to her?

After Nadia finished her orange and cleaned her hands with a paper napkin, she checked the time. "What's taking Emma so long?"

Miyuki checked the kitchen wall clock. It was getting late. Even for Emma.

Olivia crunched on her toast as she glanced around the kitchen floor. "Must have locked up Snoopy inside her room again."

"She complained about a headache last night. I hope it didn't turn into a migraine," Emma's grandma said.

Miyuki swallowed and stood up. "I'll go check."

"Tell her if she feels bad, there's no shame in staying home from school."

Miyuki gave Grandma a thumbs-up before heading up the stairs and knocking on Emma's door.

"Emma, are you sick?" Miyuki asked. "We can take the bus if you can't drive us to school."

There was no answer.

Miyuki knocked on Emma's door again.

"Are you still asleep?" Miyuki raised her voice. "Emma, wake up!"

Still no answer.

Miyuki checked the upstairs bathroom. The door was open, and no one was inside.

She returned to Emma's front door. "Emma, are you in there? We have school today."

Nothing.

Miyuki put her ear to the door to see if she could catch some kind of activity inside the room. But it was quiet.

Too quiet.

She tried the door, and it opened.

Miyuki stepped inside. There were a few clothes lying around the floor, but that was normal for Emma. The girl wasn't exactly messy. She was only disorganized when it came to picking up stuff. One thing that made Miyuki pause was Emma's bed. The comforter hadn't been touched from the last time she made the bed. No one had slept there overnight. There was also something on the pillow. A note written on yellow lined paper.

Miyuki picked it up and began reading.

When she was done, a wave of panic swept through her. Was this a joke? Did Emma really write this? Was Emma already dead?

Miyuki was hyperventilating so fast she had to sit down on the bed. Her mind was spinning like a propeller, trying to understand what she had read. She checked the closet and under the bed. She raced to the bathroom and checked the bathtub. Miyuki then ran to the room Olivia and Nadia shared. No sign of Emma's body. If she committed suicide, where was her body?

Miyuki searched the upstairs one more time. She even checked the dusty attic for any sign of Emma, and there was none.

She raced down the stairs. Her high-tops slid across the polished-wood floor before bolting through the wall of blue beads.

"She's gone!" Miyuki shouted.

"Who's gone, love?" Olivia asked.

"Emma."

"What do you mean?" her grandma asked.

"I found this on her pillow." Miyuki placed the letter down on the table.

Everyone craned their necks to read it.

Nadia gasped and covered her mouth in horror.

"I don't believe it," Olivia said.

Emma's grandmother only stared at the yellow paper. Her eyes quivering. "Is this a sick joke? Are you girls trying to pull something on me?"

Miyuki shook her head. "It is no joke. Her bed is empty. No one has slept in it."

Emma's grandmother grabbed the letter and read it again. She took a long moment before speaking. "I don't understand this. Why—? She was here last night." Emma's grandmother shook her head. "This can't be real. Is Laura doing something with Emma that I don't know about?"

"If Mrs. B is using Emma for something, she hasn't told me about it," Olivia said. "I'll call her to make sure."

"Please do that." Emma's grandma pointed at the letter. "This isn't true. This is a lie."

"Perhaps someone has kidnapped her," Nadia said. "They want us to think she's dead."

"*Hei*, that makes more sense to me as well," Miyuki said.

Olivia stepped away from the table and made the call. She explained that Emma was missing and that a suicide letter had been left behind.

"Right, okay, we'll wait for you." Olivia put down her phone. "Mrs. B has no knowledge of any mission that Emma has been assigned to. She's coming over as soon as she can."

Emma's grandmother leaned over the letter, her body wilting, her eyes soft and on the edge of losing it.

Miyuki sat down next to her. "Mrs. B will be helpful. She'll find out what's going on."

"Emma would've talked to us, wouldn't she?" Nadia asked. "If she had thoughts about—wouldn't she try to talk to us?"

"She has been unhappy lately," Olivia said.

Everyone looked up.

"Ever since Venomous put those ideas in her head about flipping sides…she's been questioning a lot of things."

"Not Emma. She wouldn't kill herself," her grandma said. "She made it through her father's death. She had every excuse in the world to do it then, yet she fought through it because she wanted to live…for him. For what her dad did for her. She wanted to repay him. Emma wouldn't throw her life away for anything or anyone."

Miyuki nodded. Since they didn't know what was going on, she wanted to stay positive. Wanted to believe what Emma's grandma was saying about her grand daughter. Whatever the true answer was, Miyuki hoped they would find out soon.

An hour later, Mrs. B and Aardvark arrived at the house. The older woman wore a calm expression as she sat down in the living room, put up her wooden cane, and read the letter.

"May I get you anything?" Miyuki asked Aardvark.

The large man's eyes were soft, as if they were worried. He managed a polite grin and shook his head.

Miyuki knelt beside Mrs. B. "Would you like some tea?"

Mrs. B was engrossed with the letter but managed to say, "Yes, if it's not too much trouble."

Nadia gripped her leg scooter and rolled across the floor. "I'll go make some."

"I'll help you." Miyuki followed Nadia into the kitchen. She reached for the cabinet that had the tea…

"Please let me do this by myself," Nadia said. "I need to keep busy."

Miyuki could see the anxiety behind her eyes. An anxiety she shared.

Nadia leaned against the counter and removed the tea tin from the cabinet. She opened it and searched through the different packets of flavors. Miyuki watched her fingers dance through four rows of tea, then start on the first row again.

"Do you think Emma killed herself?" Nadia asked, out of the blue, her fingers still searching for tea.

"I don't know. I don't think she would," Miyuki said.

"Yes, I mean…she's not here. However, there's no evidence that she's dead. We only have a piece of paper. She—she could have written that when she was mad. Have you ever done that? I have. Write angry and hurtful things when you're angry, if only to make yourself feel better. You don't mean any of it."

Miyuki nodded. "My ex-boyfriend has read such a letter, but I meant to say everything in that."

The comment made Nadia grin, which then melted. "We've all done that. The letter was Emma just blowing off steam. She must have taken a drive to reason things out. She does that a lot." Nadia continued searching through the tea. "I don't know which flavor to pick."

"Pick something relaxing. That will help everyone."

"Relaxing, yes…" Nadia finally selected four bags of the same tea, then filled the kettle and flipped on a burner.

Miyuki prepared four tea-cups and had some milk and sugar ready.

Nadia eased herself down on a chair in the breakfast nook table. Miyuki sat with her. They were both quiet as they waited.

Until the doorbell rang.

Nadia and Miyuki glanced at each other. They went back into the living room. Olivia was at the front door, letting in two California highway patrolmen. Miyuki could tell because their uniforms had different colors than the Berkeley police officers.

Emma's grandmother took a moment before getting to her feet. Her hands were shaking.

One of the patrolmen cleared his throat. "Mrs. Bernadette Rothchild?"

"Yes."

"Do you own a white Mercedes AMG coupe?"

"That's my grand daughter's car."

"And what's your grand-daughter's name?"

"Emma Rothchild."

The officer checked some of his notes on a pad. "Mrs. Rothchild, we found your grand-daughter's car…underwater in a cove just off the Pacific Coast Highway. There's some evidence that leads us to believe that it wasn't an accident. That she intentionally drove off the road."

Emma's grandmother yelped and made the most horrible moan Miyuki had ever heard a woman make before collapsing. Aardvark and Mrs. B helped her into a nearby chair as the woman curled up like a cat and cried.

Miyuki's heart broke for her; then she realized that this was real. Her friend was dead.

Nadia leaned so heavily against Miyuki that she had to hold her up as tears streamed from her eyes.

Her friend did commit suicide.

Now Miyuki felt weak. Her cheeks were damp. She guided both of them over to the couch to sit down.

Olivia was still standing, but there was shock on her face. No tears. No crying. But she was motionless, as if an electric shock had turned her off like a robot.

Aardvark concentrated on the floor.

Mrs. B rose to her feet and put her arm around Olivia as she addressed the patrolman. "Have you found Emma's body?"

"Not yet, we found some of her clothes. Her phone. And a purse. But we do have dive teams working on that," the patrolman said.

"She wasn't found inside her car?"

"No, however there's a large hole in the windshield, and her driver's side window was also down at the time of the crash. But we'll find her."

"My poor little grand-daughter," Emma's grandma said, still curled up.

Miyuki left Nadia on the couch and knelt near Emma's grandma, touching her leg, just to let her know she wasn't alone in her grief.

"Did Emma give any of you an indication that she wanted to harm herself?" the patrolman asked.

"Patrolman, may I speak to you privately?" Mrs. B asked.

Both patrolmen followed Mrs. B outside.

A loud whistle came in from the kitchen. It was the kettle for the tea.

Miyuki went in and flicked off the burner as she moved the kettle off, although she wondered if anyone really wanted to drink tea right now. Miyuki drifted away from the counter. She moved back to the breakfast nook table but didn't sit down. She didn't feel like doing much of anything right now. What was the point? Miyuki felt numb. Almost detached from reality.

Her foot kicked something that jumped across the floor.

Miyuki looked down. It was Snoopy's plastic food dish. Why did Emma take Snoopy with her? Why didn't she leave him here? Emma loved that dog and she knew how they all felt about him. That little dog would have been so well taken care of if anything happened to Emma.

So why did she take him with her? Emma wasn't that selfish. Not when it came to an animal.

Her thoughts were interrupted as a shouting match broke out in the living room.

Miyuki went back in and saw Emma's grandma back on her feet and yelling at Mrs. B.

"This is all your fault! You brought her into your sick world of secret codes and handshakes. You destroyed her life!"

"Bernadette, would you please calm down," Mrs. B said.

"You poisoned her mind with your fascist organization. I will never forgive you for this." Emma's grandmother began gasping for breath as she fell backward into a chair.

Miyuki and Olivia rushed over to her. The old woman was having trouble breathing.

"She's hyperventilating," Mrs. B said. "Someone get her a paper bag."

Olivia raced into the kitchen and came out with a bag. She gave it to Miyuki, who placed it under the old woman's chin.

"Please breathe into the bag. It will help," Miyuki said, helping her cup the bag over her mouth. The bag crinkled as it expanded and contracted with every breath. The bag seemed to be working.

"Aardvark, please stay here and assist Mrs. Rothchild while I speak with the girls." Mrs. B made her way to the front door, then waited for the three of them to join her.

Miyuki was the last one outside. She noticed the highway patrol cruiser pulling away and heading down the street.

"Did you show the officer Emma's suicide note?" Miyuki asked.

Mrs. B paused. "That's why I spoke with the men outside and flashed my FBI badge. I told him this case was of interest to the government. He'll contact me with any more details."

"Ma'am, you have an FBI badge?" Olivia asked.

"A gift from Ed, the assistant director. When the highway patrol contacts the FBI, the fake name will signal to them that we're involved. Ed will play along if I keep him in the loop. Besides, Emma's letter mentions some sensitive information that neither the highway patrol nor the FBI need to know about." Mrs. B scanned the faces of all three girls. "I can imagine the emotions that are sweeping through all of you right now."

"Did you lie to her?"

The words fell from her mouth, and Miyuki was shocked to hear her own voice behind them. Yet a part of Miyuki's mind was confused and wanted clarity as to why her best friend chose to die.

"Excuse me?" Mrs. B asked.

"My apologies. But did you lie about her mother's death?"

"Don't be daft. Of course she didn't," Olivia said. "Why would she?"

Mrs. B rested her hand on Olivia's arm. "I spoke with Emma about her mom and how she died. I told her everything I knew. Emma seemed relieved, and she was glad we had the conversation."

"Then why did she mention that on her suicide note?" Miyuki asked.

Mrs. B hesitated. "To be honest, I'm not yet convinced that she's dead."

"They found her car in the ocean with some of her things," Nadia said.

"*Hei*, and that suicide note was written by her," Miyuki said. "I recognize Emma's handwriting."

"Do you think someone forced her to write that note?" Olivia asked.

Mrs. B crossed her arms, her mind working over the question. "Until they find her body, we should treat this as a kidnapping. I'll have Aardvark look into Emma's phone records to see whom she spoke to and what she did forty-eight hours prior to the crash. No matter what, we need to investigate and make sure this was either a suicide or something else."

CHAPTER 9

It was late in the day as the Western Limited rolled across the Nevada desert. The sun was halfway tucked behind the horizon, causing the bright orange star to appear gigantic. It was beautiful. It reminded Emma of a landscape painting. Something people hung in a museum to marvel at forever. But even this breathtaking view from her window couldn't distract her enough.

Emma had to glance at her image in the roomette's side mirror once again. Her gorgeous blond hair was now dark black with curls. Her eyebrows were black. And she wore a darker shade of makeup as well. Emma had all day to kill on the train, so giving herself a radical new look was a priority. Thanks to all her work in the theater—plus all her spy training on disguises—Emma was able to transform into a different person. She wasn't sure if she was a fan of the look. It was a little too Gothic for her personal taste, but it would do for now. When she reached New York, Emma would change her look again. This time into something that she could live with for the rest of her life.

Snoopy had made himself comfortable on her lap. She petted him again, and his tail began whacking against her thigh.

They'd probably found her car by now. Everyone was probably upset. Emma could understand that, but they would all get over her death. The quickest one would be Olivia. The girl never liked her anyway. Since she got her three-girl team back, Olivia could now order everyone around to her heart's content. Nadia wouldn't be far behind. She was closer to Olivia anyway, so Emma doubted the girl would burn a candle in the window for her.

Miyuki might take it hard. Emma wished there was a way to make it easier on her, but contacting her would create a huge burden. To honor Emma's secret, Miyuki would have to lie and keep on lying to hide the truth from the other Gems and Mrs. B.

Emma didn't want to put that burden on her.

This would be painful, but Miyuki would bounce back. Time has a way of doing that. Emma learned that after her father died. It was painful for her to go through. and it took time, but she had come to terms with her father's death. That was why she was on a train to New York, right? To begin a new life. Killing herself wasn't an option. Not after everything her father did to raise her. To set up a situation where she wouldn't have to worry about money for the rest of her life. Her dad wanted Emma to succeed in life. To be given every advantage that could be stacked in her favor.

And that life was never meant to include the Gems or the Authority.

There was a knock on her sliding glass door. Emma pulled back the privacy curtain and saw the AmRail conductor who scanned her ticket. She slid open the door.

The conductor did a double take when he saw Emma's new look. Snoopy then barked at him.

"Of course I remember you," he said to the dog. "Are you enjoying your trip with us?"

Snoopy barked again.

"Glad to hear it." The conductor smiled politely at Emma. "Does he have enough treats?"

"You know what," Emma said. "I forgot to bring his treats...or food for that matter."

"Oh, I think we can scrounge up some food and a treat or two for such a fine passenger."

"Thank you," Emma said. She could see the questions forming in his eyes. Did he suspect something? A complete makeover in eight hours might look a little odd. "You must think I'm a horrible dog mom."

The conductor smiled. "If you had this animal caged up and stuffed inside a storage compartment, then you and I would have some issues. Don't worry about it."

"I wanted a change," Emma blurted out.

"I'm sorry?"

"The hair. The makeup. I wanted something different."

"I see. What you do inside your cabin is your own business, miss," the conductor said. "I do apologize for bothering you, but there's been a schedule change for the train."

"A schedule change?"

"Yes, once we arrive in Wichita, the train will be stopping for at least one hour, possibly more. Some flood-water has damaged a railroad trestle on our route. Crews are repairing it now, so once we get to Kansas, we hope the delay will be minimal."

"Oh, okay." Emma couldn't have cared less. She was looking at a five-hour wait in Chicago for her connecting train to New York anyway.

The conductor left for about fifteen minutes and came back with a clean plate and a couple of pouches of easy-to-open dog food. He also brought Snoopy a chew toy and a can of bacon treats.

Emma thanked him as he left. She gave Snoopy one of the bacon treats, and he licked her face for a thank-you.

Wichita. Why was that city so familiar? Emma took a moment to dig it out of her mind. Wait, that was where Ryan's mom lived.

She'd forgotten all about Ryan.

On the bridge of the *Falcon's Claw*—when the Royal Navy missiles were on their way and it seemed like both of them were about to be wiped out from existence—Ryan had kissed her.

The kiss was so deep and loving that the world fell away. The anxious voices on the bridge. The blaring alarms.

It all fell away.

When that boy thought he was about to die, Ryan thought about her and only her.

Ryan would take the news of her death hard. How could he not? It might even devastate him.

However, Emma couldn't tell him the truth.

Another thing she'd learned on the *Falcon's Claw* was that Ryan had a dark side. A part of him that couldn't walk away from Venomous. He was trapped like Emma was. But unlike Emma, he was unwilling to break free. He wanted the power. He accepted the greed. He wanted the attention and strength Asset One and Venomous gave him. To move ahead with her own life, Emma would have to turn her back on him and never look back.

And that was exactly what she planned on doing.

CHAPTER 10

That night, the Jeep was naked. The roof and the doors had been removed, allowing fresh air to sweep through the Jeep as it moved along the street. Miyuki had volunteered to go pick up Thai food for dinner because no one felt like cooking. Emma's grandmother even allowed Miyuki to borrow her Jeep for the task. The temperature outside was cool, but Miyuki didn't mind because the crisp air reinvigorated her after a long and stressful day. She was able to nudge her worries to the side and enjoy the moment.

Of course she was still worried.

Of course she was still trying to absorb the possibility that her best friend was dead.

Miyuki wasn't used to feeling this way. She always preferred happy thoughts. Fun thoughts. Adventurous thoughts, which were always percolating inside her mind. Every day in your life was supposed to be fun. Something you should always look forward to. The smell of pancakes for breakfast. The air filled with cherry blossoms as the breeze carried them off the trees. The thrill of jumping a motor-bike over a mound of dirt. The pride and satisfaction of ending the final quest of your favorite video game. The voice of your best friend saying that you look cute today.

Now she was sad again.

Miyuki pulled into the empty driveway. Since Emma's Mercedes was gone, she parked the Jeep in the middle since there was plenty of room, although she wished there weren't Miyuki gathered up the two large paper bags of take-out food and headed inside the house. Mrs. B was still in the living room with her laptop. She'd sent Aardvark back to Napa Valley so he could help coordinate the investigation there. Nadia and Olivia were still on the couch, watching television. Emma's grandma was missing.

"I have yummy Thai food!" Miyuki announced, trying to lighten everyone's depressed mood. She carried the bags into the kitchen and began putting the entrees out on the counter. The delightful fragrance of the food made Miyuki so hungry.

Olivia was the first one in the kitchen. The girl was obsessed with Thai food. "That smells fantastic, love. Thanks for fetching it." She grabbed her entree and a set of plastic-ware.

"You should hide that plastic-ware before Emma's grandma sees it," Nadia said, rolling in with her leg scooter.

Olivia tossed the plastic-ware back in the bag and took out some silverware from a bottom drawer.

Miyuki went ahead and took Mrs. B's order along with some silverware and hand-delivered it to her in the living room.

Mrs. B placed the entree next to her laptop. "Thank you, Ruby. Sorry...Miyuki. I keep forgetting we're not at headquarters." She continued working.

"That's okay. May I call you Laura?"

The woman paused. Her brow lowered. "No, you may not."

Out of habit, Miyuki went into a deep bow towards Mrs. B. "I apologize if I have offended you." Insulting your supervisor was a big no-no in Japanese culture. A lesson Miyuki's father had drummed into the heads of his children. Miyuki could hear his stern voice already correcting her.

Mrs. B put her attention back on Miyuki, then smiled. "That *no* came out much too strong. Thank you for going out and bringing us dinner. It's much appreciated." Mrs. B popped open the entree, then paused. "Would Bernadette prefer that we eat our meals in the dining room?"

"Emma's grandma isn't very formal. Depends on what her mood is because we sometimes eat together in the living room, in the backyard, in the dining room...her only rule for dinner is that we all eat together," Miyuki said. "By the way, do you know where she is?"

"Upstairs resting, I do believe."

Mrs. B's phone rang. She checked the number and answered. "Yes, this is FBI agent MacDonald." She winked at Miyuki, then listened. Her expression didn't change throughout the entire conversation. "Thank you, Lieutenant. We appreciate the update."

Hearing the phone ring, Olivia and Nadia were already in the living room.

"That was the highway patrol. Still no sign of Emma's body,"

Mrs. B said.

"Why is it taking them so damn long?" Emma's grandmother was half-way down the stairs. Her face was crinkled and worn, her white hair unkempt, but her eyes were burning. "Are they searching the entire Pacific?"

"They had to stop because of shark sightings in the cove, but they assure me they'll be out at first light tomorrow."

Grandma eased herself down to the ground floor. "Shark sightings? Are they saying my poor Emma was—"

"There's no evidence to suggest that," Mrs. B said. "It's only to protect the divers."

Grandma plopped herself down on a chair. "We have to find her body. We just have to…" The old woman's head tilted down as tears poured out again. "Poor Emma can't rest until we find her."

Miyuki fought back her own tears as she wrapped her arm around her. "*Hei*, they will, Grandma. They will find her." Miyuki knew she wasn't her real grandmother, yet, in a way, she was their step-grandma.

Nadia rolled in and managed to sit down next to Grandma. "We won't rest, either."

Olivia knelt in front of her. "None of us will, love."

Mrs. B's laptop chirped as a new email appeared. Her eyes scanned the message, then shut tight.

"What is it?" Miyuki asked.

Mrs. B opened her eyes. "Join me in the backyard, please."

As darkness fell on the backyard, the three Gems and Mrs. B were out on the deck. The lights were on as they sat around the birch table tucked under the lattice.

"Is it about Emma?" Olivia asked.

"Aardvark put together a schedule of Emma's whereabouts before she came home the night you all saw her. He found something disturbing. Emma used one of our pods to gain access to a Priority A thumb drive. This thumb drive contained information related to the mission her mother was on when she was killed. Information that none of you should have access to."

"Do you think that's what sent her over the edge?" Olivia asked.

"Judging by her suicide note, it's a strong possibility that—" Mrs. B hesitated, the reality hitting her as well. "That Emma did, in fact, kill herself."

Any hint of hope that her dear friend was alive...had dissolved from Miyuki's heart. She would be alone after all.

"Someone gave Emma that thumb drive knowing full well that it would poison her mind and make her turn against us," Mrs. B said, her voice rising. "Someone knew that it would put pressure on Emma. To make her question things. It was an attempt by someone to manipulate her. However, it drove Emma towards suicide instead."

"Who would do that?" Nadia asked.

"Venomous. Asset One. Maybe even Ryan," Olivia said. "I bet it's Ryan. He's so in love with her that the boy would do anything to drive Emma away from us."

"I agree." Mrs. B put her laptop to the side. "Here's what we'll do. I'll send out a priority one locate order throughout our intelligence network. When Ryan pops his little head up on our radar, I'll send you all straight to him."

"What do you want us to do?" Miyuki asked.

"Kick the living snot out of him?" Olivia asked.

"You'll kidnap Ryan and bring him back here. I want answers. And if he won't cooperate...then you get to kick the living snot out of him."

Olivia smiled. "Yes, ma'am."

"What about Emma's grandmother?" Nadia asked. "Should we be leaving her at a time like this?"

"I'll stay with her," Mrs. B said. "She shouldn't be left alone right now."

"I hope the divers can find her tomorrow," Miyuki said. "I wish we could help them."

"We can help Emma," Olivia said. "By finding that douche bag Ryan and making him pay."

CHAPTER 11

Emma drifted awake. The cheap nylon curtains couldn't hold back all that direct morning sunlight as it spilled into the small roomette. Emma sat up in bed and noticed Snoopy yawning. He glanced at her, and his tail banged against the bed sheet like a drum. Emma had actually slept well last night. It had taken a while to fall asleep, but she'd managed to stop thinking about everything, and that did the trick.

It was a new day.

Day three of Emma's new life.

Emma got up and turned the bed back into a seat. She folded up the blankets and sheets into a neat pile so the porter could grab them when he came around. For today, Emma chose some sweatpants and a dark T-shirt. She wanted to look as unremarkable as possible in the dining car, and that meant she would have to push her normal vanity to the side.

Once Emma put her dark hair up in a ponytail, she grabbed the book she was reading, left Snoopy inside the roomette, and climbed upstairs to the main level of the double-decker sleeper car. Emma traveled through another sleeper car and two coach cars before she reached the dining car. It wasn't too crowded, so she picked a booth at the far end of the car and watched the landscape roll past her window.

"Another cappuccino?" the male waiter asked.

This was her second breakfast on board, and the AmRail crew already knew what she liked.

"Oh, you know it." Emma glanced through the menu. "But I'll try the French toast today."

"With three orders of sausage links to go?"

Emma gave him a thumbs-up. The crew knew the sausages weren't for her. But the conductor told Emma that if Snoopy stayed in her roomette and if she kept him and it clean, then her furry companion would be overlooked. So far, Snoopy was doing well. Emma was able to give him bathroom breaks during some of the train stops and the conductor was always dropping by with new treats and chew toys for him.

As Emma waited, her eyes drifted over to the window. The land outside was flattening out as the train moved away from the mountains of Colorado and into the flat plains of western Kansas. She could already tell that today would be a boring one.

Emma received her cappuccino, and the warm liquid tasted delicious. The flavor reminded her of yesterday's breakfast when her morning cappuccino had been complemented by the view of soaring mountains, their peaks so high up in elevation that Emma could still see pockets of snow on top. Later that day the train had followed a beautiful mountain stream that had the clearest water she had ever seen in her life. Emma was glad she'd picked the train over flying. This was relaxing. Therapeutic in a way. On a train she could move around freely, enjoy beautiful scenery, have a cappuccino, and not worry about the train falling from the sky and crashing into the ground in a ball of fire.

A plate of French toast interrupted her thoughts. The waiter also left a plastic box full of sausage links. Emma thanked him and started on her breakfast.

An announcement came over the train's speaker system...

Good morning, everyone. I have an update on the trestle repair. The crews are finishing up their work, so there will be only a ninety-minute delay when we get to Wichita. Because of the delay, AmRail will allow passengers to disembark if they would like to stretch their legs in town. However, if you're late coming back, don't be surprised if we leave without you.

Emma wiped her mouth with the paper napkin. An hour-and-a-half wait? Oh well, she could take Snoopy out for a long walk. Let him explore the wonders of Wichita. An hour-and-a-half walk should cover most of the city. We're not talking a metropolis here. What else was there to do?

Well, Emma could call up Ryan's mom.

Ha! Wouldn't that be an interesting conversation. They could talk about the criminal organization her son was working for and how he earned all that money he sent back to her every month. If she knew the truth, would Ryan's mom still be okay with it? All that misery and violence inflicted on other human beings just so she could pay the mortgage. Would the truth make her angry enough to confront her son and make him quit since Emma had failed so miserably? Maybe his mom could do what she couldn't do.

You're seriously thinking about this? Ryan is a lost cause. You were going to turn your back on him, remember?

Emma's mind had a solid point. But that kiss...

That stupid damn kiss.

Emma's heart still wanted to try to save him.

You're stupid. You're pathetic.

Her mind shouted at her, wanting to beat her heart into submission.

Ryan Raymond is dead to us!

But if she had the opportunity to talk with Ryan's mom, then she should, right? Because then Emma could tell herself that she did everything possible to help Ryan see the light. If he failed to walk through it, then it would be on him not her. From that point on...Ryan would be dead to her.

Emma tossed the idea around. Surely an hour and a half was enough time to call Ryan's mom and have her come down to the station to meet. It wasn't like Wichita was New York. It probably took ten minutes to drive across the entire town.

But Emma did need a phone. Oh...and she didn't have a phone number for Ryan's mom either.

Okay, she would figure something out.

Emma flagged down the AmRail conductor as he walked through the dining car. "Do you know much about Wichita? I mean, do they have normal stores where people can buy electronics and stuff?"

The conductor squinted at her. "Normal stores?"

"Yeah, like an Apple store or a Macy's? Not a country store that sells horses and cattle feed."

"I do know Wichita. Grew up in nearby Newton, Kansas." The conductor paused. "Let's see...if you go past the feed store, go across the dirt street over to the blacksmith, take a right and walk past the general store and the saloon where all the cowboys hang out...then you'll find a Best Buy store."

"Do you have some paper? I'd like to write this down," Emma

said.

The conductor smiled to himself and took out a pad of paper and pen. "You can use this."

"Thanks." Emma took the pad and pressed the top of the pen. "Okay, how far is the feed store away from the train station?"

"About a mule's kick. And be careful about crossing the street, those stagecoaches rush by quick, and those horses will trample you down without a second thought."

Emma stopped writing. She was very confused.

"Oh, and you should stop by the local sheriff's office to surrender any guns you have. They don't like it when strangers come in-to town packing."

It sounded like the conductor was describing some Hollywood movie of the old west.

Then Emma put it all together and sat back.

"There's a Starbucks, a T-Mobile store, and a Best Buy all within walking distance of the station," he said. "For your information, Wichita ditched all that other stuff about one hundred years ago. Remember, be back in ninety minutes."

The AmRail conductor tipped his hat politely before leaving.

Emma couldn't believe how dumb she was. Obviously she'd insulted him. Well, how did she know? Like, she knew nothing about Kansas. Or any state in the middle of the country for that matter. Why should she assume they had things here like they do in San Francisco or New York?

Whatever…

When the Western Limited pulled into the Wichita train station an hour later, Emma kissed Snoopy goodbye and left him inside the roomette as she hopped off the train. The Best Buy store was only a ten-minute walk from the station. Since all she had was cash, Emma bought a cheap phone with one of those pay-as-you go services. She bought one hundred dollars of pre-paid minutes for it and used the store's free guest Wi-Fi to search for Ryan's mom.

Emma found a local on-line telephone directory and searched for anyone with the last name of Raymond in Wichita. She came up with twelve hits. Seven of which had male first names. The five remaining had initials before the name Raymond.

She dialed the first number and got a woman's voice-mail.

Emma sighed and waited for the prompt. "Hi, my name is—Trixie, and I'm a friend of Ryan's. If that's the name of your son, then I have something important to tell you. I'm in Wichita right now, but I have to leave very soon, so it's important that you call me back as soon as possible."

Emma killed the call, then dialed the second number. She got another voice-mail, so she left the exact same message.

The next two people were home, but they were both guys.

When Emma tried the fifth number, she hit another voice-mail. "Hi, my name is Trixie, and I'm a friend of Ryan's. If that's your son, then I—"

Her screen flashed as a new call came in. Emma ditched the message and pressed the green phone button.

"Hello?"

"Is this...Trixie?" The older woman's voice was hesitant and quite skeptical.

"Yes, yes, it is. Is this Mrs. Raymond?" Emma asked.

"You said you knew my son. Is he alright?"

"Oh yeah, Ryan's fine."

As far as Emma knew.

"What do you want?" Mrs. Raymond asked.

"Well, my train has been delayed in Wichita for an hour. And since Ryan has told me so much about you, I thought I'd ask if we could have a quick coffee together. That's if you're not too busy. I'm sorry it's so last minute."

"Where do you know Ryan from?"

"We work together."

"At American Express?"

Emma paused. "Yeah, I so love working there. All those shiny-blue credit cards and people charging things. I mean, we both love it. And Ryan is so adorable. Seriously, he makes me laugh at the office all the time. Like, I'm blowing soda out my nose because I'm laughing so hard. You must be so proud of him."

Ryan's mom paused.

Emma wanted to scream. She was usually good at ad-lib, but right now she wasn't on her best game. If she wasn't careful, Emma was going to blow it.

"Oh, and your son introduced me to the Beatles. Do you know about them? Oh my God, Paul McCartney and John Lennon? Are they not amazing song-writers?"

Another pause at the other end. She wasn't buying it. Emma had gone out on a limb with the Beatles reference. Maybe Ryan's mom hated the Beatles. Or didn't know what Emma was talking about.

"Are you at the AmRail station on Douglas Street?" Ryan's mom asked.

Emma smiled to herself. "Yes, the conductor told me there's a Starbucks nearby. I'd love to have a quick coffee with you before I have to go back on board. And your son would kill me if I had this opportunity and didn't at least check up on you. He loves you so much. Do you have time?"

Ryan's mom hesitated again. "I can meet you there in thirty minutes."

Emma retraced her route back to the AmRail station, then went north and found the Starbucks. She ducked into the bathroom and did a mirror check. She was too casually dressed to make the woman believe she was on a business trip. But maybe Trixie—her new character—was on vacation. No, better yet, she was on her way back to New York from visiting her mom in California. Yes, that'd work. Emma focused on the young woman with dark hair who stared back at her. Emma ran her finger over the buttons of her new plastic burner phone, grounding herself into her new character.

Emma sat down at a small wooden table. Five minutes later, an older woman entered the Starbucks and searched the room. She was pretty, even for her age, which Emma guested to be about late forties. The woman had dark hair, a dimpled chin, and the same deep blue eyes as Ryan.

She cautiously approached Emma. "Trixie?"

Emma gave her a warm yes and offered to buy her a coffee or tea. Mrs. Raymond picked a simple café Americano while Emma settled for a tall carmel macchiato. They sat down near a window overlooking the street. Emma told Mrs. Raymond her mom-in-California cover story. She then changed subjects and talked about what Ryan had said about his father and his criminal plot to disrupt some of the world's food supply so the Raymond Foods empire could make even more billions. A plot Venomous hijacked and exploited to almost world-wide catastrophe if it weren't for the Gems.

Mrs. Raymond scoffed. "My ex-husband, Ron—he became the

victim of his own success. He let it all go to his head. Instead of keeping himself grounded with Ryan and me—you know, his family—Ron made us into another one of his company's subsidiaries. He abandoned us long before I left him in the divorce. Ron realized this too late. By the time he tried to reconnect with Ryan, his son had already picked sides. Ryan already had a low opinion of his father, and it would've taken Ron a long time to rebuild that."

"Ryan told me that his dad never trusted him," Emma said.

"Ron thought being a dad meant toughening up your kid. Getting them ready to fly solo in the real world. But Ron went to the extreme. He wanted to cut his son off from the family's wealth. To force him to create his own life so he'd be...worthy enough to inherit his empire."

"But that made Ryan resent his dad even more," Emma added.

Mrs. Raymond nodded. "You do know my son." She sipped her coffee and continued. "Ryan only wanted Ron to care about us. Growing up, he basically didn't have a father who was around. Then, when Ron reconnected with us, he treated Ryan like an employee, not his son." Mrs. Raymond sat up. "But that's in the past. Ryan has a wonderful sales rep job at American Express, where he has a great salary and gets to travel all over the world on business. He's happy, and that makes me happy."

"Ryan tells me he sends you a lot of money from his... paycheck."

Mrs. Raymond smiled. "He's a good son. I'm a very lucky mom."

Emma took a sip of her own drink. She felt the sugar and the caffeine energizing her veins. Now came the uncomfortable part. She had to burst Mrs. Raymond's bubble.

Emma drew out a long breath and folded her hands together on the table. "When your ex-husband hatched his plot to starve out millions of people, he was assisted by a group called Venomous. They're a group of international criminals and terrorists."

"The FBI mentioned them," Mrs. Raymond said, "when they interviewed me after they arrested Ron. What has that got to do with Ryan?"

"Well, Venomous used his negative feelings towards his dad to recruit him into their organization. Venomous uses extortion, kidnapping, terrorism, violence, anything they can to earn money and to gain power. All the money Ryan sends you…that money has a lot of blood on it."

Mrs. Raymond cocked her head slightly. "What are you talking about? My son works for American Express."

"Sorry, but Ryan has been lying to you," Emma said.

Mrs. Raymond's grip on her cup tightened. "Who are you?"

"I'm Ryan's friend, and I care a lot about him. Enough to track you down and ask you to please convince him to quit. To walk away from Venomous. I know you love him. I can tell by how you talk about him, you know? Well…I care about him too, and I don't want to see him die."

"Trixie isn't your real name, is it?"

"I'm sorry, but I can't reveal my real name."

"This is all ridiculous. I don't believe you at all."

"Seriously, I'm telling the truth," Emma said. "Ryan is working for some bad people, and you can help me stop—"

Mrs. Raymond was on her feet. "Stay away from me and my son…whoever you are."

She headed for the front door.

Emma chased after her. "Ryan won't listen to me, but he might listen to you. He loves you, and you love him. Please, you can convince him."

"Get away from me." Mrs. Raymond went outside and ran to her car.

Emma followed. "You have to believe me, Mrs. Raymond. Your son is going to die one of these days."

Mrs. Raymond's car backed up and then raced out of the parking lot.

CHAPTER 12

Twenty hours later, the Western Limited hit the outskirts of Chicago. Emma searched her roomette to make sure she had everything packed and ready to go. She sat back down and poked her finger through the metal cage door of the pet carrier to rub Snoopy's wet snout. Emma relaxed and replayed her meeting with Mrs. Raymond again in her mind.

What could she have done differently? Tell the woman her real name? Would that have helped? Did the woman understand what Emma was saying about Venomous? Maybe to a normal person it all sounded crazy. Secret organizations. Plots to starve out millions of people. Why would Mrs. Raymond believe her? Emma thought that giving her a lot of personal information about Ryan would convince her that she knew her son well. But that didn't seem to matter. Like any loyal mom, her first instinct was to stand by her son.

Emma faced the truth. She was never going to save Ryan. She wasn't a good enough spy to flip him, or a good enough spy to manipulate his mom into saving him.

The train entered a tunnel, and the high-pitched whine of brakes echoed down the passenger cars as the Western Limited slowed to a halt along one of the many track platforms at Chicago's Union Station.

Emma climbed off the train with her rolling suitcase, Snoopy's soft-leather pet carrier, and her purse with her new phone inside. She followed the rest of the passengers up a flight of stairs, which led to the first floor of the station. She looked up and was greeted with a huge vaulted ceiling that spread out over a massive hall made of pure marble with large round pillars stationed along the walls. The hall was as big as a football field and much more beautiful. The style was old. But like, classic old in a cool way that Emma loved. They called it...Art Devo? Something like that. A kind of New York City in the 1930s style. But in Chicago.

Emma checked the status of her connecting train to New York on one of the departure video monitors. It was leaving in four hours.

Four hours.

She examined her surroundings. Although it was beautiful to look at, sitting here on a bench for hours after being on a train for days didn't appeal to her at all. So Emma stepped outside the station and knew immediately she'd made the right decision. Union Station was in the heart of downtown Chicago. Tall skyscrapers. Pedestrians walking across the worn and pitted sidewalks. The smell of exhaust. Angry horns. The thump-thump of rap music echoing from a car. The hustle and bustle of traffic.

If Emma closed her eyes, she could imagine Manhattan. Her old stomping grounds. That feeling of home energized her. City blocks as far as you could see. Shops and restaurants to visit. Those four hours would fly by.

Emma dug out Snoopy's leash and snapped it to his collar. The Russell terrier's tail wagged like crazy. He was excited too.

She picked him up and Snoopy licked her. "I know there's a lot of people, but you'll have to get used to it. This is what New York will be like. You'll have to be a tough little city dog, okay?"

Snoopy licked her again. He just wanted to get down and see what this place was all about.

Emma put him down and held his leash tight as they headed down one city block. It didn't take long for Snoopy's leg to go up on the nearest tree. But then he waited almost another block until he needed to squat. Luckily Emma had walked by a city dog waste container, and she'd wisely grabbed a plastic wrap from it. Shaped like a glove, Emma was able to grab Snoopy's present to the people of Chicago, unwrap her glove inside out, and dump it inside the nearest dog waste container.

Snoopy guided her away from the container and almost dragged Emma past a window display of shoes. She took charge and made the dog reverse course. This shoe store had excellent taste. Especially when it came to their dress shoes. Those leather boots were adorable too. Winter was months away, but still. She would need new boots for the winters in New York. Emma scanned the name of the shop and wondered if they had any stores in New York.

And that was when she caught a woman watching her.

If Emma scanned her surroundings, the woman wouldn't have been visible. However, the shoe store window's glass revealed her position behind a wall from across the street. The woman seemed unremarkable. Dark hair. Dark clothes. Nothing made her stand out from the crowd. And that made Emma suspicious. Lioness had told her that the best tails were the ones who could disappear into the background. They were shadows. Phantoms that you'd swear were never there.

Emma ditched her shoe shopping and walked casually down the block. She used the windows and other reflective surfaces to check behind her. But there was no movement. Nothing to indicate the woman was following her. However, that didn't mean she wasn't following her from across the street.

It was time for her to get sneaky.

Reaching a street corner with a bus stop bench, Emma sat down and put Snoopy in her lap for a dog treat. While he enjoyed his treat, Emma brought out her cheap phone and pretended to check for messages while her other hand dipped inside her handbag and took out some rubber bands. Palming them out of sight, Emma covertly unfastened Snoopy's collar and slipped the rubber bands on it, then fastened the collar back up again. She switched her phone to her other hand and petted Snoopy with her free hand while kissing his head and making a big show of it. The distraction concealed her other hand, which used the rubber bands to secure the phone against Snoopy's collar. She pressed the camera function and began recording video.

Emma put Snoopy down and this time walked back the same way she came, making sure the lens was pointing across the street. Like last time, Emma didn't see anyone following behind her and didn't notice anyone across the street either. She crossed two city blocks before coming to a large office skyscraper. Emma slipped inside the giant lobby and headed for the nearest ladies' bathroom.

"Miss, you can't bring that dog in here." The voice came from a security guard wearing a suit behind a large lobby desk.

Emma stopped and glanced down at Snoopy, who looked up into her eyes with his tongue out.

"I can if he's a drug dog." The words tumbled out of her

mouth, and Emma the actress embraced them. "And mister, you'd better hope my dog doesn't find any drugs in this lobby, or you'll be personally held responsible when I have to call in the rest of my elite drug task force to question everyone on your staff."

The man's eyes ballooned. "Oh, you're a policewoman?"

Emma had him.

"Excuse me? I'm a police *officer* who happens to be a woman. Actually, I'm a sergeant if you wanna get technical about it. Are you trying to interfere with my drug investigation?"

"No, ma'am—I mean, no, Sergeant, not at all. We always cooperate with the Chicago police."

"So far, I have a hard time believing that."

"What can I do?"

"Simple," Emma said. "You sit at your desk and let me and my dog conduct our search of the area without interference. Understand?"

The security man nodded and spoke to three other security officers who had gathered around the desk.

Meanwhile, Emma and Snoopy walked into the women's bathroom and moved into a stall. Emma shut the door and set Snoopy on her lap. She took off the phone and stopped the video recording. She rewound the video file. Then played it back.

At first, the video footage was bouncy, as Snoopy was excited to be walking again. But soon he settled down, and Emma could see across the street a lot better. The first block revealed nothing. No one was following her, at least not that she could see in the footage.

She and Snoopy then took the crosswalk over to the next street block. Emma remembered it because she'd had to hustle across because the traffic light was about to change. She hadn't had time to scan the intersection. But Snoopy's collar had recorded the crosswalk parallel to the one they used.

Emma paused the video. The HD-quality clip captured the mysterious woman dashing across at the last second. Emma played it back again. Yes, it was her. The same woman reflected in the glass.

She continued the video. The woman dropped back out of frame, but she reappeared again and again. Always trailing her from across the street until she came to an alley and broke off the tail.

Then Emma saw why. A man stepped out of a business and

resumed the tail from across the street. He had curly brown hair and wore khaki slacks with a buttoned-up shirt and a tie. He looked like a business guy on a lunch break, but he was also part of a surveillance team.

Emma let the video play out. As she reached the office building, the business-man disappeared, replaced by a large Hispanic male with a mustache.

It was a classic three-person set up. The team of three would rotate people in and out as they followed the rabbit, or target. Rotating people helped hide the surveillance from the rabbit. However, Lioness had trained each of the Gems on not only how to do proper surveillance but also how to spot it.

Now Emma knew what she was up against. A woman and two men. Were they from the FBI? The CIA? The Russians? The Chinese? Emma stopped counting the number of people the Gems had made angry during her short time with them.

But how would any of them know she'd be in Chicago? Emma had been so careful on the train, being hyper-aware of anyone who was taking an interest in what she was up to. Emma had spent some time with the AmRail conductor, but the man hadn't put up any red flags that would make her believe he was keeping an eye on her. Back home, everyone thought she was dead. And if for some reason they didn't, they wouldn't think to look in Chicago. Who else besides the conductor knew she was even on the train?

The answer was so obvious that Emma wanted Snoopy to bite her.

Mrs. Raymond must have called Ryan and told her about the weird teen girl who met her near the train station. And Ryan wasn't stupid. Even if he heard about Emma's suicide, he could put together enough clues to know it was her and she was still alive. Ryan must have called up some of his Venomous buddies to see what Emma was up to. Did Ryan tell Asset One that she was alive? Maybe the team was working under Ryan's personal orders. Maybe he wanted to prevent Emma from disappearing before he had a chance to talk to her.

You're an idiot!

Emma's brain was right. She shouldn't have contacted his mom. Now there was a Venomous surveillance team on her butt.

Snoopy barked, taking Emma out of her thoughts. He craned his little neck to see her face. He looked concerned too.

Emma squeezed him gently in her arms and kissed his head. "We're going to have a new life together. No more spies. No more scary people in our lives. I promise."

Snoopy barked again.

"Yes, dog mommy promise."

Emma stowed away her cheap phone and used the rubber bands off Snoopy's collar to pull her long black hair all the way back into a pony-tail. Next she took Snoopy off his leash and put him back into his pet carrier. Next, her T-shirt came off and was replaced by a pink sweater that she had in her suitcase. She also dumped her jeans in favor of a skirt, although she kept her sneakers and socks on in case she needed to run. Last thing to do was to wash off all her makeup, leaving her face bare and ordinary. Emma wasn't sure if it was good enough to fool the surveillance team, but it might confuse them enough to give her time to lose them.

Emma prepared herself. She would calmly leave the bathroom and head back outside to continue walking. Then she would find an alley where she could disappear quickly and haul ass to another street block. If they didn't follow, Emma would run to the next block just to make sure before making a circle back to the train station.

Emma took a moment to calm herself before stepping out of the ladies' room. She dragged her rolling suitcase behind her as she balanced the strap from her purse on her shoulder. Snoopy and his pet carrier sat on top of the suitcase; that way they were out of view behind her.

Emma walked through the lobby. The security man at the desk was still watching the bathroom for a long-haired Emma and her drug dog. But ugly Emma with a pony-tail and a pink sweater with no dog managed to slip right past the man and leave the building without one eyebrow raised.

Now came the hard part.

Emma left the building behind. It was tempting to do a street scan right after she stepped outside, but that would make her stand out to anyone casing the entrance. All Emma could do was hope they missed her appearance change and continued to wait at the building for her to come out.

Emma waited until she reached the intersection before doing a proper 360-degree scan of her surroundings.

So far, so good.

The light changed to green, and Emma followed the other pedestrians across the crosswalk. When she reached the other side, Emma checked her phone. She still had almost three and a half hours to kill. But if she could shake off her tail, then Emma had some time for lunch. A sushi sign down the block drew Emma's attention as she walked toward it. All this spy stuff was giving Emma an appetite.

She was only about fifty yards away from the sushi place when she noticed the Hispanic man with a mustache walking right towards her on the same sidewalk. Right out in the open.

Emma stopped. He wouldn't be doing that unless…they knew their surveillance team was blown.

She reversed course and picked up her pace. Surely they wouldn't do anything out in the open like this. There were far too many witnesses.

The Hispanic man picked up his pace as well.

Emma broke into a jog as she zig-zagged through slower foot traffic and arrived at the next intersection. It was a red light of course. She scanned the area.

Across the street, the woman who was following her was on a bus bench. When their eyes met, the woman stood up, holding a large purse. One of her hands gripped something hidden behind the purse. The woman angled it so only Emma could have a better look at her black gun with a silencer.

Emma's heart revved up a few beats. These people weren't messing around.

She scanned the crosswalk to her right. That light was green, so she scampered across it.

The light changed. The Hispanic man tried to follow her across but had to retreat because of the new flow of traffic.

But the woman had already crossed over the street on her side, putting her on Emma's side of the block. The woman closed in.

Emma ran down the street as fast as she could, keeping away from the woman with the gun.

The Hispanic man attempted to jaywalk across to Emma's side of the street but had to retreat again.

If Emma could get around the next corner, she'd have more options to break away from them.

But she was so concerned with her two pursuers that Emma

failed to notice the business-man in khaki slacks until he stepped right in front of her.

The man grabbed her arm and pulled her off the street into a narrow alley.

"Asset One sends his regards," the man said.

CHAPTER 13

The narrow street alley Emma found herself in was barely wide enough for one small car. The business-man with khaki slacks and a nylon tie gripped her arm uncomfortably tight. "Asset One sends his regards. He wants to have a conversation—"

Emma kneed the man in the crotch as her purse fell to the ground. As the man reeled from that, Emma followed up with a palm strike to his nose, making him break his grip on Emma and fall back against a brick wall.

Emma grabbed her purse and her suitcase with Snoopy's pet carrier on top and ran down the alley as fast as she could, not stopping until she popped out on the other side, which emptied on to another major street. She went left and jogged quickly down the sidewalk as the suitcase rattled and rolled behind her. Emma walked another zig-zag pattern down each city block and even re-traced some of her steps, trying her best to shake off her pursuers.

After about ten minutes of non-stop jogging, Emma collapsed on a bench. Satisfied that she was safe for now, Emma put Snoopy's pet carrier on her lap and opened it. When she brought him out, the dog looked worried but wagged his tail anyway.

Emma squeezed Snoopy to her chest. "I'm sorry. Your doggy momma didn't mean to bounce you around like that."

Snoopy blinked his eyes, then looked up. She rubbed her fingers across his fur, giving him as much attention as she could.

Emma checked the time. Still three and a half hours until her train to New York left. Plenty of time for those three Venomous agents to search the streets for her. She needed to hide out somewhere and waste a lot of time. Those agents couldn't search every downtown building in Chicago.

Emma glanced around the block. There was a spice store across the street, but Emma didn't know if she could waste hours in there.

To her left was a sandwich shop. Thanks to all the running, Emma was hungry enough to chow down on a foot-long. But it was a small local place with huge windows. If one of her "friends" came down this block, it would be too easy to spot her enjoying lunch. Plus staying there for a few hours was out of the question. Emma hated it, but she'd be safer if she waited to eat until she got on the train, where she could relax her guard.

Damn it. Would she have to walk aimlessly around Chicago for three straight hours?

A door opened behind her as two older women stepped outside, laughing. They were having a great time, oblivious to the stress Emma was under. The two woman each carried a book bag.

A book bag?

Emma turned around. There was a mom-and-pop bookstore literally right behind her. It was like the clouds had opened up and a ray of light pointed Emma towards sanctuary. She could kill three hours in a bookstore. Heck, she could kill a whole day in one. It was perfect.

Emma gave Snoopy one final pet before putting him back in his carrier. She whispered, "You're going to have to be a good dog for three hours, okay?" To bribe him, Emma popped in three doggy treats to keep him busy as she opened the front door and stepped into the book-store.

Three hours later, Emma checked the time, then used her cheap phone and the bookstore's free Wi-Fi to locate where she was. According to Ooogle maps, she was about eight blocks away from Union Station, and it would take her about twenty-five minutes to walk. Emma wanted to get to her train in plenty of time to board; however, she didn't want to leave that much time for those agents to pick her up either. She would have to split the difference.

Emma emerged from the book-store. She couldn't resist buying two books but had to stuff them in her rolling suitcase since adding a fourth thing to carry when you're trying to run from bad people is never a good idea.

On her phone, Emma set up a directions track on her Ooogle Maps app just in case she needed to reference it in a hurry and started out.

Well, first she ducked into the first convenience store she saw and picked up some chocolate mini-donuts for later. It was her favorite go-to junk food, and after all this stress, Emma told herself that she deserved a treat.

Now Emma was ready.

She headed south, walking as briskly as she could without drawing attention as she scanned her surroundings like a hawk. The first two blocks showed no sign of her "friends." Emma had to wait at the next light, but once it was green, she took the crosswalk and traveled four more blocks without any trouble.

Where were they? Did Emma have them so confused and disorganized that they gave up?

Emma didn't wait to find out. She walked the last two blocks and stopped at another red light. She could see the entrance to Union Station and it looked clear. Emma took her time to scan the area again. Once satisfied, she crossed over on the green light and went inside the station. Emma kept scanning as she descended the wide marble staircase that led down into the huge waiting area with the high ceilings and gorgeous pillars. Reaching the floor, Emma approached the big standing old-time sign with the words TO ALL TRAINS pointing the way.

And that was where she stopped.

Near the ticket office and the public bathrooms and the entrance to track three were mustache man, the mysterious woman with a gun, and khaki-slacks business-man. Of course they didn't chase after her in a huge city the size of Chicago. Why do that when they could wait for her to come to them? They must have observed Emma get off the train and check the departure monitor, reasoning that she must have a connecting train.

Great. Now what was she going to do?

Emma needed another option.

She moved away from the middle of the giant waiting room and kept close to the wall until she could think of something. Two AmRail maintenance workers went past Emma and opened a nearby door. The sounds of a train horn and a rush of cold air whisked across her face. The men stepped through and shut the door. Emma wondered if that was an access door that led downstairs to the tracks.

She examined the door. It was marked for *Authorized Personnel Only* and had one of those card scanners that would unlock the door. A card Emma didn't have. However, Emma noticed the door was ajar and not flush within its frame. She touched the toe of her sneaker to the edge of the door, then did a quick scan of the waiting area before using her toe to pry open the door.

Awesome! The men hadn't pushed the door shut to allow the automatic lock to work.

Emma stuck her phone in the door gap to keep it from locking and gathered her things. She shoved open the door and ducked inside before retrieving her phone. She let the door close on its own. Yup, the door needed to be pulled in for the lock to properly engage. Or that was what the warning sign said that was taped to the back of the door for all the AmRail employees to see and follow.

Emma found herself at the top of an all-metal flight of narrow stairs. It was dark, with only a handful of lights to help guide a person down them. She took the stairs anyway. And when she reached the bottom, her skin could tell the air temperature had dropped by several degrees, and she found herself inside a tunnel. The strong scent of diesel was in the air. The tunnel had a set of train tracks that went around a blind curve. This must be where the trains came into the station.

Across the tracks there was another *Authorized Personnel Only* door. That was where the men probably went.

If she followed these tracks, wouldn't it bring her right to the main boarding platforms? That would bypass her "friends" waiting upstairs. Emma decided it was worth a shot. She took a moment to re-orient herself. The door she went through was on this side, so the upstairs board-all-trains sign was to her left. That meant she should go left down the tunnel. Cool.

Snoopy barked and whined behind her. He wasn't in love with the tunnel.

Emma pulled his soft-leather pet carrier off the suitcase and peered through the front. "We'll be on the train in a sec. Hang in there, buddy." She put the strap over her shoulder, then realized her purse was on that side too. Emma brushed it off; she could carry both for a small distance.

Emma started off down the tunnel, walking in between the tracks as she dragged her rolling suitcase behind her. It was oddly quiet. Quiet enough that Emma could hear water dripping from the ceiling and the crunch of the gravel under her sneakers. Emma began to fantasize about how delicious those mini chocolate donuts would be with another AmRail cappuccino, when an air horn echoed through the tunnel.

Emma slowed her pace. Was that from one of the platforms? Or was that from another tunnel?

The horn blared again, only louder.

Emma could hear another sound, like a motor humming. A big continuous motor.

And it was getting closer.

Emma scanned the tunnel. The walls were made of smooth concrete. She wasn't sure how much room there was between them and the tracks.

Another horn pierced Emma's ears as she noticed the tunnel glowing white ahead of her.

Where was a door? Surely there was a door she could use? Or a walkway?

Emma quickly realized she was trapped. The AmRail locomotive came around the blind corner. It filled up the tunnel as it glared down on Emma with its dual headlights. The monster must have weighted a thousand tons. Enough to crunch a teen girl and her dog like they were peanuts.

Emma hopped over a rail and jammed her back against the concrete wall as much as she could as the noise of the engine overwhelmed her ears.

The train was so big, and the tunnel was so small. Emma knew it would scrape her body across the wall like a bug.

Oh my God. She was going to die. And she was going to take poor Snoopy along with her.

Emma shut her eyes. The next image she would see would be Jesus.

Or God.

Or maybe Satan.

Yes, she was about to kill an innocent dog, so going to hell was a gimme.

A blast of wind hit her face as the clatter of steel wheels rang inside her ears. Emma waited for the train to rip her face off or crush a limb or two.

The clatter of steel went on and on and on.

Finally, the wind died as the wheels of death rattled down the tunnel.

Emma opened her eyes. She was still in the tunnel. She was still alive. She gasped for breath and allowed herself to cry a little. She looked around and noticed her suitcase was missing. Emma gripped the two straps still on her shoulder. Snoopy's pet carrier and her purse were still stuck to the side of her hip.

She stepped over the rail and peered down into the tunnel. Torn and tattered bits of clothing were scattered all over, as if her suitcase had exploded on impact. The spine of one of her new books was bent, causing the pages to shed all over the tunnel like a tree in the fall. Emma had no idea where her actual suitcase was. She assumed whatever was left of it was on its way to either Seattle or New Orleans.

Emma wanted to break down and cry. All those clothes. Her favorite tops. Her favorite pants. Her favorite skirts. Dresses. She had packed the cream of the crop. The best clothes she had for an essential wardrobe. Some items were so exclusive you couldn't buy them anymore. Emma checked her neck and felt the diamond necklace still there, thank God. It was the necklace her dad gave her. Emma did have it in her suitcase, but while on the train she had decided to put it on. She sighed; at least it wasn't a total disaster. Yet…

Emma broke out in a run. She wanted to get out of this tunnel as soon as possible.

However, a familiar series of barks made her stop and turn around.

Snoopy was fifty feet away from her, standing in the middle of the tunnel, wagging his tail. He barked again.

Emma checked the pet carrier. The metal cage door was wide open. It must have popped open when she shoved herself against the wall in terror.

"Snoopy, come here!" Emma yelled.

Snoopy waddled to the side of the track and lifted his leg.

"This is no time for a pee-pee break."

The dog felt differently as a stream of piss glazed the rail.

"Well, hurry up or we'll miss our train."

Snoopy barked and then squatted.

"Seriously, you have to do both now?" Emma asked.

Snoopy grumbled at her, as if to say…*duh, you've kept me in a cage all afternoon. you evil girl.*

Emma waited as a distant horn sounded behind Snoopy. Another train was coming, but this time into the station.

"C'mon, Snoopy. Let's go!"

Snoopy dragged his butt along the gravel, taking his time.

Emma moved towards him. This portion of the tunnel was long, and Emma could see a light at the end coming in their direction.

Fast.

"Snoopy, come here!"

The dog wagged his tail and ran away from her.

"We don't have time to play chase the doggy," Emma yelled. "Now come over here!"

Snoopy barked and bounced along the tracks, wanting her to chase him.

Emma could see the face of the locomotive. Its cyclops headlight loomed ten feet above the rails. Its motor hummed along the walls.

Snoopy stopped. He tilted his head at the strange object barreling towards him.

Emma ran towards her dog.

The locomotive filled up the tunnel. A blast from its horn sent Snoopy scampering towards Emma in terror.

She reached out to grab him, but the dog ran between Emma's legs, causing her to fall down in the gravel between the rails.

The horn screamed, and the ground shook as the powerful locomotive closed in on her.

Emma was about to find out what her suitcase felt like.

CHAPTER 14

The air horn scared the crap out of Emma, so much so she couldn't think of anything else besides Snoopy. She scrambled up out of the gravel and leaped towards her dog. She scooped him up and threw herself against the concrete wall of the tunnel, causing a sharp jab of pain to go through her body as her head grazed the wall.

The train flew past. The smell of diesel filled her nose as the rush of wind hit her face again. Emma closed her eyes and let more tears fall down her face. The clatter of steel wheels returned, overwhelming her ears. The noise went on and on. Soon the train disappeared around the blind curve, leaving behind only an echo.

Snoopy quivered in her arms. His face looked terrified, but the dog still managed to get in a few thank-you licks. Emma scratched his head, causing his tail to wag again. Then she touched the back of her own head. It was sore and quite tender, but her fingers had no blood on them.

Emma found her purse and Snoopy's pet carrier battered and abused, yet they were still stuck to her shoulder. Emma put Snoopy back in his carrier and double-checked the door. She then hauled butt down the tracks as quickly as she could without falling over. Soon the tracks led Emma to a large underground facility. The track she was following split up into a yard of multiple tracks, all leading to Union Station's various passenger platforms.

Emma located platform three. From track level, there were no access stairs up to it, so she first apologized to Snoopy as she threw his pet carrier up to the platform before climbing up to it herself.

The speakers on the platform came on…

All aboard AmRail's Lake Erie Express with service to Toledo, Cleveland, Buffalo, Syracuse, Albany, and New York City. All aboard at this time, please.

Passengers lined up to start boarding. On this train, Emma only had a coach seat, so she found the coach cars and got in that line.

The conductor checked her ID and paused when she saw Emma's face. "To your left there's a bathroom. You can use it before we leave." The conductor scanned her paper ticket and moved on to the next one in line.

Emma thought that was odd. She climbed on to the coach car and noticed the bathroom. She went inside and activated the lighting.

Oh my God.

In the mirror, her face was a mess. Pieces of gravel and dirt were stuck to her skin, making her face look like the outside of a tire. But her dark hair didn't look too bad.

Emma washed her face and hands. She began taking off the rubber bands holding her pony-tail together when the sharp pain returned. She touched the culprit, a large bump where she'd hit her head on the wall of the tunnel. The bump made it difficult to take off the rubber bands, but Emma took her time and managed to free her poor hair. She brushed it out, being careful to avoid touching the bump.

Now satisfied she didn't look like a troll digging through the tunnels of Chicago, Emma found her coach seat, but she had to ask the man sitting next to her to let her in. The man was nice, and soon Emma had Snoopy's pet carrier stowed right in front of her legs as she sat down and relax. Finally Emma broke out the mini chocolate donuts inside her purse.

They tasted like heaven.

Out of her window, the Lake Erie Express eased out of Union Station, making its way through the scary tunnel before emerging out into the daylight as it raced through the fields of Northern Indiana.

After donut number six was safe in her stomach, Emma watched the rolling scenery for a couple of hours. She flagged down the conductor for some aspirin and a bag of ice for the back of her head, which was still throbbing. She then took Snoopy out of his pet carrier and gave him some more yummy treats along with some love for another hour. After she put Snoopy back, Emma relaxed and played a couple of free games on her phone, which killed a few more hours. Soon the throbbing in her head stopped, and Emma drifted off to sleep.

CHAPTER 15

When Emma woke up, her outside window was dark, as night had fallen across the landscape. This allowed the reflection of the lit-up AmRail coach interior to shine against the glass. Emma retrieved her cheap phone from the front seat pocket and checked the time. Her little nap had lasted over two hours at least.

"Feelin' any better, darling?"

The girl's voice had a distinct Irish accent. An accent Emma recognized.

Bridget O'Malley sat in the seat right next to her, tilting her head in a rather sympathetic gesture. The girl's long red hair hadn't changed since Emma had last seen her in Africa, but her vanilla skin had darkened a few shades. Sitting on the girl's lap was Snoopy, who looked up at Emma and wagged his tail.

Where was the man who was sitting there?

"Did ya bonk your head?" Bridget asked, referencing the ice pack.

Emma reached for Snoopy, but Bridget angled him away. "Now don't make a fuss. He's being a lovely dog. Don't force us to do something sad to him."

"Why does your pup have that brace on him?" another Irish voice asked from the seat in front of Emma. Sophia O'Malley turned around and leaned over the back. "Did he hurt his back?"

A fire burned inside Emma. "If you harm that dog, I will hunt you down and—"

"You'll murder us in our sleep. Got it. Does he have a weak back?" Bridget asked.

"Yes, I hit him with my car."

"Ya poor thing. And you're worrying about us tryin' to hurt him?"

"Why did ya hit him with your car?" Sophia asked.

"It was an accident."

Sophia reached over the seat and scratched Snoopy's head, causing the dog to wag his tail even faster.

Emma didn't like either of these girls touching her dog. "What do you want?"

"The boss wanted a word, but ya ditched his welcoming committee in Chicago," Bridget said as she petted Snoopy too.

"They showed me a gun and tried to drag me off the street," Emma said.

"You overreacted."

"And ya interrupted our Caribbean holiday," Sophia added with disgust.

"St. Maarten was so grand," Bridget said. "The water was blue. The college boys on the beach were hot. And I was starting a nice tan."

"Then we had to fly to fecking Cleveland to board a fecking train to babysit Miss America and her mutt."

Bridget grinned. "My sister's a bit pissed at ya."

"I figured that out," Emma said. "Well, it's not my fault because I didn't ask for anyone to 'have a word' with me. I wanted to be left alone."

"Yeah, nah, that's not happening." Bridget typed out a text and sent it. "The quicker we get this done, the quicker we get back to the ocean."

Emma blew her off. Whatever. She glanced at Sophia. "How's your concussion?"

"My what?"

"After the *Falcon's Claw* sank, you had to go to the hospital in Africa. You were out cold. I was wondering if you were okay."

Sophia raised her chin. "Why do you fecking care?"

Emma shrugged. "It looked serious at the time. I mean, they had to get an ambulance for you and everything."

"My, what a sweetheart," Bridget said. "She actually gives a piss about ya, Sophia, darling."

"Well, I don't give a piss about her."

"Fine. Sounds like you made a complete recovery anyway," Emma said with a sarcastic grin.

Sophia glared at Emma, then looked over at Bridget. "Is she insulting me?"

Bridget's phone rang. "Give it a rest. Important call coming in." She hit the green button. "Asset One-three-zero here." Her eyes flicked to Emma's. "Yes, sir. She's right here." Bridget handed Emma the phone.

Emma rolled her eyes but took it. "What?"

"You're a hard young woman...to pin down," Asset One's voice began. He was in no hurry. Like he had all the time in the world. "As soon as I heard of your...death...I was disappointed. But now...I understand."

"I want to be left alone," Emma said. "Seriously, why can't you understand that?"

"Currently, there's a large operation in motion...against the Authority. Right now...we're attacking some of their facilities. Destroying safe houses and bases...that we know of. With your help, we could wipe them all out."

What was Asset One talking about? What major operation?

Emma shook off the questions in her mind. "I don't care about what you're doing. I don't care about the Authority anymore. I only want to disappear."

"We...can help you with that," Asset One said. "Anywhere in the world...that you wish. Let us help."

"I don't want anything from you."

"Ryan is coming to New York this weekend. He very much wants...to speak with you. Remember, Emma, you're running out of friends. Once Mrs. B finds out you faked your own death...she will be furious. She will send everything at her disposal...to hunt you down. Including your own friends."

That last sentence gave Emma pause. Would Mrs. B do that? Make the Gems hunt her down?

Sophia waved her hand in front of Emma's face.

"What?" Emma asked.

"Answer his question," Sophia said.

Emma snapped out of it. "Sorry, what was the question?"

Bridget sighed. "Asset One wants you to wait for Ryan when he comes to New York and hear what he has to say before running off."

Ryan was the last person Emma wanted to see. She needed a clean break, like, never ever seeing him again. Emma's "begin a new life" plan was unraveling like a ball of yarn.

"Okay, I'll wait for Ryan," Emma lied.

"Excellent," Asset One said. "In that case, Asset One-three-zero...you and your sister will escort Emma...and make sure no harm comes to her in New York."

Sophia shook her head and pretended to bash her face against the back seat cushion repeatedly.

Bridget frowned. "We understand, Asset One. Consider it done." She killed the call.

"Ah, I'm going to murder myself," Sophia said.

"It's only for the weekend, darling. The beach will still be there when we go back."

"Can we throw her off the train...accidentally?"

"I'm peckish," Bridget said. "Let's head for that dining car."

She handed Snoopy back to Emma, who kissed his head and placed him back into his pet carrier before standing up and following Bridget down the aisle. Sophia fell in right behind Emma, keeping a close eye on her.

Emma played along for now, but once they arrived in New York, she would find a way to ditch her new travel companions.

CHAPTER 16

The sun was out, painting the city park with natural light. As Emma walked through it, the blades of grass felt warm and soothing as they brushed against her toes. She reached a blanket covering the grass and flopped down on it.

Her backpack was there. It was wide open and contained a stack of college textbooks about acting, theater makeup, and lighting. An NYU-labeled water bottle sat half-empty as Snoopy rolled around effortlessly in the grass without his back brace.

"Hi, Em!" A girl that was close to her own age ran up to her. It was Hailey, her best friend from New York. She had long brown hair with curls and wore an NYU college sweater over her cream-colored skin. "I'm heading back to the apartment. Do we still need soy milk?"

Our apartment?

Emma glanced at her sweater. Oh, yeah. They must be college roommates. That made sense.

A shadow appeared over Emma and the blanket.

Hailey smiled at someone. "Hi, Mr. Rothchild."

Emma turned and saw a man with golden hair like hers. He now sat on the blanket too and flashed her the warmest smile.

"Welcome back home, Emma. I've missed you," he said.

It was her dad. He was alive!

But before Emma could reach out and touch this new reality... his image disappeared.

Someone tapped her on the shoulder.

Emma turned again and saw Sophia O'Malley sitting next to her.

"You've got drool all over your chin," she said with a little too much glee.

Emma shook herself awake and scanned her surroundings. She

93

was still inside the AmRail coach car as it rolled through the state of New York. It was daylight. The morning sun hung low over the horizon. Emma touched her chin and felt the sticky drool. She pulled out her purse and took out a Kleenex to fix the problem before allowing herself time to think about the dream she'd had. A dream of what could've been.

Emma thought about her dad. Those warm eyes that loved her. Those strong hands that held her when she was little. That confident voice that would scold her. That gentle voice that would forgive her. Those large arms that would embrace her. Those thoughts and feelings were still vivid in her mind, as if the man had walked the earth only a day ago...but Emma reasoned that her emotions were lying. That man existed no more.

But maybe Emma could salvage a part of her wonderful dream. She could live in New York. Go to school in New York. Be a New Yorker again. Maybe regain pieces of her old life back.

Emma wondered if Hailey still decorated her room with dolphins. If she still wore that necklace made of seashells. If she was still dating Drew Marshall and still snorted when she laughed.

It would be nice to see her again.

Through the window, the scenery changed as the train approached the outskirts of New York City. The land was swallowed up by rows and rows of tall buildings that reached up to the sky. The train went through more tunnels as it twisted its way south. When the train broke out into the open, Emma recognized some of the buildings. They were in Manhattan, heading down the island along the Upper West Side.

Central Park came into view as a giant patch of green spanning across dozens of city blocks, its borders surrounded by buildings.

Soon Emma could pick out the Lincoln Center for the Performing Arts.

Mount Sinai West Hospital.

Rockefeller Center.

The Empire State Building.

Emma felt goosebumps forming on her skin, the excitement brewing in her stomach. The landmarks reminded her of a not so distant past. The happy times. A young girl with the island of Manhattan as her playground. A young girl with a dad who exposed her to art, culture, music, and fascinating people. A young girl who was sometimes expected to be a big girl and take care of herself when Dad was away on business.

Emma forgot how much New York would remind her of him.

Sophia leaned in to the window. "Geez, how big is this stupid place?"

"As big as it gets," Emma replied.

"I'd rather be in Dublin."

"You'll have to settle for Woodland Heights."

"What's that?"

"The most Irish neighborhood in the Five Boroughs," Emma said, her hometown pride coming out.

Sophia appeared confused. She got Bridget's attention in the seat in front of Emma.

"Is she messing with me?" Sophia asked. "Are there Irish people in New York?"

"Oh bejesus, Sophia, you're such an egg at times. Of course there are," Bridget said. "Haven't ya heard about our people migrating through Ellis Island and all that?"

Sophia only blinked. Clearly she hadn't.

"Do ya know where this Woodland Heights is?" Bridget asked Emma.

"Yes, of course."

"Ryan texted me. Says he won't be here until Sunday morning…so we have some time to kill," Bridget said. "Doesn't a proper Irish lunch sound grand, Sophia?"

Sophia actually smiled. "Oh, that'll be nice. I could do with a taste of home."

"Okay, then once we get off at Pennsylvania Station, we'll need to take the subway," Emma said. "I'd say we'd be there in about an hour."

"That's a sound idea," Bridget said. "Then we can do some shopping."

Emma's attention kicked up a level. "Shopping, what kind of shopping?"

"On *the Falcon's Claw* you said we had horrid taste in clothing," Bridget said. "Now's your chance to make it up to us."

"I'd rather kick myself in the face than go shopping for clothes," Sophia said.

"How would you know?" Bridget asked. "I bought everything you've ever worn, ya muppet. Without me, you'd be wanderin' around the world naked like a clueless git."

Normally Emma would jump at the chance to go clothes shopping, especially in New York City where she knew every shop —at least in Manhattan—but Emma wanted to buy new clothes for herself, not help two crazy girls who thought cat-suits were on the cutting edge of fashion.

"Sure, that sounds like fun," Emma lied.

Once AmRail's Lake Erie Express pulled into New York's Pennsylvania train station, Bridget and Sophia didn't leave Emma's side. After disembarking, they all went into the ladies' restroom together before emerging outside into the sunshine.

It was a warm day in Manhattan. The skyscrapers went on for miles and miles in every direction. It was like downtown Chicago all over again. More pedestrians walking across the worn and pitted sidewalks. More smells. More traffic. More angry horns. More rap music echoing out of car windows.

But Emma could smell the pizza. The good kind that you can fold the crust using only one hand. She recognized the hot dog carts with the yellow and blue umbrellas. She recognized the street signs. She knew where all the subway stops were without even glancing at a map or a sign. And she knew to watch out for the bright yellow cabs that always tried to run you down in the crosswalks.

This was her city.

Emma took it all in. Her heart beat faster. Her body soaked up the energy of the city block they were on.

It was New York.

And it felt so good.

Someone took away the strap to Snoopy's pet carrier.

"I'll keep this for now," Bridget said, slipping the strap over her own shoulder. "Just in case you're thinking of ditching us."

Emma wasn't happy about that. Poor Snoopy didn't deserve all this stress in his life. Maybe she should have left him in California. The twins knew that she wouldn't go anywhere without him. How could a mom abandon her little furry baby? Emma told herself to be patient. Maybe an opportunity would come her way, so she had to be ready for it.

Emma led the way to the Thirty-Fourth Street subway station. Using a self-service machine, Bridget bought them each a twenty-dollar MetroCard which Emma said would help them get around New York much more easily. From Thirty-Fourth Street, Emma had them take the Uptown Express A subway all the way up to 125th Street. Then she had them transfer to the Bronx Express D subway that would take them north into Woodland Heights.

As the Bronx Express wormed its way through the underground tunnels under Manhattan Island, Emma scanned the row of advertisements that were above the windows on the opposite side of the subway car for the one hundredth time. She still didn't know what she was going to do.

Ditching the twins at the next subway stop would be the easy part. Emma was confident of that. She remembered that crazy running-in-circles trick she'd used on the bus in Montreal when a Venomous agent was tailing her and Ryan. It was a trick Emma learned here, riding the subways with her girlfriends, who loved to goof around when they traveled through Manhattan. But Emma couldn't come up with a way to do that trick and swipe Snoopy's pet carrier away from Bridget.

Emma sighed and read the Broadway show advertisement again, this time imagining her own name on the featuring actor credit.

"Hey, is that a dog?" a tall man asked from the other side of the car. He pointed at Snoopy's pet carrier resting on the seat between Bridget and Sophia. The tall man had wire-rimmed glasses, a button-down shirt with a collar, and slacks. Emma pegged him as a corporate drone from the financial district who was single and didn't know how to relax or dress himself on a Saturday.

"I don't know, is it?" Bridget asked.

"Can't have a dog on the subway. It's against the rules."

Bridget made eye contact with her sister. "Did ya hear that? We're breaking the rules."

"We tend to do that a lot," Sophia said.

Bridget crossed her legs. "So what if he is a dog. What are ya gonna do about it?"

The tall man's lips pressed together. "I'll report you to the cops. These subways have enough smells on them. We don't need a dog adding to the mix."

"Don't be such an egg," Bridget said.

"Mind your own fecking business, why don't ya?" Sophia asked with a glare.

The tall man didn't let it go. He pulled out his phone.

"Who ya calling?" Sophia asked, rising from her seat.

The tall man didn't answer. He put the phone to his ear. "Yes… I'm on the Bronx Express D Northbound, and I want to report a —"

Sophia grabbed the man's phone and tossed it down to the opposite end of the subway car.

"What the hell's wrong with you!" the man yelled as he moved over to retrieve his phone.

Bridget clamped down on Sophia's arm and guided her back down to her seat, then shot her sister a look that said; *chill out.*

Emma was surprised at how short a fuse Sophia had. The man was acting quite normal for a New Yorker. Every person in the city had a pet peeve about something, and New Yorkers were never shy about letting others know about it. Growing up here, Emma had learned to ignore it and let that person get it out of their system so they'd feel better.

The tall man picked up his phone. "Damn it. You broke my phone."

Bridget squeezed Sophia's arm. It was amazing to Emma how the twins could read each other. Sophia pressed her lips together while her cheeks inflated. She wanted to say something so bad.

"No worries," Bridget said to the man. "Give us your address, and our parents will buy you a new phone. Honest to G."

The tall man slipped the phone into his pocket and went through the connecting door to the next subway car.

"What an *eegit*," Sophia said.

"Why did ya throw his phone?" Bridget asked. "Are ya tryin' to get us arrested, ya git?"

"He wouldn't shut his mouth."

"Welcome to New York," Emma said. "You'd better get used to that."

As she tried to explain the Big Apple's social norms to the twins, Emma caught a glimpse of the tall man re-entering the subway car with a New York City transit cop.

"Oh swingin' Jesus," Bridget said. "He's got a cop with 'im now."

Having the police involved certainly complicated things.

And it gave Emma an idea.

CHAPTER 17

Inside the moving subway car, the tall man with wire-rimmed glasses pointed towards Sophia and Bridget. "Those two girls, officer. Right there."

The New York City transit cop was a short woman with pale skin and strong cheek-bones, her hair folded up inside her police officer's cap. The officer analyzed the twins with her trained eyes. "So what's the story? Are you girls harassing this man?"

Emma could detect her strong Queens accent.

"Nothing of the kind, officer," Bridget said, turning up her Irish accent. "If anything, he started in on us first."

"They have a dog. That's against the rules," the tall man said.

The officer tilted her head at the pet carrier. She held two fingers up to the door, and Snoopy's friendly tongue poked out to lick them.

"Well, hi there, little guy," she said to Snoopy. The officer then straightened back up. "That a Jack Russell?"

"Who's Jack Russell?" Bridget asked.

Emma tried her best not to smile. "Yes, he's a Jack Russell terrier," she said.

"The size of the dog doesn't matter," the tall man said. "Dogs are not allowed on the subway."

The officer stepped back to address the man. "That's true, sir, if the dog is not inside a carrier. But as you can see, this animal *is* inside a legal dog carrier, which is not against the rules. For it to be an issue, the dog would have to be free."

"But what about my phone?" The man pointed. "That girl threw it against the wall and broke it. I want to press charges against her."

The officer sighed. "Let me see the phone, please."

The tall man gave it to her. The officer turned the phone on and flipped through it. "Your phone isn't broken, but there's a crack in the screen here. Are you saying she damaged your phone?"

"Yes, fine, she *damaged* my phone."

"Anyone see what happened between this gentleman and these girls?" the officer asked as she scanned the subway car for any takers.

Everyone in the car looked away. No one wanted to get involved.

"I saw what happened, officer," Emma said.

The twins both shot her a look.

"Wonderful. Come with me, miss." The officer led Emma to the back of the car where no one was sitting. "Suppose you tell me what's going on here?"

The idea dropped into Emma's mind like an apple from a tree, and the actress inside her pounced on it without hesitation.

"Those two girls jumped me at the station on 125th Street. They took my dog and I chased them on board this subway. But then, one of them pulled out a knife while the other forced me to sit down next to them to keep quiet. They're only waiting to ditch me at the next stop and flee."

Again, Emma tried her best not to smile. She was so wickedly good at improv.

The officer crossed her arms. "Run that by me again. So you're saying…those two girls jumped you?"

Emma lowered her voice and let the emotions of her new character slowly take over. She told the officer again, but this time her voice sounded scared, her body joining in on the charade by quivering and showing stress.

The officer studied Emma's face for a long moment.

Emma loved acting on the stage. But there was a certain exhilaration when she used her skills in the field. In a real-life situation. A situation that could go horrible for her if Emma failed to convince her audience of the fake reality that she wanted to sell.

The officer grabbed the radio that was hanging off her shoulder. "Charlie Seventeen to Charlie Eleven."

Go ahead Seventeen.

"You available?"

Affirmative. What's the problem?

"Not sure. Meet me in car five? Over?"

On my way, Charlie Seventeen.

The officer put her radio back up. "Sit on the opposite side of the girls, okay?"

Emma nodded and did exactly that as the officer approached the twins.

"So are you going to arrest her?" the tall man asked.

"Sir, sit down over there." The officer pointed to an empty seat at the other end of the car. "I'll be with you in a moment." The officer turned her attention to Bridget and Sophia. "Put the dog down on the floor."

Bridget glanced over at Sophia, then put Snoopy's pet carrier down on the floor.

"Let's break out those IDs," the officer said.

Bridget hesitated, then handed the officer her passport. Sophia did the same.

The officer scanned them. "Citizens of Ireland, huh? Sounded like you two were from Boston."

"We'd fancy a visit to Boston some day," Bridget said. "I hear it's quite grand."

"Better not say that too loud around here," the officer said with a grin. "You here in New York to visit family?"

"Yes, our cousins. They live in Woodland Heights," Bridget answered.

"Oh yeah? What part?"

"They live right off the subway entrance."

"Which stop?"

Bridget paused.

Emma hadn't told them what stop they'd be getting off at. This would be interesting to watch.

"One Hundred Thirty-Fifth Street, ma'am," Sophia said with an innocent smile as her hand discreetly tucked her phone back into her pocket.

Emma was impressed. Sophia must have had their subway route already on her phone and picked a random spot in Woodland.

Clever girl.

The officer thought about it. "Can you tell me their exact address, but without looking at your phone this time?"

Sophia's smile evaporated.

The connecting door swished open again as a second police officer stepped into the subway car. He was a big dude with a baby-like face and a flat haircut. When he reached the first officer, he put his cap back on. "What's up?"

The first officer glanced at Emma, then returned her attention to the twins. "I'm still not sure yet. Can you watch these two as I search them?" The female officer had Bridget stand up and face the windows as she spread her arms and legs. She padded Bridget down and found a switchblade. She gave it to the second officer.

"That's for personal protection," Bridget said.

"Sit down on your hands," the female officer instructed.

"What?"

"Sit down on your hands, miss."

Bridget did what the female officer said.

It was now Sophia's turn. The girl grumbled but followed her sister's example.

The female officer patted down Sophia's jeans and stopped. She rolled up her pant leg, revealing a long knife sheath. "Well, look at this, would ya?" The female officer pulled out the knife blade which was at least four inches long. She gave that to the second officer as well.

"Damn," the second officer said. "What's a young lady like you need a knife like this for?"

"Because men are bastards," Sophia said.

The second officer lost his grin.

"Sit on your hands too," the female officer said after she finished with Sophia.

Sophia hesitated, then complied.

"How do you two know this girl?" The female officer pointed at Emma.

Bridget and Sophia exchanged looks.

"She's our friend," Bridget said. "We're all going up to Woodland Heights together for lunch and to visit with my cousins whom she knows." Bridget looked over. "Isn't that right, Emma?"

Emma was already committed. There was no turning back. "I've never met either of you before in my life. At least, not until you jumped me and stole my dog."

"Get off the grass. That's a fecking lie," Sophia yelled.

Bridget kept her anger in check. "Now, Emma darling, don't be making a fuss. I know you're pissed at us from the other day, but lyin' to this friendly police officer isn't gonna do either of us a bit of good. Remember, bad things always happen when people lie."

Bridget's eyes put an exclamation point on that last sentence.

Emma's heart tightened. Did Bridget mean they would kill the police officers? Or they would kill Snoopy? Or her? Or would the twins do all three?

She prepared herself. If the twins made a move on the officers, Emma would have no choice but to try to prevent that. She couldn't let these officers get hurt because some guy on a subway didn't like dogs.

"What do you wanna do?" the second officer asked.

The brakes hissed, and the wheels began a low squeal as the subway was slowing down for its next stop.

The female officer sighed. "Let's take 'em all off and interview them separately at the next station. See if we can get a clearer picture."

"I'm with ya." The second officer grabbed his microphone. "Charlie Eleven to dispatch. Have another unit meet us at...the Astoria station on Seventy-Ninth. Over?"

"Listen up," the female officer said. "When we come to a full stop, I want you girls to follow Officer Burns out of the subway in a single file. You're not under arrest, but we wanna ask more questions, okay? Let's all cooperate, and we'll have no problems, got it?"

Emma nodded.

"What about me?" the tall man asked from a couple of rows away. "Don't you want to ask me questions too?"

"Yes, sir. Just follow us out."

The subway came to a stop, the automatic doors slid open, and people emptied out.

Snoopy's pet carrier was still on the floor.

Emma swallowed. She had to at least try.

CHAPTER 18

The doors of the subway car were wide open, but the policeman with the baby face blocked one set of doors as he held up the next round of passengers trying to board. "Wait a second, people. Police business coming through. Make a hole, please."

Snoopy's soft-leather pet carrier sat right there on the floor.

Emma launched herself towards it, doing her best to keep as low as possible as she grabbed the strap.

The female officer swung around and tried to grab Emma but only got a handful of her T-shirt.

Feeling the pull, Emma rotated her body and shoved the officer's arm away, causing the woman to lose her balance and fall to the floor. This almost made Emma fall backwards as well, but she grabbed on to a standing bar to balance herself before pushing herself to the other end of the car, towards another subway door.

"Stop!" the baby-faced police officer shouted.

Emma ran out of the subway car and weaved through the crowded underground station. She saw two flights of stairs and ran up them as fast as she could until she popped outside to street level. Emma raced down the sidewalk, bumping into people, who gave her dirty looks. Soon, Emma settled down into a steady walk, her mind jumping around various ideas on what to do next while her lungs screamed for a rest.

Her lungs won; Emma dropped herself on a steel bench to catch her breath. She checked on Snoopy. He gave her a couple of barks, his eyes begging her to let him out of his carrier. But at least her fur baby was safe and by her side again.

Emma closed her eyes. She didn't have much time. What would a spy do in this situation?

She had to change her look completely, like Emma had on the train out of California. But how? She had no extra clothes thanks to that near-death experience in the tunnel.

Emma had to find a clothing store.

A siren wailed as a NYC police car zoomed past her bench, no doubt on its way to the subway station. It wouldn't take them long to swing back around. This got Emma off the bench and kept her moving. She crossed over a few streets and went down a couple of blocks until she found a small alley to duck into. She pulled out her cheap phone and did a search of clothing stores near her. There was a Goodwill store. That would have a lot of different clothes for a lot of different disguises. However, it was ten blocks away. Hardly ideal. Emma needed somewhere closer. Every minute she was on the street looking like this gave the cops more time to find her.

She then found a store on the map calling itself a boutique. That was around the next corner. Emma would try that one first.

As she emerged from the alley, another NYC police car rolled slowly down the street.

Emma retreated up the alley and hid behind a metal trash bin as the patrol car continued its slow cruise. By how slow they were moving, Emma was convinced they were looking for someone. Most likely a girl with dark hair who ran out of the subway.

Carefully, Emma moved out from behind the trash bin and peeked. The police cruiser made a right turn and disappeared. However, Emma was convinced that it would return. They hadn't even looked down the alley she was in. Which meant they would fix that mistake on their next pass.

She was running out of time.

Emma glanced down the road to see if she could make it over to the next block when she saw an I LOVE NYC tourist shop on the corner. It was one of those places New Yorkers typically ignored because only gullible tourists would shop in junky stores like that. But to this New York girl, it might save her butt.

Emma crossed the street and headed inside I LOVE NYC. The store was as much of a tourist trap as Emma had thought it would be. The walls were covered with T-shirts. Statue of Liberty. Empire State Building. Radio City Music Hall. New York City this. New York City that. Maps of Manhattan. The Bronx. Queens. Brooklyn. Mugs. Caps. Pens. Key chains. Whatever piece of junk you could put a New York logo on, it was sold here.

Emma searched around this cornucopia for something to wear,

but every shirt made her want to vomit. None of it appealed to her. She couldn't even find a color that halfway did her figure justice.

Finally, she found a black T-shirt with a picture of the old Twin Towers that said, *9/11 We will never forget.* It was in her size, and the black would go with almost anything. Plus the shirt wasn't stupid. In fact, she agreed with it one hundred percent.

Emma folded the shirt around her arm and made it halfway to the cashier before she stopped. On the other side of the store, there was a sports apparel section that had New York Yankees baseball jerseys.

Jackpot.

Emma bid the 9/11 shirt a respectful goodbye before jogging over to the jerseys. She had been a Yankees baseball fan ever since she was little, and going full out now to show her loyalty to the team was the best idea ever. With her emergency cash still in her purse, Emma bought a Yankees jersey, a cap, sweatpants with the team's logo tastefully added on the side, pin-striped socks, and—oh my God. Emma found the cutest New York Yankees doggy shirt she ever saw.

"Do you have a bathroom I can use?" Emma asked the cashier.

Once inside their single-room bathroom, Emma went to work. She popped open her purse and took out all her beauty stuff. First she washed all the coloring out of her hair, turning the inside of the sink black. She then removed her makeup and decided to go all natural with only some added lip gloss. Once her hair dried, she combed it back and placed the Yankees cloth cap on top of it, allowing the strands of her blond hair to spill out over the back of her neck. Emma clipped off all the tags and changed into her new wardrobe.

After stuffing her old clothes inside Snoopy's pet carrier, Emma checked herself in the mirror. She looked New York Yankees adorable.

Out of his carrier, Snoopy was excited to be free. But once Emma slipped him into his new outfit, Snoopy protested with a series of whines.

"You'll have to be a big dog and suck it up," Emma told him.

Next she clipped on his leash, and Snoopy's tail began wagging again.

Emma then emerged from the bathroom as a new woman. She walked back out on the street with renewed confidence as she made her way back to the alley, where she tossed Snoopy's soft-leather pet carrier in the trash bin.

Emma headed down the street with Snoopy waddling along on a leash, as happy as can be.

After traveling at least two blocks, Emma spotted another NYC police cruiser rolling slowly down the street.

She tensed up, then told herself to relax. Her fingers gripped Snoopy's leash, the actor grounding herself into her new character. A character that was familiar to her. As Emma walked down the sidewalk, she kept her attention on Snoopy and the places she was walking past, doing her best not to give the policeman any attention at all.

But the cruiser fell in behind her, still on the street. Were they trailing her?

Emma focused on her trade-craft. Spying 101...the art of pretending not to pay attention to your surroundings even though you actually were.

The cruiser was rolling beside her, keeping pace. Any moment now the officers would burst out of their vehicle and tackle her like a criminal.

"Miss, hey, miss?" a voice to her left asked.

Stay focused. Stay in character, Emma told herself.

"Not interested," Emma said as she continued walking.

The cruiser moved on ahead and slipped into an empty parking spot by the curb.

Emma continued towards them, not changing her course at all.

"Miss, we'd like to talk to you." The voice came from the open passenger-side window of the cruiser.

Emma could see the police officer now. He had dark skin and glasses. "Oh my God. Sorry about that, officer. Thought you were some dudes harassing me. Guess I should look next time, right?" She could feel that New York attitude flowing back into her veins.

"Where you headed?" the officer asked.

"Nowhere. Around the neighborhood. Taking my Snoopy out for a walk."

"Seen anyone with one of those leather pet carriers with a strap? You know, that look like a bag or a piece of luggage? Or a teen girl with dark hair, jeans, and a white T-shirt?"

Emma thought about it. "Nah, ain't seen no one like that. Is she a runaway or something?"

"Something like that. If ya see anyone who fits that description, give us a call," the officer said. "Seen anything weird or unusual since you been out?"

"It's New York. Where should I start?" Emma flashed them a knowing smile.

Both police officers laughed.

The black officer pointed at her Yankees jersey. "Is Valdez pitching tonight?"

Emma was so busy this month that following the Yankees' new baseball season had gotten away from her. But the girl wearing this baseball outfit would know the right answer. Damn it.

Emma told herself not to panic. Pick a pitcher. A veteran. Someone she hoped they hadn't traded in the off season.

"Thought Simmons was on the mound tonight," Emma said, secretly crossing her fingers.

"He pitched Thursday night. Their bullpen is much deeper than last season, so I doubt he'd come back in the rotation that soon."

"You're probably right."

"Appreciate your time," the officer said as the police cruiser rolled away. It moved down the street and disappeared into the urban jungle.

Emma felt a great weight lift from her shoulders. That was too close. She took out her new dark sunglasses and slipped them on to complete her disguise. Another proud New Yorker...walking in America's greatest city.

CHAPTER 19

The backyard of the abandoned home was quite large. Big enough to set up a ramp made of old plywood and a mound of dirt. The grass had long since died, leaving behind only dirt. The bank held the deed and was in no hurry to fix the place up for whatever reason.

Miyuki pumped the pedals so hard her Yeti trail bike was flying across the dirt. She leaned her body to the left as she let the toe of her sneaker drag along the ground to force the Yeti into a 180-degree sliding turn. Keeping her momentum after the turn, Miyuki pumped the pedals even more as she gained speed, approaching the ramp of plywood. As her bike launched up into the air, Miyuki kicked the side of the bike under her as she held on the handlebars, letting the Yeti do a 360-degree rotation under her before she landed on the opposite ramp of plywood.

Miyuki then slid her bike to a stop.

Her audience of twelve-year-old boys sat on their bikes in pure awe.

Miyuki's eyes touched the ground, embarrassed she was drawing so much attention to herself. She missed her motorbike in Japan. Emma's grandmother wasn't a fan of motorbikes, so out of respect, Miyuki had settled on a nicely equipped trail bicycle. It wasn't fast. But the bicycle could still do some cool tricks that would get you killed on a motorbike. Although motorbikes were great for jumping large mounds of dirt at speeds higher than 120 kilometers an hour.

Still, Miyuki needed to go outside. Needed to go fast and jump over things. Needed a distraction from reality.

"Do that again!" one of the boys yelled.

"*Hei*, would you like me to do a flip this time?" Miyuki asked.

The boys nodded.

Miyuki pumped the pedals again, raced around a circle to build up momentum, then she bolted for the ramp. Soon she was in the air, leaning her body all the way back and bringing the bike along with her as she did a flip in mid-air. She landed hard on her front tire and almost lost it on the ramp, but Miyuki settled the bike down and rolled off the ramp to a stop.

"I think I'm in love," another boy said, making the others crack up.

"You too young for me," Miyuki said.

"But you're old enough for me."

The boys cracked up again.

Feeling the testosterone rising to an uncomfortable level, Miyuki said good-bye to her admirers and pedaled down the street.

It was Saturday. Four days since Miyuki had found Emma's suicide note.

Four days since one of her best friends in the world had committed suicide.

Four days of numbness.

Aimlessness.

Hopelessness.

Feelings that made Miyuki pump the pedals faster. And faster. Causing the Yeti to fly over the pavement.

It wasn't fast enough.

Miyuki pushed herself harder. Pumped harder. Pushed the Yeti to its limit.

She saw a stop sign at an intersection. Miyuki didn't care. She sailed through it.

Brakes squealed. A few angry horns.

Miyuki ignored them. She had to keep moving. Had to keep pushing. Had to keep forgetting.

At the next intersection, Miyuki turned right and followed the road as it climbed up a steep hill. But Miyuki didn't care. She pushed her legs. Pushed her body. Shoved that bike up that hill.

The Yeti went slower and slower.

Miyuki grunted, forced her legs up and down.

Harder.

Push.

Get over the hill.

She could hear herself breathing. Gasping. Almost grunting. Forcing the bike over the hill like it was a building that she could somehow push over the edge by her sheer will.

The frame of the Yeti shook. Or was it her body?

The bike slowed to a crawl as it veered towards the curb.

Miyuki screamed at herself.

Push.

Faster.

Faster.

Then her body let go.

The Yeti nudged the curb, and Miyuki let herself collapse on top of the cool grass. The tears leaked out. The sadness spilled out. The anguish. The love of a friend who never said goodbye. Miyuki sobbed on the grass, allowing herself a moment to flush out the pain in her system.

It felt good.

Miyuki sat up and wiped her cheeks before brushing off her pants. She took in a long breath before standing back up and retrieving her bicycle. She coasted down the hill and headed back home.

As she rounded the corner, Miyuki noticed a strange car parked in front of their house. It was an older model car. Nothing fancy. The passenger door opened, and out stepped a short teen girl with red hair and freckles. It was Kayla. She carried some kind of baking pan wrapped in plastic.

Kayla noticed Miyuki rolling her way and stopped.

"Hi, Miyuki." Kayla's normally bubbly personality was subdued, as if she were on a sedative. "I made some chocolate-chip cookie squares for Emma's grandmother. I mean…you all can have them too. It's for everyone." She offered the pan to Miyuki.

"Would you like to come inside and deliver them yourself?"

"I don't want to get in the way."

"You're not in the way," Miyuki said.

Kayla glanced at the car. "My mom's waiting on me. After this, she's taking me out for a driving lesson to get my mind off…" Kayla hesitated, letting the sentence trail off into nothing. "Sorry, I talk too much."

"*Hei*, I understand. Believe me. I understand."

Kayla searched Miyuki's eyes, noticing something familiar there. "It's only been a few days…but it's like…I miss her already. It hasn't been a week yet, and I feel like she's been gone for months. Does that sound crazy?"

Miyuki knew what Kayla was saying. Every hour of every day seemed to drag on forever. Miyuki's world had indeed slowed to a crawl. Magnifying the waiting until they could find Emma's body. Until they could have a proper funeral. Until everyone could start to heal.

"It doesn't sound crazy to me. Not at all," Miyuki said.

The two girls exchanged another look.

"Hugs?" Kayla asked with a tiny crack of a smile on her lips.

"*Hei!*"

The two girls hugged it out before Miyuki took the pan from Kayla, who retreated into her mother's car and drove away.

Miyuki brought the pan of cookie squares into the house. She set the pan down on the dining room table, which was already crowded with food that people had brought them in the wake of Emma's death.

Miyuki wandered into the living room. Emma's grandmother was still lying on the couch, her arms crossed, her eyes wandering across the ceiling. The non-braided ends of her white hair went everywhere, like an old mop squished to the floor. She hadn't read one book all week, and the three Gems were worried about her.

"There you are," Olivia said. "We've been waiting."

"For what?" Miyuki asked.

"You'll need to pack an overnight bag," Nadia said.

Olivia took out her phone and showed Miyuki the message she received…

Found Ryan. Go to airport now. Jet is waiting. Information on the way. Pack light.

A twin-engine business jet waited on the private aircraft tarmac at Oakland International Airport. Miyuki was the last of the three Gems to climb the air stairs before the engines spooled up and the jet taxied for takeoff.

Once they were in the air, Mrs. B appeared on the cabin's video screens.

"We have new information about Ryan Raymond. Our Berlin station received word that he'll be on a Lufthansa flight arriving tomorrow morning in New York. I want the Gems to kidnap Ryan and bring him back here so we can have a word with him. This jet is equipped with a security cell in back, and the crew are quite capable of handling prisoners. The captain and first-officer are also trained field operatives, so make use of them if you can. Good hunting."

CHAPTER 20

The tall buildings of the Midtown East section of Manhattan surrounded Emma as she emerged from the underground subway exit. The street corner here was familiar, one that Emma had passed through again and again. She was on her old turf. East Fifty-Seventh Street down to East Forty-Second and all the places in between. Emma felt safe. She knew these streets as well as anyone here and it felt so good to be back.

Emma walked a few blocks and found herself in front of the main doors of Van Dorn Hall, her old school. The building itself was closed for the weekend, but Emma could peek through the glass and see the old main hallway, along with a set of metal lockers. Her old locker, number 31, was still there. She wondered if it still had the same combination.

She continued down the block to Horowitz's Deli, her old after-school hang-out. Emma's stomach remembered their corned beef and swiss sandwich on rye as it poked her repeatedly with hunger pains. A reminder she hadn't eaten much for breakfast.

Emma only had twenty dollars left, which she was saving in case of an emergency. But even though she didn't have her credit cards, and this trip to New York had already cost more than she anticipated, Emma knew she could count on Hailey. Once Emma reached her old neighborhood, Hailey's mom would put her up for free in their penthouse without blinking an eye-lash.

She relaxed. Everything was going to work out fine.

Emma went inside the deli. Her fingers lingered on an old iron wall rail as the whiff of chicken noodle soup caught her nose. The lunch crowd was winding down, but there were still a lot of people inside. Emma stood in line. The men behind the deli counter shouted orders and danced around each other like a ballet company performing *Swan Lake*. Each man knew where to be and where not to be at any given moment. It was a well-oiled machine. This deli had been in the Horowitz family since they came over on a boat from Europe.

"What'll ya have?" a middle-aged man behind the counter asked loud and direct.

The couple ahead of Emma studied the menu. The older man wore a college football hat from Oklahoma. His wife, a T-shirt that read Manford High School...wherever the heck that was. They moved so slowly that Emma had them pegged as tourists who were in way over their head.

"What sounds good to you?" the woman asked her husband.

"I don't know," he said. "Wonder if they have soup."

"Do you have soup?" the woman asked.

"Soup's under there." The man behind the counter pointed at the large wall menu. "Meats and cheeses there. Kinds of breads we have are there. What'll ya have?"

"Is there a soup of the day?" the husband asked.

"No. Soup's listed there. Meats and cheeses there. Breads are here. What'll ya have?"

"I don't know. There are so many choices," the wife asked.

The couple continued their browsing.

"Folks, the meter is running here," the man behind the deli said. "We got lots of hungry people behind ya. It's all good food. I promise ya."

The couple glanced back at the line. Emma could feel their stress. They weren't used to such pushy people.

"Their chicken noodle soup is fantastic here," Emma said. "Seriously, homemade noodles, big chucks of chicken—hands down, it's the best on the island. Get that and a full Reuben; that way you can split the sandwich because it goes great with the chicken noodle. I guarantee you'll be happy."

The man behind the counter pointed. "Listen to that young lady. She's showering you with golden words of wisdom there."

The wife smiled. "Oh, well, thank you for the recommendation." She checked with her husband, who shrugged. The woman faced the counter. "We'll get...whatever she just said."

"You got it. Number seventy-one. Two orders of the best damn chicken noodle soup on the island. One big Reuben sandwich. Want drinks with that?"

The couple glanced at each other again.

The man behind the counter sighed and tossed a knowing look at Emma. Tourists.

"How 'bout some iced tea?" the man asked the couple. "Who doesn't love iced tea, right? I'll just give ya folks two iced teas on our dime. How's that grab ya?"

"That's very nice of—"

"No problem, you folks have a nice day." The man moved over to Emma. "What can I get ya, sweetheart?"

"A corned beef and swiss on rye with a Coke."

"Cup of chicken noodle with that?"

"You know it."

"Anything else?"

Emma shook her head and went back to a table in the back to wait for her order. Snoopy waited for her on a chair; she had slipped his leash under one of the heavy metal legs, preventing him from taking off while she was in line.

"Number seventy-two?" a woman yelled.

Emma went to the counter and was about to pick up her tray of food when a voice made her look up.

"Is that Emma Rothchild?" The question came from an old man with a food-stained apron. His skin was wrinkled to the point of leather. His eye brows were bushy and white, just like the large carpet of hair still on the man's scalp.

Emma smiled. "Oh hi, Mr. Horowitz."

The old man leaned in. "Thought ya moved out west to be with your grandma."

"I did do that, but I'm back in New York."

"Still going to school at Van Dorn?"

"Maybe I—you know, I don't really know right now."

"Number seventy-two," the woman repeated, then addressed the old man. "Let the poor girl enjoy her meal first before you bore her to death."

"Do ya hear that, Emma? Do ya hear how my family treats their grandfather?" The old man winked before he threw his arms up towards the people behind the counter. "Keep it up, you schmucks. I swear I'll give ya this deli in my will, and then you'll all be sorry."

"We're already sorry," the man who served Emma yelled with a smile.

Everyone behind the counter laughed.

Mr. Horowitz followed Emma to her table. He petted Snoopy,

and the dog clung to him as Emma began eating. Mr. Horowitz flagged down one of his relatives and had them bring over a plate of meat for Snoopy.

"How's that sandwich?" Mr. Horowitz asked.

"As good as I remember," Emma said.

"Is your grandma movin' out here with ya?"

"She's staying in California."

"Then you stayin' with some other family out here?"

Emma hesitated, then drank some Coke.

"Yes," she lied.

"My word, Emma, you're a young woman now. Grown up so fast." Mr. Horowitz watched her for a moment or two. "Remember those Saturday morning breakfasts with your pops? Now that man could tell a story. You know, he never once acted like one of those Wall Street types. Nah, your pops was a straight arrow. Great business-man. Treated everyone with respect. Always one of my favorite customers."

Mr. Horowitz took a long look at her.

"Did he take good care of ya, Emma? You know, in the will?"

"He did."

"Ken was a good guy. He died much too young."

The old sadness returned. Emma could feel the despair pushing against her emotions. The depression. The heartache.

"Shit, I'm sorry, Emma. I can be a sentimental old fool sometimes." Mr. Horowitz rose from the table. "I'll leave ya alone. If you need anything, you know where I'll be."

As Mr. Horowitz moved away, Emma reached out and squeezed his hand. "Thanks for listening to my dad. He always enjoyed talking to you."

"The feeling was mutual, my dear."

Emma took her time, enjoying her sandwich and the delicious chicken noodle soup. Snoopy wanted more meat, so Mr. Horowitz brought him another small plate. Once Snoopy was finished, his eyes were heavy as the dog yawned. He'd had enough adventure for one day, and Emma agreed with him.

Emma searched her purse and found the slip of paper with Hailey's number on it. She dialed the number on her cheap phone and waited.

"Who is this?"

It was Hailey's voice. Emma knew it immediately.

"Hey, what are ya doin'?"

Hailey screamed. "Em, is that you?"

After settling Hailey down, the two girls talked up a storm. Hailey asked her about California and San Francisco. Emma talked about her grandma and the UC campus in Berkeley.

"I didn't know she was a professor," Hailey said. "Whoa... you're not going to college out there, are you? What about our plans for NYU?"

"They're still on," Emma said. "In fact, I'm back in New York. For good."

"No, shut up. Are you serious?"

"Yeah, and I need a place to stay."

There was a pause.

"Oh, Em...we're in Bermuda right now."

"Seriously?"

"Yeah, but we're coming back tomorrow night. Why don't you —crap, I gotta go to school on Monday, or my mom will freak out. Hey, come back to the deli after school, and we'll hook up then. My mom will let you stay over Monday night. She adores you."

"Thanks, but what do I do for the weekend?" Emma asked.

"I'd call Keisha, but she's upstate with her parents this weekend," Hailey said. "What about your dad's friends? The ones you babysat for?"

"The Goodens."

"Yeah, call them. Didn't you say your two families were tight?"

Staying with Hailey was always part of the plan. A week with her would give Emma plenty of time to relax and figure out how she was going to convince Ben to help her create a new life in New York City. Since Emma and her grandmother had appointed Ben Gooden CEO of the Rothchild Industries, his loyalty would be with Emma's grandmother, meaning that he might rat Emma out and send her back to California if she failed to convince him.

Emma wasn't ready to talk to Ben. Yet sleeping on a bench in Manhattan all weekend with poor Snoopy looking up at her, wanting food, was too much for her to bear.

"Em, are you there?" Hailey asked.

Emma parked her worries and continued to talk to Hailey for a while. Soon, they said their goodbyes, and Emma promised to see her on Monday after school at Horowitz's Deli. She then got a refill of Coke and sat back down. Snoopy rested his head on her leg and closed his eyes. His warmth made Emma feel better since she was not looking forward to the next call.

Emma turned over the piece of paper with two more phone numbers written on it. She called Rosa's number first. It rang a couple of times.

"Hello?" a female voice answered.

"Hi, Rosa. It's Emma."

"What—what did you just say?" the woman asked.

Emma hesitated. "Isn't this Rosa?"

A pause.

"Yeah."

"I know Ben likes to sneak in-to the city and work in his office on Saturdays, so I took a guess that you might be with him."

"How do you know about that?" Rosa asked.

"You told me that you love reading in his outer office on the weekends because it's so quiet. This is Emma, remember?"

"Look…I don't know who you are, but this is in extremely bad taste. Emma Rothchild is dead. God rest her poor soul."

Oh yeah. Emma kinda forgot about all that.

"Rosa, what if I told you…that she's not dead, or to be more accurate, right now I'm sitting at a table inside Horowitz's Deli."

There was a long pause on the other end of the line.

"Hello?" Emma asked.

"Girl, don't be messing with me. If you're messing with me, so help me—oh, I'll hunt you down, and bad things are gonna happen. Do you understand?"

"I'm not messing with you, Rosa. Seriously, it's me. I kinda—well, I faked my death."

More silence.

"Hello?"

"Hold up," Rosa said. "Hold up. What are the names of our daughters?"

"Nicolle and Naomi," Emma answered without hesitation.

"What's their favorite food?"

"Mac and cheese with slices of hot dogs mixed in. And Naomi loves snicker-doodle cookies, which Nicolle hates because she's a chocolate-chip traditionalist and loves to tell you about it."

Another pause.

"Emma…my God, child. Is that really you?"

"I swear it's me."

Emma could hear sobbing on the other end. It started to make her feel guilty.

"You say you're at Horowitz's Deli on Forty-Ninth Street?"

"Yes."

"Stay right there. We'll be there in a few minutes."

CHAPTER 21

A half hour later, a black Lincoln SUV pulled up to the curb near Horowitz's Deli. Emma came outside and helped Snoopy into the back seat before slipping in herself. Before Emma could put her seat-belt on, Rosa Gooden climbed over her passenger seat and gave Emma a big hug. The woman's perfume gave off a fresh scent of lilacs. Her dark hair was curly like Olivia's but more braided. Her dark brown skin was accented with plum-colored lipstick and dark eyeliner. She was a large-framed woman but still in great shape.

Ben Gooden judged Emma through his rear-view mirror. The man was in his late thirties and wore a New York Knicks basketball jersey over some nice dark jeans. "I can't wait to hear this story."

"Sorry to bother you on a Saturday, Ben," Emma said.

"That's what you're apologizing for?" Ben asked.

Rosa sat back down. "Let's hear what she has to say first."

"All right." Ben shot a look at Emma. "This'd better be good." Ben pulled the Lincoln back into traffic and headed uptown so he could cross the Queensboro Bridge out of Manhattan.

"Is this Snoopy?" Rosa asked.

"Yeah, I couldn't leave him behind."

Rosa reached over and petted him. "He's so cute."

"Still haven't gotten my story yet," Ben announced to everyone in the car.

Emma sighed.

"Honey, maybe you should start talking, huh?" Rosa asked.

Emma began by saying how difficult it was living in California. How much of an adjustment it was. How lonely at school it sometimes was. Then she was recruited as a Gem.

"At first, it was great. We helped bring my dad's killers to justice. We kept millions of people from starving. And I had three new girl friends. I never had a brother or a sister before. But, all of a sudden, I had three sisters who looked out for each other. On our missions and while we're at school."

Emma told them about Ryan and Venomous. About how aggressively they were trying to recruit her. About how much pressure she was under to try to flip Ryan.

"Man, I can see why Ken walked away from all that," Ben said. "He didn't need all that secret-society drama on his plate while running a major corporation. Hell, I'm working sixty-hour weeks just to keep up."

"Is it too much work?" Emma asked. "I can talk to my grandma, and maybe we can find—"

"Don't let him fool you," Rosa said. "He loves being a CEO, and he loves working too much."

"I do not."

"Then if it's too much, why don't you have people helping? You're the boss, sugar. Delegate that work."

"Rosa, baby, it's not that simple."

"Oh, it's simple." Rosa turns to Emma. "You know why he doesn't do it? He's just like your dad. Convinced if he doesn't have his nose in it, whatever it is won't get done."

"I'm not that bad."

Rosa shot him a look.

Ben shifted in the driver's seat. "People sometimes can't follow direction."

"You mean they don't do it the way you want it done."

"Exactly."

"Even though the outcome is the same," Rosa said.

"Companies are like playoff basketball teams. You have to build them up into a well-oiled machine. Each player contributing to the team in a certain way."

"*Your* certain way. Face it. You can be a control freak at times."

Ben pressed his lips together and focused on the road.

"Sometimes you have to let a player throw that three-point basket," Rosa said. "Even when you told them to always be passing the ball."

"Appreciate the advice, Charles Barkley. Now…let's get back to why we're in this car." Ben flicked his eyes to Emma in the rear-view mirror. "Why did you fake your death? All I'm hearing is that your new life was difficult. So you wanted to escape? Run away from it all? Is that what I'm hearing?"

"I had to get away from them. You don't understand, Ben. Faking my suicide was the only way I could get out of the Authority and start a new life."

"Wait a minute. Hold on. Your grandmother and I had a long talk about this when you first asked her about joining those people. Your grandmother told me that you had the option of getting out anytime you wanted. They promised her that."

"Mrs. B lied to me. They were all lying about a lot of things."

"Who's Mrs. B?" Rosa asked.

The way Ben glanced at the rear-view mirror told Emma that he already knew. Her grandmother Bernadette most likely told him.

"What did they lie about?" Ben asked, steering the conversation away from Mrs. B.

Emma sighed. She didn't care anymore. She was sick of secrets.

"Mrs. B is my grandmother."

Rosa looked confused. "Bernadette is caught up in this secret Authority society too?"

"No, my other grandmother, on my mom's side. Her name is Laura."

"I thought Angela's mother was dead."

"She's not," Ben said.

"You knew about this?" Rosa asked.

"Bernadette told me when Laura approached her about the Authority."

Rosa looked at Ben.

"It's not something you spread around. Laura—she's as serious as I am about her business."

"So you're saying, your other grandmother lied to you," Rosa said. "About what?"

Emma talked about her mom. About the mission that killed her. About the report that blamed Mrs. B for everything.

"Seriously, my mom died for nothing," Emma said. "Mrs. B told me she sacrificed herself to save millions of lives. She was only saying that to recruit me."

Rosa sat back. "That's not right."

"I felt betrayed. I was told we were the good guys, you know? That what we did mattered. That we were doing things that helped people around the world. But it was all crap." Emma petted Snoopy, who felt her vibe and rested his little head on her lap. "I was trapped. If I tried to leave, Mrs. B would pressure me into staying, or make the girls pressure me into staying. I couldn't just quit. I had to disappear." She looked out over the New York City skyline. "I should've never left New York."

"I'd be lying if I said we didn't miss ya too," Rosa said.

"I need your help. I want a new life. I'll have to change my name. Get a brand-new look. Do whatever the FBI does to hide their informants, you know? Relocate me somewhere in New York. There are millions of people here, and I'll slip right in and disappear."

"I'm assuming you want an advance on your trust money?" Ben asked.

"Only to get myself settled. You can charge me interest or a fee —whatever you want."

"There's a reason Ken wanted your trust to be released only when you turned twenty-five."

"I wouldn't be running away from the Authority if my dad hadn't been involved with them."

"Girl's got a point there," Rosa said.

"Emma's too young to be getting all that money," Ben said. "She's not ready for it."

"I only need enough to get by," Emma said. "Enough to go back to school. Maybe college at NYU. I could be your third daughter."

Rosa melted. "Nicolle and Naomi would love a big sister."

"Baby, don't let Emma weasel her way out of this." Ben glanced into his rear-view mirror. "Aren't you forgetting that your grandmother Bernadette took you in and made it her personal responsibility to raise you? Are your forgetting that that poor woman thinks you're dead right now?"

Emma hesitated.

"That poor woman could barely tell me over the phone that you were dead. She tried four times to get the sentence out. That's how upset she was."

Rosa frowned, then nodded along with her husband.

"I won't agree to anything concerning you staying here on a permanent basis unless your grandmother gives me the okay," Ben said. "That means you'll have to call her and explain everything. And you'd better hope that she forgives you. Because if one of my daughters did this to me...I'd kill them or turn my back on them for the rest of their lives. Do you understand where I'm coming from?"

Emma petted Snoopy. Her eyes moistened as she realized that she never once thought about how her grandma would react to the news.

"I was planning to tell her, Ben. Seriously, once I got settled, I was going to call her—"

"You don't treat people you love that way, Emma. You wouldn't leave Snoopy alone on a subway and expect him not to think you had abandoned him."

Snoopy closed his eyes, enjoying her warmth. Ben was right. Doing that to Snoopy would be torture for her. Unforgivable. She would never forgive herself for doing such an awful thing. But she'd just done it to her grandma without a second thought.

"You have to call her," Ben emphasized.

Emma glanced out the window. "Okay, I will."

"It's still only four thirty in the afternoon in California."

The despair bubbled up quickly inside. Maybe it was the stressful day. Maybe it was confessing all her problems out loud. Maybe it was Ben's refusal to go along with her wishes. Whatever the cause, the despair overwhelmed Emma, forcing her cheek against the glass of the window as she quietly sobbed.

"Do you want us to call her?" Rosa asked.

"Baby, no. Emma has to be the one. She's gotta take responsibility. She's gotta own this." Ben glanced up at the mirror towards Emma. "Are you calling her?"

"Ben," Rosa said.

"What?"

"Drive us home."

"But Emma needs to—"

"You made your point. Let's go home first."

Ben sighed and turned his attention back on the road as they made their way across the Queensboro Bridge on their way out to Long Island.

CHAPTER 22

On Sunday morning, the arrivals section of Newark International Airport was filling up with people waiting for their loved ones to clear United States customs. Miyuki joined them, sipping on a paper cup of honeysuckle tea that she'd purchased from a coffee kiosk inside the airport terminal. The warm liquid kept her energized and ready to face whatever the new morning would bring.

"Where is he?" Olivia asked, her voice coming from the hidden ear-piece Miyuki wore. "Ryan's plane landed an hour ago."

Miyuki smiled to herself. And everyone thought she was the impatient one in the group.

"A woman near me told her daughter that it took them over fifty minutes to go through customs," Nadia's soft voice announced over the radio. The girl waited in her electric wheelchair, wearing an old sweater. Old jeans. And a pair of dated glasses. What took Nadia's disguise to the next level was the white-haired wig she wore that complemented her makeup, which aged the teen girl seventy years at least. It was an outstanding disguise. Miyuki was so impressed that she was tempted to take a picture. But since they were working, she resisted the urge.

Miyuki's disguise was simple. A long, dark-colored dress and a face with no makeup. A look that blended in with the boring airport.

"Hope you're right, Sapphire," Olivia said. "If we somehow missed him, I'll—shit."

Miyuki giggled. Sometimes Olivia was funny, even when she wasn't trying.

"I see them now," Nadia said.

What were the girls talking about?

Miyuki pretended to rub her nose as she spoke into her all-black Seiko dive watch that had a microphone inside. "What is it?"

"They haven't made me yet. Stand by," Olivia said.

"Sophia and Bridget," Nadia answered. "Next to the beverage machines."

Miyuki bent down to scratch her ankle before glancing to her left. Bridget was typing on her phone, standing near one of the soda machines as Sophia was buying a drink.

Miyuki leaned back in her chair and rubbed her nose again. "Bridget's texting someone. Probably Ryan."

"They must be here to pick him up," Nadia added. "Do we continue?"

"We have to," Olivia said. "This is the only chance we have to nick him before he disappears again."

"What do we do about the twins?" Miyuki asked.

"I'm thinking," Olivia said.

Miyuki watched as Sophia popped open her drink and took a sip while she moved over to where Nadia was in her wheelchair. Still concentrating on her phone, Bridget drifted over to Sophia.

"Sapphire, don't look up. Sophia is standing right next to you," Miyuki warned.

Nadia didn't move. She only lingered there like a helpless old woman.

Sophia's eyes did a once-over on the woman in the wheelchair; then she leaned against the wall and enjoyed her beverage while she scanned the room. Miyuki glanced away before Sophia could catch her.

"Emerald—is Sophia watching me?" Miyuki asked softly.

"Not directly. But she's casing the arrivals area all right. Better not make a move until I tell ya."

"Ten-four, good buddy."

Miyuki pretended to glance at her own phone while her heart increased its beats.

A new cluster of passengers were arriving. From where Miyuki was, she could see them coming down the ramp from customs through the clear glass security wall, which separated both areas. Miyuki could make out a young guy wearing a V-neck T-shirt and a dark cap. Under the cap, she could make out Ryan's face as he was moved along with the crowd.

"Target spotted," Miyuki said. "He should be on our doorstep any minute."

Having all three Gems converging on Ryan and taking him by surprise was the cornerstone of Olivia's kidnapping plan. But since the twins were here, Miyuki wondered what they were going to do.

"Right. We'll have to improvise," Olivia said. "Ruby, I want you to stand by and copy what I do. Sapphire, think you can snag the target if we get the twins off your back?"

"Do I have a choice?" Nadia asked in a low whisper, almost too light to hear.

"You'll do great, love. Don't worry about us; just grab the target. Ruby, follow me."

Miyuki scanned the room and caught Olivia out in the open. She was in disguise as an airport employee, complete with a fake airport ID lanyard swinging around her neck. Miyuki got up and made her way down the aisle she was sitting in. She could feel Sophia's eyes already on her.

To Miyuki's surprise, Olivia went right up to Bridget, who was still messing with her phone.

But Sophia intercepted her. "What do ya think you're here for?"

Bridget chuckled. "Hi, Olivia, what a pleasant surprise."

"You two girls had better bugger off if you know what's good for ya," Olivia said.

Miyuki came up behind her. "*Hei*, what she said."

Sophia got into Olivia's face. "I'm up for it if you girls are."

"Now, we wouldn't want the police to get involved, do we?" Olivia asked.

Bridget pulled her sister back gently. "Of course not." She glanced at Miyuki. "Where's the other one?"

"Sapphire had to sit this one out. She has a broken leg, remember?" Olivia asked.

"Too bad. Honest to G. I think Sophia would've been keen on breaking her other leg," Bridget said. "So, Olivia, darling, how do ya propose we solve this? You're obviously here for Ryan, and we can't let you have him."

"We should go outside and discuss it," Miyuki said. "That way we can come up with a compromise that benefits everyone."

Sophia appeared confused. "Is that code for let's fight outside?"

"Why do we always have to fight? Why can't we discuss this?"

"I agree," Olivia said. "Let's move this outside and discuss it like young mature women."

"Discuss it? What's there to discuss?" Bridget said. "Ryan's coming with us. The question is…do ya girls wanna get hurt if ya try to interfere?"

"Because we can make that—"

With no warning, Olivia tackled Sophia to the floor.

Bridget and Miyuki froze, both surprised by the move. They met each other's eyes. Miyuki then lunged for Bridget, who stepped to the side and knocked Miyuki off course into the wall as she slid to the floor.

"Monkey balls!" Miyuki spat out in frustration.

Bridget towered over Miyuki, shaking her head with a smirk. "Pathetic."

Miyuki then caught Nadia's electric wheelchair moving off as it lined up on a collision course towards Ryan, who had emerged into the arrivals area.

Bridget followed her eyes and saw the wheelchair. But as Bridget began to move—

Miyuki swept her leg under Bridget, causing her to crash to the floor.

Sophia saw the wheelchair too. She jumped up and stumbled forward a few feet before Olivia tackled her again.

"Hey! Stop it," an airport security officer yelled as he rushed towards the group.

As their "fight" was drawing the room's attention, Nadia fired a special dart from her modified wheelchair. It struck Ryan in the lower back. He felt the sting and stopped walking. He reached around and searched for the culprit. When he found the dart, Ryan ripped it out of his back. But not before the dart injected a generous dose of its contents into his body.

Ryan tried to break into a run, but Nadia was right on his heals with her wheelchair as they disappeared behind the crowd that was forming to watch the "fight."

Bridget was on her feet first, so the airport security officer grabbed her arm. She gave him a hard knee to the stomach before breaking off and running through the crowd.

The officer grunted in pain as he dropped to his knees.

Miyuki chased after Bridget.

After clearing the crowd, Miyuki could see Ryan stumbling around and having trouble with his legs. That was when Nadia "bumped" into Ryan, and he fell into her lap like a kid. Nadia then spun off down the terminal as Bridget raced after her. Miyuki was shoved to the floor again. It was Sophia, running across the terminal in pursuit of her sister. Olivia ran after her.

Miyuki hopped to her feet and chased after all of them. She followed Olivia through the sliding glass doors that led outside to the arrivals pick-up area. The cool morning air chilled her face as Miyuki ran down the sidewalk, dodging passengers waiting for their rides.

Olivia cupped her hand around her ear as she spoke into her own Seiko watch. "Emerald to Hospitality One. Over?"

"Hospitality One," the captain of their jet answered inside Miyuki's ear piece.

"Expedite our pick up. Sapphire has the target. But she's being pursued."

"Roger, stand by."

A minute later, a hotel mini-bus weaved through the four lanes of traffic before slamming its brakes next to Olivia. The bus passenger door flipped open, and Olivia and Miyuki climbed inside. The captain, who was behind the wheel, flipped a switch to close the passenger door. Miyuki held on to a metal grab bar as the mini-bus took off. The traffic on the arrivals side of the airport was moderate, but the captain did his best to navigate around it as fast as possible.

Olivia pointed. "There she is!"

Miyuki leaned forward to see through the windshield. In the lane farthest from the terminal, Nadia was moving fast with her special wheelchair while Ryan was passed out on her lap. But the twins were keeping pace, running after Nadia like they were in the New York City marathon. Miyuki was impressed. Those girls were in great shape.

"Get up ahead of her," Olivia said.

The captain accelerated the mini-bus past Nadia and put some distance on her.

"Pull over here."

The captain did.

Olivia turned to Miyuki. "We need to go buy them some time to put Nadia in the bus."

"Don't worry about that," the co-pilot said, pulling out a gun.

The captain put the van in park before pulling out his own gun. "We'll have a talk with those girls. You two help your friend."

"Right, be careful," Olivia said. "Those girls can be quite vicious."

The two men shot each other a look, as if Olivia's warning were cute.

"We can handle them," the captain said as he and his co-pilot exited the mini-bus.

Miyuki followed Olivia out as she activated the wheelchair mechanism. A door in the back of the mini-bus popped open as a metal ramp slid out and settled on top of the road, ready to receive its passenger.

Nadia maneuvered her wheelchair around the two pilots before heading for the van.

Miyuki watched as the two pilots stood there like a wall, each with a gun in their hand.

Bridget approached them first, almost out of breath before she stopped. Sophia was about to pass by, when Bridget reached out to stop her. Both girls caught their breath while they stared the men down.

Nadia skidded the wheelchair to a stop. Miyuki helped Olivia drag an unconscious Ryan up into the mini-bus while Nadia drove her wheelchair up the ramp. After Ryan was secured into one of the bus seats, Miyuki and Olivia came back outside. Since Nadia had secured herself in the bus, Olivia activated the ramp-retrieval system, closing up the rear door and the ramp.

That was when Miyuki saw Bridget finishing a side kick across the captain's face, putting him on the ground. The co-pilot nursed his right arm, which had a knife sticking out of it. Sophia was grinning and admiring her handiwork as the co-pilot's gun sat on the road.

Miyuki didn't hesitate. She ran towards the gun and slid across the concrete on her butt.

Sophia realized what Miyuki was after. As she bent down for the gun…

Miyuki plowed into her, pushing Sophia away from the weapon as she grabbed it for herself.

As Bridget regained her balance from the side kick, she raced over to Miyuki and was about to kick her in the stomach when… Miyuki pointed the gun in her face.

"Call off your sister," she yelled.

"Whoa, darling. Easy there," Bridget said, showing her hands as she put down her leg.

But Miyuki sensed that Sophia was up and moving behind her, so she aimed the gun off to the side and fired off a round, causing Bridget to jump. Miyuki then corrected her aim.

Bridget dropped her smile. "There's no need for that. Come over here, Sophia darling, where she can see ya."

Slowly, Sophia came back around into view, the anger and hate in her eyes quite genuine.

The captain rubbed his jaw as he glared at Bridget, who winked and blew him a kiss. He checked with his co-pilot, who nursed his injured arm.

"Airport police probably heard that gunfire. We need to move," the captain said as he carefully removed the bloody knife from his co-pilot's arm and tossed it over a security fence before helping him back into the mini-bus.

Miyuki stood up. Still watching the twins like a hawk, she backed away towards the mini-bus.

The twins didn't move.

Miyuki was the last one to climb into the mini-bus before the captain sped away. He weaved around traffic again as they headed out of the Newark airport perimeter and joined the highway, heading northeast.

"Is he still out?" Olivia asked, taking off her fake employee badge.

Miyuki gently moved Ryan's cheek towards her. His eyes were closed, and he was still breathing.

"*Hei*, the boy's having a nice nap." Miyuki turned her attention to Nadia. "Need any help?"

With her wheelchair stowed in the back of the mini-bus, Nadia had already taken off her white wig, and she was brushing back her long black hair. "I'm fine. Thanks."

"Ryan will receive a pleasant surprise when he wakes up in a cage at thirty-five thousand feet," Olivia said. "How long is it to Teterboro?"

"GPS says about forty-five minutes," the captain answered. "Should be in the air within the hour."

Miyuki saw the co-pilot opening a first-aid kit. "May I help?"

The co-pilot nodded, and Miyuki helped clean up the man's cut and bandaged his arm.

"You weren't kidding about those girls," the co-pilot said. "We blinked, and they were both on us."

"It's because twins can read each other's minds," Miyuki said.

"Ruby, there's no scientific evidence of that," Nadia said from the back of the mini-bus.

"The fact is…we have Ryan, and the twins can disappear off the Earth for all I care," Olivia said.

"You'd better care," the captain said. "Because those girls are on a motorcycle coming up fast."

CHAPTER 23

Inside the mini-bus, Miyuki rushed to the back, holding on to the metal standing bar as she peeked out through the window. On the far left lane of the three-lane highway, a street bike was approaching with two girls on board, their long red hair snapping in the wind. Miyuki could feel the mini-bus accelerate, but the street bike was still gaining.

"What kind of motorbike is that?" Nadia asked, still sitting in her wheelchair, which was stowed in the back.

When the motorbike reached the mini-bus, Miyuki could see why they were gaining so fast. Bridget had managed to steal a Ducati motorcycle. It was expensive, Italian, and fast. Sophia held on to her sister with one hand while she used her other hand to hold a gun.

Miyuki then remembered Bridget kicking the captain, who must have dropped his.

"They're right behind us!" Miyuki called out.

"And Sophia has a gun," Nadia added.

Olivia went to the back. "Don't worry. She won't fire into the mini-bus. Not with Ryan inside."

Bridget weaved the Ducati back and forth and gunned the engine to get their attention. Sophia then showed the Gems her gun and motioned for them to pull over.

"Are they right behind us?" the captain asked.

"They are now," Olivia said.

"Brace yourselves."

"For what—?"

Olivia and Miyuki fell backwards against the next row of seats as the brakes came on full.

The motorcycle missed the back of the mini-bus by inches, thanks to Bridget, who veered away at the last moment. She then fought for control of the motorcycle as the abrupt maneuver made it unstable, causing the motorbike to gyrate all over the right two lanes. Bridget slowed way down as the mini-bus passed her. But soon the Ducati settled down as Bridget took back control. She gunned it forward and caught up with the mini-bus again, but this time she kept the motorcycle in the adjacent lane. Sophia thrust two fingers up into the air.

Miyuki pointed. "What does that gesture mean?"

"It doesn't mean V for victory," Olivia said.

Miyuki didn't understand.

"It means...up your bum," Nadia said with a grin.

Miyuki giggled.

The mini-bus suddenly swerved into the twins' lane, causing Bridget to take evasive action.

At the wheel, the captain swerved again, trying to shove the motorcycle against the highway guardrail.

Bridget had to back off.

"What are you trying to do?" Miyuki asked the captain.

"I'm trying to get rid of them," the captain said. "Unless one of you girls wants to borrow my co-pilot's gun."

Olivia moved down the aisle of the swaying mini-bus to the wounded co-pilot, who handed her the automatic pistol.

"Should have twelve rounds in the magazine," the co-pilot said.

Olivia nodded as she took the weapon from him and checked the chamber. Once satisfied it was loaded, Olivia joined her friends in back.

Miyuki gave her a look.

Olivia read her mind. "Only as a last resort," she said. "Let's hope the twins still have some common sense."

The Ducati's motor roared as Bridget popped a wheelie. She then maneuvered around the back of the mini-bus and popped another wheelie, with Sophia holding on tight. Miyuki was impressed by Bridget's motorcycle skills. Controlling her bike so well on a highway like this at these speeds took some talent. And also a total lack of fear.

Bridget popped a third wheelie, but instead of dropping her wheel back down on the highway, she inched the bike over enough to where Sophia grabbed on and pulled herself aboard the mini-bus.

"Mother trucker," Miyuki said in amazement. She pointed.

"Emerald!"

One of Sophia's legs was sprawled against one of the rear windows as the girl pulled herself up to the roof. Bridget was back on two wheels and alone. Now in the adjacent lane, she gunned the Ducati forward and zoomed past the mini-bus.

"Flipping hell," Olivia said to herself before turning to the captain. "Oy, she's on the roof. Take evasive action!"

The captain aggressively threw the mini-bus around as Olivia and Miyuki held on to the back of some seats to prevent themselves from being thrown around. Even though Nadia's wheelchair was secured to the floor, the girl's brown face was looking a bit pale.

"I'm getting sick on this ride," Nadia said.

"You and me both, love," Olivia said.

The captain went through another series of aggressive swerves. Miyuki could feel the mini-bus on the edge of rolling over. Normally, she would be enjoying this…if she were the one driving.

Suddenly, two sneakers hit a side window. The toes pressed against the glass, trying to gain traction on the window as Sophia hung on to the edge of the mini-bus's roof. Miyuki was amazed at her determination but wondered what the girl was trying to do. Maybe Sophia was an adrenaline junkie like she was and couldn't resist the urge to hang on top of a vehicle at a high rate of speed without falling off and killing yourself. Miyuki would be lying if she said she had never done such a crazy thing before.

The answer to what Sophia was doing came quickly as her sneakers burst through the driver's open window and kicked the captain out from behind the wheel.

Sophia plopped down in the driver's seat. Her first instinct was to hit the brakes.

The captain slammed into the passenger side dashboard while everyone else was thrown against the back of the seats. Except for Ryan and Nadia, who were still belted in.

Sophia floored the gas pedal, pulling everyone back. She removed the pistol tucked under her belt and pointed it at the captain. The man's nose was broken and gushing blood, but the captain still looked like he wanted to crush Sophia like an accordion.

"How's that for a brake check, ya muppet?" Sophia asked. "Almost made me and my sister into road sausage back there."

Despite the pistol, the captain inched towards Sophia.

"Ya think I don't have the stomach to pull the trigger?" Sophia asked. "Bugger off, or I'll give ya two mouths."

Olivia slipped into the seat next to Ryan.

Miyuki slipped into the row opposite her. Wait, did she see Ryan's head move? It was like he reacted to Olivia's presence. Miyuki wondered if the effects of the drug were starting to wear off.

"Stand down," Olivia yelled. "Or I'll shoot Ryan."

Miyuki couldn't believe what she said. Shoot Ryan? What was Olivia doing?

Olivia touched the butt of her pistol against Ryan's head.

Miyuki's heart beat faster and faster. She knew Olivia well enough to know that the girl was serious.

This kidnapping wasn't going well at all.

"Everyone needs to calm down," Nadia yelled from the back. "No one wins if we start shooting each other. Let's calm down and work this out. Please pull the bus over, Sophia."

Sophia laughed. "I have a better idea."

The mini-bus picked up speed.

"Let's play Russian roulette. I'll drive this bus off the motorway, let it roll a few times, and we'll see who lives and who dies."

Sophia yanked the wheel back and forth, making everyone hang on for dear life. "Bejesus, a big lorry. Hope I can avoid him." Sophia swerved the mini-bus into the semi-trailer truck. The impact caused the large truck to begin weaving all over the highway before the vehicle finally jackknifed and rolled over in a cloud of debris. Sophia maneuvered the bus out of the way.

She laughed. "Ooops."

This girl had no regard for innocent people. Miyuki knew that if they didn't stop her, someone would die. Including them.

"Emerald," Nadia called out from her wheelchair, "you might have to shoot her."

Sophia veered the bus over three lanes of traffic, causing two cars to smash into each other.

"Pull the bus over," a male voice called out.

At first, Miyuki couldn't make out whom the voice belonged to.

"Get another tranquilizer dart," Nadia said from the back. "He's coming back around."

Ryan was still strapped into his seat, but his eyes were drifting open. He was waking up.

"Go grab my purse," Olivia yelled to Miyuki. "It's on the seat over there. I should have two tranquilizer pins left."

Miyuki managed to hang on to the seats of the swaying bus as she made here way over to Olivia's purse. She took out the tranquilizer pin and moved behind Olivia and Ryan. Miyuki uncapped the pin and was about to stick it in Ryan's neck when his hand came up and touched her arm.

"No drugs," he said, straining to get the words out. "Tell Sophia—tell her to pull over the bus—tell her—direct order."

"What are you waiting for?" Olivia asked. "Stab him with the pin."

Miyuki hesitated.

Ryan peered into her eyes. "Order her...before she kills all of us."

"Ryan's awake," Miyuki yelled. "He orders you to pull the bus over, Sophia."

The girl in the driver's seat laughed. "Don't be daft. I'm not falling for that trick, ya muppet."

Miyuki gripped the back of the seat as Sophia steered their vehicle towards a Greyhound bus.

Ryan cleared his throat as he summoned some energy. "Stop this bus, Asset One-three-one," he yelled.

Sophia's hands gripped the wheel as her body tensed up.

"Pull the bus over now." Ryan's forceful voice was a few octaves lower than normal. A voice that made you flinch and listen.

Sophia's body language changed. The carefree and overexcited girl who was living on the edge crawled back inside her body. She slowed down the mini-bus. "I'll get off at the next exit." Her voice sounded disappointed.

CHAPTER 24

Earlier that Sunday morning, Emma stared at the steaming cup of coffee. Rosa had fixed it up how Emma liked it. Even adding a dash of cinnamon, the brown flakes of which still floated on the surface. The aroma smelled enticing, but she couldn't bring herself to enjoy it. Fearing that if she enjoyed the coffee, it would give her another excuse to put off what she knew she had to do.

"Why are you so sad?" Nicolle asked.

The Goodens' two little girls watched Emma like baby hawks at the breakfast table.

"Yeah, you look sad," Naomi added.

"Girls, eat your breakfast." Rosa joined them at the table with a bowl of cereal and some toast.

Ben was all suited up as he worked on a piece of bacon. "Call your grandmother yet?" he asked Emma.

"It's five in the morning there," Rosa said before taking another bite of her cereal.

"Is her grandma okay?" Nicolle asked.

"She's fine," Rosa said. "But Emma didn't ask you to be nosin' around in her business. But if you must know, Emma needs to call her grandmother because she's worried about where she is."

Nicolle looked shocked. "Emma didn't tell her grandma she was visiting us?"

"You're in trouble," Naomi said.

"But Emma's gonna do the right thing and call her." Ben glanced over at his girls. "Because I'd expect nothing less from the two of you."

"Okay, Daddy," Nicolle said. "We'll call you."

"Yeah, don't be trippin' on us," Naomi added.

Ben cocked his head. "Did you say...don't be trippin'?"

Naomi laughed. "Yeah."

"That's it." Ben got up and put his empty plates in the sink. "From now on, we only play jazz in this house."

"Okay, right now, Daddy's trippin'," Rosa said with a grin.

The two girls laughed. Emma caught herself smiling.

"Fine, I'm punting the ball." Ben made his way around the table as he picked up his soft briefcase. "I'll go enjoy my jazz in the car. Where it can be appreciated." He hesitated near Emma, expecting something.

"She gets up at six," Emma said. "I'll call her then. Promise."

"Text me when you do." Ben gave her a quick hug, then did the same for everyone else.

"Where you going?" Rosa asked him.

Ben hesitated. "Work."

"Baby, it's Sunday."

Ben was confused, then thought about it. He rolled his eyes before he laughed at himself. "Daddy *is* trippin'."

The two little girls laughed again.

When Emma finally finished her coffee, she washed out the porcelain cup in the sink and wandered into the living room as the grandmother clock announced the quarter-hour chime. It was after nine in the morning. Her grandmother should be awake.

Emma picked up the Goodens' home phone off its charger and stared at it. Emma sat down on the couch and rested her sock-covered feet on the table.

She then put her empty coffee cup back in the kitchen where it belonged and sat back down on the couch again.

Emma curled her legs under her. Then folded them back out again and rested her socks on the table again.

She hesitated.

Emma knew she was wasting time but couldn't seem to stop herself.

Finally she wandered inside Rosa's sun-room with all its beautiful roses, tulips, ferns, ivy and other plants in various stages of bloom. The brightness of the room along with all the growing plants gave Emma some encouragement. She sat in one of the chairs with the phone in her hand. Her thumb hit the call icon next to Bernadette Rothchild's contact entry. The phone connected and dialed. Emma waited, her stomach twisting into a knot.

Click.

"Rosa?" her grandma answered. All the attitude and enthusiasm the old woman normally carried with her was missing. "Hello?"

Emma swallowed. "It's me, Grandma."

Silence. Maybe too much silence.

"Um…I'm in New York with Ben's family. Oh…Snoopy is with me too."

Still nothing.

"Grandma?"

Emma could now hear the sobs through the phone.

"Grandma, it's okay. I'm fine. I'm good. Ben and Rosa are taking good care of me."

"You're alive?" her grandma finally asked.

"Yes, I'm alive. I'm great. I'm sorry you've been worrying about me."

Another pause.

"Grandma?"

"Worrying about you? My God, you left us a suicide note. You wrecked your car. We thought you were dead."

"I'm so sorry about that. Seriously, I totally made a huge mistake. I didn't want to really commit suicide. It was fake."

"You faked it?" Grandma asked with an edge to her voice.

"Hear me out. I've been stressed out about a lot of things lately, and I needed—"

"Do you realize what you've done?"

Emma paused. At this moment she wasn't too sure.

Grandma continued. "Your friend Kayla has been stopping by every day to see if I need help with anything. She tells me your entire school is traumatized by your suicide. Your school counselor called me last night to apologize for not seeing these suicidal tendencies in you and getting help. Not to mention the poor girls. Miyuki is taking it very hard. Nadia and Olivia are depressed…"

Grandma paused.

"I'm so mad at you right now that I could—infuriated would be more accurate. How dare you do this to us. And on purpose to boot."

Emma wiped away the tears. "I was overwhelmed, Grandma."

"Overwhelmed? With what? What would make you do such an awful thing to us?"

Emma broke down and told her the truth about her mom's

death. What she had read in the secret report. That her mom had died because of a lie. She also told her why her father had shunned Mrs. B during the funeral.

"I left because I felt trapped," Emma said. "I wanted to hit the reset button. Go back to where my life was fantastic." Emma then realized. "Not that living with you has been horrible. No, I'm so happy you took me in. It's just—I don't trust Grandma Laura anymore. I don't think she'll ever let me leave the Gems."

"Let me get this clear," her grandma said before repeating what Emma told her.

"Yes, Grandma. I know it sounds stupid, and I messed up how I handled it all. But I still had to do it."

Grandma sighed. "Laura and her capitalist stooges. I knew this would happen one day."

"Please don't say anything to her," Emma said.

"Young one, I can't go on with this lie. Especially when it comes to your friends at school. It's not fair to them or to the three girls who have been your close friends for over a year. Running away from your problems is not going to work. If you tell Laura, face-to-face, what's bothering you...I'm sure some kind of agreement can be reached between the two of you."

"I can't call her. Seriously, I don't want her to know where I am."

"Don't worry," Grandma said. "I'll give her a piece of my mind about your situation, and we'll make sure you can come back home safe and sound."

"Grandma, she's not going to listen to you."

"I said don't worry. Laura and I have an understanding. You stay right there. And please thank Ben and Rosa for me. We owe them one."

"No, Grandma, please don't tell her where I am."

The phone disconnected. Emma wasn't even sure if her grandma even heard that last sentence.

CHAPTER 25

Later that Sunday, Ryan Raymond was confused. A few hours ago he had been enjoying Lufthansa's excellent first-class breakfast service when Bridget sent him an email saying they would pick him up at the airport. Ryan assumed "they" meant Sophia, Emma, and Bridget. That was the entire reason Asset One made the girls ditch their vacation and fly back to the US, so they could pick up Emma and keep an eye on her until he could get there.

The last time he saw Emma, Ryan feared for his life because he'd decided not to kill the Gems on that pier in Africa. It was a decision that he was sure would attract the wrath of Asset One. However, to his surprise, Bridget didn't rat him out. Even though he almost hit her in the face for not following his orders. He was lucky. And Ryan decided to use that luck by jumping into a new Venomous operation where he could redeem himself in the eyes of Asset One. Show him that he was still valuable and could make the organization money.

As for Emma, he honestly didn't know where he stood. Those days when he and Emma had spent time together on Asset Twelve's training island were some of the happiest days he'd ever experienced in his life. They had great chemistry together. They could relate to each other. They were both ambitious. They both had unique talents. And they looked so good together. They were a perfect couple. They really were.

Did they have issues to work out? Sure they did, but the situation was far from hopeless. All he needed was to find that one thing that would win her over. To help her over that last hill so Emma would trust him without question.

Emma felt this too. How could she not? He remembered that little wave she gave him as she walked away from the pier. She didn't want to let go of him either. Why else would Emma go visit his mom in Wichita? It pissed Ryan off because she had no business outing his secret in front of his mom. That was his responsibility. That was his secret to carry. Now his mom was worried about him. He spent hours on the phone trying to calm her down. To convince her that the people he worked for were not as bad as Emma had led her to believe.

However, no matter the problems she caused, it was a sign that Emma was still trying to help. Still trying to "save" him from Venomous. Still trying to make what they had together stick. He had to admire her for that.

Why was he in love with Emma?

The girl had him wound up around her little pinkie. Even now Ryan was craving her like a drug. If he was truly ruthless, he would make himself focus on work. This new Polish operation looked quite promising from a money standpoint. Something that would make him look good in front of everyone. It was the smart play. A real man wouldn't let a woman hurt his career. To keep him from greatness.

If he had a few more months of work to distract him, Ryan could have purged himself of Emma. At least enough to resist the pull she had on him.

But when Asset One had heard about Emma's visit with his mom—especially after the girl was reported dead—it led the man to believe that Emma was preparing her own exit out of the Authority. That all the work that Ryan and Asset One did to woo Emma to their side was finally bearing fruit.

Ryan doubted his boss's thinking. Emma could be stubborn, determined to do things her own way. However, that didn't mean she was doing all this for him. Emma was quite capable of doing all this for selfish reasons as well. Still, when Asset One told him to go to New York City to see what Emma's intentions were, he went without question.

Anyway, Ryan had assumed that Bridget and Sophia had Emma with them. But when he emerged from US customs, someone shot him in the back with a needle. Before he could figure out what the hell was going on, he lost all feeling below his waist and had trouble walking. Before he could even find a chair...some old lady in a wheelchair scooped him up like he was a present. Like she wanted to marry him before he could remember how to say no. It was freaking embarrassing.

However, as Ryan regained his wits, he began to add things together. "Grandma" was actually Sapphire, who broke her leg on the *Falcon's Claw*. The Gems had kidnapped him from the airport. But his big question was...

"Why did you girls go to such trouble to kidnap me anyway?" Ryan asked.

Ruby and Sapphire glanced over at Emerald. She was always the bossy one of the Gems.

"We have questions we want answers to," Emerald said. "We assumed you wouldn't cooperate."

Ryan scanned the interior of the mini-bus. The two Authority lackeys disguised as pilots were quiet, but still stewed with anger. Especially the tall one, who had two pieces of tissues stuck up his broken nose, which no doubt did plenty of bleeding. His partner got off with only an injured arm. There was no doubt who the two individuals were who gave them their "gifts."

Bridget and Sophia sat on either side of Ryan. Still watching his back. Even though he'd yelled at Sophia, she obeyed. She knew the rules. She knew the consequences of breaking them. And she knew Venomous was excellent at enforcing its own rules.

"You still with us, love?" Emerald asked him.

"Yes, sorry about that," Ryan said. "Where were we?"

"You agreed to answer our questions."

"Correction, I agreed to listen to your questions. If I can, I'll answer them."

"Whatever," Emerald scoffed. "Right, did you have anything to do with Emma's death?"

Ryan was confused again. Surely they knew Emma was still alive.

Or did they?

"Emma's death?" Bridget repeated, sounding just as confused as Ryan.

He quickly slipped his arm around Bridget's torso and gave it a gentle squeeze. Bridget responded with a surprised grin. As he gently pulled her over, Ryan brushed away her red hair with his free hand so he could whisper in her ear. "Don't say anything. I don't think they know." To seal her cooperation, Ryan's free hand rested on the girl's cheek before he sat back. When he tried to withdraw his arm, Bridget pressed her back against the seat and pinned his arm there, not wanting him to remove it.

Ryan found that anytime he gave Bridget attention, the girl melted like butter. He shouldn't take advantage of her like this, but sometimes controlling your subordinates with love was better than violence.

"What was all that about?" Emerald asked, rightly suspicious of their private conference.

Ryan ignored the question. "No, I had nothing to do with Emma's death. In fact, I was quite upset when I heard about it."

He was telling the truth. When he first heard about Emma killing herself, Ryan had been devastated. He'd blamed himself for putting too much pressure on Emma and wondered if he was the one who pushed her over the edge. Privately, that first day, he'd cried as he looked through all of Emma's pictures that he took on his phone. Blubbering over them like a kid who lost his dog. Even after her death, Emma made him weak. Vulnerable. A love-sick boy instead of a man who spit in the face of death. It was the one thing he hated about Emma. She could melt him. Make him do things that he didn't want to do. It wasn't outright manipulation. Ryan knew people inside Venomous who were masters at manipulation. No, Emma knew how to access his softer side. His weak side. The side that wanted Emma to guide him away from the life Ryan knew he deserved. A life that would never be given to him. It was a life and a future that had to be fought for.

Ryan told the Gems only about his shock and the possible blame he put on himself for Emma's death. However, the private things were still kept private. Reading the faces of Ruby and Sapphire, they believed him.

"After you met Emma in Montreal, did you give her a thumb drive?" Emerald asked.

Ryan hesitated, pretending to be reliving his thoughts about Emma. The girl who was "dead."

"I don't think so," he said. "No, I never gave her such a thing. Why? What does that have to do with anything?"

Emerald slapped him. Hard. "Don't lie to me."

Bridget stood up, her eyes fuming.

Ryan freed his arm and touched hers. "Bridget, please."

Bridget drilled her eyes on Emerald before easing herself back down.

"I'm not lying," Ryan said. "I was with Emma most of the time, and I never saw anyone give her a thumb drive. If they did, I never saw it."

"I still don't believe you."

"What was on this thumb drive? Maybe I can help you find out who did give it to her."

"It contained information that we think caused Emma to kill herself," Sapphire said. "Whoever gave it to her knew it would mess her up."

Ryan was curious about this thumb drive. The contents must have been shocking to send Emma into hiding.

"Any more details than that?" he asked.

"It's not necessary," Emerald said. "What's important is that it was a murder weapon that drove her to suicide. And when we find out who gave it to her...they'll pay."

"A quest for revenge," Bridget said. "Sounds grand."

"It's justice. Not revenge," Emerald corrected.

"If I knew it would upset Emma to the point of committing suicide...I definitely wouldn't have given this thumb drive to her," Ryan said. "Any more questions?"

Ruby pointed at Bridget. "They would have."

Emerald crossed her arms. "What about you two?"

"Piss off," Sophia said.

"Yeah, nah," Bridget said. "Ya wanted to ask Ryan some questions, not us, Olivia darling."

"So you're not denying it?" Emerald asked.

"You muppets aren't cops, so piss off."

Emerald turned to Bridget. "Does your sister have an off switch?"

"Girls..." Ryan said.

"Ya fat English cow," Sophia said. "Run away before I use your scruffy hair to mob up the floor of the bus."

"You little red-headed—"

"Girls, this is a truce. Stop it," Ryan said. "That's an order."

"This is getting stupid," Bridget said. "Fine, I'll answer your little question, straight up. We don't know anything about a thumb drive. We spent most of our time with all of you, not Emma. Don't ya remember that, Olivia darling?"

Emerald relaxed. "Yes, I remember."

"Then...are we done here?" Ryan asked.

Emerald checked with Sapphire and Ruby before addressing him again. "Don't suppose you would voluntarily come with us to

San Francisco?"

"*Hei*, we have a private jet," Ruby added.

"Are you girls asking me out?"

Ruby giggled and covered her mouth.

"My, you're a cheeky bloke, aren't you?" Emerald stopped and took out her phone. Ryan could hear the device vibrating for an incoming call. Emerald checked the screen. "I'll take this outside. Don't go anywhere." The girl then disappeared off the mini-bus.

"I'm fecking bored. How long do we have to sit here?" Sophia asked.

Bridget's eyes slid over to Ryan. She was right. They were wasting time here. If they could reach Emma before the Gems, then Ryan could help her disappear or at least find out what her plans were. That was if Emma had a plan.

"How about lunch?" Ryan asked.

"Lunch sounds grand," Bridget said. "Think you're up for a bite, Sophia?"

"I vote for Chinese."

"Chinatown it is, then," Ryan said, trying to keep his grumbling subordinate happy.

Emerald climbed back onto the mini-bus. Her face was in total shock.

Ryan stood up, and the twins followed. "This was fun, but we're going to Chinatown for lunch. Without you, of course. So if you would please—"

"Emma's alive," Emerald said.

Sapphire and Ruby froze.

Emerald continued. "Mrs. B said that Emma called her grandmother earlier this morning and told her that…she faked her own suicide."

"Are you kidding?" Sapphire asked, dumbstruck.

"She's alive?" Ruby asked. Her eyes watered as tears streamed down her face. The girl collapsed into one of the bus seats, then began laughing and crying at the same time…as if a great burden were removed from her shoulders.

Emerald leaned against one of the seats, closing her eyes and absorbing the news.

Sapphire began wiping tears off her own cheeks.

Ryan was disappointed. His advantage was gone.

"Oh, swingin' Jesus," Sophia said, watching the water-works.

"Can we please get off this bus before I vomit."

Bridget smiled as she pulled Ryan along. "Let's get out of here."

Sophia walked past the Gems and their two wounded lackeys as she went down the stairs and out through the double doors. Bridget was right behind her with Ryan in tow. She made it to the bottom of the stairs before Emerald turned around.

"Hang on, Ryan. Did you hear what I just said?"

Ryan stopped at the top of the stairs. Bridget tugged at his arm, but Ryan didn't budge. "Yeah, Emma is alive."

Emerald tilted her head. "You don't seem very surprised."

She caught him. Emma was important to him, so hearing that the girl he loved was still alive should've received more...emotion from him. Rushing off for Chinese food was a bit too casual for the situation. But maybe he could still salvage the situation by knowing Emma's whereabouts.

Ryan let go of Bridget's hand and stepped inside the bus. "We already knew Emma was alive."

"I knew it," Emerald said. "You were lying."

"Only about Emma being alive. We intercepted her on a train coming to New York." Ryan turned to Bridget, who was stepping back on the bus too. "By the way, what happened with that? I thought you two had Emma under control."

"Can we talk about this some other time?" Bridget asked.

Ryan blew her off. "Sophia and Bridget were asked to chaperone Emma until I was able to get into town."

"Who asked them? Asset One?" Emerald asked. "Is he trying to recruit her again?"

"Look, Emma obviously wants to be left alone. She's here in New York, where she feels safe. I think we should both stay away from her and give the girl time to think things through."

"*Hei*, I agree," Ruby said. "Emma is going through a difficult time. We should respect her wishes."

"Enjoy your lunch," Emerald said to Ryan. "We won't be needing you anymore."

But Ryan still needed them.

"Tell you what," he said. "Why don't we all go meet Emma together and see what she has to say. And whatever Emma wants to do, we'll respect that."

A big smile formed on Emerald's face. "That'd make it easy for you, wouldn't it, love?"

This girl read him like a Burger King menu. She knew where Emma was and he didn't.

"What if—"

"The truce is off," Emerald said. "Better go enjoy that lunch."

Bridget tugged at Ryan's elbow. "Let's go. For real this time."

Ryan reluctantly followed her down the steps as the engine of the mini-bus turned over again. Soon the bus rolled away from the convenience store parking lot.

"Want me to follow them on the Ducati?" Bridget asked. "Sophia put a tracker on the bus."

"Waste of time," Ryan said. "They'll ditch that bus as soon as they can. Plus they'll be on the lookout for tails, so the chances they'd lead us straight to Emma are small."

"What do we tell Asset One?"

"We tell him nothing. I have another way to find Emma."

CHAPTER 26

On Monday morning, Emma nursed another porcelain cup of coffee as she stood on the upstairs balcony of Ben Gooden's mansion on Long Island. The balcony overlooked a clear-blue swimming pool and a wooden platform that stretched out to a dock on Hayground Cove. There were many such docks that led to expensive homes all around the cove. It was a nice area. A place where Emma wouldn't mind visiting for a while.

Yesterday's confession took a lot out of her. The guilt. The sadness and despair her grandmother had experienced. Emma was still reeling from the call. It made her question everything she had done over the past week.

Emma took another sip of coffee as she breathed in the salty air coming in from the Atlantic Ocean.

"Nice, ain't it?" Ben asked as he stepped on to the deck, wearing a suit and tie, all dressed for his CEO gig. "This is a nice spot. Rosa and I like to come up here with a glass of wine at the end of the day."

"How long have you lived here?" Emma asked.

"Moved in about a year ago. A few months after my promotion."

"You and Rosa deserve it."

"Does that mean you're not pissed off that I made you call your grandma?"

Emma hesitated. "You did what you thought was right. Me, on the other hand—if Grandma doesn't let me back in the house, can I stay with you until I find my own place?"

"Do I have a choice?" Ben asked.

Emma looked at him. Was he being serious?

Ben laughed. "It's your corporation. That's what your grandmother said. So you're my boss."

Emma scoffed. "Not until I'm twenty-five."

"Well, I have to keep my future boss happy so I have a cushy corporate job to retire from."

"I think your future is safe. I don't wanna run the company."

Ben chuckled. "You're only sixteen, Emma. Along the way, you may change your mind about that."

"Shouldn't you be going to work so I have a corporate empire left to inherit?" Emma asked.

Ben's smile melted a little.

"What is it?"

"Laura called. Asked for my permission to come by the house and talk to you. Said I'd ask you first."

Emma sighed. She was hoping for a little more time before confronting Mrs. B with what she'd done. But that woman didn't believe in waiting. She wanted to dive into battle with her cane swinging.

"Sure, whatever. That's fine."

"I'll tell Laura to come over, then."

Emma nodded.

It was late morning when Rosa came upstairs and told Emma her friends were waiting downstairs. She followed Rosa down the long spiral staircase and through the open-spaced living room to get to Rosa's sun-room. Miyuki was the first one up from her chair. She rushed over to Emma and wrapped her arms around her. The girl was sobbing, making Emma's guilt inflate.

"I'm sorry," Emma managed to say.

"You make me upset. Big time," Miyuki said. "But I forgive you."

Nadia crawled back on-to her leg scooter and moved over to Emma. "I'm not sure if I can forgive you yet." Her eyes softened. "But I'm still happy you're alive." She offered Emma a hug, and she took it.

Olivia stood up. To Emma's surprise, she gave her a hug too. But the girl then stepped back and crossed her arms. "I'm so flipping pissed at you. We all thought you were dead. What the hell is going on, Emma?"

Emma took in a deep breath. "I didn't think everything through. Well, I did think a lot on the suicide part, but not so much on everything else after that. Seriously, I'm sorry for not including you in my plans."

"What plans?" Olivia asked.

"I wanted to leave. To run away, I guess. I felt I had to do this."

"Why?" Olivia asked.

Emma's eyes drifted over to Mrs. B, who was still seated with Aardvark on the couch.

Mrs. B read her eyes but showed no reaction. "Mrs. Gooden, your sun-room is absolutely beautiful."

Rosa smiled. "Thank you."

"It's seducing me to stay longer. May we have some of those refreshments that you offered us earlier?"

"Sure thing." Rosa headed for the kitchen.

"Girls, please thank Mrs. Gooden for her hospitality when she comes back." Mrs. B used her cane to move off the couch and face Emma. "Meanwhile, let's you and I talk outside."

The sun was out over Hayground Cove as a sailboat moved out to sea with its mainsail flapping in the strong wind. Mrs. B led Emma across the wood planks to the Goodens' boat dock. Mrs. B leaned against the railing as she referenced the cove. "Look how graceful they are."

A group of swans were coasting across the surface, about twenty of them at least. One would think that that many birds would be making a lot of noise, but they weren't. The birds were quiet. As if they could appreciate tranquility like humans can.

After the swans glided past the dock, Mrs. B turned her attention back to the water. "Who gave you that report?"

Emma faced away from the water. "You lied to me."

"Are you referring to the top-secret report you were not allowed to read?" Mrs. B paused. "Tell me, who gave it to you?"

"You ordered my mom to die."

"That's only one interpretation of that operation. The committee who created that report had no idea what was at stake —"

"My dad was part of that committee," Emma said. "You don't think he knew what was at stake? It was his wife's life."

"Your father should never have been involved in that investigation. He couldn't judge the operation without a bias."

"Oh yeah, because you should be able to get away with killing his wife."

Mrs. B's eyes burned into Emma. "Watch yourself, young lady."

Emma moved a few steps back and faced the water. "You should've told me the truth about my mom before you ever recruited me."

Mrs. B sighed. "I did tell you the truth. Your mother died a hero."

"Is that why my dad left the Authority? Because he was proud of my mom's heroic death?"

"Emma, sometimes people interpret things differently. Sometimes there are no right or wrong answers to a situation. One makes a decision and hope they make the correct one."

"But you didn't."

Mrs. B was silent for a moment. "I refuse to live in the past."

The woman regained her composure. "Who gave you that thumb drive?"

"Why is that so important?" Emma asked.

"Was it Ryan? Is he still trying to flip you?"

Emma closed her eyes. "This is why I did it. This is why I faked my suicide. It's because of all this…shit." Emma opened her eyes. "I'm done. Seriously, I've had enough of Ryan and you and Venomous and the secrets and the lies about my mom—." Emma moved closer to Mrs. B. "Ever since I've been involved with you, my life has gone completely nuts. The only place where I feel normal, the only place that's not making me crazy is here, in New York."

Mrs. B absorbed her words.

"I want out," Emma said.

"This is my fault," Mrs. B said. "I misjudged you. I thought you were ready."

The two women stared over the water, not saying anything for a moment or two.

"Are you gonna let me leave? Or is Aardvark going to drown me in this cove?"

"We don't need to go through such theatrics," Mrs. B said. "I want you to promise me—literally on your grandmother Bernadette's life—that you will never tell a soul anything about our organization. Nothing about our Napa Valley station. Nothing about the people who run it. And nothing about the Gems. It was like we never existed in your life. This promise must last your entire lifetime."

"Okay."

"If you violate this verbal agreement, we will not hesitate to come after you or anyone else in your life. I'm not playing around, Emma."

"I understand."

Mrs. B turned her attention back to the water. "The Gems will move out of your grandma's house, and you both will be left in peace. You have my word on that."

"Thank you," Emma said with relief.

"We should break the news to your grandmother together. Gather your things, and we'll head for the airport."

"Right now?"

"I have a job to get back to and items that need my attention. You're not my only headache to worry about today."

Emma hesitated. "Tonight, I can fly back commercial and we can tell my grandma in the morning."

"You have my word. We won't kidnap you right off the plane."

That made Emma grin. "It's not that. I already called my friend Hailey, and we're hanging out this afternoon. I haven't seen her in ages, and she'd hate me forever if I flaked on her."

"For security reasons, I'd feel better if you came with us on the jet," Mrs. B said. "So I'll give you the afternoon with Hailey then we'll leave tonight."

CHAPTER 27

That afternoon, Emma did some shopping in Manhattan. She needed something cute to wear since her suitcase was gone and her New York Yankees costume was way too much. When her friends and Mrs. B came to visit, Rosa was nice enough to let Emma borrow some of her old jeans and a blouse Rosa had worn when she was in her twenties, but those clothes didn't fit her body that well. So Emma bought a nice skirt with a pretty top to match it along with some pink sneakers that were perfect. The outfit was casual, cute, and looked nice.

But the shopping had made her late.

When Emma rushed back inside Horowitz's Deli, the place was hopping with Van Dorn students who were out of school. Emma's eyes searched the packed tables.

"Em!" a girl shouted as she waved her hands in the air. Hailey Gold jumped up from a table of girls. She raced around a bunch of kids to intercept Emma with a hug. Hailey was shorter than Emma and still had her curly brown hair. She wore a lot of makeup, but the girl knew how to make it work for her.

"Oh my God, Em. Missed you for, like, forever. Oh my God." Hailey stepped back and did her fashion assessment. "You're, like, the only one who can make that look work. I'm so jealous of your gorgeous blond hair. Have I ever mentioned that to you?"

"Ever since we were ten." Emma laughed. "And look at you, glamor cat. Bold accessorizing with your school uniform. And you're rocking that hair. Did Niles do that?"

"Of course, and he's gonna freak when he hears you're back in town." Hailey grabbed Emma's hand. "Come say hi to everyone." Hailey pulled her through the deli like a kid with a new Christmas toy. In her haste, Hailey knocked Emma against one table where two short-haired girls were eating, almost spilling both their drinks.

"My bad," Emma apologized, even though it wasn't.

Hailey dragged her over to a large table full of familiar faces from Van Dorn Hall. There was Jackie, Morgan, Cassie, Sienna, and Keisha Williams. The girls went crazy when they saw Emma. So many welcome-back hugs. So many smiles. It was like Emma had been gone for decades.

Hailey then offered her an empty seat. "I've been holding it for ya."

Emma sat down and was bombarded with questions...

How are you?

How was California?

Emma told them how different San Francisco was from New York. The cultural differences of the people. How she and her grandmother could never find a decent bagel or slice of pizza there. "Plus, you have to drive everywhere. Walking to the grocery is, like, a sin in California. Like, I was forced to get a driver's license."

"Wow, you're driving now?" Hailey asked.

"Yeah, but not very well. I already hit a dog."

"Oh no." Hailey cupped her hands over her mouth. "You didn't kill the poor thing, did you?"

"I rushed him to the vet, and he's fine. In fact, he's my fur baby now."

A collective *ahhhh* surrounded the table.

"Do you have pics?" Keisha asked.

"I lost my phone back in California. I only have a cheap temporary one now."

"Why haven't you posted them on your Faceplace account?" Hailey asked. "You didn't un-friend me, did you?"

"Never," Emma said. "Seriously, I know. Like, I've been a bad long-distance friend to all of you. I've been super busy over the last year, and...I haven't been posting as much as I should."

"Busy with what?" Hailey asked.

Emma hesitated. "My life has gotten a lot more complicated."

Hailey examined her. "Oh my God. Are you in trouble?"

"Why do you say that?"

"We've known each other since kindergarten, Em. I know every expression on that face, and there's something else on your mind."

"She's right," Keisha added.

"You're wrong. This is the only thing on my mind. Being here with all of you."

Hailey's eyebrow went up. "Don't use your actor tricks on me. I'm immune to your efforts of deflection. C'mon, what is it? Is it the reason you're here in New York without a chaperone?"

Her old bestie could read her mind too well.

"I can't say."

Hailey smiled. It was like throwing a bucket of blood-soaked fish into shark-infested waters.

"But you sooo want to."

The girls all laughed.

"Seriously, it's better if you don't know," Emma said.

Hailey dropped the smile. "If you're in serious trouble, let me help. My dad knows everyone here. The US district attorney. The mayor. The governor—I have your back, Em."

"Thanks for the offer, but I think all of my problems will be worked out soon." Emma paused. "There's a chance I might even move back here."

"Shut up!" Hailey playfully shoved her. "Don't mess with me like that."

"That would be awesome," Keisha said.

"I have to talk to my grandma first, but—at least I could maybe spend the summer here."

"Hey, you can stay with me and my mom." Hailey referenced a girl with dark skin and a pony tail. "Keisha's family has that summer house in Martha's Vineyard. We could, like, hang out there."

"Hailey, my parents don't want all of us out there," Keisha said. "They bought it for them."

"You can talk them out of it," Hailey said with a mischievous grin.

Everyone at the table laughed. It was great. Emma felt so relaxed. So chill. It was like she never left for California. Like her father had never died. Like her life was still filled with sunny horizons. That was when Ryan stepped in front of their table.

Emma couldn't believe it. How dare he show his face here. This was Emma's spot. It was private. It was for her real friends. Friends who gave her no conditions for their loyalty. Friends who were dying to catch up on her life because they actually cared about her.

Ryan flashed Emma a friendly smile, putting on the same old charm he would always use. A charm Emma was becoming numb to.

"Hi there," Hailey said. "You don't go to our school, do you? Let me guess, Monte Cassino?"

"He could be from Henderson," Keisha said.

"Oh, good guess. Which is it?" Hailey asked.

Ryan's focus didn't wander. "Can I speak with you?"

Emma sighed.

Hailey leaned over. "Oh my God. Is this the 'trouble' you were talking about?"

"Part of it, yeah."

"What do ya wanna do? You know we got your back."

Emma thought about it. The deli was crowded with lots of witnesses if things got crazy.

She crossed her arms and sat back. "What do you want?"

"Can we go talk?"

"Ryan, whatever it is, I'm not interested."

"You owe me a conversation."

"Oh, do I?"

"I want to address a few of the things you told my mom. Things you had no business telling her."

"What did you tell his mom?" Hailey asked.

The table listened for an answer.

The guilt seeped out of Emma's heart and burned her chest. Yeah, maybe contacting Ryan's mom wasn't such a great idea either.

Emma lifted herself from the table. "Anywhere but outside, okay?"

Ryan nodded and moved farther back into the deli. Emma followed him cautiously. She could see an empty table near the wall, but Ryan veered away from that and chose an occupied table. The one with the two short-haired girls whom Emma had bumped into earlier. What was he doing?

"Sit down, Emma."

She gave Ryan a puzzled look.

"Do as he says, ya muppet," one of the short-haired girls said.

Emma took a closer look at her face. It was Sophia. She was wearing a dark wig along with a perfect camouflage of makeup.

"Cool your sneakers, Miss America," the second girl said. She was obviously Bridget. "We have some unfinished business with ya."

CHAPTER 28

Ryan wasn't too sure what he was feeling right now. His mind was in conflict. Pieces of it fighting against each other. One piece wanted Ryan to be a man and tell this girl to leave him alone. Emma made him weak. Made him look stupid in front of his peers. And through her meddling, put a strain on his relationship with his mom. He needed to stop following his puppy-dog heart and start embracing his balls. You don't become the top dog of Venomous by embracing your feminine side.

Yet the other piece of his brain told Ryan there was another way to become powerful. The concept that two heads were better than one. Emma had talent. Had a financial empire she would inherit. In this day and age, there was nothing wrong with a power couple. A couple who only trusted themselves and shunned everyone else who opposed them. If he could get Emma to see that potential, Ryan could have both. A girl he couldn't live without and a partner who would help him rise to the top. To become a greater man than his father could have ever been. Asset One saw the potential Emma offered. That was why she had been treated as a guest on the *Falcon's Claw*. That was why he had been assigned to look after her. To charm her. To change her loyalty. But Ryan didn't want Asset One to have Emma. He wanted that privilege. A powerful couple was no match for a strange man who played with falcons all day.

"How did you know I'd be here?" Emma asked.

Ryan caught himself staring at her soft lips. Even now, he could feel the power she had over him.

"You told me, remember? How you would always go to Horowitz's Deli after school with your friends. Van Dorn Hall, right? The private school down the street," Ryan said. "Was that Hailey?"

"What do you want, Ryan?"

"Asset One wanted me to talk to you again. He assumes you faked your suicide to escape from the control of the Authority, so he wanted to extend another offer to join us."

"I'm not interested. Seriously, none of this has anything to do with Venomous."

"But if you didn't go through all this for us—"

"Us?" Emma asked. "Like, are we talking about you and me... or them?"

"What's going on with you?" Ryan asked. "First you fake a suicide then you show up in Wichita to tell my mom that I've been lying to her. What the hell, Emma? What made you think you had a right to even approach her?"

Emma hesitated; clearly the accusation bothered her. "I didn't plan it. My train had an unscheduled stop in Wichita, and I remembered what you said about your mom, and I thought... maybe if she knew the truth, she would convince you to leave Venomous." Emma softened. "I did it for you."

Sophia rolled her eyes.

"Can we have the table, please?" Ryan asked.

Sophia was already on her feet when Bridget said, "Yeah, nah. I wanna hear all this."

"Too bad. Leave."

Bridget stayed put. These sisters were becoming aggravating. Why did they always question everything he did?

"That's an order," Ryan added.

Bridget met his eyes, studied him. A grin formed along her lips as she stood up. But instead of walking away, Bridget moved behind Ryan, and he felt her hand running down his chest, her nails digging into the fabric of his shirt. "Don't be such an egg. Could be fun for ya to let me give the orders for once, Ryan darling." Her hand withdrew from his chest and messed up his hair before she left.

"So...you did that for me?" Ryan asked, regaining his cool by combing his hair back in place. "Telling my mom?"

Emma waited to make sure Bridget was gone. "Before I disappeared, I wanted to do something that would help you."

"Disappear? Is that why you faked your suicide?"

"Ever since we got off the *Falcon's Claw*, I've been thinking about the future and what I want and what's possible—right now, I

161

don't want to be a Gem anymore. I don't want to be a part of your group. I only want to go back to when my life made sense."

"Okay, so you're saying that you don't want to spend your future with me?"

"Not like this. Not having to look behind each other's backs all the time. I want to be normal. I'd love it if we could be normal. I mean, if you left Venomous—"

"That's not possible."

"Hear me out, Ryan. Seriously, if you left Venomous and could go into hiding with your mom, you could escape all this. And then maybe when things are safe, you could go to college. And one day I might run into you at college. And then we could make plans and have a future together."

"And your friends at the Authority would help me set this up?"

"It could be the last favor I ask." Emma reached out for his hand. "I know there's good in you, Ryan. You keep saying that you don't have a choice. But you do. I know it won't be an easy one, but it's the right one for you and your mom."

"But what if you're wrong? What if Venomous is the best opportunity for both of us to be happy. Emma, together, we could be unstoppable. Who wants to be normal? I want to be exceptional. I want to change history. I want to move mountains. You have wants and desires too. Let me bring them to you. Let me be your champion. Let me be your king. I will give you everything that you have ever wanted in your life. I promise you that. But you have to trust me."

"Ryan, I love you. Not Venomous. The trouble is…I don't think you can separate the two."

"You're wrong."

"Am I?"

She didn't believe him. How could she not believe him? What else did he have to say to convince her?

Bridget and Sophia were back and standing over the table.

"I'm not done yet," Ryan barked.

Bridget leaned over and retrieved her phone from the chair she was sitting in. The speaker-phone was activated, and the phone was connected to another line. "Was that enough for you, sir?"

Ryan froze.

"Yes, Asset One-three-zero…I heard enough." It was Asset One. Bridget had allowed him to hear their entire conversation.

Shit.

He was dead.

"Asset Ninety-five, it sounds like your charms are... ineffective...with this young lady. Since Emma's answer is no, I have no use...for her now. My apologies, Asset Ninety-five, but we must leave...a strong message to Emma's friends. Asset One-three-zero?"

Bridget straightened. "Yes, sir."

"I want you and your sister...to kill Emma."

The order shocked him. At first, Ryan wasn't sure if he interpreted the man's words correctly.

Beaming like a little girl on a horse, Sophia withdrew a large hunting knife from its sheath hidden under the waist of her school uniform skirt.

Bridget didn't wait. She unrolled a set of utensils on the table, grabbed the knife, and was about to plunge it into Emma's stomach before Emma grabbed her arm and pulled Bridget across the table.

Ryan jumped back as Emma used Bridget's body as a shield against Sophia trying to stab her.

"Stop it," Ryan ordered.

No one listened.

Emma dumped Bridget to the floor and ran through the deli, knocking people over in a rush to get out.

Sophia jumped over her sister and took off in pursuit. As Bridget got back to her feet, Ryan grabbed her arm.

"Don't kill her. Emma still could be valuable as a—"

Bridget pulled his arm behind his back and shoved him against the wall with her foot. He then felt her body pressing against his. "Shove Miss America out of your head, would ya? She's not worth your time anymore."

As Bridget released him, Ryan swung around and grabbed her again. "No!"

This time, Bridget kicked him in the crotch. The intense pain made Ryan collapse to his knees. Instead of laughing at his misfortune, Bridget kissed him on the forehead. "I know you have strong feelings for this girl. So don't worry, darling. Sophia and I will do what must be done."

Bridget weaved her way through the crowd that was forming around this part of the deli.

"Where did Emma go?" Hailey asked, her friends closing in on Ryan.

The intense pain lingered, making it difficult for Ryan to stand back up. But he pushed through the pain as he stumbled through the crowd and out onto the sidewalk. But even this small amount of movement was too much. Ryan had to surrender to a bench at a nearby bus stop. He gingerly sat down, sparking an objection from his tender coconuts.

Ryan glanced down the street and saw no signs of either Emma or the twins. He closed his eyes, trying his best to soak up the pain. To force his body to recover enough so he could run after them and maybe save Emma's life.

Someone sat down next to him, causing Ryan to open his eyes. It was an older woman with a cane who stared.

"Ryan Raymond, a thorn in my side since day one," the old woman said.

A massive arm seized Ryan's throat as it squeezed his head into a choke hold.

"My name is Mrs. B," the woman said. "You and I have a lot to talk about."

Ryan gasped for air. He felt sleepy as darkness closed in around him.

He tried to fight against it. But he couldn't.

Soon that darkness overtook him into unconsciousness.

CHAPTER 29

Through the window of the passenger van, Miyuki leaned her forehead against the glass as she watched the street in front of Horowitz's Deli. Emma had gone in about twenty minutes ago, and Miyuki already missed her. She wished they could have come in with her, but Mrs. B had made it clear that this stop was a private one for Emma, and the Gems had to stay in the van. It was a strange request because at West Berkeley High Emma had showed them around her school and introduced them to all of her high school friends. But since they'd discovered she was alive, Emma was acting strange, placing herself at arm's length to them, as if Emma knew something they didn't. Miyuki hoped that everything would get back to normal once they got back home to California.

"Do you think I was too hard on Emma?" Olivia asked, sitting in the row in front of Miyuki. "I think she needs to know how upset we are about what she did...but do you think I overdo it sometimes?"

It was rare for Olivia to ask her such deep questions. Usually she reserved them for Nadia, who kept many things between them private. But it was refreshing that Olivia was asking her for a change.

"I feel you could better connect with Emma if you gave her more compliments."

"More compliments?"

"Start with small things like...her hair looks nice. Or the outfit she's wearing is cute," Miyuki says. "Emma responds better if she feels that you're making an effort to make her feel good."

"Why doesn't she make an effort to make me feel good?" Olivia asked.

"You have to give before you can receive. If you make love to the world, then the world will love you back."

Olivia hesitated. "Make love to the world?"

"*Hei*, embrace life. Make love. Give love. Then...you receive love," Miyuki said.

"So basically, I should be nicer to Emma."

"Show her that you care about what she thinks. That you value her as a person. As a friend."

"That makes more sense to me, love."

"Good." Miyuki smiled. "And don't be so bossy."

"What?"

Miyuki covered her mouth. She'd said too much and had embarrassed her friend. She bowed. "Sorry, I didn't mean for that to come out...in that way. Please forgive me."

"I'm not that bossy." Olivia then studied Miyuki's face. "You disagree?"

She shouldn't say it. It wasn't polite. Yet Olivia did need to hear it.

"It is a...difficult subject," Miyuki began. "You might find it... offensive."

Nadia turned her attention to the window.

"I'm a big girl," Olivia said. "I can take some constructive criticism."

"That is most helpful." Miyuki hesitated. "When it comes to Emma and me, you sometimes are very bossy. More so than you ever are with Nadia."

"No, I'm not." Olivia then thought about it.

Miyuki caught herself bowing, as if silently apologizing again. Making a person uncomfortable on purpose was foreign to Miyuki. Her Japanese parents would never approve of such behavior. However, in the West, offering helpful criticism to a good friend in a kind, non-confrontational style can lead to positive results for everyone involved.

"Nads, did you hear any of that?" Olivia asked.

Nadia shrugged but didn't peel her eyes away from the window.

"Are you saying she's right?"

Nadia slowly acknowledged the question. "Sometimes—and I would stress, not all the time—however, sometimes you do tend to boss around Emma and Miyuki more than me. Not that I'm complaining about the special treatment."

"But I'm the leader of the group. I can't play favorites," Olivia said.

"Bingo!" Miyuki said. It came right out of her mouth without a filter. Just like Emma would say.

Nadia giggled, then tried to stop when Olivia frowned at her.

"Do you and Emma feel the same way?" Olivia asked Miyuki.

"We all can improve ourselves. I know I did. I've learned so much being a Gem. I'm not the same girl I was when I joined. Nadia is different too. You're different as well. *Hei*, you have more confidence in yourself. I'm only saying…you can love and respect your friends and still be our leader."

Olivia thought about that.

"Where's Emma going?" Nadia asked.

Miyuki looked out the window and caught Emma running down the street.

"Look over there!" Olivia said.

A girl wearing a school uniform with dark short-hair was running after Emma with a large hunting knife.

"Mother trucker…what's going on?" Miyuki asked.

"C'mon, let's go help her!" Olivia used both hands to pull open the sliding door. Miyuki was right behind her as they both jumped out of the van.

Mrs. B was in the front passenger seat. She was already on the radio calling in reinforcements as Miyuki and Olivia crossed the street.

Before they reached the other side, another girl ran outside the deli. She ripped off her short-haired wig, allowing her long red curls to drop down. It was Bridget. The girl ignored them as she ran as fast as she could in the same direction as Emma.

Olivia took the lead as they both chased Bridget down the block.

As they turned a corner, Miyuki could see down the sidewalk a few blocks. Emma was about to cross another intersection when a large city bus moved in and blocked the crosswalk, forcing her to a dead stop.

This allowed Sophia to close in on her with the knife.

"Emma!" Miyuki yelled at the top of her lungs.

She swung around and dodged Sophia's knife, which bit into the side of the bus. Emma responded with a back kick that threw Sophia against the side of the bus.

Emma ran towards Miyuki.

But Bridget appeared between them with another knife.

Emma turned back around and saw Sophia approaching her from that side.

Both O'Malley sisters closed in on her like two pieces of an Emma sandwich.

Emma glanced over at the set of stairs that went up to the door of a brownstone home. That was a dead end.

Next she glanced over at the busy one-way street with its lanes of moving traffic.

Emma ran into traffic. A box truck jammed on its brakes as its fender knocked Emma forward. She stayed on her feet and zig-zagged through all four lanes of traffic.

Sophia ran after her, dodging cars and determined to use that knife.

Miyuki followed them. A taxi came right at her, causing the girl to jump in the air and roll across the hood of the car. Luckily for her, she was able to avoid the windshield and get back on her feet.

A bus came at her next. Miyuki couldn't jump over that. So she flattened herself on the ground as the massive vehicle passed over her.

Miyuki came back to her feet and managed to dance past the other two lanes of traffic to the other sidewalk. She checked to see if Olivia was following. But her friend was stuck on the other side with Bridget right on top of her. The two girls were swinging legs and arms, each trying to out-maneuver each other in a fight.

Miyuki was on her own.

She ran down the sidewalk and picked up Sophia's trail. The Irish girl was closing in on Emma again.

As Emma ran over another crosswalk, she caught her foot on the curb and fell down.

Sensing the opportunity, Sophia put on a burst of speed to reach that crosswalk.

Miyuki pushed herself hard, moving around two boys playing catch with a baseball.

Emma slowly rolled over on her back, as if she were injured.

As Sophia reached the crosswalk, Emma was the perfect target. The girl stood over Emma with the hunting knife, ready to treat her like a roast.

Miyuki knew she couldn't get there in time.

When the neighborhood boy tossed his baseball back to his friend, Miyuki caught it in mid-air. "Sorry, I must borrow." Miyuki got into her pitching stance and hurled the ball as hard as she could. The ball was low, but it hit Sophia square in the back with enough force to drop her to the ground.

The two boys stared at Miyuki with wide-open mouths.

She agreed. It was a good pitch. Perhaps the Tokyo Giants would draft her now.

Miyuki ran over to the crosswalk. Emma's eyes were open, and there was some blood oozing from her lip.

Sophia was rolling around on the ground, her face in agony. "You fecking, *eegit*! Ya broke my damn kidneys."

Miyuki picked up the girl's knife from the sidewalk. "You should be nicer to people."

Emma sat up. "Nice throw to first base."

"Thank you." Miyuki knelt down and examined her chin. "You split your lip. How's your chin?"

Emma nodded. "It's okay."

A car screeched to a stop as two men got out. Miyuki recognized them as part of Mrs. B's security detail.

CHAPTER 30

Mrs. B's security detail made quick work of the situation. They gathered up all the Gems, Mrs. B, Aardvark, and Ryan before stuffing them all in the van and rushing them all to Teterboro airport. Once there, the large private jet spooled up its engines and took off with wheels up in less than ten minutes.

Miyuki was impressed with their efficiency. She later learned that some of the men had worked for the US Secret Service back in the day.

As their jet leveled off, Miyuki enjoyed a *Brain Milk* energy drink. It was the beverage that almost destroyed the company her father worked for. However, since taking over the reins, her father took out the bad, mind-altering chemicals of *Thunderdog* and replaced them with good-for-the-brain natural ingredients that made it one of the healthiest new energy drinks on the market.

"Is that your dad's new drink?" Emma said.

"Oh, I'd like to try it," Nadia said.

"Are you bonkers?" Olivia asked. "The way that stuff scrambles your brain."

"But Miyuki's dad took all that bad chemical stuff out, right?" Emma asked.

"*Hei*, this all natural. Very good for you." Miyuki went back to the jet's fridge and brought the Gems three more cans and placed them on the table that faced their four seats. "I'm so proud of him."

Soon the Gems relaxed and talked about the twins. Olivia did a play-by-play of her fight with Bridget. Although it sounded like the fight was more of a draw, especially when Mrs. B's armed security detail showed up and convinced Bridget to leave. Miyuki told the Gems about Sophia reaching Emma. And how she had to think of something fast.

"You hit her in the back with a baseball?" Nadia asked.

"From across the road, love?" Olivia asked.

Miyuki nodded.

"Oh, that's fantastic. Wish I were there to see that."

"Was she hurt?" Nadia asked.

"I hope so," Olivia said.

"She'll have a nasty bruise on her back," Miyuki said. "But she was moving her arms and legs, so I don't think it was that bad."

"When Sophia reached you, Emma, did she say anything?" Nadia asked. "I can't imagine how scared you must have been."

Emma was watching the clouds, her mind somewhere else.

"Emma?" Miyuki asked.

She turned. "Yes, what?"

"Did Sophia say anything to you? After you fell on the sidewalk?" Nadia repeated.

Emma faced everyone. "She didn't use any words. The girl kind of sneered at me with this grin. It was bizarre." Emma patted Miyuki's hand. "Thanks for digging me out of trouble."

"We all sisters," Miyuki said. "We all stand up for each other."

"I promise it'll be the last time."

"Last time?"

Emma frowned and closed her eyes. When she opened them, Emma began by saying, "I'm not staying in California. I'm going to move back to New York and live there." She told them how overwhelmed she felt. How being a Gem had consumed her life, and she wanted to step away from it. Hit the reset button. That was why she'd fled to New York City in the first place.

"I know I botched it all up. I should have planned things better, you know? I should have told all of you what was going on inside my head. But I'm used to keeping it all inside because I don't want anyone to worry about me. I mean, I got through my father's death, so I figured that I could cope with moving to California and going to a new school and becoming a spy and…"

Emma let that sentence die. Her fingers mindlessly played with the energy drink can.

"Turns out…I can't handle it. Not without creating chaos with everyone else's life." She scanned their faces. "I'm sorry I let you all down. I thought I wanted to be a Gem. But I think I'm a better rich girl than I am a human being."

A wave of sadness washed over Miyuki. Her heart sank lower

and lower. Her best friend was leaving. The only Gem who fully understood and loved Miyuki for who she was. She'd be alone once again, still trying to convince Nadia and Olivia to like her.

"Did you ask Mrs. B what she thought of all this?" Olivia asked, her voice softer as she glanced to the front of the cabin, where Aardvark and Mrs. B worked on their laptops.

"We came to an understanding," Emma said. "Once everyone moves out, my grandma Bernadette and I will be left alone."

Miyuki enjoyed California. She loved Kayla and Lewis and everyone in her gaming club. And Grandma Bernadette was like her American aunt. Someone who loved them and looked out for them while they were away from their own parents. Now, the three of them would be living somewhere else.

Again.

Emma dug into her purse and handed Miyuki a tissue. Miyuki dotted her wet cheeks with it.

"May I borrow one too?" Nadia asked.

Emma gave her the pack of tissues. Nadia took one out and patted the corners of her own wet eyes.

Even Olivia couldn't hide her disappointment. "When do we move out?"

"After we land, I guess," Emma said. "I don't know for sure."

Olivia cleared her throat. "That's too bad. I felt like—well, we were all starting to gel. The four of us. It was beginning to feel like a team, you know? We needed someone who could help the three of us sharpen our skills at maintaining a solid alias. Someone good at picking out wardrobes and creating believable characters. Someone with theatrical experience who could teach us professional acting techniques because she was such an experienced and talented actor."

Emma wiped a tear from her own cheek. "You think I'm a talented actor?"

Before Olivia could answer, Emma sprang from her seat and hugged her tight.

Miyuki fought back her own tears. She didn't want to ruin this moment.

Emma leaned back, took a tissue, and blew her nose. "Since we're being honest, I wish you were flying this jet, Olivia. Because you're the only pilot I trust. Like, I'm super nervous to be on board this thing right now."

Aardvark came to their table; he had to lean down since he was taller than the plane's fuselage. The man typed on his phone, and the digital reader came on…

Ryan is asking for you, Emma. Mrs. B requests that you see him and make it "short and sweet," as she phrased it.

CHAPTER 31

The small metal cage that Ryan found himself inside was surprisingly comfortable. There was a small cot with clean sheets and a fluffy pillow. A crescent-shaped chair, which had excellent back support. The aircraft toilet was small but first class in terms of flying toilets. The wall that was part of the fuselage of the aircraft was reinforced with metal as well. Ryan was sure the floor was metal too; however, there was a nice carpet underneath so the floor wouldn't get too cold up in the air. For a prison cell on a private jet, it wasn't half bad.

However, being captured by the Authority was the least of Ryan's worries now. He was sure that he was a dead man.

Dead man walking.

Wasn't that what they said in prison movies? The one inmate who had a target on his back because he stood up to the wrong guy or snitched to the guards about one of the prisoners having contraband in their cell?

Ryan was sure that Asset One had lost all his faith in him. Worse yet, the man probably thought that Emma had compromised him. Made him weak. Made him a risk to Venomous. Asset One wouldn't tell him any of this face-to-face, because Asset One wasn't a man who talked about his feelings. Asset One didn't conduct staff reviews to evaluate everyone's performances. Every operative would have to read in between the lines, and if they got it wrong…a falcon would visit them. A falcon fitted with special claws that were sharp enough to dig into human skin. A falcon that was trained on how to attack a human being. Ripping their flesh open like a cat attacking a roll of toilet paper. Hitting the victim near arteries and other vital areas…such as a person's eye.

There was a knock at the door that separated this part of the jet from the cabin. The Authority lackey who was guarding Ryan looked up from his science fiction novel and gave the person permission to enter. Ryan was pleased to see who it was.

Emma let herself into the compartment. The guard excused himself so they could have some privacy. Well, fake privacy because there was a camera in the corner monitoring Ryan's every move. Most likely that old woman with a cane would be listening in.

Emma sat down on the guard's chair with her arms cradling her chest. She still looked beautiful. She still made his heart thirst for her.

"Why am I here?" she asked.

"I wanted to talk to you," Ryan said.

"We both said enough at the deli. Don't you think?"

"Our discussion was interrupted."

"It was basically over," she said.

"You said…either pick me or Venomous, right?"

Emma didn't answer.

Ryan smiled. "Okay, I pick you. I love you. I do. If your friends can help me get out, then yes, let's do it. Venomous means nothing to me now. As soon as Asset One finds out I've been captured, he'll want me dead. I've messed up enough that I don't think I can prevent that from happening even if I somehow escaped." Ryan exposed his wrist. "Remember that implant I told you about? If Asset One wants to, all he needs to do is activate it using our satellite network and it will trigger a heart attack. So I need the Authority to help me get it out before that happens. You need to talk to your friends and convince them I'm worth saving. I know you can do it. If anyone can, it would be you."

Emma watched him; then her eyes wandered as her mind processed things.

"This is everything that you wanted from me, right?" Ryan said. "Complete commitment to you. I'm ready. I'm ready to make that promise now."

Her eyes scanned his face again.

"Please, Emma. I'm begging here. You're my last hope."

Emma's chin lifted, as if her mind had come to a conclusion. "So you wouldn't quit Venomous voluntarily for me. But you'll do it because they don't want you anymore."

"Emma—"

"You'd still pick Venomous over us, wouldn't you? Of course

you would, because having power is more important to you than me."

"It's not more important. We can have both."

She pointed. "There it is. That's your choice. It's always been your choice, Ryan." Emma stood up.

"Emma, I'm scared. You don't know the things Venomous will do to me if you don't help me get out of this."

"Ryan, I'm done. I'm going to go live in New York. Finish high school. Maybe go to college and forget that I ever came to California. Or that I ever met you."

"So what are you saying?" Ryan asked.

"I'm saying…this is goodbye."

CHAPTER 32

After they landed in Oakland four hours later, Emma watched as Ryan was taken off the jet in handcuffs. He kept his eyes glued to the airport tarmac. His body slouched as he walked. The confidence, the energy, the swagger of the boy she knew in Montreal was gone.

Aardvark put Ryan into the van himself, then climbed inside. A member of the security detail opened the van's passenger door for Mrs. B; then her men all got in as the van drove away.

Emma wondered if that was the last time she would ever see Ryan again. If the boy had half a brain, he would cooperate with Mrs. B so she could get him out of the situation he was in. But Ryan wasn't Emma's problem anymore.

This is goodbye.

She meant those words too, even if a part of her still wanted to put a candle in the window for him.

Emma knew she had to move on.

"Are you ready, miss?" a driver asked.

The other three girls were already inside the limo that would take them to her grandma's house...for the last time.

"Yes," Emma said as she climbed in.

The four-hour time difference between New York and California meant that it was still about six o'clock in the early evening by the time the limo arrived at her grandmother's house. There was also a cargo van and two men waiting outside to help the Gems move their things out.

Sometimes Mrs. B was a little too efficient.

Emma went inside the house first. Her grandmother emerged from the doorway of blue beads and wiped the tears from her eyes as she embraced her granddaughter for a very long time.

"Please, young one, never ever do that to me again," Grandma Bernadette said. "You'll break my old heart."

"I'm sorry, Grandma." Emma heard her voice cracking. "Please don't hate me for being stupid."

"I'm only mad at you for being selfish, but I love you enough to forgive the stupid."

Emma laughed.

Grandma touched Emma's face, then turned her attention towards the others. "Didn't know the plan, but I made dinner anyway if anyone is hungry."

Miyuki bowed to her. "Thank you for your kind offer. However, we had dinner on the flight."

"We still could have some tea," Nadia said. "I think we have some biscuits left."

Olivia frowned. "Mrs. B wanted us moved in at headquarters by tonight." She glanced at Grandma Bernadette. "I'm sorry, ma'am, but I don't know how long it will take us to move out."

"I can be done in twenty minutes," Miyuki said.

"Olivia, it won't take that long," Nadia said. "We can spare it. Besides, I think Mrs. B would understand."

"Sometimes it's okay for the boss to bend the rules," Grandma Bernadette said.

"And listen to her people," Olivia added. "Right, I'll put the kettle on, then."

The five of them gathered in the kitchen. They drank tea and ate cookies. No one brought up Emma's trip. No one brought up moving. Emma didn't talk about New York. But they all talked about Thai food night. About those nights when all of them sat outside around Grandma's fire-pit that made being outside on cool nights tolerable. About Grandma's weekend culture trips when she took all of them to the opera. To art exhibitions. To the symphony. To Asian-American festivals. Native American festivals. Mexican-American festivals. Then Miyuki brought up the time at school when Emma dressed up Kayla and realized she had made the poor girl a literal clone of herself.

"Seriously, I still can't believe I did that," Emma said.

The other Gems laughed.

"The look on your face, love—that moment you realized it—was classic," Olivia said.

They talked about school. About classes. About their normal after-school activities that most teens took for granted, but for Olivia, Nadia, and Miyuki were brand new and refreshing. They would miss going to a normal school. They didn't touch on too many things they all would miss because no one wanted to spoil this moment. The final moment before goodbye.

Olivia and Nadia went upstairs to their room to pack. Emma followed Miyuki up to hers. Soon a few boxes were filled. Suitcases and duffel bags were packed. The two men took the boxes and the suitcases and the duffel bags and placed them inside the cargo van. Soon the job was done.

The three remaining Gems said their goodbyes to Grandma Bernadette, each receiving a long hug in the process. No one had dry eyes.

"Hope to see you on the telly one day, love," Olivia said as she hugged Emma.

"That means television in the Queen's English, right?" Emma asked with a smirk.

Olivia grinned. "Piss off."

"If I don't make it there, come see me on Broadway," Emma said. "I'll always have three tickets waiting for you at the box office."

"I'm hoping you star in a big science fiction movie," Nadia said. "As the hero, not the man's cute side kick."

Emma gave her a hug. "I'll tell my director to hire you as our science consultant. And I'd better find you working at NASA some day."

"I'll do my best," Nadia said.

Miyuki's sad eyes looked up. "I don't want to say it."

Emma wrapped her arms around her.

"Do you really want to do this?" Miyuki asked.

Emma closed her eyes. "I have to. I'm sorry."

"Maybe you can't contact us," Miyuki said. "But you can send me an email through my father. He will know where to send it so I will receive it."

"I'll do that."

"Please do. It would make me...happy, *hei?*"

Emma nodded. "*Hei.*"

Miyuki returned her nod as she put on a weak smile.

With that, the three Gems waved as their limo drove off with the cargo van following it.

Her grandmother sighed. "I'll miss them. What a sharp group of young women."

"Am I making a mistake?" Emma blurted out, her mind still not able to let some things go.

"Under the circumstances, I think you're making the right decision." Grandma Bernadette faced Emma with her arms folded. "However, I think you're making a huge mistake by wanting to move back to New York."

"Don't worry. Ben and Rosa will treat me like their third daughter. You know I'll be in safe hands."

"Why on earth can't you stay here and go to college in Berkeley? The University of California is one of the best schools in the country. I should know because I teach there. Not to mention you'll be paying cheaper in-state tuition as well as taking advantage of my vast knowledge of the school. I know every dean. I know every professor. Every teaching assistant. I can steer you away from all the idiots and help you get into the brilliant ones."

"Grandma—"

"Besides, you made a lot of friends over at West Berkeley High. Wouldn't it be easier to just stay?"

"Hailey's father is already setting her up for NYU, and I wanna go to NYU. They have a great film program. Plus New York is where I want to study acting."

"University of California has a film school. There are acting classes here. And Young One, Los Angeles isn't that far away. As I recall, they have plenty of actors studying acting down there."

"Grandma—"

"Your thinking doesn't make any sense to me."

"I knew it."

"Knew what?"

"I knew how difficult you would make this." Emma paused, feeling her emotions bubbling up. "I love you, Grandma, but you have to let me go sometime." Emma ran back into the house, letting the door slam shut.

CHAPTER 33

Two days later, Miyuki woke up to Olivia running her hair dryer. She rolled over on her side as she lifted her heavy eyes. Both bunk beds on the opposite wall were empty, but the cotton sheets and comforters were scrambled up, indicating they'd been slept in. Miyuki sat up and dangled her feet over the bed frame. She'd picked the top bunk and left the bottom one empty because she liked climbing things. Also, it was fun jumping off the top too.

Now living deep under California wine country, the three Gems were assigned one of the larger of the two sizes of "apartments" that were available inside Authority headquarters. It wasn't a luxury unit by any stretch of the imagination. The unit had two sets of bunk beds. A bathroom with a shower. A small living area with a couch and a chair. A television. And an old-school telephone wired to the wall. The phone had a screen that sometimes told you the extension of the person calling. It also alerted you if there was a message waiting. Miyuki was surprised that anyone still used such old things.

"Did I wake you?" Nadia asked, her cast resting on her leg scooter as she worked on her laptop. Her headscarf was gone as she wore her *Girl Scientists Rock* T-shirt.

"You didn't." Miyuki leaped off her bed and landed on her feet. "What are you doing?"

"Mr. O gave me a puzzle to solve. This super-encrypted network server some Russian hackers are using. This group keeps trying to hack into online control systems to take over public water facilities."

"What will you do if you get in?"

"Seize control of their computers, steal all their personal information so we can identify them, then fry their computers."

"That sounds mean," Miyuki said.

Nadia stopped typing. "They're trying to mess up people's drinking water. They're criminals. They need to be stopped and put in jail."

"Oh, if they're bad guys, then I guess it's okay," Miyuki said, even though she thought Nadia was a scientist at heart. Wanting to help solve future challenges that mankind faced. But maybe girl scientists had hobbies too.

"What are you up to this morning, love?" Olivia said, brushing out her large curly hair.

Miyuki shrugged. Since going to school was on temporary hold until Mrs. B could schedule a full-time tutor to take over, the three of them had plenty of time to kill.

"Mrs. B starts her interrogation of Ryan today. From what I heard, she's a master at it. Looking forward to watching her in action. Do you wanna come?"

Miyuki would've rather gone surfing. Or load up a good RPG and go on an adventure with some of her online friends. Or ride a motorcycle through the twisty hallways of the Labyrinth at ridiculously high speeds. But since she didn't have those options...

"*Hei*, as long as we have breakfast first," Miyuki said.

After the three of them had breakfast, they parted ways. Nadia rolled her leg scooter over to the "jungle" to use one of the empty green pods to work on her laptop, as well as taking advantage of the pod's fantastic sound system for music.

Miyuki followed Olivia inside the Labyrinth. They followed a series of dark blue corridors to a room with a single monitor and a few aluminum chairs scattered around. The monitor's screen showed a small room with two chairs and a table mounted to the concrete floor. To Miyuki, it reminded her of the room Volleen Woo had used to interrogate them in China.

It hadn't been a pleasant experience.

Soon a man came inside their room with a laptop. He plugged into a network connection on the wall and began typing before Mrs. B and Aardvark arrived.

"Are you here to grade my performance?" Mrs. B asked.

"We wanted to observe, ma'am," Olivia said.

"If it bothers you, we can leave," Miyuki added.

"Nonsense," Mrs. B said. "It should be quite an education."

She checked with the man with a laptop. All the equipment inside the other room was ready to go. Mrs. B told him to begin recording and have them bring in the prisoner. Five minutes later, Ryan Raymond showed up on the monitor as he was brought into the small room and sat down. He was chained to the metal table and left alone.

Mrs. B didn't take one step towards the other room. She diverted her attention to Miyuki and Olivia instead.

"Did you girls sleep well?" she asked.

Mrs. B then asked them what they had for breakfast. How they were fitting in to their new quarters. And also mentioned that Friday was make-your-own-ice-cream-sundae day in the cafeteria.

Finally she glanced at the monitor. "It's like waiting for the dentist. The growing dread. The worry. The uneasiness. I haven't stepped one foot inside that room for fifteen minutes, and Ryan's mind is already softening up his defenses." Mrs. B used her cane to get up. "Time to begin."

Aardvark opened the door into the corridor, allowing Mrs B to leave before following her out. Soon Mrs. B and Aardvark reappeared in the monitor. Mrs. B sat opposite Ryan, and Aardvark stood in a corner behind Ryan, looking menacing.

"I'll start by saying...I don't like you at all. You've caused havoc within my team, and I'd rather get rid of you once and for all. Perhaps I should give Emma that honor." Mrs. B's eyes slid to Aardvark. "Do you think Emma would enjoy pounding this boy with a baseball bat?"

Ryan lifted his chin. "Emma would never do that."

"Perhaps not," Mrs. B said. "However, her friends might like a go. They're watching us right now. Chomping at the bit to do some nasty things to you. On the plane they were so keen on the idea that I had to order them to stay away from you. But here. Now. There are no police. There is no government that's willing to step in on your behalf. It's only you. And us."

"Thanks for telling me what I already know."

"That's an excellent place to start. Tell me, what do you already know?"

"About what?" Ryan asked.

"Asset One. The sinking of the *Falcon's Claw*. How close were we in killing him?"

"About as close as you were to killing me and Emma."

"That was a calculated risk. Emma knew what I was asking from her. She accepted the risk."

"You mean your failed attempt to flip me?"

"Young man, you flatter yourself," Mrs. B said. "I believe you're a toad. An ugly, back-stabbing ego-maniac who's on the Autobahn to hell. What Emma sees in you is an enigma to us all."

"It's because Emma has more intelligence than you give her credit for."

Mrs. B hesitated. "Intelligence? My dear boy, Emma is the dumbest girl I've ever met."

Miyuki shot Olivia a look. *What was Mrs. B saying?*

Olivia shrugged.

"The girl's suicide attempt was laughable," Mrs. B continued. "Emma dropped her car in one of the shallowest inlets on the California coast. She put her wallet in the armrest storage compartment yet took out her driver's license. Why would someone committing suicide do that? She also took her small suitcase with her. Not to mention a package of dog treats for her soon-to-be-dead canine." Mrs. B chuckled. "Even Inspector Clouseau could have seen that evidence and deduced that her suicide was faked."

Miyuki was confused. Emma's car had been found in a deep cove that emptied out to the sea. It wasn't shallow at all. And Emma's grandmother hadn't found any missing dog treats. However, the statements about the suitcase and the driver's license were true. Emma did make a couple of mistakes, but no one put it all together until Emma called her grandmother.

"What is she doing?" Miyuki asked. "Emma isn't stupid."

"It's a tactic." Olivia grinned. "Let's see how Ryan reacts."

"Emma was a disaster," Mrs. B said. "The girl thought her acting skills and her good looks would make her a great spy. She was lazy. Refused to work hard. Didn't master any of the trade-crafts. Emma was the weakest spy operative I've ever seen in my twenty plus years in this business. However, she did manage to play you like a helpless marionette. Making you dance around the world like a love-sick little dog only because she smiled at you once."

Mrs. B paused. "I suppose you and Emma both have some things in common. Two rich kids who were handed the keys to their fathers' golden kingdoms. Two rich kids who never saw their parents come home tired after working an overnight shift at a factory or a twelve-hour shift at a hospital. You two don't know what the word struggle means, do you?"

Ryan focused on a crack in the wall.

"My father worked in a British Leyland auto factory. It wore him down to a nub," Mrs. B said. "My mother worked in a shop part-time. We knew what the words 'struggle to make ends meet' actually meant." She glanced at him. "And that's what makes me sick about the super rich. They look down on common people. Think they're all expendable. That's what your father thought, wasn't it?"

Ryan shot her a look. "Don't go there."

"Your father planned to starve out millions of people…so he could make even more money. That's appalling."

"I'm nothing like my father."

"Your father collaborated with Venomous to help with his grand financial scheme. And then you used Venomous to betray him. Why did you do that?"

Ryan didn't answer.

"Did you betray your father because he was doing something morally wrong?" Mrs. B asked. "No. You betrayed your father because if he ever died, you wouldn't receive daddy's financial empire. Isn't that right?"

Ryan's gaze stuck to the ground.

"You did it for selfish reasons. Envy. Spite. You wanted that money. As the only son, the Raymond Foods empire was yours by birthright. Your father cut you off from your golden ticket. So you had to do something. So you took advantage of a sweet and vulnerable young heiress and tried to seduce her into not only joining Venomous but to fall in love with you. That way, you could steal Emma's financial trust and set yourself up for life."

"That's ridiculous."

"My dear boy, face the truth. Emma is naive enough to trust your manipulative advances. But in hindsight, you're the truly pathetic one. Only a pathetic little boy would go to such lengths to blind himself to the fact…that he's daddy's biggest disappointment."

Ryan jumped up as the metal chain around his hand cuffs snapped him back into his seat. His eyes burned. "My father's the pathetic one. He hung himself like a coward. Unable to face his crimes like a man. Fuck him. I never needed his money. I don't need Emma's money. I don't need anyone's charity."

Miyuki took a step back. The anger was so intense that even through the monitor it was too intense to watch.

"Blimey, she's cracked him wide open," Olivia said. "I almost feel sorry for the bloke."

Mrs. B waited calmly. Her face cold. Unreadable.

Tears squeezed out from the corners of Ryan's eyes, but he held on tight to his emotions. No crying. No bawling. He stared down Mrs. B, trying his best not to break. However, his body quivered ever so slightly, as if it wouldn't take much to tip him over.

Mrs. B used her cane to stand. "That's all for today. We'll continue—"

The lights inside their interrogation room went all red.

Miyuki noticed it wasn't only the interrogation room. Their room lights were now red also. The phone on the wall rang. The man with the laptop picked it up. By then, Mrs. B and Aardvark were back inside the observation room.

"What's going on?" Miyuki asked.

The man handed the phone to Mrs. B.

"Do you know what's going on?" Miyuki asked Olivia.

Her friend shook her head and looked just as concerned.

"How many men?" Mrs. B asked as she listened to the phone. Her face looked worried. "How did they get through our defense perimeters so quickly?" As she listened, the woman closed her eyes. "I see. Have all the automatic security protocols been activated?" Mrs. B asked. "Right. Yes, I don't see we have much of a choice now. Order all divisions to initiate scramble alerts. Inform the other stations that we are going dark."

"Ma'am?" Olivia asked.

Mrs. B turned to Aardvark. "Mr. O reports that we have a major security breach. Approximately two hundred heavily armed men have broken through all four defense perimeters."

Aardvark tilted his head.

"Yes, all four. And I don't understand how that happened either. I've ordered the entire complex to evacuate. Meanwhile, let's head to my office so I can activate the SDM."

"What's SDM?" Miyuki asked.

Mrs. B frowned. "The self-destruct system for the base."

CHAPTER 34

Miyuki couldn't believe her eyes. She'd never seen the Labyrinth crowded with this many people in the hallways. Everyone was moving. Some had weapons; others carried either laptops or other items through the once dark blue corridors that were now flashing red because of the security breach and the general scramble order. But no one was running. There was an urgency to move but no cause for panic.

"Ruby!" Olivia yelled as she came back and pulled her around a blind corner.

"Sorry, Olivia. I was distracted," Miyuki said.

"You've got to keep up. And don't forget to use our code names when we're inside headquarters."

Miyuki thought observing that rule in the current circumstances was ridiculous. They had more important things to worry about, like making sure Mrs. B got to her office so she could activate the self-destruct system and literally bury all their secrets.

Aardvark cut a path through the corridor using his large body as Mrs. B, Olivia, and Miyuki trailed him. After turning a few more corners, and letting a squad of security officers pass them, the group reached Mrs. B's office.

She swiped her ID card, and the air escaped from the door as the seal unlocked and the door opened. Mrs. B used her cane to hurry inside as the others followed. The phone on her desk was ringing. But Mrs. B ignored it as she sat down next to her laptop. "Emerald, answer my phone, please." The woman began typing on her laptop as Aardvark stood over her.

"Mrs. B's office," Olivia answered, then listened. "It's Mr. O, ma'am. He's asking about the SDM system."

"Tell him I'm on it," Mrs. B said.

"She's on it, sir."

Mrs. B sighed and closed her eyes. "The system is off-line. I don't have access to it. Ask Mr. O if he has access from his division."

Olivia repeated her request. She shook her head. "He has no access either. Plus Mr. O says he must abandon the upstairs offices." Olivia pulled the phone from her ear, like someone blasted a horn through it. "I hear gunfire, ma'am." Olivia cautiously put the phone back to her ear. "The line is dead now."

Try the command systems in each of the divisions, Aardvark's phone said as he finished typing the text.

"Good idea." Mrs. B focused on her laptop.

The phone on the wall flashed as a general announcement went out through the speaker...

General Scramble Order still in effect. TA division is now under code scarlet. TA division is now under code scarlet. The following sections are currently under code scarlet...

Miyuki listened to the automated announcement. There were a lot of areas of headquarters that were now compromised by a security breach.

"Do you have access yet, ma'am?" Olivia asked. The poor girl was trying to project an image of calm, but Miyuki could tell she was nervous.

"It's no good, I'm afraid. The SDM system is not accepting any computer commands, which I find strange since we purposely designed the system so the command programs can't be accessed remotely."

Unless we have a traitor among us, Aardvark's phone said.

Olivia flashed Miyuki a worried look.

"That's a distinct possibility, Aardvark."

"If you can't access the system, what should we do now?" Olivia asked.

"There's a way to manually activate the SDM system. Two hidden keypads." Mrs. B used her cane to stand up. "Follow me."

The four of them emerged back into the corridors of the Labyrinth. The red lights still flashed on and off as more automated announcements were made over the speakers. More areas under code scarlet. Miyuki noticed the traffic in the corridors was much lighter as more people escaped out of the underground complex. This allowed the four of them to make good progress through the twists and turns of the Labyrinth's dizzy system of corridors.

Soon they reached the entrance that connected the Labyrinth to the large open atrium that connected most of the areas of the headquarters together.

Suddenly, a bullet ricocheted off a wall near Mrs. B.

Aardvark yanked her back inside the entrance as Olivia and Miyuki crouched down.

A torrent of automatic weapons fire sprayed down on the floor of the atrium. Three Authority people hid behind toppled pieces of large furniture. Two men and one woman. They tried their best to return fire on those upstairs, but they only had two pistols and one rifle.

Miyuki inched out slowly, doing her best to keep close to the outer wall next to the entrance. She took a peek upstairs.

The glass walls of the TA division were all shattered. Many of the desks and chairs were overturned and being used as cover by at least twenty heavily armed men wearing black. With their commanding position upstairs, they dominated the atrium.

Miyuki withdrew.

"What do you see?" Mrs. B said.

"Twenty bad dudes upstairs. Armed to the teeth. They can see all over the atrium."

"That's most inconvenient," Mrs. B said. "One of the panels is inside the relaxation area."

Miyuki glanced across the atrium. On the far side was the entrance to the relaxation area. The entire area was exposed to— right then, a burst of gunfire took out one of the men hiding behind the furniture. He died before he hit the ground.

Miyuki covered her mouth in horror.

The woman behind the furniture pointed out Mrs. B to the man with the rifle. He nodded as they both ran towards the Labyrinth's entrance.

Another burst of gunfire. The last man dropped to the floor with a bullet in his back as his rifle slid along the tiles. The woman made it over to them, and she caught her breath.

"What's your situation?" Mrs. B asked.

The woman was shaking a little, but she swallowed and composed herself. "All the divisions have scrambled. We delayed the intruders inside the TA division as long as we could...but we had to retreat downstairs. That did give a lot of people time to escape. However, we're getting reports that most of the exits have been cut off by the intruders. Although, the wine barrel exit is still open, but those men above us are blocking us from that exit. I'm afraid we're trapped down here, ma'am."

"Any word from Mr. O?"

"I haven't heard," the woman said. "The gunfire was pretty intense. He still might be up there hiding out somewhere, but I don't know." She paused. "We lost a lot of people in our division."

Mrs. B reached out and laid her hand on the woman's arm. "I understand."

"What are your orders?" the woman asked.

Mrs. B gazed across the atrium. There were already a few dead bodies sprawled across the floor tiles. The thought of dashing across the atrium while people rained bullets down upon you didn't much appeal to Miyuki at all. The idea was too crazy. Even for her.

"I can't stress this enough," Mrs. B said. "It's vital…that one of us gets across to the relaxation room, finds the hidden keypad, and puts in the proper code to activate the SDM system. If we allow these intruders to gain access to our secrets inside the Labyrinth… it will compromise our entire organization. We can't allow that to happen. Does everyone understand?"

Everyone nodded.

Mrs. B then had them memorize the six-digit code. "The keypad is hidden under an electrical outlet in the northwest corner of the room. Is everyone clear on that?"

Another round of nods.

"Look out!" The woman with the pistol brought it up to a firing position as two armed intruders were coming down the steps.

She fired two rounds into the first man. The second returned fire, spraying the walls near the Labyrinth's entrance with more bullets before retreating upstairs.

"Scouting party," Mrs. B said. "Soon they'll be down here in force."

"I volunteer to run across, ma'am," Olivia said. "Let me go first."

"What are you doing?" Miyuki asked.

"Someone has to do it."

"I'll go second," the woman with the gun said.

"I appreciate the brave offers," Mrs. B said. "However, I have no stomach for a D-Day assault on the beaches of France approach to this. On the contrary, we only need a good distraction." Mrs. B brought up her wooden cane. She twisted the handle a couple of clicks, unleashing a secret compartment that popped open as springs clicked a small rocket-propelled grenade into place.

Miyuki thought it was the most awesome gizmo she ever saw.

Mrs. B pointed at the floor. "Emerald, try to retrieve that rifle without getting shot, please."

Olivia bent down and paused. She then scrambled forward, grabbed the end of the rifle, and pulled it back as bullets pelted the floor around her. Olivia took in a deep breath, then checked the rifle and its magazine. "I have a few rounds left."

"Excellent," Mrs. B said. "When I give the word, please give me covering fire. Empty your magazine if you must. Just give me time to fire this upstairs."

"Should I fire that for you?" Miyuki asked.

"Ruby, are you implying that I'm too old to use my own cane?"

Miyuki bowed. "No, I wasn't. My apologies."

"Ladies, if you please."

The woman with the pistol glanced at Olivia, who nodded. They both stepped out and fired upstairs, peppering it with bullets.

Mrs. B moved out behind Olivia. Aardvark stepped out in the open too, to give the men a bigger target than a small old lady. Mrs. B aimed her cane upstairs with the coolness of a sharpshooter, as if too old to worry about such things as dying. She fired the grenade, and it blasted through a plate of cracked glass. Then there was an explosion as white smoke enveloped the upstairs office area.

"We should hurry," Mrs. B said as she led the way across the atrium.

Miyuki and Olivia followed her. As did Aardvark, who was holding his shoulder as he ran behind them. The woman with the pistol guarded their rear.

As Mrs. B reached the entrance to the relaxation room, Miyuki heard gunfire behind them. She whipped around to see the woman firing a round into one intruder who had appeared from the stairs. A second intruder fired back and hit the woman, who fell down.

On impulse, Miyuki ran back into the atrium to help her. She knelt beside the woman and felt her pulse.

The woman was dead.

The smoke from Mrs. B's grenade had rolled down into the atrium itself, creating a gray haze around the stairs.

"Ruby!" Olivia called out from behind the entrance to the relaxation room.

Miyuki now realized she was in the middle of the atrium. Through the smoke, the outlines of heavily armed intruders were twisting down the staircase. Soon they would reach the floor of the atrium.

Miyuki stood up, ready to charge into them, hoping she could at least give Mrs. B enough time to get to the keypad.

But Bridget O'Malley stumbled from the smoke first, wearing a cat-suit with thin pieces of Kevlar over her chest. The girl was coughing as she held a gun in her hand.

Miyuki charged. Running at full speed, she jumped into the air and twisted her pelvis to bring her foot around for one sweeping kick against Bridget's arm, throwing her gun clear across the floor.

Bridget fell over, still trying to recover from the smoke and the surprise attack.

Miyuki was at the base of the stairs. There was no time to think.

The Venomous goons came at her one by one. As soon as they emerged from the smoke, Miyuki attacked. A bicycle kick here. A palm strike there. Even a kick in the coconuts if she could manage it. Those men collapsed in pain at the base of the stairs. The smoke caused confusion as men were rushing forward, even trampling over their fallen comrades to get at whatever was attacking them downstairs. Soon, this caused a bottleneck at the base of the stairs as panic was setting in. Rifles began firing randomly, even though the goons couldn't quite see what they were firing at.

After a few minutes of non-stop fighting, Miyuki was getting tired. She backed away from the stairs and realized the Venomous goons were distracted quite enough without her help.

She was quite pleased with herself as Miyuki retreated into the relaxation room. But that positive attitude took a nose-dive.

In one corner of the room, Olivia and Sophia O'Malley were trading kicks and other nasty hits to each other in a fierce fight.

In another corner, two Venomous goons armed with knives were closing in on Mrs. B.

The final blow was a middle-aged woman, wearing the same Kevlar cat-suit as Sophia and Bridget...who did a Bruce Lee round-house kick into Aardvark, sending the large man against a salt water fish tank, which shattered under his weight and dumped its contents all over the floor.

This middle-aged woman had green eyes, short dark hair, and a brownish shade to her skin that was similar to Nadia's. She was in top physical shape and held herself like a force to be reckoned with.

The woman noted Miyuki's presence and smiled. "*Kon'nichiwa. And what challenges do you offer me?*"

Her Japanese was as flawless as her swift movements.

The woman was on Miyuki in seconds.

CHAPTER 35

Inside the relaxation room, Miyuki's heart was pumping like a piston. She was forced to retreat as the middle-aged woman attacked with a series of palm, elbow, and knee strikes that seemed to come at her all at once. Miyuki did her best to block them. However, the skill and accuracy of this woman's attacks told Miyuki she was dealing with a master. Miyuki continued to retreat, almost stepping out of the room as the woman kept up her offensive.

Miyuki ducked under the woman's leg as it tried to knock her out. Miyuki tried to counter with a kick to the woman's side, but her opponent's body wasn't there. The older woman was a blur, already anticipating her kick as she twisted her body out of the—

An elbow nailed Miyuki in the chin, throwing her head to the side as the woman kicked her hard in the back, throwing her to the floor.

When the older woman smiled, Miyuki noticed her dark orange lipstick. None of it was smeared. Miyuki found that strange, like the woman put on makeup so she would look good in a fight. The woman came at her again. Miyuki was about to try a crazy somersault to try to surprise the woman. But a soaking-wet Aardvark unleashed his own surprise.

The woman sensed he was behind her, so she twisted around for a kick...but he grabbed her leg and used her momentum to slam her body to the floor. The woman recovered quickly, jumping off the floor and kicking Aardvark in the face. The large man shook it off and showed his own moves as the two of them fought.

Miyuki was happy to let Aardvark have a go with her. She scanned the room to see who needed help.

Sophia kicked Olivia to the floor.

Miyuki came from behind and kicked Sophia to the floor,

knocking the wind out of her.

"Thanks, love," Olivia said, panting as she stood back up.

"Need more help?" Miyuki asked.

"Oy, Mrs. B!" Olivia pointed.

Miyuki whipped her head around to see Mrs. B fighting off two Venomous goons with her wooden cane. What amazed Miyuki was...Mrs. B standing in a classic fencing stance as she waved her cane around like an expert swordsman. Her legs seemed to be working just fine.

One goon tried to stab Mrs. B, and she whacked him in the arm. She was holding them off, but that was all.

Miyuki and Olivia rushed over and attacked the men, knocking out their knives before knocking out their heads.

"Your assistance is much appreciated," Mrs. B said before turning her attention to the wall. And the outlet with the SDM keypad behind it.

A gunshot spun Miyuki around. She saw Aardvark grimace and fall to his knees as he slumped to the floor.

Bridget lowered her pistol, with a hint of surprise on her face. But her finger was on the trigger.

Miyuki ran over to Aardvark and turned him over. He was bleeding from his gut. But his eyes blinked. He was still breathing, but in discomfort. The man wasn't dead. Yet.

"That wasn't necessary." The older woman he was fighting wiped her mouth, her orange lipstick now smeared with blood. "I was winning that fight."

"Sorry, Asset Twelve," Bridget stammered, her normal confidence a little rattled. "I thought he was going to hurt you."

"He was a worthy opponent," the woman called Asset Twelve said. "He should die with respect."

Bridget saw something that caused her to run over to Mrs. B. The girl touched the pistol to her head. "Don't move or I'll shoot ya too."

Mrs. B froze. The outlet door on the wall was open, revealing the SDM keypad.

Miyuki wondered if she was able to put in the code.

Olivia took a few steps towards Bridget.

Miyuki got ready to help her. But she didn't see Sophia behind her with a rock from the busted aquarium.

The blow knocked Miyuki out completely.

CHAPTER 36

Miyuki shook off the drowsiness as her mind woke back up. The back of her head throbbed, a not so subtle reminder that someone had knocked her out cold. Miyuki tried moving her arms, then realized her hands were bound behind her back. As she got her bearings, Miyuki realized they were in the middle of the central atrium. The smoke was gone. She sat on the cold, tiled floor along with many Authority personnel who had been captured in the attack.

Mrs. B and Olivia were sitting on either side of her. Next to Mrs. B was Lioness and then there was Mr. O, an Indian man in his mid-forties who was the head of the TA division. Like hers, all of the prisoners had their wrists tied in back with plastic zip ties.

About twenty feet away was Aardvark. Still on his back. Still bleeding from his gut. His broken nose slowly oozed blood as well. There were other bodies strewn all over the tiles of the atrium, mostly Authority personnel who fought back to buy time for everyone to evacuate.

"Is Aardvark still alive?" Miyuki asked in a soft voice.

"I do believe so," Mrs. B said. "However, he needs serious medical attention."

"Hey, Bridget?" Olivia called out.

"No talking!" a Venomous goon shouted, gripping his assault rifle. There were a couple of dozen of these heavily armed men watching over them.

Bridget turned her head, then cautiously moved over to Olivia with her hand resting on the grip of her holstered pistol. "Yeah, nah. We're not gonna let ya muppets go. Do ya have another question?"

"Our friend over there. The one you shot. He still needs a doctor," Olivia said.

Bridget glanced at him. "Wasn't my fault. He was attacking a woman."

"They were fighting, Bridget. And it wasn't like she was a helpless puppy. She broke his nose and a rib, then shoved him into a glass fish tank."

"Asset Twelve is one of the best," Bridget said. "She trained me and Sophia. I wouldn't want to fight her."

"Can you do your former roommate a solid and find someone to treat our friend, please?" Olivia asked.

Bridget laughed. "And what have ya done for me lately?"

"Are you joking? We saved you and your sister from dying, remember? We could've left you unconscious on your boss's sinking ship, but we didn't, did we?"

"And she didn't want to help you at first either," Miyuki said. "We had to talk her into it."

Olivia shot her a look.

"But it didn't take that long," Miyuki added.

"So…you're sayin' I owe ya one, darling?" Bridget asked.

Mrs. B stepped in. "Young lady, you owe that man you shot some medical attention. That's if you have any humanity left inside that twisted mind of yours."

The woman with short dark hair and orange lipstick approached them. "Is there a problem here?"

"No, Asset Twelve," Bridget answered. "Well, they're worried about their wounded chum over there. They want us to do something to help 'im."

Asset Twelve scanned Mrs. B's eyes as both women sized each other up.

"Are you making this request?" Asset Twelve asked.

Mrs. B waited a moment. "I am."

"The man was a great opponent. He should have died by my hands. Not shot like a common soldier." Asset Twelve fired a look at Bridget, who looked away. "Out of respect to a fellow warrior, I'll allow a doctor to treat him."

"Thank you."

Asset Twelve turned to Bridget. "See if Dr. Knox is in Asset One's helicopter. If so, bring him down here."

"Yes, ma'am," Bridget said before disappearing upstairs.

Asset Twelve moved away with Sophia and a Venomous goon trailing her.

Finally left with some space, Mrs. B leaned towards Lioness and Mr. O. "What the hell happened? All four of our security perimeters failed? In such a short period of time. That's impossible."

Lioness scanned the room before talking. "Before he was killed, Wombat alerted me that the attack was too well coordinated. Their men knew exactly where to hit us. Every checkpoint. Every manned defense point that was part of the level one defense perimeter."

"I would surmise," Mr. O whispered, "they were able to disable both our outside power connections and our internal power generators to shut down the level two perimeter. However, our battery power was still online."

"Then how on earth did they get through the two remaining levels?" Mrs. B asked.

"I don't know how. They're self-contained systems," Mr. O said, looking around. "One can't disable them from the outside."

"Those automated defense pods should have kept any intruder busy for hours at least."

"Agreed," Mr. O said. "And the blast doors to seal us from the outside failed to operate as well."

Mrs. B sighed. "They must have gained access to those systems somehow."

Another large platoon of armed Venomous goons emerged from the upstairs and came down the long circular staircase. Leading the way was Asset One himself, wearing dark sunglasses with thick white frames. His extra-long blond hair hung straight down each side. The man's square face contained a slight grin.

His falcon, Sunchaser, swooped into the large atrium, happy to find such an open space to stretch its wings.

"What a glorious day," Asset One said. "Everything went well...more so than I could have ever imagined."

"What's our operational status?" Asset Twelve asked.

"We have secured all the exits. Their headquarters...is ours."

Another squad of armed Venomous goons emerged from the entrance to the Labyrinth with a freed Ryan. Bridget ran over and gave him a hug. Ryan acted more embarrassed than grateful.

"Ah, our family...is now complete," Asset One said. "I see that you have...prisoners, Asset Twelve." The man with long white hair grinned with delight as he walked along the line of people sitting on the ground and stopped. "Why, the infamous Mrs. B. The woman who tried to have me killed. Now she has been captured...inside her own headquarters. That amuses me." He looked around. "For years, I've dreamed of this moment. The moment of time...when I stood on the ground of my enemy. Capturing this jewel on top of the Authority's crown...a major headquarters with all of its secrets...is priceless."

Asset One turned. "Think of it, Asset Twelve...now we can compromise their entire spy network. Perhaps their information will compromise...the world's largest intelligence organizations as well."

"Or have them pay us billions to keep their secrets quiet," Asset Twelve added. "Extortion at the highest level."

"Indeed. Mrs. B and her friends...have given us so many lovely presents to put under our company Christmas tree."

"You won't be opening any of my presents," Mrs. B said. "You'll never gain access to the network drives. They run through a separate and isolated security system with anti-tampering devices. Any attempt to access them inappropriately and without proper authentication...will trigger security protocols. The drives will be magnetically erased, and fire systems will melt down the drives to goo."

"Clever. Ruthlessly clever. I would expect that from an enemy...of your caliber, Mrs. B. Therefore, to make our poker game fair, I had to bring an ace up my sleeve." Asset One turned his attention to Lioness. "Remove her bindings. Lioness has much more work to do."

A Venomous goon snapped off the bindings holding Lioness's hands together. The goon then helped the woman to her feet as she rubbed her sore wrists.

"Your work so far has been invaluable. Do you know how to remove...these security protocols as well?"

Miyuki couldn't believe it. Everyone along the floor was in shock. Lioness must have been the one who helped Venomous get through all the base's defense systems.

Mrs. B's seething eyes burned into Lioness. So much so that the Russian woman couldn't even look in her direction.

"Yes, I know how," Lioness said, without emotion.

"Excellent. You're beginning to drift...over to my good side," Asset One said. "I reward those who stay on my good side."

Asset Twelve and some Venomous goons escorted Lioness deep into the Labyrinth.

Mrs. B and Mr. O exchanged looks. They were worried.

About twenty minutes later, Asset Twelve came back to the atrium and informed Asset One that the security protocols for the servers were now disabled.

"Excellent, have our portable servers moved inside... immediately. We shall drain their computer servers for every kilobyte...of information."

A service elevator went into action as a squad of Venomous goons brought down rolling carts filled with portable servers. Each cart had a laptop attached to manage those particular servers as well as a Venomous tech guy trailing it. Miyuki was amazed at how organized it all was.

Someone stood in front of her.

It was Ryan. "Do you know where Emma is?"

"Leave that poor girl alone," Mrs. B said. "She's done with you."

"I wasn't talking to you." Ryan focused on Miyuki again. "Did our men capture her?"

"She's no longer one of us. She quit," Miyuki said. "Please let her go, Ryan. If you truly care about her, you'll let her walk away."

Ryan was quiet for a moment.

"Don't torment her like this," Miyuki added. "Emma is my friend. I beg you...please forget her."

Bridget then approached Ryan. "The girl's onto it. You should listen. Miss America was never gonna be a reality for ya, Ryan, darling." She came up from behind and embraced Ryan, sitting her chin on his shoulder. "But I'm real. And I'm spot on when it comes to making decisions. When I see something I want...I grab it." Bridget hovered near his ear. "Straight up, you're just like me, you beauty. You know it. I know it. Together, we'd be invincible." Bridget slipped herself in front of him. "But don't take too long. I don't cry over boys." She patted him on the cheek before walking away.

Miyuki waited until Bridget was out of earshot. "I would stay away from her too."

Ryan smirked. "Thanks." The boy drifted away, choosing to be on the far end of the atrium from Bridget.

Olivia got Miyuki's attention. Mrs. B leaned forward...

"Ruby, Emerald, that panel I was trying to access in the relaxation area...if you put in the code, it will manually trigger the self-destruct system for the base. Promise me, if you get the opportunity, activate the system. We must protect our secrets at all costs."

"What's the code, ma'am?" Olivia asked.

While Mrs. B gave them each the code, a large crate was brought down in the service elevator. Miyuki noticed it because it looked completely different from all the racks of computer servers that had been rolling past them. The Venomous goons placed this crate in the middle of the large atrium.

Curious, Ryan moved over to the crate. "What's that?"

Asset One drifted over to him. "My final present to the Authority. A send-off present...if you will." Asset One waved his arms. "Come around, my children."

Asset Twelve and Sophia joined him with a handful of Venomous goons who were curious as well.

"Asset One-three-zero, please, come join us."

Bridget left the doctor who was treating Aardvark's injuries. Once she joined the group, Asset One ordered his men to open up the crate. As the sides were taken away, what remained was an aluminum device about as big as a small washer. It had wires going everywhere and a timer. To Miyuki it looked like a—

"Is that a bomb?" Sophia asked. Her mouth hung open in amazement.

"It's more...than a simple bomb, my dear," Asset One said.

"Ah, the nuclear warhead," Asset Twelve said. "The one you've been saving for a special occasion."

"Can you think of a more...special occasion than this?" Asset One asked.

"What are you doing?" Lioness asked, cutting into the group. "You said nothing about using a nuclear bomb."

"That was on a...need-to-know basis, my dear. Don't worry, you can come with us. You've earned your family's freedom."

"Why do we need to use this?" Ryan asked. "It wouldn't take that much C-4 explosives to bury this place."

Asset One put his arm around Ryan. "You fail to see...the big picture. A low-level nuclear blast that kills millions...is traced to a secret Authority base. We then leak some of their secret information to the world. The people of the world…will be terrified of them. It will cripple the Authority's power. All their allies around the world will abandon them. The Authority will then be labeled…as a terrorist organization. Every government will hunt down their operatives. And they'll find them using our leaked information. It's the perfect plan."

Lioness backed away from her conspirators, her mind preoccupied.

Miyuki hoped she felt regret. Because for whatever reason, Lioness had helped Venomous plant a nuclear bomb only fifteen miles away from over seven million people.

CHAPTER 37

Inside the atrium, Ryan watched Asset One's technicians as they switched on the bomb's arming system. The series of wires and cables that were housed inside the bomb's aluminum casing didn't make any sense to Ryan. One of the techs mentioned an anti-tampering device that would trigger the bomb in case someone tried to disarm it. The tech sounded like they knew what they were doing. As soon as Asset One gave the order, the nuclear device would be armed, and from what he gathered from the techs, it would then be only a matter of time before the bomb would detonate.

There was no doubt that Asset One had an evacuation plan for his people. They would be free and clear long before the bomb would go off. However, the millions living around the bay area wouldn't be so lucky. Ryan remembered those old videos he saw on Utube. The nuclear test films from the 1950s. The bomb blasts that turned the Nevada desert bright orange. The radius of the blast slamming into buildings and cars, blowing them into bits like they were Legos. The images of Hiroshima and Nagasaki in Japan after the US dropped two atomic bombs. The cities had been basically flattened. Wiped from existence. San Francisco, Oakland, and every place surrounding them would surely be obliterated.

Was Emma still here in town? If she was, she'd be with her grandmother.

Emma was in danger.

Asset One wanted her dead, so there was no way he would allow Ryan to take the girl with them to safety. Even if Ryan slipped out to save her, Asset One would hunt him down and kill both of them. Right now, the man seemed to have forgiven him for his past mistakes. And Ryan planned to keep it that way. So what would he do? Let Emma die to protect himself? Ryan couldn't bring himself to do that. There had to be a way to warn Emma without getting himself into trouble.

Why don't you just call her?

Yes, it was as easy as that. Well, he needed a phone first, one that would have the phone number to Emma's grandmother programmed inside since Emma's phone had suddenly gone out of service after her "suicide."

Ryan quizzed one of the guards, wanting to know if the prisoners had been searched.

"Of course, sir," the guard answered.

"Where are the items you confiscated?"

Ryan followed the guard up the spiral staircase. Among the shattered glass and wreckage of the previous morning's fight, there was a table containing phones, knives, guns, radios, and other contraband the guards felt too dangerous to leave with the prisoners.

"The two girls next to Mrs. B. Did you find anything on them?"

The guard searched the table. "Yes, I remember searching them. This right here. Two phones and some cosmetics. Asset Twelve told us their cosmetics were possibly weapons—if you believe that."

Ryan picked up both phones. One was purple and had glitter-like stones all over it with some Japanese anime stickers. The other phone was plain white. Ryan tried the white one first. But the screen was locked. He didn't know the password. Normally, he would go to the girls and threaten them to open up their phone. But causing a scene like that downstairs would draw Asset One's attention to what he was trying to do.

Ryan tried the purple phone. When he swiped his thumb across the face, the menu opened. There was no screen lock. Ryan went into the contacts menu and raced through the entries.

Emma's Grandmother

Jackpot. This phone must belong to Ruby, the Japanese girl.

Wait a minute...two girls? If Emma wasn't with the Gems anymore, that meant there were only three girls left, right? Then where was the third girl?

Ruby and Emerald were downstairs.

What was her name? The girl in the wheelchair who kidnapped him at the airport?

Sapphire.

Where was she?

"Is there something wrong, sir?" the guard asked.

The screen flickered off, so Ryan woke it up again and noticed the phone only had a fifteen percent charge left. If he wanted to warn Emma…

"I'll see to it when I return. Show me the quickest way outside."

The guard took him to an elevator, which opened up. As they stepped inside…

"Watch your step." The guard pointed at a pool of blood on the floor of the elevator. A reminder of the attack and the real humans who died defending the base. The elevator doors closed.

When they opened, Ryan saw the beautiful rolling hills of Napa Valley stretched out before him. As he stepped out of the elevator, the ground was soft and had grass. He turned and saw a massive tree, its trunk hollowed out to hide the elevator. It was the only tree on this one hill, making it an ideal spot to see around the valley.

The guard pointed at a hidden button on the trunk. "When you're ready to come back down, sir." The doors closed and disappeared inside the tree.

Ryan was alone. A warm breeze tickled his neck as he scanned the horizon. He could see wineries all over the place, their fields littered with vines and grapes as outdoor water systems kept them moist and growing. After today, it all would be ruined.

He dialed the phone number.

"Hello, Miyuki?" an older woman answered. "Thought Laura said you wouldn't be calling us anymore."

"Is this Emma's grandmother?" Ryan asked.

The voice on the other end paused. "Who wants to know?"

"My name is Ryan, and I'm a friend of Emma's."

"From school?"

"Yes, we're in chemistry together." Ryan wasn't sure Emma was taking chemistry, but he went with it.

Emma's grandmother told him to wait. Soon he heard Emma's lovely voice.

"Hello?"

"Emma?"

There was a long silence. Then a sigh.

"Oh my God, Ryan. Please leave me alone!" Emma said, almost shouting. "Did I not get through to you on the plane? Seriously… dude…we're done."

"Emma—"

"I'm ending the call now."

"Emma, don't. There's a bomb."

"A what?"

"A nuclear bomb."

Ryan told Emma about Asset One capturing Authority headquarters. About holding all her friends prisoner. And how Asset One planned to out the Authority with a bang. "As soon as he's done stealing all the data from the Authority servers, he's going to set the bomb and leave. Emma, you and your grandmother are in danger."

"Oh my God, why don't you stop them, Ryan? This is horrific. Evil. How can you let this happen?"

"Asset One won't listen to me."

"Forget about him," Emma said. "Steal the bomb and lock it up somewhere so they can't arm it."

"You don't understand. Asset One has a small army here. I can't fight them all—look, you're wasting time. Please, you and your grandmother need to pack up and hit the road right now. You could still make it to Nevada if you hurry. You should be safe if you're that far away from the blast."

"Who is going...to Nevada?"

Ryan turned around.

The tree elevator was open. Asset One and four armed guards stood there. One of the guards was the one who escorted him up here. He must have told someone. And now Asset One had heard everything.

"You're speaking with Emma again...isn't that right?"

Ryan didn't answer.

"I'm disappointed, Asset Ninety-five. You are smart. Ambitious. Useful. Effective in generating revenue for us. I brushed aside your weaknesses toward Emma because...you are young. And Emma's financial empire could have been useful to us. I would have even allowed you to marry her...as long as Venomous had an equal partnership in that union."

A shadow passed over Ryan. Sunchaser was in the air, circling above him, his deadly modified talons glinting in the sunshine.

Asset One continued. "However...you failed to turn Emma. You failed to capture her. You failed to kill her. So much failure. You know this organization...does not tolerate failure. It also does not tolerate...weakness. Especially weaknesses towards our enemies. I'm afraid that your usefulness...has ended."

The four guards pointed their assault rifles at Ryan.

"Ryan, what's going on? What's happening?" Emma's voice pleaded from the phone.

He placed the phone back to his ear. "Listen to me, Emma. I love you. I'll always love you for the rest of my life."

Ryan braced for the bullets and the waves of pain he was sure would follow.

But Asset One motioned the men to lower their weapons. "That would be...too humane."

Asset One looked towards the sky as Sunchaser glided over the wind.

He yelled some phrases in Arabic.

Sunchaser did an abrupt turn and dived straight at Ryan, ripping its special claws across the back of his neck. Ryan heard himself yelp but held on to his emotions. The wound stung, but he could take it.

The falcon came at him again. Ryan used his arms to protect his head as the talons tore across his arms. Ryan grunted, but he swallowed the pain as he looked around for cover. Somewhere he could hide from the falcon.

But the hill was empty. The only such cover was under the elevator tree, which the four armed guards were now protecting.

The falcon dived. Ryan protected his head again, but instead of hitting him in the arms, the falcon circled near the ground and hit him across the stomach, ripping his shirt apart. The level of the bird's training was impressive. Asset One must have spent months perfecting the bird's killing technique.

Focus, Ryan. What else can you do?

Maybe he could make it to some faraway shelter before Sunchaser could do any serious damage.

"Say something! Ryan, you sound like you're in pain. What's going on?" Emma asked, her voice frantic and worried.

Ryan gripped the phone and stumbled a few feet away from the tree.

Sunchaser attacked, this time across his back. The falcon's strike was hard enough to push him over.

No, it wasn't the strike that did it. Ryan was feeling weaker. The strength was leaving his body. The back of his neck burned. His left arm burned.

Ryan was confused. He wasn't gushing blood. Why was he losing so much—

The falcon's special talons must contain some type of poison. It must be in his system. The burning pain was spreading. Soon the threshold of pain would be too much for him to endure. Something Asset One obviously intended.

It was hopeless.

This was how he would die.

Ryan gripped the phone. "Emma..."

"Oh my God, what's going on? Are they torturing—"

"Emma...please tell my mom...that I faced death like a man. That I didn't give up like my father did. That I lived life on my own terms with my only disappointment being...that I couldn't share my life with you."

The falcon swooped across Ryan's face, which now stung.

Ryan dropped the phone. His body felt weaker. He was having trouble breathing. Nevertheless, the boy stood his ground. Forcing his legs to keep him upright. To face what awaited him.

Every vein was now burning. The pain made Ryan grit his teeth. But he forced himself to look into Asset One's eyes and lift his chin.

To stare him down as an equal.

To not give the man any satisfaction of watching him cry out for mercy. Even as the darkness surrounding him reached out... and pulled Ryan through.

CHAPTER 38

Back at her grandma's house, Emma could only hear the wind blowing through the phone now. She strained her ears for any sign that Ryan was still there. That he was still alive. Or better yet, that this was all one big horrible joke.

Someone then picked up the phone.

"Ryan, is that you?" Emma asked.

"Nevada sounds…perfect. I recommend Lake Tahoe. You and your grandmother should have…a pleasant time there."

Emma's entire body clenched up. She knew that voice.

"You are one…lucky young woman," Asset One said. "I did want to kill you. But that pleasure is small compared to…what I'll accomplish on this day. So flee to Lake Tahoe with your grandmother…with my compliments. Protect yourselves from the coming storm. However…if you cross my path again…be assured that you'll meet the same fate as all your Authority friends."

Emma gripped the back of her grandmother's sofa, trying to literally prop herself up. "Can I speak to Ryan, please?"

Asset One hesitated. "My apologies…the boy is dead."

Emma fell against the back of her grandmother's sofa, dropping the portable house phone to the floor. She gripped the end of the sofa and allowed gravity to pull her down to the floor as she wailed. The grief flowed out of her.

Her grandmother ran over to Emma and peppered her with questions. But all Emma could do was cry, so the old woman cradled Emma like a kid, letting her get it all out. When Snoopy came over to check out the commotion, he licked Emma's face as well. The wet tongue helped Emma lift herself from the pain as she realized something. All of them were in grave danger.

She wiped her eyes. "We have to go."

"Can you fill me in, young one?" Grandma Bernadette asked. "Who was that on the phone?"

Her grandma didn't know about Ryan, and Emma didn't have the time nor the strength to talk about him right now.

"Someone I care about just died." Emma almost lost it again.

"Oh no. I'm so sorry." Her grandmother brushed her hair out of her eyes.

"But we have to go now. We're in danger."

"What danger?"

"If we take the Jeep, we can reach Nevada in a few hours," Emma said.

"Nevada, what in blazes are you talking about?"

Emma went ahead and told her about their secret base getting captured and the nuclear bomb that was going to be detonated.

All Grandma Bernadette could say was, "Dear God."

"I know."

After the death of her father, it was now officially the second worst day in Emma's life. Ryan was dead. The Gems would be next. Maybe Grandma Laura, whom she was only now beginning to get to know. Emma couldn't take much more death in her life.

"You have to warn people, young one," Grandma Bernadette said. "Call the police. Call the government. Millions of people need to start evacuating."

What was she going to do? As if the cops would listen to a teenage girl ranting about nuclear bombs and secret bases under a winery in Napa Valley. They wouldn't believe her.

"It's too late for that," Emma said. "Seriously, grab some clothes. I'll pack stuff for Snoopy. We have to hurry."

Grandma didn't move. "Can't Laura do something? She knows people in the government, doesn't she?"

"Yes, but the terrorists already have her. She can't contact anyone." Emma raced up the stairs but slowed down as she reached the top. Her mind was kicking her in the butt, trying to get her emotions to shut up and listen. Emma gripped the railing. Mrs. B did know that one guy in the FBI. What was his name?

Ed. His name was Ed.

That's not helpful.

Snoopy whimpered, reading his human's nervous behavior. Something was going on.

Emma picked Snoopy up. Without a last name, how would she

know which Ed was the right Ed? Ed was too common. There must be thousands of Eds inside the FBI. Wouldn't they just label her a crank and hang up? She needed someone to call on her behalf. Someone the FBI would take more seriously. Emma hurried downstairs and borrowed Grandma's cell phone.

"Hey, Bernadette. What's shaking?" Ben Gooden asked.

"It's Emma. Who does the company know in the FBI? Someone high up. It's urgent. Super important I get in contact with them."

"Whoa...step back. The FBI?"

"Yeah, I need to talk to someone in the FBI. His name is Ed, and he's an important FBI dude. But I don't know his last name or anything else about him. Please, Ben. I know I sound crazy, but I'm not. This is a credible threat. Trust me. Millions of people could die if I can't get a hold of him."

Ben didn't answer.

"Seriously, Ben. You have to trust me."

"Damn, Emma." Ben sighed. "All right, I know a guy. I'll see if I can track him down. Keep this phone with you."

"Thanks, Ben."

Emma slipped Grandma's phone in her pocket.

Millions of people could die.

That sentence still lingered in the air. Her mind holding on to it. Begging her to act. Emma knew where the winery was. How to get inside. Maybe she could do something. Maybe she could even stop the bomb from going off.

You've done it before, remember?

In Norway she'd cut the correct wire, preventing another bomb from going off and killing Miyuki and Nadia. But that hadn't been a nuclear bomb, and she had been lucky.

Emma's heart pushed back. Snoopy and Grandma needed her. She should help them escape. She wanted to keep them safe.

But if the FBI stormed Authority headquarters, wouldn't they need someone on the inside who knew the place and could get them in quickly to disarm the bomb? She was the only one who could help them.

Emma petted Snoopy as he wagged his tail. If she took the Jeep, there would be no escape for him and her grandmother. She would be risking their lives as well. Emma's eyes fell on her grandma, who was studying her.

"Ben is calling the FBI. They might need my help to get inside the facility. But if you want me to drive you to Nevada, then—"

"Take the Jeep," Grandma Bernadette said without a pause. "If you can help the FBI, you should try."

Emma hugged her grandmother tight and lingered inside her warm embrace, hoping this would not be the last time.

"I'm proud of you, young one," Grandma said. "Always have been. Remember that."

Emma grinned. She then gave Snoopy a hug and a kiss before heading outside, jumping into Grandma's Jeep, and taking off down the road.

Emma's mind was racing faster than the Jeep's engine as she sped through the streets of Berkeley, California. Images of Ryan's smile as they walked the streets of Montreal together. Ryan sharing his MP3 player with Emma as the music of the Beatles swept into her ears and captured her heart. The bright days spent together on the beach when she was Ryan's guest on the Venomous training island. Ryan confessing his love for her before the missile wrecked the bridge of *the Falcon's Claw*. Ryan showing up in New York. The look on his face when she said it was over between them on the plane. The message he wanted Emma to tell his mom before he died.

She couldn't shake it out of her head. The pain ached throughout her body, making it difficult to concentrate on—

Her foot hit the brake pedal, causing the Jeep to skid halfway into the crosswalk. She swore that red light was green a second ago.

The traffic became heavier as Emma got closer to the highway. She weaved through traffic, gunning the Jeep around like a crazy mom who was too obsessed with making soccer practice on time.

Grandma's phone rang. Emma had to fish it out of her pocket while still trying to drive. It wasn't easy.

"Hello?"

"Hi, Miss Rothchild, this is Special Agent Walton of the FBI's New York bureau. Mr. Ben Gooden contacted us and said you had some information about a possible terrorist threat?"

"Yes…yes, that's me. My codename is Black Opal…well…it was my code name, but I quit—"

Emma swerved to avoid a delivery van. "Sorry, I'm driving way too fast right now. Anyway, my code name was Black Opal, and I was a member of the Gems. Tell Ed that Mrs. B needs his help. He'll understand."

Walton didn't answer.

"Oh my God, did I lose you?"

"Miss, are you reporting a credible threat, or is this some kind of joke? Do you know we can arrest you on federal charges for making a false report?"

"This isn't a false report. Seriously, I need to talk to Ed. Can you please go get him?"

Special Agent Walton scoffed. He wasn't taking her seriously at all. "Which Ed would you be referring to?"

"You know...Ed. He's, like, one of the head FBI guys over there, isn't he?"

Another pause.

"Miss, are you referring to Edward Wilcox, the assistant deputy director?"

"Yes, that's got to be him! Please transfer me."

"I'm not bothering the deputy director with something like—"

"Sorry, but could you please shut up and listen to me? Tell Edward Wilcox that someone is about to set off a nuclear bomb in Napa Valley. If he wants to do something about it...please have him call me as quickly as possible."

Emma was so focused on her phone call that she didn't notice both lanes of traffic ahead of her were stopped.

When she did, Emma fought the impulse to hit her brakes and swerved the Jeep away from the last car in line. Her front wheels hit the street curb hard and uneven, causing the Jeep to lose its balance. Emma found herself in a store's parking lot, careening out of control towards some parked cars.

Emma cranked the wheel to avoid them, but that was too much for the Jeep, and it rolled over and smashed into the cars with a loud crunch of metal and glass.

CHAPTER 39

Emma opened her eyes and realized she was hanging upside down inside the Jeep, thanks to her seatbelt, which kept her in the driver's seat. She craned her neck to look around. The roll bars had done their job, preventing Emma from getting squashed like a red pancake.

An older Hispanic man dipped his head inside the Jeep. He wore a construction hat and a thick black mustache.

"Are you hurt, *senorita?*" he asked in a thick Spanish accent.

She wasn't too sure. "I think I'm okay. Can you help me get out of here?"

The man with the mustache had Emma brace herself against his shoulder as he unlatched her seatbelt and lowered her out of the seat. He went ahead and carried her out of the wreckage. Emma then asked him to stand her up. When he did, Emma could feel her legs, and they didn't hurt. She checked the rest of her body. Besides a couple of new rips in her already pre-ripped jeans, Emma was fine.

"Did I hit anyone? Is anyone else hurt?" Emma asked.

The man called out to his co-workers in Spanish. His construction crew were searching around the park cars. They all shook their heads.

"No, *senorita*. You were very lucky."

Emma knew better. Her luck was evaporating quickly. Now she couldn't get up to Napa Valley to help the FBI save millions of people or use the Jeep to go save her grandmother. No wonder she quit the Gems. She was no hero. She was a disaster.

At that point, some girl shrieked. At first, Emma thought they'd found someone dead, and she was going to totally lose it…but it was a short teen girl with red hair and freckles. It was Kayla.

Her friend from school vibrated with excitement as she ran

towards Emma. "What happened? Are you alright? Did anyone die? Oh my God is that your grandma's Jeep?"

Emma relaxed. "Yeah, I totaled it."

"You poor thing. It was an accident, right?" Kayla said. "You weren't trying to…" Kayla didn't finish her sentence and glanced at the ground.

Kill yourself again? Kayla meant to add.

"What are you doing here?" Emma asked.

Kayla grinned and shook a pair of car keys. "I'm in the middle of a driving lesson with my mom. Well, I was until this Jeep came out of nowhere and—sorry, I bet your shaken up by the accident. I would be. I'd be totally freaked out of my mind. Like, driving is stressful enough without crashing. Shit, I'm sorry. You don't want to hear about that. Are the cops gonna throw you in jail for this?"

An older woman came up behind Kayla. She looked like a mom, so Emma introduced herself.

"Hi, Kayla's mom. I'm Emma."

"Oh…hey, Mom," Kayla said. "This is my best friend from school."

Kayla's mom frowned. "Is this the one who faked her own suicide for attention?"

"Mom."

"Um…I didn't exactly do it for attention."

"Don't put her on the spot, Mom," Kayla said. "She'll tell me why. Because we're best friends." Kayla whipped around to Emma. "We are best friends, right? Because you were planning to tell me, right? Because you wouldn't fake your death and not tell your best friend about it. No…wait…you didn't tell me anything about it, did you?"

"You're pissed at me," Emma said.

"Why would I be mad at you…for not telling me you weren't dead or for those many sleepless hours of crying I did…thinking you were dead."

Emma sighed. If she survived the end of this day, Emma told herself she needed to buy Kayla a brand-new wardrobe on top of a big, heart-felt apology.

"Do you need an ambulance?" Emma's mom asked.

"I'm fine."

"*Senorita?*" The man with the mustache was back with a ringing phone in his hand. "Is this yours?"

Emma swiped it out of his hand. "Thank you...*gracias*." She walked away from Kayla and her mom. "Sorry, I have to take this."

She answered the phone.

"Yes, this is Ed Wilcox, FBI assistant deputy director. Is this the young woman claiming there's a bomb in...Napa Valley?"

"Oh my God," Emma said. "I'm so happy I found you."

"Young lady, why would someone want to blow up a bunch of vineyards?"

"Didn't that Walton guy tell you who I am?"

"Agent Walton said that a distressed girl was reporting a plot to blow up Napa Valley. Which makes no sense. And if you don't convince me that this isn't some kind of joke...I have all the information I need to find the owner of this phone and have them thrown in jail."

Emma was sick of having to explain herself. Like, no one in the world was taking her seriously.

"I used to be a member of the Gems. My codename was Black Opal. We've met before. That one time you found Robert—that top-secret military drone—in Utah, remember? You stopped that crazy CIA guy from grabbing us. I also watched the meeting in the park between you and Mrs. B when you discovered that we had Robert. You were relieved because the Pentagon was putting pressure on you to find him."

Ed paused, putting all the pieces together. "What's the situation?"

"Venomous has taken over our base. I think Mrs. B and some of her people are being held prisoner while they clean out all their secrets from the computers. When they're done, Asset One plans to detonate a nuclear bomb. I can tell you where the base is so you can stop them."

"Are you sure it's a nuclear device?"

"Ryan said—I trust my source. They have one and are prepared to use it."

"When did you last contact this source?" Ed asked.

"I don't know...thirty minutes ago."

"If they plan to escape the blast, Asset One will need time to get himself and his people out of the way. That means he'll need a couple of hours at least to get away. That buys us some time," Ed said. "I'll send people there to deal with the bomb. Can you get me in contact with Mrs. B?"

"Not now. But I'll try my best to get inside the base and make that happen."

"Good. Keep this phone on your person. We'll track its location and use it to find your headquarters."

Emma thanked Ed and slipped the phone back into her pocket as she walked back to Kayla.

"Kayla, I'm so sorry for all the grief I've caused you. I know I owe you big time, and I'll pay you back. I promise. But...I need a huge favor. Can I borrow your mom's car?"

Kayla glanced at the keys in her hand. She looked confused.

"Beg your pardon?" Kayla's mom asked.

"It's an emergency. That's why I was speeding in my Jeep. It's a matter of life and death, I promise."

Kayla glanced at Emma, then at the keys in her hand. "It's our only car. My mom is still making payments."

"I'll be very careful."

"Careful?" Kayla's mom scoffed. "You just plowed through a parking lot and totaled your own car."

"I'll pay more attention. I promise."

Reluctantly, Kayla held out the keys for her.

Emma took them.

"What are you doing?" Kayla's mom asked.

"Which car is it?" Emma asked, moving away.

"The blue sedan," Kayla said. "The engine rattles a little, but don't worry because it doesn't leak oil anymore since Mom got it fixed."

"Why did you give her the keys?" her mom asked, her face in shock.

"Mom, she's my best friend. You always help your best friend when she asks. It's the rules."

Emma didn't wait for the argument to end. She slipped into the blue sedan. The engine rattled as Emma took off down the road, got onto the highway and headed north to Napa Valley.

CHAPTER 40

An hour later, Emma slowed the blue sedan way down as she passed by the public entrance to the Burlington Winery. The wooden fence gate to the empty parking lot was closed along with a sign that gave the normal business hours of the winery. Since she couldn't enter the parking lot, Emma kept driving until she found a spot on the shoulder to pull the car off the road. She shut off the engine and took a moment to think.

So far, no nuclear holocaust. Emma hoped Asset One was still inside; that meant she still had time to do something. But what?

She could wait for the FBI to show up. They'd have people who knew what to do in situations like this. They might even give her a bullet-proof vest if she went in with them. That would be the smart thing to do.

But Emma had promised Ed that she would try to find Mrs. B and have her contact him. That meant going inside before they arrived. Besides, during Emma's spy training, Lioness had hammered the concept into her head that the Gems weren't trained to sit back and watch. They were trained to act. If the lives of innocent people were at risk...the girls were always expected to act.

What if Emma just sat here in the car and the world literally blew up under her? No bullet-proof vest would save her. Or the millions of people living miles away from the blast.

She was expected to act.

Emma climbed out of the blue sedan to look around. The large Burlington Mansion itself, which housed the winery's gift shop and most of the storage barrels, seemed empty of people. The winery's offices upstairs also showed no movement inside the windows. The barns in back of the mansion also looked abandoned.

Emma didn't remember too much from the training materials Mrs. B had made her study after joining the Gems, but there was something called a "sector scramble." An official order given to areas of headquarters to evacuate in cases of fire, spilling of dangerous material...things like that. Maybe when Venomous attacked, the order had been given in time for the people at the winery to evacuate.

But where did Venomous attack the base? If it was here, there was no sign of violence. No bodies. No blood. Even the Burlington winery mansion looked untouched, not one brick out of place.

Emma kept hidden as she made her way around the fenced perimeter of the "winery." She reached one of the secret back entrances to the facility. The first "gate" where Emma would be screened before driving to the garage was occupied by four men in dark fatigues, carrying rifles. There was no sign of Skip, the friendly hippie guy with glasses who normally greeted her. Emma hoped he wasn't dead. She kept moving around the perimeter.

Emma recognized the barn with the hidden car elevator. A dozen men in fatigues stood there with about a dozen vans disguised as Bamazon delivery vehicles. She saw bullet holes peppering the outside wall of the barn. Then someone's car had been moved out of the way. The windshield was shattered with holes, and something dark red stained the car's white hood. The image made her stomach tighten as reality settled in.

Emma kept moving.

Each of the six hidden entrances to the facility had been attacked and breached. Further evidence of blood and bullet holes indicated to Emma that it was a fierce battle, but one the Authority had lost. There were armed guards at all these entrances. Unarmed, there was no way she could get through them. Emma returned to the blue sedan and called Ed's number.

"What's your status, Black Opal?" Ed asked.

She told him where roughly each of the six secret entrances were. How many men she saw guarding each one. And about the Bamazon delivery vans.

"They'll try to use those vans to escape. That means the countdown hasn't started yet, which means we have time to hit them."

"How soon can you get here?" Emma asked.

"I have a SEAL team about an hour out. Army Rangers coming in right behind them along with FBI strike teams. We have your location. Stay right there. Since it's too dangerous, I don't want you to go into the base itself."

"Okay."

The call ended.

An hour out? There was so much that could happen in an hour. Like all her friends getting killed.

She couldn't just sit here and wait. Emma had to try to do *something*.

It was obvious that Venomous knew about the secret entrances around the perimeter, but the main winery building looked untouched, as if it were closed for the day. Did Venomous know about the wine barrel entrance? It was an entrance that Emma had used when she showed up for her first day and actually went into the winery gift shop instead of using one of the secret entrances that everyone else used. If Venomous did know about that entrance, where were the guards? They put them at every other entrance. Why not outside the winery building itself?

Maybe they thought that part of the base was only a front, a wine business made to hide the fact that there was a secret facility under it. Maybe they thought the winery itself had limited access to the base under it.

Emma thought it was worth checking out.

She left the safety of the car and eased her way to the gated entrance to the winery. She hesitated, wondering if Venomous was watching any of the numerous cameras that she knew were covering the parking lot and main winery building.

She had to take that chance.

Emma climbed over the wooden gate and sprinted across the lot to the front door of the gift shop. Again, there were no signs of broken windows or bullet holes in the building, and no one glancing through the windows.

She tried the door, but it was locked. Emma remembered some of her lock-pick training but didn't have any of the tools. She checked her pockets. No, she had nothing that would do the trick. As she was summoning the courage to break a window...the front door opened, and someone pulled her inside. It was so abrupt that Emma fell on her knees.

When she looked up, Emma saw Skip, the man with round glasses and a wine smock around his waist. His left hand gripped a pistol while his right touched a finger to his mouth, signaling to

Emma not to scream.

Emma nodded.

"Good to see you again, sister," the man whispered, still sounding easy-going, which in this situation was kinda weird. "But you can't go in. Base is under lock-down. Someone attacked the entrances."

"I know," Emma said. "Venomous took it over. Asset One captured a lot of our people. Plus he's going to detonate a nuclear bomb."

"Ah, man. That's heavy," Skip said. "Was working the gift shop when the scramble went out. Lots of people used the barrel entrance to get out. Thought it was a fire or something. Then I heard gunfire and went outside to look around. Someone was attacking the other entrances, so I retreated here to the mansion. Did everything I'm supposed to do during the scramble; then I hung out to make sure everyone split."

"Were you supposed to stay?"

"Nah, sister. I had nothing better to do. Thought I'd hang tight until someone gave me the lowdown on the lock-down. Then I saw you."

"We need to make sure Asset One doesn't arm that bomb," Emma said. "I think that's what Mrs. B would want us to do."

"I'm down with that. I've been watching the barrel. No one else has come out of it in a while. My guess is the Venomous dudes don't know about it."

"Yeah, that's what I was thinking too," Emma said. "Will you help me?"

"I'm down with that too." The man checked his gun magazine. "Rock and roll."

CHAPTER 41

Emma slipped through the employees-only door and moved into the large warehouse inside the mansion. A row of giant wooden barrels lined each side of the warehouse. Skip was trailing her, his gun drawn as he scanned the area for trouble. As they went further inside the building, Emma had to stop. "Which one was it again?"

"Barrel twenty-one," Skip answered.

Emma found the barrel and climbed up the metal stairs to the scaffolding that allowed access to the top of the barrels. Skip followed her, and they both stopped at the hatch to barrel 21.

"Wanna open it, sister?" he said. "Don't want my masculine assumptions to overshadow your value as a strong and capable young woman. You dig?"

Emma had no idea how any of that was related to digging, but thinking of her was a nice gesture.

"You can open the hatch," she said. "I'll let you know if you try to...overshadow my value as a capable young woman."

"Right on." The man moved a lever to the side, causing the seal of the hatch to pop. As Skip swung open the hatch, some air blew in their face. He glanced up at her.

"You first. You have the gun," Emma said.

Using another ladder, the man climbed down into the hatch. Emma then followed him down into the barrel. The inside of it was lit up, revealing a curved floor of polished oak. As Emma reached the bottom of the ladder, she saw the elevator at the back of the barrel.

Skip produced a key that was around his neck. "Had to manually shut off this elevator when people stopped coming out. When they activate the security protocols, the elevators are supposed to shut down, but I don't know what happened." The man inserted his key into a slot near the elevator buttons. Soon the lights came on, and the elevator powered back up.

The doors soon opened, prompting Skip to move into a firing stance. But no one was inside the car.

"Ladies first...or do you wanna flip a coin?" Skip asked, being absolutely serious.

Emma laughed as she stepped inside the elevator. "I don't mind ladies first...just never say ladies last."

"Right on, sister." The man joined her inside. "Don't know what we'll see when these doors open again. Could be rough. You ready?" Skip gripped his pistol, aiming it down to the floor.

Emma got serious and prepared herself. "Rock and roll."

When the elevator doors opened, the adjacent hallway was empty. Emma allowed Skip to go first, keeping his gun aimed down the hallway. Then she stepped into the hallway too. They were now inside the headquarters facility itself. A sign directed people to the TA division, which was on the first level, above the main level.

Her eyes then discovered a body on the floor. A security officer. Shot in the head. She glanced down the other side of the hallway and saw two more dead security guards.

"Never left their posts," Skip said. "Allowed everyone else to escape through the elevator. Must have stayed until they were overwhelmed." He bent down and searched them. "Sorry, sister. All their weapons are gone."

"That's okay. Let's keep moving."

As Emma and Skip entered the office area for the TA division, they had to jump behind a desk as four armed Venomous guards stood around some of the shattered glass partitions. There were pieces of glass all over the office floor here, as well as dead people. Emma had never seen such a sight before. It was freaking her out a little.

"Any ideas?" Skip asked in a whisper.

Emma collected her thoughts. "I should go look inside the atrium. See what's going on. Can you watch my back?"

"Right on."

Emma tensed up, then ran over to a far desk near the edge of the office floor. She ducked behind it and gathered her breath.

The goons didn't see her.

She moved to the side of the desk, away from their line of sight.

Then felt a sharp prick. She bit her lip and turned over her palm. A piece of broken glass had pierced her skin. Emma pulled it out and grunted as the wound stung her hand.

Emma found herself at the edge of the Threat Assessment office, which was upstairs and overlooked the main atrium. Usually this floor was walled off with thick glass, but due to the intense firefight, many of the walls were shattered, making it too easy to take a wrong step and fall thirty feet against the hard-tiled floor below.

Emma scanned below her. Two lines of people sat on the floor with their legs folded under them; their arms were all tied behind their backs like prisoners. She could pick out Miyuki and Olivia. Then she saw Mrs. B and Mr. O. For some reason, Lioness was standing away from the others, and her hands were free. She was watching as—Emma's heart melted as she saw Aardvark unconscious on the floor. Some man was treating him, so maybe he wasn't dead. But the look on Lioness's face told Emma he wasn't doing well at all.

Asset One's long blond hair was visible as Sunchaser sat on his padded shoulder. The sight of him made Emma's blood boil. The hate seethed through her body. She'd never felt this much hate towards a human being before. She wanted that man dead. After what he did to poor Ryan…she felt capable of doing it herself.

Emma swallowed her anger and analyzed the situation. Emma recognized Asset Twelve, the Turkish woman who ran Venomous's training island. No doubt she was here as Asset One's trusted second-in-command. And of course…the twins were here as well.

There was a metallic-looking device off by itself but surrounded by four guards. This indicated to Emma that it was most likely where the nuclear device was.

So there was Asset One. Asset Twelve. The twins. And at least twenty-five heavily armed guards in the atrium area alone. How in the world could she get to that bomb? Or release the prisoners to help her? There was no way she could sneak down that open staircase without getting shot to death. Using the slide would be faster, but that wouldn't prevent the men from shooting her as soon as she popped out at the bottom.

She needed to find another way downstairs.

Emma made her way back to Skip and told him the situation.

"There is another way." The man guided Emma away from the shattered office area and back into the hallway with the elevator. He pointed up at an air vent. "You're small enough to fit, but not me." He offered her the pistol, and Emma took it. He also slipped an extra magazine into her pocket. Skip then crouched and cupped his hands together to boost her up.

Emma raised her leg...only to put it back down again as she read the warning sign near the vent...

**Electrocution Danger. Vent ducts contain security nets.
Maintenance crews must contact security before doing any work.**

Emma pointed. "What's that about?"

"Oh, don't worry about that," the man said.

Emma paused. "Why not?"

"Before their attack, Venomous shut down all the security protocols."

"What about after the attack?"

Skip thought about it.

Emma scoffed. "So they could have switched some of them back on, right?"

"You know, that's a good question. I still think you'll be okay. Why turn them back on when you went to so much trouble disabling them?"

There was some logic to his statement. But did Emma want to trust her life on that?

"What kind of shock are we talking about?" Emma asked. "Like...rubbing your socks across the carpet and touching the door handle or—?"

"Yeah, well, basically, I don't remember how much juice an electric chair uses, but—"

"Dude, I'm not going in there," Emma said.

"No, honestly, I think it's all turned off."

Emma glared. "You're super-stressing me out right now with your lack of confidence in that statement."

"You'll be fine," Skip said.

Emma sighed.

"I think."

Emma closed her eyes.

"If you wanna wait for the feds, I understand," he said.

Emma wanted to but…Aardvark didn't look good at all. If he needed to go to a hospital, every minute of delay could mean life or death. And who knows how many other people were wounded downstairs and needed medical attention. Waiting was dangerous too.

"Please help me up," Emma said reluctantly.

The man smiled with encouragement as he boosted her to the vent. Emma hesitated before touching the metal grating around the vent. No shock. No nothing. Emma dug her fingers in and pulled the vent out and handed it to Skip.

"You're right. It's off," she said.

"They don't electrify the grating. Look for wiry-looking curtains at all the junctions. Good luck."

Emma wanted to kick him in the face, but she restrained herself. Well, she was kind of committed now. So Emma used her elbows and knees to pull herself into the vent shaft.

After scooting along the vent tunnel, she soon arrived at a "curtain" made of what almost looked like icicles from a Christmas tree. Emma moved within inches of the curtain and paused. She didn't hear a hum or anything that indicated electricity was being passed through it, but did that mean anything?

Emma bit her lip, then reached out with her hand and touched the curtain with one finger.

Nothing.

She ran her fingers through the entire length of the curtain.

It was off.

Emma smiled to herself and pushed through the curtain to the next section of vents. Soon she figured out which vents would lead her down. After about fifteen minutes, Emma peeked through the grating of one vent and noticed the sea of green pods that were located in the "jungle." That would be an excellent place to hide and observe.

Emma pushed the vent cover off. It almost dropped to the floor, but she managed to grab it in mid-air before it clattered against the floor. Finally she lowered herself out of the vent and touched the floor with her sneakers.

Moving around one of the large green pods, Emma parked herself behind one of the fake jungle trees and scanned the area. This place was quiet. No sign of any guards. No sign of bodies or any evidence of fighting in this area of headquarters. Emma held her pistol with both hands as she slowly made her way through the jungle.

Emma pressed her back against one of the pods as she scanned the entrance to the jungle. There were six guards at the threshold of where the atrium joined the jungle, but their attention was on the prisoners inside the atrium. They must have already searched the jungle, thinking it was secure.

Emma decided to retreat into the jungle and think. What was she going to do? She was in a good position to create a diversion, but there was no way she was close enough to do anything about the bomb, which was on the other side of the atrium.

A mechanical noise made Emma spin around as one of the green pods opened up. Emma aimed her gun and slowly walked towards the pod. To her astonishment, Nadia hopped out on one leg with her laptop tucked under her arm. She then took out her leg scooter and rested herself on it. She casually walked towards the atrium, almost oblivious to everything.

Emma ran up to her. When Nadia opened her mouth, Emma clamped her hand over it. Nadia protested with a muffled sound meant to be a question.

"Shhhh," Emma whispered. "Don't cry out or yell, okay?"

Nadia looked confused.

"Seriously."

Finally she nodded.

Emma grabbed Nadia's arm and moved her back to the green pod. She helped Nadia inside the pod, and they both sat on the large couch.

"What's going on?" Nadia whispered. "What are you doing here?"

"How long have you been in here?" Emma asked.

"You mean in the pod?"

"Yeah."

"I don't know. Not that long. I've been working on some code. Why?"

As Emma filled her in on what was going on, Nadia turned as white as fresh snow.

"I had no idea," she said. "Now I feel so stupid."

"These pods are sound-proof. You couldn't have known."

"Olivia, Mrs. B, Aardvark…I could have helped them."

"Or you'd be captured too," Emma said. "Seriously, I need your help. As soon as Asset One gets all the information from those Authority servers, he'll arm that bomb and leave. We have to waste his time so the FBI can get here. Do you know where the computer servers are?"

"Inside the Labyrinth?" Nadia asked. "Yes, I do."

"Can we get to them from here?"

"Not without going through the atrium. All the lower levels are connected through the atrium," Nadia said. "How did you get down here from the winery entrance?"

"The air vents. The security protocols are off." Emma brightened. "Can we use the vents?"

"You can." Nadia glanced down at her leg cast.

"Oh, yeah." Emma didn't think about that.

"Wait a moment. You said Mrs. B issued a scramble order, correct?"

Emma nodded.

Nadia brightened. "Follow me."

Emma followed her friend out of the pod and deeper inside the jungle area. Soon they came upon a wall with an open hatch.

"Where did that come from?" Emma said. "There's no door in this wall."

"Yes, there is," Nadia said. "Didn't you read the Authority manual Mrs. B gave you? The chapter about scramble alerts?"

Emma balked. "I skipped that part. I mean, we don't work in the building, so why should I know about emergency procedures."

Nadia tilted her head, like a mom. "During a section scramble, all emergency exits are activated. The map in the manual shows all the exits inside a given sector of the base. Normally the Labyrinth only has one main entrance. But in an emergency ten exits are activated. Many of them go above ground, but a few empty inside the atrium. Like this one."

"Seriously, some of these open up outside?"

Her friend nodded.

Emma wanted to kick herself. If she had read that stupid book, getting into the base through one of the emergency exits would've been a no-brainer.

"This exit should lead us into the Labyrinth," Nadia said. "The server rooms are located inside the CAC zone. But if all the security is off, we should be able to get into the server rooms fairly easily. What are we going to do once we're in there?"

"Stop them from transferring the data," Emma said.

"How?"

"Oh my God, Nadia, I can't come up with all the answers. Once we get in there, we'll just have to…improvise."

"I don't like that word."

"Whatever happens, the show must go on."

"If we die, Emma, the show stops," Nadia said.

"You're missing the—forget it. Let's go before you talk me out of this."

Emma followed Nadia on her leg scooter as they navigated through some of the dark and empty hallways of the Labyrinth. Soon they came to an open door. There was a dead security officer on the floor who had been moved out of the way. Emma gripped her pistol and checked the open door.

There was a series of rooms, each room attached to the other by a door. As if one had to pass through several layers of security in order to access whatever was beyond all this. The sign next to the door identified this place as the main CAC computer servers.

But all the doors were wide open.

Emma moved into the first room. It was the first security check-point. A few bullet holes were in the wall. Blood was all over the desk. Emma paused, then glanced at Nadia on her leg scooter.

She nodded.

Emma went forward into the next room. Same story. Bullet holes. Blood. Another body pushed to the side.

Every room or checkpoint had a similar story. There had been quite a fight in this area, as security guards had stayed behind to defend this area to the last.

Finally Emma reached the last one. Through the next open door, she could hear voices talking, but couldn't make out the exact number. The hum of hundreds of fan motors also competed with the voices.

"Can you see anything?" Nadia asked.

Emma took a peek around the corner. The room itself was large. Rows and rows of cabinets containing rows and rows of computer servers went on for what seemed like forever.

"I see rows of computer stuff," Emma said. "I hear people talking, but I don't know how many."

"Do they have guns?"

"I can't see them. They could be right around the corner here."

"Should we take the chance?" Nadia asked.

"Well, we have to do something." Emma checked her pistol, then pointed it towards the ground as she got herself ready. Emma smiled. "Isn't improv fun?"

Nadia rolled her eyes.

Emma took in a deep breath, then ran around the corner.

CHAPTER 42

As Emma cleared the corner, she found herself in an open area surrounded by aisles of computer servers. Seven men stood around four large carts, each cart of portable servers was wired up to an aisle of servers. Emma pointed her gun at them, causing these men to freeze in total shock.

Nadia rolled in behind her.

"Who else is in here?" Emma asked, trying to sound confident.

The seven men only gawked at her. Their clothes were ultra-casual. No dark fatigues like the armed goons she'd seen inside the atrium had on. Many of them had light unkempt beards that signaled to Emma that they didn't take their grooming seriously. Why didn't they answer her?

"Hey, I'm asking a question…who else is in here?"

One of the men glanced at the others. "Only us, I guess." He wore a T-shirt with a Nintendo logo.

"And who are you?"

The men checked with each other.

"Who are *you*?" the Nintendo man countered.

"I'm the girl with the gun," Emma said. "Are you working for Venomous?"

"I don't know. We're only contract workers. Some lady recruited us for a job."

Nadia examined one of the carts. "Are these your servers?"

Nintendo man took a few steps in her direction.

"Stay right there," Emma yelled. "I didn't give you permission to move."

The man stopped. "Wow, you're serious."

Nadia pulled off the connection cables to all four of the carts.

"Wait a minute. We're not done yet," Nintendo man said.

"Sapphire, you'd better move away from there," Emma said.

Nadia looked confused but rolled away from the carts.

Emma paused, then swung around, firing a round into each of the four laptops attached to the carts. She then aimed her gun at the men. "Well, you're done now."

Nadia's mouth hung open slightly. She didn't see that coming, but then a shallow grin formed on her lips.

The men's faces were gripped with horror.

"That was a two-thousand-dollar I-Book," one of them said.

"Let's kick her ass," Nintendo man said.

Some of the men nodded.

Emma gripped the pistol. She didn't want to kill anyone. Didn't these idiots understand how this went? They were supposed to listen to the person with the gun because she had the power to kill them.

The men hesitated, waiting for one of them to make a move.

Nintendo man stepped forward.

On impulse, Emma stepped back as her finger touched the trigger of the weapon. She didn't want them to do this. She wanted them to stop.

"You idiots!" Nadia yelled, her face filled with disdain. "My friend just shot four laptops dead center and didn't miss once. What makes you think she can't do the same with four of your heads?"

The men froze.

Emma was impressed. Where did that come from? Maybe Olivia's take-charge attitude was rubbing off on Nadia.

Nadia straightened her back. Even with the leg scooter, the girl crossed her arms and acted like she was in control. "Sit on your hands. Now!"

The men looked at each other.

"Do what she says," Emma barked, waving the gun around as a reminder.

The men physically wilted as they sat on their hands. Nadia used some computer cables to tie up their hands and feet. After the men were secure, Emma and Nadia gathered the four carts together.

"Without their laptops, they can't access the servers, right?" Emma asked.

"Yes, but all they need is another computer," Nadia said.

"They've already collected hundreds of gigs of classified information."

"Okay, so let's hide these portable servers until we can destroy them. How about upstairs in the winery?"

"The large barrel entrance? Good idea," Nadia said. "There's a cargo elevator near where our quarters are. We can take these up to the first level from there."

"And Skip can come down and help us with the rest of the carts." Emma glanced at their prisoners. "I hate leaving them alone, but I need your help finding the elevator."

"I don't think these boys are going anywhere," Nadia said. "Let's make sure they can't make any sounds while we're gone."

After confiscating the man's Nintendo T-shirt, Emma ripped it up into sections to use as gags, tying them across the mouths of each of the men to keep them quiet. With that accomplished, Emma and Nadia left the server room with one of the carts, pushing it through the open door checkpoints and down one of the dark corridors of the Labyrinth.

Emma was surprised how easy it was; no one seemed to be inside this area of the Labyrinth. Maybe some of the Venomous goons didn't want to take a chance of getting lost inside these endless hallways that all looked the same. Luckily, Nadia was with her. The girl was smart and had an excellent sense of direction. Besides, Nadia had been living at this base before Emma was even a Gem, so she was happy to let her do the navigating.

Soon they found the cargo elevator and rolled the server cart into it. Nadia hit the up button and Emma felt the elevator rise.

"So far, so good," Nadia said.

"Yeah, if we can hide all four of these carts and make Venomous waste time trying to find them, that should give the FBI plenty of time to get here."

When the elevator reached the first level, Emma aimed her pistol at the door, just in case. The elevator door opened, revealing the shattered upstairs office area of the TA division.

"Stay right here," Emma said, remembering the guards up here from earlier. She jumped out of the elevator and ducked behind a desk. Emma then poked her head up. She was in a different area of the office than before. Across from her, about two hundred feet ahead, was the hallway that went to the elevator Skip had taken her down in. If they could get the cart to that elevator, they could store it inside that wine barrel while Skip switched off the elevator.

Where was he?

Emma scanned the office again.

And where were those guards who were here earlier? Did they go downstairs to the atrium? Or down into the Labyrinth?

Emma wasn't going to wait for them.

"Let's go." Emma pointed. "The elevator to the winery is that way."

Nadia and Emma moved the cart through the upended desks and other debris as the wheels crunched through pieces of glass on the floor. The cart itself was noisy. Emma swept her eyes across the large room, convinced the entire base could hear them moving across the floor. Emma was tempted to run over to the edge and check on Mrs. B and the other prisoners. But she resisted the urge, keeping her eyes peeled for anyone coming up the stairs.

Finally the cart rolled down the hallway, past the electrocution warning sign from earlier. There was still no sign of Skip. Maybe it was safer for him to hide inside the elevator or upstairs in the gift shop.

Emma pressed the up button, and the elevator responded. She was happy it was still turned on.

"One cart almost done. Three more to go," Emma said.

"Let's hope the FBI gets here soon so we don't have to move all of them," Nadia added.

The elevator doors opened.

Skip was on the floor, unconscious.

Before Emma could rush over to him…someone struck her in the mouth, the blow hard enough to throw Emma against the far wall.

Asset Twelve stepped out of the elevator. The older woman kicked away the pistol that Emma dropped.

Bridget and Sophia were right behind her with their guns out.

Nadia showed them her hands.

Finally, Asset Twelve stood over Emma, leering at her like she was a cockroach. "Asset One will not be happy to see you again."

CHAPTER 43

Immediately, Emma's hands were pulled tight behind her body as Bridget zip-tied her wrists together. The girl made it so tight the plastic was biting into her wrists.

"Is that snug enough for ya, darling?" Bridget asked.

"It's a little tight," Emma said.

"Hurting your wrists?"

"Yeah."

"How grand." Bridget then grabbed a fistful of Emma's hair and pulled it back. "Because you'll pay for what ya did to Ryan."

"What *I* did?"

Bridget got into her face. "You got him killed. You tried to manipulate 'em. Tried to convince Ryan to turn on us so you two could be a happy little couple. You corrupted his mind. Confused him. Led him to the edge of a cliff and then abandoned him."

"Ryan knew what he was doing. He knew the risks involved and took them anyway," Emma said.

Because he loved me.

"If Asset One doesn't kill ya, I will. That's a promise, darling," Bridget said in a calm, matter-of-fact way. But as she backed away, a small tear trickled down her cheek. A sign that Emma wasn't the only one upset over Ryan's death.

Soon Asset Twelve and the twins escorted Nadia and Emma down the steps to the ground floor of the atrium. When they saw them, Olivia and Miyuki wilted, while Mrs. B closed her eyes.

"Why did you...come back?" Asset One showed his back to Emma. "I was going to leave you alone. To allow you...an exit strategy." He slowly turned to face her. "Why did you? Was it...for your friends? For Ryan? For revenge...against me?" Asset One took a few steps towards her. "You're a silly little girl...a blond puppet too stupid to know…when she's been given a golden parachute."

The man moved away from Emma. "So be it. You'll be made an example of." He pointed at Nadia. "Put that one…with her friends."

Bridget and Sophia moved Nadia over to Mrs. B and the other prisoners.

Asset One turned his attention to the ceiling. Emma followed his gaze to see Sunchaser circling above them. The man called out an order in Arabic.

The falcon dived at Emma, causing her to hit the floor as its talons ripped into her back, making the girl scream in pain.

"Painful, isn't it?" Asset One asked. "Now you know…how Ryan felt. Soon, you'll feel the poison…seeping into your own body. The grim reaper…is coming around the corner. And he's looking for you…Emma Rothchild."

Even with her arms still tied up, Emma managed to balance herself on her knees.

The falcon came at her again.

Emma tried to avoid it, but its talons raked her cheek, and she heard herself yelp. Her back started to burn, and she remembered Ryan. How he sounded over the phone. How his voice went up a few octaves as Ryan did his best not to cry. Not to show weakness as he held back the pain.

The next strike was to the back of her neck. It came out of nowhere and made her scream in shock.

Emma collapsed to the floor, rolling on her side. Her cheek burned. Her neck stung. Her back felt numb and tingly. That had to be the poison. It was already attacking her body.

She had to move.

She had to hide.

But her body wouldn't respond. It was terrified. It was in shock. It only wanted to lie there because it wanted to give up.

Emma finally agreed. There was nothing much else for her to do.

But die.

CHAPTER 44

Their Napa Valley headquarters was now in shambles. Broken glass. Broken doors. Broken people.

Blood on the floor.

Death on the floor.

It was horrible. Sights that Miyuki would never be able to push out of her mind. And if that wasn't bad enough, Miyuki watched as a falcon ripped up her best friend. Piece by piece. Making her suffer. Torturing her. Punishing her for trying to help them.

Emma's eyes were half open, still fighting the effects of what Miyuki assumed was poison coming from the falcon's talons. She could see the aluminum glistening on the modified talons as the bird circled above, ready for another dive attack.

Miyuki's hands were tied, but she did try to stand up. Only to sit back down when behind her, Sophia tapped her shoulder with an automatic pistol, warning her not to intervene. Bridget also stood behind Olivia and Nadia, assuming correctly the three of them would be the ones most likely to try to help Emma.

Miyuki felt trapped. She wanted to help Emma so badly it made her heart ache. It also made her angry and frustrated. How long could her friend survive? Especially with all that poison being injected into her system.

Miyuki then noted Lioness standing nearby. The traitor had drifted in Emma's general direction, as if the poor girl's torture fascinated her. Miyuki thought the woman was sick and twisted. Not only did Lioness betray Mrs. B's trust...but she also was a mentor to Emma. She'd taken the girl under her wing and trained Emma personally. Emma looked up to Lioness, wanting to please her. Wanting to be the best spy that she could be. And Lioness had been patient with Emma, not going off on her like she did most of the people in her training division.

Miyuki still didn't understand why. How could Lioness do this to them?

The woman's face was neutral. Did Lioness have any feelings? Was she a robot, unable to show emotion or empathy towards a girl she'd trained?

"Take a good long look," Mrs. B said to Lioness, her face tight and unforgiving. "That's my granddaughter dying over there."

Lioness hesitated as her eyes fell to the floor.

Sunchaser hit Emma again.

Emma screamed again.

Miyuki couldn't take it anymore. She had to do something.

She went over the move in her head...then executed it.

Leaning far forward first, Miyuki threw herself backwards, freeing her legs out from under her.

Sophia fired her gun, but Miyuki's twisting body was already under the girl.

Now able to use her legs, Miyuki grabbed on to Sophia and flung her forward, causing the girl to flip and smack her back against the floor like a pancake as her gun slid across the tiles.

Miyuki rolled to her side and scrambled to her feet as quickly as she could with her hands still bound.

Sophia's gun fired again.

Miyuki yelped, assuming the bullet was meant for her. But when she looked up...

Lioness held Sophia's gun. The muzzle was pointed towards the ceiling. There was an audible thud as Sunchaser dropped to the floor.

The room went quiet. As if everyone was in shock.

"You traitorous bitch!" Asset One yelled at the top of his lungs. His face red. The veins in his neck rigid. "I'll execute your entire —"

Lioness fired again.

Asset One clutched his chest and collapsed to the floor.

The Russian woman's eyes burned. "That was for threatening my family, you *mudak*."

The room was in shock. Did that just happen?

"Lioness," Mrs. B yelled, "you can still do your duty."

The Russian woman paused, nodded, then ran straight for the relaxation room.

"Kill her!" Asset Twelve yelled as she took out her own gun.

The guards were slow to react, but two of them managed to turn around, bringing up their rifles.

Lioness quickly shot both of them down before entering the relaxation room. She reached the electrical outlet in the corner, popped it open, and typed in a code on the self-destruct keypad.

A trio of guards soon sprayed the room with bullets, hitting Lioness in the process. She died instantly.

But not before she pressed enter.

A loud rumble began as a series of muffled explosions came from the direction of the Labyrinth. The ground under Miyuki shook as a cloud of dust belched out from the Labyrinth's main entrance, causing everyone to cough.

"What was that?" Bridget asked.

Asset Twelve coughed into her arm. "Obviously part of a self-destruct system has been activated." Her eyes moved over to Mrs. B. "Any more surprises we should be aware of?"

"I won't tell." Mrs. B raised her chin. "However, if I were you, I'd move along. Who knows what else could explode."

Asset Twelve studied Mrs. B again, both of their eyes speaking to each other without using one word.

"Should I go check on the computer geeks?" Bridget asked.

"Don't bother," Asset Twelve said. "They're buried along with all the rest of the Authority's secrets."

Sophia knelt before Asset One and checked his pulse. She shook her head at Bridget.

"Asset One is dead," Bridget said, her voice wavering a little. "You have the highest rank here, Asset Twelve. What are your orders?"

CHAPTER 45

Every prisoner in the atrium, including Miyuki, watched to see what Asset Twelve would do next.

The Turkish woman glanced at Asset One's body; then her eyes wandered over to Mrs. B, who smiled like a grandmother who just won the lottery.

Asset Twelve sighed. "Order all our people to evacuate as planned. Asset One's intelligence-gathering operation has failed. However, our leader's death will not be in vain. We shall arm the bomb and leave it behind as a lasting reminder of our power. No matter who leads Venomous into the future...the world will still fear us."

It took the twins fifteen minutes to round up all the Venomous personnel still left inside the facility while Asset Twelve armed the nuclear warhead.

"An hour should be sufficient. Our jet should be over Oregon by then." Asset Twelve faced Miyuki and the rest of the captives. "Be thankful you'll be caught up in the blast, not suffering from radiation sickness or cancer for the rest of your life." With that, Asset Twelve was the last one to leave the atrium as her small Venomous force evacuated through one of the breached secret entrances.

Mrs. B immediately took charge. "Find something sharp to cut off these bindings."

The captives all scrambled to get back on their feet. Several people went off in all directions.

Miyuki ran over and knelt beside Emma. The girl's eyes fluttered open. She looked weak and helpless, but she was still breathing.

"Hold on, Emma. Please hold on."

Olivia plopped down next to them. "We're here, love. We're

going to get you help."

"Is she still breathing?" Nadia asked, rolling over on her leg scooter.

"*Hei*, but she's having difficulty keeping her eyes open," Miyuki said.

Mr. O stood over them. "It's the poison."

"Poison? What poison?" Nadia asked.

"Through the claws of the falcon. It's Asset One's calling card, I'm afraid," the older Indian man said. "Emerald, go upstairs to my office. Right side of my desk. There's a vial of liquid there. Grab that and a medical kit. That's assuming we can get these bindings off."

Mrs. B joined them. "Did you take some antidote from the lab? That's against regulations."

"It's a long story," Mr. O said.

"If we live through this, I look forward to reading that report," Mrs. B said. "How soon can we recall our bomb techs?"

"They'll be scattered all over Northern California by now. It could take hours to get them back here. Not to mention the time they need to figure out the damn thing and disarm it."

Mrs. B scoffed.

"We could reach the airport and be in the air in thirty minutes. It'll be a tight fit, but we could get everyone here on board."

"And what about the millions of people we leave behind?" Mrs. B asked.

Mr. O paused. "If I had a better idea, I'd recommend it."

An Authority office worker ran up to Mrs. B, holding up scissors with her freed hands. Soon people's hands were free of the plastic ties. Emerald ran upstairs for the antidote as Miyuki laid Emma's head on her lap, combing her long blond hair back.

"I need to check on Aardvark's condition," Mrs. B said. "Once you give Emma the antidote, we'll evacuate."

A few minutes later, Emerald was almost out of breath as she handed the medical kit and vial of antidote to Mr. O. He swabbed Emma's arm before injecting it. "There we go. She should be on the mend now. The poison is painful, but its slow. Designed to torture the individual before killing them. Hopefully it hasn't done any permanent damage to her system."

Miyuki heard a large disruption going on upstairs as a group of men in tactical gear took positions overlooking the atrium, their rifles pointed down.

"Don't move," a man yelled from above. "Move and you will be fired upon."

After that, a scouting team cautiously came down the stairs, the letters FBI displayed on their Kevlar vests. They waited for a second scouting team to join them before the first team searched the relaxation area.

Mrs. B walked towards the staircase as her eyes followed a man coming down the steps. "Is all this male bravado necessary, Ed?"

The man she called Ed smiled. "Do you know how long I've dreamed about finding this place?"

Miyuki recognized him. He had been the FBI guy at the National Park when Robert was first taken away by the US Army.

Ed walked around the atrium like a kid in a chocolate factory. "I can't wait to go through this place. You'll give me the full tour, of course."

"Maybe later," Mrs. B said. "But we have more pressing matters."

As if on cue, a group of US army technicians dressed in protective blast gear hurried down the stairs and set up their equipment around the bomb.

"Specialists from Texas. The best in the business," Ed said. "If they're using a stolen Russian warhead as their device, these boys should be able to disarm it."

Mrs. B moved over to Ed. "How did you know?"

"Black Opal. She told me everything. Why did you let Asset One take over your base?"

"I don't air my dirty laundry to anyone. Including the FBI."

"Fair enough. But since I'm about to save your ass, you might not have much of a choice." Ed craned his neck. Intrigued, the man moved over to Asset One's body. "Is that who I think it is?"

Mrs. B drifted away from Ed. "Yes, it is."

"Nice work. I won't be missing that guy."

One agent in FBI tactical gear came jogging up to Ed. "Most of the hallways and caverns on that side of the facility are caved in."

"Is that where you're hiding all your candy, Laura?"

Mrs. B leaned her back against a wall on the other side of the atrium. "I don't know what you're talking about, Ed."

Ed laughed. "Okay, I don't mind digging for treasure. The good news is...I'll let all of your friends go. Then, after you give me the guided tour, I'll let you go too. Sound fair?"

"Does our gentleman's agreement include you ransacking my place for secrets?"

"J. Edgar Hoover's agreement says we can exchange information and work together when it was appropriate. Yet there's nothing about keeping our eyes shut if your secrets drop right into our laps." Ed glanced at her. "It's all fair game, Laura."

Thirty minutes went by as the army technicians worked on the bomb. Miyuki could tell that Emma was looking better. Olivia and Nadia had treated all of her wounds as the antidote neutralized the poison in her system.

Miyuki still held her friend's head in her lap, still talking to her.

Emma finally opened her eyes. "Oh my God…I feel just awful. What did I miss?"

As Miyuki filled her in, Ed approached the bomb squad.

"Cutting it kinda close, guys," he said.

One of the technicians wiped away sweat from his scalp. "We're close. Once we isolate this one relay…"

"Got it," another technician said. "Now cut the line."

With a snap, the device went dark.

"Are we good now?" Ed asked.

"Yes, sir. The device has been neutralized."

Miyuki clapped her hands. She was so happy today wasn't going to be Armageddon Day.

Suddenly, the atrium lighting turned red as a new alarm sounded.

Now Miyuki thought she was wrong.

"What is that alarm for?" Ed asked.

"It's a warning bell for the next self-destruction phase," Mrs. B said. "We have twenty minutes to evacuate the facility before it explodes."

Ed ran towards Mrs. B. "How did you trigger the—?" Ed stopped as he saw a secret panel open. He then cursed at himself. It was no coincidence that Mrs. B was leaning against that particular wall.

"Sorry to spoil your treasure hunt, Ed."

***

Twenty minutes later, Miyuki and Olivia held on to Emma as they sat her down on the back bumper of a US Army ambulance. Aardvark was carried on a stretcher towards another army ambulance. Once on board, that ambulance left the scene.

Miyuki and the other survivors from the Venomous attack were now behind a military barricade across the main road that went past the Burlington Winery. Thanks to Mrs. B activating the self-destruct system, the FBI had ordered everyone to evacuate the facility.

Mrs. B allowed herself a simple grin as she approached Emma. "You're looking better."

"Yeah, the burning stopped. Still feel like a cheese grater attacked me though."

"How are you doing, ma'am?" Olivia asked.

"Better, knowing that Aardvark and Emma are on the mend," Mrs. B said.

Ed approached them all as he checked his watch. "Thought you said twenty minutes."

"I did. Your watch must be fast, Ed."

"Laura…if you lied to me—"

A massive explosion rocked the horizon. Miyuki could see the Burlington Winery mansion surrounded by a wall of debris that had been blown into the air. Soon the mansion itself exploded into a ball of flame as the land around it became an inferno.

"Damn," Ed said.

"A special wine is pumped into all the caverns and rooms, even the ones buried under rubble inside the Labyrinth. This special wine contains over seventy-five percent alcohol. As you can see, it's highly flammable."

Ed smiled to himself. "Even if we dug up your entire complex, everything would be scorched."

"Or melted down," Nadia said. "Depending on the location and internal temperature of the fire."

Ed turned to Mrs. B. "So instead of sharing your candy, you'd rather melt it all down."

The woman smiled. "I'm a greedy little girl."

CHAPTER 46

The next morning, Emma was surprised that she fell asleep last night at all, since thoughts about Ryan and Lioness made it impossible for her to relax. The only good thing about having them on her mind was that it blocked out her own traumatic attack. Emma was convinced she'd be now terrified of birds for the rest of her life.

Emma stirred in bed and received a few jabs of pain in response, a reminder that she was still covered with wounds. After the army medics treated her, Emma refused to go to the hospital. Thanks to the antidote, her young body bounced back from the poison quickly, and after everything she went through, all Emma wanted to do was to go home and be with her grandma again. That was why she was waking up this morning in her own bed with Snoopy yawning on the pillow right next to her.

"How do you feel?" Miyuki asked.

Emma rubbed her eyes and followed the voice over to the window. Miyuki stood there wearing a grin.

"Okay," Emma said. "Did you just come in?"

Miyuki pointed to a sleeping bag on the floor. "I stayed here last night."

"You didn't have to do that."

"Last time I came into your room, I thought you were dead. This time, I make sure you stay alive. At least for one night."

"You found my note?"

Miyuki nodded.

"You didn't deserve that. Seriously, none of you did," Emma said. "I'm a horrible friend."

"Why didn't you talk to me? All the things you talked about in your note...I would've listened to you. Maybe help you work things out." Miyuki hesitated. "I'm mad at you because you never trust me enough to let me try to help."

"You're right." Emma paused, scoffed at herself. "Before I left, I thought about doing that, but my self-indulgent ego pushed me right past that idea."

"Americans and your egos," Miyuki said. "Get you into plenty of trouble."

There was a knock on the door as Nadia and Olivia popped their heads inside.

"We heard some talking," Nadia said. "How are you?"

Emma reassured everyone that she felt better, even though Olivia still maintained she should go see a doctor. Emma's grandma then appeared in the doorway with a breakfast tray. Emma moved into a sitting position and paid the price with more sharp jabs of pain.

"Are you still hurting, young one?" Grandma asked, setting the tray down on Emma's bed.

"Yeah, can I have some more aspirin?"

"She needs to see a doctor," Olivia repeated. "Your wounds could all be infected. You don't want to get gangrene and die, do you?"

"She's right, we shouldn't take any chances," Grandma said. "Eat your breakfast; then we'll take you over to the hospital."

"Oh my God, I don't want to go to the hospital. Seriously, I'm feeling much better."

"I checked her bandages last night," Nadia said. "There's no evidence her wounds are infected."

"Did you graduate from medical school, love?" Olivia asked. "Oh, that's right...you watched a Utube video."

Nadia placed her hands on her hips. "A video made by a nurse with over thirty years experience in medicine. Her examples of skin infections were very detailed and quite informative."

"Did I come at a bad time?"

Everyone turned to see Mrs. B standing in the doorway.

"My apologies. We rang the front door, but no one answered. Only wanted to make sure everyone was safe." Mrs. B then stepped to the side. "I took the liberty of procuring a doctor to check out our newest heroine."

The doctor nodded. There were six other men behind him, all dressed up in suits and ties.

"Are those FBI guys?" Emma asked.

"My new security detail," Mrs. B said. "We're still picking up the pieces from yesterday. Which reminds me, Bernadette, thank you for allowing the girls to stay here overnight on such short notice. Fortunately, we've made some temporary arrangements elsewhere."

"Why can't we stay here?" Miyuki asked.

"Emma's grandmother has been most patient with us over the last year. We've intruded into her life for long enough."

"But does Emma want us to go?"

"We've already talked about this," Mrs. B said. "The decision has been made."

"That was before Emma came and saved us. If she didn't convince the FBI to come disarm the nuclear—"

"Miyuki, that's enough. Emma's grandmother doesn't need to know the details."

"Might as well keep the dirty clothes hamper open, Laura," Grandma said. "I already know about the nuclear bomb. If I put the pieces together, I can also figure out that my Emma went through a lot to save the day...no thanks to all of you. She's done enough for the Authority. Emma needs to live her own life now."

"I quite agree," Mrs. B said.

"I haven't heard Emma say that." Miyuki knelt beside Emma. "Is that what you want?"

A part of Emma wanted to bend. The old Emma wanted Miyuki to be one of her best friends for the rest of her life. But the new Emma, the young woman who grew up during the cross-country trip to New York, the young woman who longed for turning twenty-five and taking charge of her own life...she knew it was her last chance to walk away. To free herself from Grandma Laura. The Gems. And her parents' past. It was hard. But it was necessary.

"Yes. That's want I want," Emma said.

Miyuki paused, not expecting her to say that. Slowly the girl rose to her feet. "*Hei,* I will...honor your wishes."

Emma felt guilty for saying it. But it was the truth. And it was too late to change anything.

Mrs. B reached into her pocket. Her phone was buzzing as a call came in.

"Yes?"

As the older woman listened, her posture stiffened. "Yes...yes, of course. They would be delighted." Mrs. B glanced around the room. "As a matter of fact, I'm with them right now." Mrs. B nodded. "Saturday night will be fine. Of course. Thank you for the invitation. I'll tell them." Mrs. B lowered her phone. "Doctor, do you mind giving us the room for a moment?" Mrs. B flicked her eyes to her security detail. "Keep him company."

All the men left the room, leaving the Gems and Grandma Bernadette behind.

Mrs. B shut the door. "There's a group of people who would like to meet you, Emma."

"That's kind of vague."

"You've been asking to speak with this group for some time. Well, they're ready to see you now."

Emma thought about it. What was Mrs. B talking about? What group did she want to—then it hit her.

"The Century Group?"

Mrs. B nodded.

"You didn't have to arrange that. I mean, it's kinda too late now."

"I told you. I can't arrange meetings like this. Basically the group summons whom they wish to summon. This Saturday night, they've requested to see all four of you."

"All four of us, ma'am?" Olivia asked. "Why do they want to see all of us?"

"Are we being punished for letting Venomous take over the base?" Nadia asked.

"No, that responsibility is mine and mine alone," Mrs. B said. "If I were to guess, I'd say they wanted to speak with Emma. Perhaps they want you all there when they do. I'm not sure."

Emma's brain overloaded with questions. Everything she had ever wanted to ask about her dad. About her mom. About why the Century Group formed the Authority. Who were these people? What were their motivations? And the biggest question of all…why did they want to see her?

"I thought you wanted to live your own life now?" Grandma Bernadette sat on the edge of Emma's bed, reading her granddaughter's eyes. "You have to shut the door on these people now, young one. If you go to this meeting, you'll be opening yourself up to them again. There's also a risk that you'll fall so far down that rabbit hole you won't be able to crawl back out again."

Emma thought about her grandma's warning.

"Now is the time to walk away. You're already a remarkable young woman. You don't need to prove that to anyone."

"That's not why I joined," Emma said. "I did it for my mom."

"Then you don't mind quitting for your dad," Grandma Bernadette said. "And for yourself."

Emma sighed and shook her head. "I can't make that decision until I've had my questions answered. I have to go."

Her grandmother released a heavy sigh.

"On Saturday we'll fly out at noon," Mrs. B said. "It will be a formal dinner meeting, so please bring your best dress for the occasion."

Grandma Bernadette stood up from the bed. "I have an old cocktail dress. Don't know if it still fits, but I'll give it a whirl."

The room paused as everyone stared.

Grandma Bernadette didn't even blink. "Emma needs a voice of reason with her, so I'm coming along."

"You can't go, Bernadette," Mrs. B warned. "You weren't invited."

"Then Emma doesn't go either."

"Bernadette—may I speak to you in the other room?" Mrs. B asked, trying to stay calm.

"No, Laura, you may not. I'm dead serious. Emma's not going if I can't go."

"They will not allow you into the meeting."

"They will if these people want to see Emma."

"The organization doesn't operate that way," Mrs. B said, slightly holding back her irritation.

"Well, they're going to start."

Mrs. B shut her eyes as her face tightened. The woman was about to blow her top like a volcano. But soon the frustration passed as she opened her eyes again. "Do whatever you must. However, be warned that I can not guarantee your safety."

"Laura, I'm old enough to read between the lines," Grandma Bernadette said. "So where is this shindig going to be at?"

***

The Boeing 767 business jet leveled off at thirty-five thousand feet. The aircraft itself was what they called a wide-body, capable of fitting seven seats in a single row. But this cabin didn't resemble a normal passenger jet at all. The cabin's interior was a luxurious living room with large leather seats that swiveled around. Wood-finished tables. Couches. Expensive carpet. A modern design that all went together to provide its passengers with premium comfort.

Emma's hands still had a death grip on the corners of her leather chair. The size of the jet helped convince her brain that old and more experienced pilots were the only ones capable of flying such a big jet like this, even though her heart was still acting like she was on a small jet that would spin out of control and crash.

"Can you fly one of these?" Emma asked Olivia, who was sitting in another chair, wearing a cocktail dress, heels, earrings, and a light eyeshadow with lipstick that made her face pop.

Olivia scanned the interior. "I'd love to give it a go. If I can land an Airbus A380 in Paris, why not a Boeing too, eh?"

"Speaking of Paris...where are we going?" Nadia was all dressed up too as she relaxed in another comfy chair. She didn't wear her headscarf but chose to pull back her long hair and tie it together with a beautiful bow that matched the color of her dress.

"You can go ask Mrs. B, love. She won't tell me," Olivia said.

"I hope we go to England," Miyuki said. "They have all those extra fancy dinner parties inside those big old manors. Like the ones on that television show Downtown Addy."

Emma laughed. "It's Downton Abbey."

Miyuki covered her mouth and giggled at herself. Her dress was very short, but Miyuki had an athletic body that filled it out well. So well in fact, that it reminded Emma how tight her own dress felt against her body. Emma was convinced that because of all her stress eating, she had gained ten pounds on her way to New York.

"God, that would be dreadful. No upper-class twits dinner party for me, thank you very much," Olivia said. "A nice beach barbecue by the ocean would be lovely."

"In Tahiti," Nadia added.

Olivia closed her eyes and smiled. "In Tahiti."

Miyuki grinned as well. "Someday we'll go back."

"Have you talked to Robert lately?" Emma asked, knowing full well that not only did Nadia have a giant crush on the boy, but also that the Gems had helped Robert and his other android friends relocated to the Pacific, where they could live free and in peace.

Nadia hesitated. "We text each other."

"Oh yeah? What do you text each other about?"

"Yeah, what do androids like to talk about?" Miyuki asked, very interested.

"It's private."

"Oh, come on," Emma said.

"Is he sending you dirty pictures of himself?" Olivia asked.

"Of course he isn't," Nadia said. "He's programmed to be a gentleman."

"So…what does a gentleman android like to talk about?" Emma asked.

Nadia kept her mouth shut as she scanned her friends' curious faces. But then she relaxed.

"We play on-line chess together," she said.

The other three Gems paused.

"You mean that game with knights and kings and Middle Age looking things on a board with squares?" Emma asked.

"Robert discovered the game, and he can't get enough of it. He enjoys the logic and the complex strategy of it all, so he asked me to play him. While we're playing, we message each other."

"And what do you talk about while playing chess?" Emma asked.

"I told you, that's private," Nadia said, crossing her arms.

"I see," Olivia said. "So you're the one sending dirty pictures to him."

Miyuki giggled and covered her mouth.

"Can we please stop talking about my private life?"

"We're only messing with you, love," Olivia said.

Nadia looked away. The comments were still bothering her. Emma knew how close Nadia was to Robert. The unique bond they had with each other. Maybe they shouldn't tease her about it, but one had to admit that being friends with an android would be a unique experience, worthy of people asking you questions about at least.

"When is Laura going to grace us with her presence?" Grandma

Bernadette was at the open bar, making herself another rum and Coke.

Emma wondered that too. Before they took off, Mrs. B greeted them briefly before retiring to a closed office in the back of the aircraft to get some work done, promising to join them later. That was a half hour ago.

"How many drinks is that for your grandmother?" Olivia asked in a whisper.

"Three," Emma said. "I've never seen her drink like this."

"She's nervous," Olivia said. "Well, I'm nervous too. I mean, we don't know where we're flipping going and—"

"We're on our way to New Orleans," Mrs. B said, finally emerging from the back office. "My apologies. Since my office has been destroyed, I've had to use the one on board for the time being. Ah, I see that Bernadette has found the bar."

"You're out of rum," Grandma Bernadette said, grabbing on to the furniture to balance herself.

Mrs. B found a large chair near Emma and sat down, crossing her ankles. She studied the Gems. "My...you all look beautiful."

"Should we be worried?" Olivia asked.

"Worried about what...the meeting?"

"Yes, ma'am."

"Don't worry. You all will do fine." Mrs. B then paused. "May I have the room with Emma and her grandma for a moment?"

The three Gems exchanged glances before standing up.

Mrs. B waited for them to leave the cabin. "Bernadette, would you be so good as to make me a screwdriver, please?"

"Make that two," Emma said.

"I'll make that one," Grandma Bernadette said as she went to the bar and whipped up the drink. She handed it to Mrs. B, who downed half of it before Grandma Bernadette sat down.

Mrs. B closed her eyes, as if allowing the alcohol to cleanse her throat. She took another drink, then put the glass on a nearby table. "I have something to say to both of you."

She took Emma's hand and pressed it in between both of hers. The warmth of her hands against Emma's skin was strange because it was the most intimate gesture her grandma Laura had ever made towards her.

Mrs. B concentrated on Emma's eyes, but not in her usually intimidating way. There was a softness in them. A vulnerability inside. "I confess that...I've lied to you. When I first recruited you, I didn't tell you the whole truth about your mother. And because of Ken—your father's wishes—I should have been more open about it. You see, to me, Angela was a hero. She died because she took actions thinking that what she was doing would save lives, even though she knew that her chances of dying were significant. Yes, the information about the crate was bad. Yes, I made a horrible miscalculation that resulted in not only the death of your mother but the death of many policemen as well."

She glanced down at her hands. "I must live with that mistake for the rest of my life. I must live with the fact that...I killed my only daughter." The woman paused. Her eyes watered. "Forgive me."

Mrs. B closed her eyes, taking a moment to seize back control.

She cleared her throat. "I killed my daughter. I drove her husband away from the organization. And I drove her daughter away as well. These mistakes will haunt me forever. I don't say these things out of any solicitation for your pity. I understand that you and Bernadette can never forgive my actions. Nor should you. Because I don't forgive them either."

Mrs. B gave Emma's hand a slight squeeze. "I want you to know that whatever you decide—you'll always be in my thoughts."

The woman tried to withdraw her hands, but Emma held on to them, almost without thinking.

Mrs. B glanced up at Emma.

The two searched each other's eyes.

Grandma Bernadette was leaking like an old drain-pipe, brushing back tears.

Emma glanced down at their hands, then returned her gaze up to Mrs. B.

"I forgive you...Grandma," she said.

Mrs. B swallowed hard as a tear trickled down. She responded with a simple nod.

Suddenly, Mrs B withdrew her hands and stood back up, as if pretending everything was business as usual. "Now, if you would excuse me, I'll head back to my office to finish up a few more items before we—"

Grandma Bernadette stumbled forward. At first, Mrs. B backed away, as if she were about to attack her. But then the woman embraced her in a hug.

"I'm so sorry, Laura. I know how much you loved Angela."

"That's not necessary—"

"Hell yes, it's necessary. I should've said it at the funeral. I should've yelled at Ken for not speaking to you back then. He lost his wife. But damn it…you lost your daughter, and treating people like that during such a terrible time of grief…that's uncalled for. So I'm sorry, Laura. Maybe I can't forgive you for some things…but that doesn't mean we shouldn't treat each other like human beings."

"Thank you for saying that." Mrs. B stepped away and swallowed again. "I should leave."

"You sit right there," Grandma Bernadette said. "I'm making you another screwdriver, and you're gonna drink it."

CHAPTER 47

The French Quarter of New Orleans was vibrant with activity. The night life was on full display as people shuffled along the streets, carrying all kinds of alcoholic spirits. Bottles of beer. Mixed drinks. Giant plastic glasses with weird shapes and colors. Some drinks even glowed in the dark.

The scene was amazing to Emma. All these people standing around the street and drinking without the cops busting them. According to her grandma, this spectacle was nothing compared to the days of the Mardi Gras celebration when these same streets would be choked with people.

Mrs. B guided their well-dressed group through the crowd. Two men from Mrs. B's security detail also followed them, wearing tourist clothing. Soon they came upon a small restaurant called *Mr. Pelican's*. The glass double doors showed drawings of a sophisticated pelican with a top hat, a fancy cigarette holder, and a monocle. There was also a large CLOSED FOR RENOVATIONS sign in the nearby window.

Mrs. B knocked on the door. A large Latino man in a suit answered. He had a clean-shaved head.

"I brought along some friends," Mrs. B said.

"Are they allergic to shellfish?" the Latino man asked.

"No, but one is allergic to bee stings."

"Which one?"

"Black Opal."

The Latino man nodded and allowed them to come inside. All the tables of the restaurant were empty except for six huge men who equaled the size of the Latino man. When these men moved around, Emma spotted gun holsters tucked inside their well-tailored suits.

A woman stepped out from an employees-only door. She wore

a gorgeous black cocktail dress and had a body to complement it.

"What a wonderful surprise." Mrs. B gave this woman a hug. "How are you?"

"Excellent, ma'am. It's been far too long," the woman said.

Mrs. B turned to Emma. "Black Opal, this is Black Widow. A colleague of ours from the London station."

Emma and Black Widow exchanged hellos.

"Black Widow trained Emerald and Sapphire."

Black Widow nodded towards her former students. "So far, I've heard nothing but excellent reports. Keep up the good work."

"Thank you, ma'am," Olivia said, only giving the woman a courtesy smile. Emma could tell there was something deeper there. Something that demanded a deeper conversation among close friends. Emma made a mental note to explore that some other time.

"May I search you?" Black Widow asked Mrs. B.

After Black Widow did a thorough body search of Mrs. B, the woman paused at the sight of Grandma Bernadette.

"Who is this woman?" Black Widow asked.

"She's an uninvited guest," Mrs. B said.

"I'm Emma's grandmother. You can call me Bernadette," she said, moving towards Black Widow. "Tell your friends that Emma talks to no one unless I'm in the room with her."

"Grandma—" Emma said, sensing these people were not used to hearing demands…but making them.

"Hush, young one," Grandma Bernadette said. "I'm not backing down on that. You want to see her? Then I come along too."

"Who's Emma?" Black Widow asked.

"Emma is Black Opal," Mrs. B said.

"Ah, yes, I see now." Black Widow's lips moved to the side. "This is most irregular. One can't simply go in without being invited in."

"Well, you see…I'm inviting myself in."

The large Latino man simply flicked his eyes, and two of his large men placed themselves behind Grandma Bernadette.

Emma's muscles tightened. Her heart began beating fast. Her body getting ready for a fight.

Black Widow's eyes moved over to Emma. "So you're Black Opal. The girl who saved San Francisco. The group has been looking forward to meeting you. Unfortunately, we don't allow uninvited guests to be in the presence of the Century Group."

"You'll be making an exception in my—"

The two large men picked up Grandma Bernadette like she was a harmless teddy bear.

"Stop it," Emma yelled. "Put her down."

"I warned both of you," Mrs. B said. "I have no power here. The rules are the rules."

Emma moved towards the men, but Black Widow blocked her. This made Emma's stomach burn. She made a move to push Black Widow out of the way, but the woman scooped up Emma's legs and put her back to the floor so fast that the world seemed to spin.

Out of instinct, Miyuki took a step forward.

"I wouldn't try anything, love," Olivia said. "Black Widow's father was in British Special Forces."

Black Widow drilled her eyes into Miyuki. "To be precise, he trained the 1st Parachute Regiment of British Special Forces."

"And his daughter," Mrs. B added.

Miyuki retreated.

Black Widow released Emma and stood up. "Your grandmother will not be harmed. However, she'll have to wait in the kitchen."

Emma slowly stood up, brushing her dress off.

"It will be necessary to search all four of you," Black Widow announced. "Let's avoid any future attempts at violence, shall we? Would be a pity to ruin such a lovely evening with a trip to the casualty ward."

Reluctantly, Emma allowed Black Widow to search her, then came Miyuki, Nadia, and finally Olivia.

"Are you ladies ready?" Black Widow asked before leading the five of them down a hallway of the old restaurant.

Soon that hallway emptied into a giant dining room, decorated like a set from *Gone with The Wind*, but with a Louisiana flavor. Lots of gold-trimmed furnishings. Several nineteenth-century chairs and couches with time-appropriate decorations done up with luxuriousness. All the furniture in the room surrounded a giant oak dining table that was all set to serve dinner to at least fifty people.

If the room itself didn't blow Emma's mind, it was the group of people who were gathered inside it. They were all dressed in their finest clothes. Tuxedos, designer dresses, top-dollar suits…it was a scene out of Emma's childhood. The fancy dinner parties her father would take her to in New York, where rich people could relax and enjoy the company of their own kind. But this party was different. Most of the people here wore masks over their faces, as if it were some masked ball. Some wore black ones. Some wore white. Some wore a fancy color like pink, blue, or purple. One lady wore a dazzling gold mask.

As Black Widow escorted them through the party, Emma's ears picked up several different languages. French, Russian, Spanish, Japanese, Arabic, and a few others she didn't quite recognize. Yet not everyone wore a mask.

As they approached him, Mr. E bowed. He was a middle-aged Japanese man wearing a crisp black suit. He was the head of the Tokyo station and had helped the Gems during their Thunderdog mission. Miyuki went up to say hello, followed by Mrs. B and Black Widow.

Emma was more interested in people watching.

"What a unique group," Nadia whispered.

"I'd say more bizarre than unique," Emma said.

"Oy...not so loud," Olivia said. "They might throw Black Widow and her goons on us if we start making—"

The lady wearing the dazzling gold mask approached them.

"*Bonjour*, would you happen to be members of the Gems project?" the woman asked in a thick French accent.

"Yes, we are," Emma responded. "*Bonjour*, it's a pleasure to meet you. And what's your name?"

The woman wagged her finger. "Naughty, naughty, I can't tell you that. It's a secret."

"Members of the Century Group can not disclose their identities to those outside the circle," a man said in broken English. He wore a dark green mask covering his dark-skinned face. "We appreciate that you girls were able to join us this evening."

"Thank you for inviting us, sir," Olivia said.

"On behalf of the group, you're welcome." The man in the dark green mask turned to the French-woman. "We should get started. Unfortunately, our agenda is long tonight."

"I quite agree," the French-woman said. She turned around, causing her golden dress to sparkle under the lights. The woman stepped towards the giant dinner table and called out for the room's attention. She then said...

"It is time."

All the unique or bizarre people took their seats around the giant oak table, leaving Emma, the three other Gems, and Mrs. B standing by themselves.

Emma leaned over. "Are we supposed to find a seat or—?"

"They will tell us," Mrs. B said. "Just listen and do what they ask."

Once everyone settled in, the man with the dark green mask stood up from his seat. "This meeting of the Century Group is now called to order. Everyone is accounted for. Who would like to start?"

A white man with a black mask raised his hand. "Because of our special guests, I propose that we move our main agenda until after we've had dinner. What do y'all think?"

Emma placed the man's Southern accent from either Alabama, Georgia, or maybe even South Carolina.

"That's most considerate," the woman in the golden mask said. "Do I have a second on the proposal?"

Another woman in a teal mask lifted her hand.

The woman with the golden mask then conducted a show of hands around the table. "Very well. The proposal has been approved. We will move Mr. E's report concerning last week's attacks upon our Authority stations until after dinner." The woman turned her attention to their guests. "Black Opal...Sapphire... Emerald...Ruby...would you four please approach the group?"

The four Gems exchanged glances with each other before moving towards the giant table.

"Black Opal," the French-woman with the gold mask began, "the Century Group wanted to show our gratitude for your brave and selfless actions that prevented the deaths of millions in California. You are an inspiration and the finest example of why the Authority exists."

"However...this dinner is not for you," the man with the dark green mask said. "It's for all four of you. The Gems project has been a triumph. Each one of you has performed beyond our wildest expectations. Collectively, your missions have saved thousands of lives around the world."

"We are grateful for what you've achieved and look forward to your future accomplishments," the woman with a gold mask said. "Tonight it's only dinner, but I hope the four of you interpret our gesture as an appreciation of everything you've done for the Authority."

One member began clapping. Soon the gesture spread around the large table as members stood up and applauded their appreciation to the four girls standing in front of them.

Emma's ego skyrocketed. The clapping. The standing ovation. The actor inside her stood up taller and soaked in the adulation. She was a hero. She was a rock star. And she did almost die. Then Emma noticed poor Nadia. Her cheeks were red, and her eyes pointed at the ground…as if the girl were embarrassed by it all. As if she wasn't worthy of the praise.

That was crap. Emma knew that without Nadia's brain, the Gems wouldn't have accomplished anything.

Emma rested her hand on Nadia's shoulder and gave it a reassuring squeeze. This made Nadia lift her eyes. Emma flashed her a smile, and that brought out her friend's smile.

"You're a rock star. Enjoy it," Emma said.

Olivia gripped Nadia's hand. "You deserve this too, love."

Nadia lifted her chin and gave a bigger smile to the room.

Suddenly, Miyuki jumped behind them and bear-hugged all three girls, causing them all to laugh.

When the applause finally died, Olivia spoke up…

"We couldn't have done anything without Mrs. B's help," she said. "She's the glue that keeps us together."

The remaining Gems all nodded.

However, the mere mention of Mrs. B's name created a strange pause that went through everyone at the giant table. The members then took their seats.

Something was wrong.

The man with the dark green mask folded his hands together on the table. "Black Opal…we have been told about your reservations concerning the organization. That you question the sincerity of our mission. That you feel we have compromised our values in order to serve our bank accounts and quench our thirst for power."

"Would that not be a fair summary of your doubts about us?" the woman with the gold mask asked.

Emma was surprised. How many people did Mrs. B tell? These people just gave her a standing ovation, but since Emma had talked trash about them, would they now do something bad to her? Like, sacrifice her during some crazy secret ritual involving goats and pentagrams.

Emma hesitated.

About fifty pairs of eyes watched Emma through their masks. Not one of them was smiling.

Emma swallowed. Did she sabotage the Gems victory parade? Was she now going to be stamped as a traitor and hunted down like a non-believer?

"Please answer them, Emma," Mrs. B said.

Emma took in a deep breath. This was her only chance to ask the questions that she wanted answered. No matter how much it might piss them off.

"Well, yeah. I only want to know the truth. What do each of you get out of all this? I mean...the satisfaction of saving the world? Are you really being serious?"

There was a silence across the room. It was so loud that Emma feared they would kill her right there and then for asking such a question.

The woman with the gold mask leaned back in her chair. "Look around, Emma. Can you guess the combined net worth of all the men and women seated around this table? I can assure you...that dollar amount is in the trillions. I don't say this to impress you. I say it because there comes a point in each of our lives when money is not enough. We see awful things that happen in the world and think to ourselves...something must be done. Some wealthy people focus on charities in order to help solve the world's problems. We feel this is only part of the solution."

"Some families of wealth use their money to buy power and influence so they can manipulate governments," the man with the dark green mask said. "Usually for their own benefit, not for the benefit of the people."

"You see, Emma, the big trouble is...governments all have their own agendas," the Southern man said. "Sometimes they can shake hands and do the right thing for everyone, but most of the time, they bump heads. Or worse, they attack their own people."

"The point we are making is...the world needs a champion for its people. Someone who protects them," the man with the dark green mask said.

A part of Emma was fascinated and wanted to keep on listening, but the other Emma had to say something...

"Well...no offense, but...who gave all of you the power to

make those decisions for mankind? I'm sorry, but why are you a better judge of what mankind needs?"

The people around the giant oak table studied Emma, taking in her comments. Some of the people chuckled to themselves. As if Emma was an idiot because she just didn't get it. Some reacted as if they themselves had been insulted. A handful grinned in response to Emma's spirit.

"I can't speak for my colleagues," the woman with a gold mask said. "I only can speak for my family. My great-grandfather used his construction company to help remove and bury tens of thousands of bodies that lay upon the battlefields of France after the First World War. Even though the Allies won, the human cost of that war was unimaginable at that time. It shook my great-grandfather's generation to its core. And he wasn't the only man of wealth who felt this way. Other such men saw that war as a failure of civilization. Patriotism mixed with militarism had led Europe to the edge of oblivion. Along with my great-grandfather, these men of wealth decided something had to be done. They formed the Century Group. A private alliance that vowed to use its vast financial resources to prevent mankind from destroying itself. My great-grandfather also recommended the creation of a secret organization that would be the instrument of that alliance."

"The Authority," Emma said.

"I'm here because of my grandfather," the man with the dark green mask said. "He joined this group in the 1970s because no government wanted to help his people overthrow a brutal dictator who was murdering thousands of his own citizens. But the Authority did help. And their intervention saved many lives and provided stability to my country."

"Did anyone give our families permission to do these things?" the woman with the gold mask asked. "No. Do we feel morally superior to everyone else? Of course not. But can we allow ourselves to stand by and do nothing while a country or an organization or even an individual allows their ambitions to once again threaten the stability of our civilization? The world is becoming smaller. More and more people realize that we need each other to survive and to prosper. That the future challenges our world faces demand that we all work together. The world needs us now more than ever. And we need young people like you to help us carry on with that great work."

"My family has been a member of the Century Group since the 1920s," the Southern man said. "In fact, one of my grandfather's closest friends inside this group was...Henry P. Rothchild."

Emma shot him a look.

"Yes, your great-grandfather Henry. Our two families were close back then. We recruited men and material that formed the building blocks for the Authority here in America. And even though the Rothchilds were a bunch of Yankees...we still found common ground on how we viewed the future. So our two great-grandfathers served the Century Group for the first dozen or so years. They were replaced by our grandfathers. Then our fathers after that. And then...I served with your father, Ken."

"A Rothchild has always been a member of the Century Group," the woman with a gold mask said. "When your father quit, we all were very disappointed. He was a natural leader. The man who would help our cause grow in the new century. However, we understood his grief and allowed him to part with the organization on good terms." The woman with a gold mask paused. "Now we come to you, Emma. Your father expressed to this group that he didn't want you involved with us. However, Mrs. B expressed that your mother held the opposite opinion. She wanted her daughter to know about the cause she died for. So we agreed to let Mrs. B approach you. Now you've expressed the desire to leave us as well. Is that correct?"

Miyuki, Nadia, and Olivia collectively wilted, their eyes waiting for the answer they knew was coming.

Emma stood there for a long moment. She was going to quit. A part of her wanted to quit. Then another part listened to these people. Money didn't solve all the world's problems. Sometimes it took action. Sometimes it took courage to do the right thing. Sometimes it took one girl to stand up and refuse to give up, no matter how dark the world seemed to get.

Remember, Black Opal. A Gem doesn't call for help. She is the help.

The words from Lioness still whispered inside her head. The woman could have saved herself. Doing nothing guaranteed her safety. But she chose to defy Asset One. She chose her loyalty to Emma and her duty to Mrs. B over her own life. Lioness made what she thought was an acceptable sacrifice.

Like her mom did.

When she thought that little girl was in danger, Emma went

263

after the kidnappers without a second thought. Like, it was in her blood. It was in her DNA. She had to help. She wanted to help. She wanted to make a difference in her life.

The entire dining room was watching her. Waiting for her answer.

Emma scanned all the masked faces watching her from the table before her eyes rested on Mrs B.

The older woman then lifted her chin and smiled. She could see the answer in Emma's eyes.

"I still want to be a Gem," Emma announced.

Her three friends screamed their relief as they gang-hugged Emma, almost knocking her to the floor.

Once their screams died down...

"We are most delighted to hear that." The French-woman with the gold mask scanned the faces around the table. "We should have dinner now."

Black Widow and two of her large henchmen appeared with a new section of table. The Century Group moved out of the way as the new table leaf was inserted. Waiters came in to setup new place mats. Soon, everyone sat back down, leaving four empty places.

"Please join us," the woman with the gold mask said.

The four Gems sat down as waiters brought out drinks and the first course.

Emma noticed that Mrs. B was still standing. Olivia did too.

"With respect, ma'am, we'll need another place mat for Mrs. B," Olivia said. "We can squeeze her in next to us."

The woman with the golden mask frowned.

"Mrs. B," the man with the green mask said, "I do believe you'll be dining with Black Widow in the kitchen. We will hear your report after dinner."

"Of course," Mrs. B said with a slight bow. The older woman then followed Black Widow out of the dining room.

Emma was confused. Why did Mrs. B have to leave?

"Why isn't Mrs. B eating with us?" Miyuki whispered to her friends.

"I think she's in some sort of trouble," Olivia said softly.

"Why is she in trouble?" Nadia asked.

"Because our base had to be destroyed," Olivia said. "And during her watch, Venomous managed to flip Lioness and almost snatched all the Authority's secrets. I get the feeling Mrs. B has a lot of explaining to do."

CHAPTER 48

A light scanned the dark horizon. The patient couldn't tell what in the hell he was looking into. Some dark void. A place of non-existence. And where was that light coming from?

The light grew brighter, stimulating his mind, lifting him out of a deep, dark place. Soon the patient's eyelids were able to separate as he squinted at the harsh whiteness of the tiled walls. His breathing was ragged. Then the patient felt the cool air being pumped into his nose.

Where the hell was he?

Then a man blocked the white tiled wall as he came into view. The man wore a suit and tie, along with an FBI ID card pinned to his lapel. The name on the ID card was Edward Wilcox.

"Can you hear us, son?" the man's voice asked.

The patient tried to nod, but he still felt groggy and unable to lift his head. He could see the room a little clearer though. It looked like a hospital room, but there was no television or window. He could smell the cleaning products they used on the floor, something he remembered from his stay at the hospital when he fell off his bike as a kid.

"Ryan, can you hear us?"

The boy had to force the words, but they came out. "Yes."

"Good. My name is Ed Wilcox from the FBI. How are you feeling?"

Ryan swallowed. "Water?"

The man poured him a glass of water and tipped the contents into his mouth. The water tasted so good that Ryan drank the entire glass. His mouth began to feel normal again.

"Feels like a bus landed on top of me," Ryan said as he got a better look at FBI agent Ed. "What happened?"

"You tell us," Ed said. "My agents found your body baking

outside in the sun. Thought you were dead, but you still had a pulse. So they rushed you to the hospital." Ed sat on the edge of the bed. "What were you doing out there?"

The attack came rushing back. Sunchaser ripping him into shreds. Nowhere to run. Nowhere to hide. His final words to Emma before...he died.

But he wasn't dead.

"I was sitting under that large tree and enjoying the view. You can see a lot of the valley from there," Ryan said. "I must have fallen asleep."

A burst of laughter filled the room as another man stepped into Ryan's view. He was a short white man with a beard. His eyes were dark, and his nose had this hook-like quality to it.

"Got to give the kid credit, he's got a sense of humor," the short man said.

Ed flicked his eyes back to Ryan. "We know you weren't there to enjoy the view. Multiple lacerations around your arms, back, face—poison injected into your blood."

"A unique poison," the short man added.

"Speaking of unique, the doctor found a device embedded in your wrist," Ed said. "A special device with access to your veins and nerves. I've never seen such a device like that before."

"But I have," the short man said. "Nasty little piece of technology. There's only one organization in this world that goes to such lengths to control its assets."

"Ryan, we know you're a member of Venomous." Ed stood back up. "You were there with Asset One to attack the Authority headquarters in Napa Valley."

"Not exactly."

"Sleeping under a tree was funny the first time, but don't insult our intelligence."

"Mrs. B captured me in New York and brought me back to their headquarters to interrogate me."

Ed glanced at the short man before sitting back down on the bed. "Go on."

"She finished one round of interrogation before Asset One attacked the base. When Venomous captured it, I was released."

"So why did Asset One then want to kill you?" the short man asked.

Ryan studied the short man. His ID card hung on a lanyard

with the word GUEST printed on it. He then motioned to Ed. "You're FBI, but who's this guy?"

"The name's Sheppard. Central Intelligence Agency." The short man crossed his arms. "That unique poison the doctor found in your blood—Asset One saves that for special people. It's a slow-acting poison that hurts like a son of a bitch. You're one lucky boy. We gave the antidote to the FBI a year or so ago. Saved your happy ass."

"We recognized the poison when the doctor told us," Ed said. "But it's not all good news. The poison wasted one of your kidneys. Damaged some of your organs, and they had to cut a piece of your stomach out. Still, you're alive."

Ryan closed his eyes. He couldn't believe it. He was sure it was the end. Then he remembered Emma.

"Did the bomb go off?"

"The one your friends planted?" Sheppard asked.

"We disarmed it," Ed said. "The danger is over. However, the consequences around this terrorist plot will still need to be dealt with."

"And since you're the only Venomous agent the FBI captured alive...you'll be the one charged with it," Sheppard said. "A home-grown boy from Missouri turned nuclear terrorist. The American people are gonna love you."

"I had nothing to do with that bomb," Ryan said. "I didn't even know we had such a weapon."

"The government might even reinstate the federal death penalty...just for you." Sheppard brought out a pack of cigarettes.

"Sheppard, you can't smoke in here," Ed said.

"Damn it. I forgot." He put his smokes back in his pocket. "Look kid, you can either be a pathetic martyr for the white-haired wacko who tried to kill you with his falcon...or you could be smart and play ball with us."

"What does that mean?"

"You made a lot of bad choices, Ryan," Ed said. "Got involved with the wrong people."

"Like father, like son," Sheppard added.

"But despite all of your numerous mistakes...we want to give you another chance."

"To make amends for all of your sins and finally serve your country for once," Sheppard said.

"The FBI needs all the information you can give us on Venomous operations within the United States," Ed said. "I'm talking contacts, safe houses, objectives, supporters…we want everything you know."

Sheppard took a chair and scooted it across the floor as he sat down near Ryan. "And when the FBI is done squeezing all that information out of you, then it's my turn."

Ryan smiled to himself. That was why they saved him. To them, he was a diamond mine full of Venomous information.

But not for long.

"You do realize, once they find out I'm alive…Venomous can send a signal to my wrist implant from anywhere, and it will trigger a heart attack."

"Your body's clean," Sheppard said. "My boys at Langley figured out a way to take those devices out without triggering the cyanide booby trap."

Ryan turned over his wrist, there was a large bandage there, and the area was sore. He thought it was impossible to remove them.

"Once you've cooperated with us and the CIA," Ed said, "then we'll drop our investigation concerning your involvement with Asset One's plot."

"You can then go home to Wichita and see your mom," Sheppard said. "But don't tell her about your new job offer."

"What new job offer?"

Sheppard flashed him the biggest smile ever. "Ryan, how would you like to work for the CIA?"

THANK YOU FOR READING!

Dear Awesome Reader,

I hope you enjoyed *Girls Always Live Twice*. This novel was a departure from previous ones in terms of action and pacing. Since this novel was a follow up to the plot line established in *Man With The Golden Falcon*, Emma's physical and emotional journey to discover more about her mother and to come to terms about the mysterious Century Group was of prime importance. I also needed to address Emma and Ryan's relationship in terms of what the future held for them. Ryan couldn't go on playing both sides of the fence in terms of pleasing Asset One and Emma. Eventually Asset One would grow impatient of Ryan's lack of progress and kill him for being too weak. So in the first draft I decided to kill Ryan off and force Emma to move on with her life. However, as I was rewriting, the CIA idea just fell in my lap and I instantly knew it was the perfect way to end the book. It will get Ryan safely out of Venomous and shake up his relationship with Emma.

Book reviews are huge to authors! You don't have to give a full book report, a sentence or two is fine. But I would love a review of this book if you have time. Love it or hate it. Doesn't matter. I would just enjoy the feedback.

What did you think about the novel? What kind of stories would you like to see in future Gems novels? I'd love to hear from you! Please feel free to write me at **doug@dougsolter.com**, or send me a tweet, or visit **www.dougsolter.com** for more options to stay connected.

Thank you again for reading *Girls Only Live Twice*!

All the best,

Doug Solter

ACKNOWLEDGMENTS

Another Gems book. Another round of sincere acknowledgments of people who help me do what I love to do.

The last act of this book would've been a disaster if it wasn't for my ace beta reader Laura Benedict. She was honest enough to help me streamline the book and make it work better. And she made me keep the final chapter. Thank you, Laura!

My cover designer for saving me yet again. After I suggested a few images that would've made a horrible cover, Travis Miles came through by ignoring many of my suggestions while still enhancing the theme of what I wanted in the final awesome cover you see now.

My long time editor Pauline Nolet, for her amazing proofreading abilities and attention to detail with a professional attitude.

The screenwriting legend Max Adams, for her unending support and her superior screenwriting classes which I highly recommend.

For their wonderful support: Shelby Badstibner, Jeff Benedict, Jerry Bennett, Lela Fox, Becky Kephart, Joe Kinkade, Trevor and Talon Lane, Valarie Lawson, Barbara Lowell, Brenda Maier, Anna Myers, Helen Newton, Ginny Sain, Sherry Spurrier, Angela Townsend, Victoria at Whitty Books, Megan Walvoord, and Ann Whitmire. All my friends at the Oklahoma chapter of SCBWI. All my screenwriting friends through Max Adams' AFW program. All the writers on the 20Booksto50K Facebook group. I appreciate you all!

Plus a special thank you to all my friends and family.

ABOUT THE AUTHOR

Doug Solter began writing screenplays in 1998, then made the switch to writing young adult fiction in 2008. His first novel *Skid* was a screenplay before it was adapted into a book. Doug has worked in television for over twenty years. He has directed rap music videos and short films. Doug respects cats, loves the mountains, and one time walked the streets of Barcelona with a smile. Doug is an active member of the Society of Children's Book Writers and Illustrators.

Connect with Doug through his website...

www.dougsolter.com

ALSO BY DOUG SOLTER

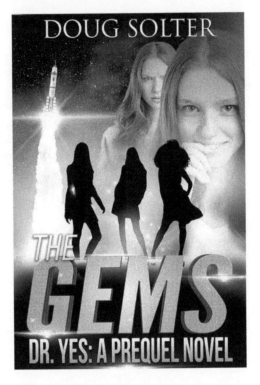

Before Emma. Before California. The three Gems met the O'Malley twins. Things didn't go well.

Keep reading for a sample chapter from the book!

DR.YES
SAMPLE

Olivia stepped into the enormous dinning hall filled with girls wearing their full dress uniforms. It was noisy as everyone was visiting across one giant table which ran the length of the room. It reminded Olivia of those long tables at Hogwarts in those *Harry Potter* movies.

Her dress flats clapped against the stone floor as Olivia followed Bridget O'Malley down the long table. Many of the girls turned and waved at Bridget who flashed them an acknowledging smile. A few of the girls even threw out compliments about her hair.

Nadia and Miyuki sat near each other, but not together. They watched Olivia pass by and didn't smile.

Close to the head of the table, Bridget reached three empty places. She tucked the bottom of her skirt under her and sat before offering Olivia the spot next to her. Olivia tucked in her skirt and took a seat.

It was a half past six when Dr. Glenn Joyce and all the school's instructors emerged into the hall wearing their best dress clothes. There was a smaller dinning table that faced perpendicular to the student table to form a large T. The instructors took their places at this table while Dr. Joyce stood in the middle.

"May I have your attention?" Dr. Joyce asked.

The girls continued their loud conversations.

Dr. Joyce tapped his knife against a water glass. The clanging noise simulated a bell as the girls become quiet.

"Thank you," he continued. "Welcome to Avondale's ninth school dinner of the semester. This is a time for us to be together as one. For fellowship. For encouragement. And for community. We are a family. Those aren't just words. It's a reality. As far as I'm concerned, you are all daughters of this school. We want to bring out the best in each and every one of you. Every young woman here has a dream. Something that calls to you and only you. The faculty and I want you to succeed beyond your wildest expectations. We want you to be stoked about the future. And if not, we'll do whatever needs to be done to help you achieve your dreams." Dr. Joyce's smile was infectious. "I also want to challenge you all to support and help each other. Remember that when you lift up another student, you lift up the class. We all rise together. A strong tide that lifts all boats."

Dr. Joyce's attention shifted to Olivia. "Before we begin our dinner together, I'd like to introduce a new student. Lisa, would you please stand?"

Olivia hesitated. She had no idea Dr. Joyce was going to do this.

"Oh, don't worry. We won't bite ya," Bridget said.

The girls laughed.

Olivia stood up.

"This is Lisa and she comes to us from Portsmouth, England. Please make her feel welcome," Dr. Joyce said.

Soon the entire room said in unison…

"Welcome to Avondale, Lisa."

The greeting was warm. Most of the girls had smiles and seemed to mean what they were saying. Olivia thought it was a nice gesture.

Drinks were served first. Then baskets of fresh baked bread that smelled delicious and made Olivia hungry. Bridget showed her a local jam that was on the table. Olivia tried it on her bread and the local fruit tasted delicious.

"It's from a farm only a few kilometers from here," Bridget said. "I'm an addict for their jams. They're absolutely class."

"It's quite lovely, thank you," Olivia said.

Finally the garden salads come out. The vegetables were crisp and fresh. The vinaigrette tasted homemade.

Olivia had eaten about half her salad when another girl with red hair came running into the dining hall.

Dr. Joyce wiped his mouth with a napkin before clearing this throat. "You're pretty late, Sophia."

Everyone stopped eating to gawk at this girl who rushed past the student table and dropped herself into the third empty seat next to Olivia.

The girl named Sophia threw back her long fiery-red hair. "Sorry…won't happen again."

Olivia had to blink twice. This new girl had a striking

resemblance to Bridget.

No, it was her twin.

Olivia's eyes bounced to Bridget who displayed the most satisfied smile. She was enjoying this.

"Who the hell is this?" Bridget's twin asked.

Bridget didn't hesitate. "She's my new roommate. Her name's Lisa and she's from the UK. So far she's been grand."

Bridget's twin Sophia examined Olivia like a new car. Her eyes judging every square millimeter.

"She has nice brown skin. Her hair's nice as well." Sophia leaned in way too close as she checked Olivia's eyes. "And she doesn't have crazy eyes like that *Eegit* Molly had."

"We'll see how she is tonight," Bridget says. "I hope she doesn't snore like a plow horse."

Flipping hell. Olivia wanted to run away. These girls were having an entire conversation about her…while she was literally right in front of them.

Sophia backed away, but not by much. "You don't snore do you? My sister hates girls who snore."

"I don't think I snore," Olivia said.

"You're not a lesbian are ya?"

"Bejesus, Sophia!" Bridget said. "You can't ask her that. It's none of our fecking business."

Sophia blew off her sister and kept her focus on Olivia. "Only asking because my sister prefers men. However, if ya want me to introduce you to some girls ya fancy, I don't mind."

Olivia was overwhelmed by the girl's aggressiveness. She didn't hold anything back. "Right, I appreciate the offer, but I'm not a—"

"You can stay in the closet if you want. My sister and I won't tell anyone," Sophia added.

Olivia froze. A part of her wanted to slap the crap out of this girl for not even trying to listen to her.

"I'm not in the closet," Olivia blurted out. "I'm not even gay."

"It's all grand, ya don't have to come out of the closet."

"Not that there's anything wrong with ya being gay," Bridget said.

Olivia sighed. "Of course not. It's lovely. But not for me."

Bridget nodded and ate some more of her salad.

Sophia sat back, still fascinated with Olivia. "What's it like to be black?"

The main entrees were brought out to the student's table.

"Oh look," Olivia said. "We're having fish tonight!"

After dinner, Olivia headed into the dorm and went upstairs to her room. She changed out of her uniform into some shorts and a T-shirt before putting away the rest of her things. Olivia sat on her soft bed and checked her phone. No word yet from either Nadia or Miyuki. Mongoose advised the two girls not to contact Olivia until they found a secure place to meet.

Olivia wanted to go downstairs and see if either one of them were there. However, she talked herself out of it. It was better to wait for their signal. She didn't want to screw up another mission because of her impatience.

Olivia scanned her new dorm room. Well, it was more Bridget's than hers right now. The girl's belongings had taken up most of the room. Olivia did have a small closet to herself. A small desk and wooden chair. And a bed. For some reason, it all made her sad. Maybe it was the strangeness of the place. Maybe it was because she was halfway around the world in a country that spoke English, but still had a foreign landscape that she was still getting use to.

Another reason was her mom and dad. Olivia hadn't seen them for quite a while. Maybe a year. She should have contacted them before she left England. It would have been nice to hear her mum's voice again.

A fatigue fell over Olivia. The stress of traveling to Avondale, meeting new people, and understanding new surroundings had taken their toll on her body.

Olivia went to bed early, hoping things would become easier as the week went on.

Dr. Yes: A Prequel Novel is not available in stores.

To get a free eBook copy go to
www.dougsolter.com/doctoryes

Also by Doug Solter

Man With The Golden Falcons

Dr. Yes

Thunderdog

Tomorrow Always Lies

Spies Like Me

Skid Racing Series

Lightning Source UK Ltd.
Milton Keynes UK
UKHW010350301121
394802UK00002B/372